DEATH

THE SCENT OF DEATH

ANDREW TAYLOR

ISIS
LARGE PRINT
Oxford

First published in Great Britain 2013
by
HarperCollins*Publishers*

Published in Large Print 2013 by ISIS Publishing Ltd.,
7 Centremead, Osney Mead, Oxford OX2 0ES
by arrangement with
HarperCollins*Publishers*

CIP data is available for this title from the British Library

ISBN 978–0–7531–9208–5 (hb)
ISBN 978–0–7531–9209–2 (pb)

Printed and bound in Great Britain by
T. J. International Ltd., Padstow, Cornwall

To Will with love

CHAPTER
ONE

This is the story of a woman and a city. I saw the city first, glimpsing it from afar as it shimmered like the new Jerusalem in the light of the setting sun. I smelled the sweetness of the land and sensed the nearness of green, growing things after the weeks on the barren ocean. We had just passed through the narrows between Long and Staten islands and come into Upper New York Bay. It was Sunday, 2 August 1778.

The following morning, Mr Noak and I came up on deck an hour or two after dawn. The city was now close at hand. In the hard light of day it lost its celestial qualities and was revealed as a paltry, provincial sort of place.

We had heard that a conflagration had broken out during the night. Nevertheless, it came as something of a shock to see the broad pall of smoke hanging over the southern end of the island, which was where the city was. The stink of burning wafted across the water. Fires smouldered among the stumps of blackened buildings. Men scurried along the wharves that lined the docks. A file of soldiers moved to the beat of an invisible drum.

"It's as if the town has been sacked," I said.

Noak leaned on the rail. "The Captain says it must have been set deliberately, Mr Savill. This is the second fire, you know. The other was two years ago. They blamed the rebels then, just as they do now."

"Surely New York is loyal?"

"For some people, sir, loyalty is a commodity," Noak said. "And, like any other commodity, I suppose it can be bought and sold."

Above the smoke the sky was already a hard clear blue. I borrowed a glass from a young officer who was taking the air on deck. Most of the surviving houses of the city were of brick and tile, four or five storeys and crowned with shingles painted in a variety of faded colours. Some had balconies on their roofs, and already I could make out the tiny figures of people moving about above the streets. Many buildings nearer the southern tip had steeply gabled Dutch façades, relics of the days when the town had been called New Amsterdam.

"I confess I had expected a finer prospect," I said. "Something more like a city."

"It looked well enough before the war, sir. But looks deceive at the best of times. Believe me, there is great wealth here. The possibility of profit. And the possibility of so much more."

I looked down at the grey-green water running with the tide along the line of the hull. The oily surface was spotted with soot carried on the south-westerly breeze. The fire had broken out in the very early hours of the morning.

A large, pale rag billowed just below the surface of the water. Seagulls fluttered above it, crying like the souls of the damned. The rag snagged on a rope trailing from the ship to a dinghy alongside. The current made the cloth twitch as if alive. A few yards away from us, the young officer who had lent me his glass was standing by the rail. He swore under his breath.

The rag had a long tail, barely visible beneath it and entangled with the rope. It made me think of a merman or some other strange creature of the sea. The officer said a few sharp words to a sailor who, a moment later, leaned over the side with a long boathook.

"Distressing," Mr Noak said, and clicked his tongue against the roof of his mouth.

I glanced at him. "What is?"

Noak nodded at the merman. The sailor had twisted the boathook into the rag. The water slapped and curled around it, growing cloudier and greyer.

Looks deceive at the best of times. Not a rag, I thought. A shirt.

The sailor heaved the boathook and its burden upwards. The shirt rose a few inches above the water. It twisted. The water around it was filthy now. There was a sucking sound as if the merman had smacked his lips. A waft of foul air rose up, forcing us to step back and cover our noses and mouths. Three seagulls swooped closer, sheering away at the last moment.

For an instant I saw the merman's face — or, to be more exact, I saw where the face would have been, had it not been eaten almost entirely away by the creatures of the deep. Nor did the merman have a tail. Instead, two legs waved behind it. I glimpsed discoloured flesh flaking from swollen thighs and I smelled rotting meat.

The body fell back into the water. The current drew it swiftly away from the ship, and with it went the smell.

"Can they not even bury the dead?" I said.

The officer had heard me. "He was probably a prisoner from one of the hulks upstream, sir. Most of them are sailors from captured privateers. They tip them over the side."

"Do they not merit something better than this?"

His round, good-natured face split into a smile. "But there are so many of the knaves, sir, and he was only a rebel, after all."

"Cheaper, too," Noak pointed out. "Though as far as His Majesty's Treasury is concerned it will come to the same thing. No doubt someone will claim the allowances due — for the shroud, the cost of committal and so on."

I looked downstream. In the distance, the seagulls danced like blackened cinders against the blue sky. The body was no longer visible. The sea was greedy.

"As I told you, sir," Noak went on, "there is the possibility of profit here, and that is true even in wartime. Indeed, perhaps more so than in peace."

This was the first dead body that I saw in New York, and the first of the two dead men I saw that very day. As an individual, this one meant nothing to me, then or now. He and I had nothing in common apart from our shared humanity. I would never learn his name or how he died or who had thrown his corpse into the East River.

4

CHAPTER
TWO

I had met Samuel Noak on the voyage from England.

Mr Rampton, my patron, had arranged my passage on the *Earl of Sandwich*, a Post Office packet of which he was part-owner. The ship's principal purpose was to carry the mails to and from North America and the West Indies. The owners supplemented the considerable income they derived from this by squeezing a handful of passengers into the cramped cabins. Most of them were, like myself, travelling on official business. But there were a few who made the voyage in a private capacity. Such a one was Mr Noak.

He and I were thrown into immediate intimacy for we were obliged to share a cabin little bigger than the commodious kennel that housed Mr Rampton's mastiff at his house in the country. Noak was a small, spare man who wore his own sandy hair with only a modicum of powder for gentility's sake and tied it with a brown ribbon. He scraped back the hair so tightly that the bones of his face seemed to poke through the skin. His figure was youthful but he might have been any age between twenty and forty. He spoke with a thin, nasal voice, and always with deliberation, in an accent that I later discovered was characteristic of his native Massachusetts. There was something of the puritan about him, a sourness of mien.

Even before we had weighed anchor, I resolved to keep a proper distance between Mr Noak and myself during the passage to New York. But I had not reckoned with the peculiar swaying motion of the ocean, let alone with the terrifying effects of rough weather.

Within a few hours of our leaving Falmouth, I descended into an abyss of spiritual and physical suffering. I was convinced that I was dying — that the ship was sinking; and my condition was so miserable that, for all I cared, the world might end in the next instant, which would at least put a period to my agonies.

It was then that I began to see Samuel Noak in a different light. For it was he who sponged my brow, who emptied my basin, who assisted me to the heads. It was he who forced me to undergo what he assured me was an old naval remedy for *mal de mer*: to wit, to swallow a lump of greasy pork again and again until the stomach no longer had strength to resist it.

Slowly, over the long days and longer nights, my symptoms subsided. Mr Noak brought me Souchong tea laced with rum and spooned it into my mouth, which eased my aching gut and at last encouraged me to fall into the first unbroken sleep I had enjoyed since leaving England.

Given Noak's kindness, I could hardly hold the man at arm's length, even if I had wished to do so. As I recovered, we slipped by degrees into a relationship that

6

was something less than friendship but much more than mere acquaintance. It is difficult not to be civil to a man who has restored you to life.

"Will you remain in New York, sir?" I asked him one afternoon. The weather was calmer now, and we were strolling on deck after dinner. "Or do you travel on?"

"No, sir — I have a position waiting for me in the city. A clerk's desk in a contractor's house. A friend of my uncle's procured it for me."

"I'm surprised you should wish to leave London. The opportunities must be far greater there."

"True," he said. "But in New York I shall be a senior clerk, whereas in London I had no hope of advancement at all. Besides, I had a desire to see my native land again."

"Where were you employed?"

"At Mr Yelland's in the Middle Temple, sir. I had been there for three years."

"I believe I know the gentleman. That is to say, I have come across him once or twice."

"Indeed?"

"I have a position at the American Department," I explained. "As you know, Mr Yelland acts as the British man of business for many Loyalists. He sometimes favours us with communications on their behalf."

That was an understatement, as Noak must surely have known. Mr Yelland was one of several London attorneys who had reason to bless this unnecessary war, for it was proving very lucrative for them. He and his colleagues kept up a steady flow of letters to the Department. London was packed with displaced

Loyalists who were convinced that the American Department owed them compensation for the losses they had sustained because of their attachment to the Crown.

"Will you stay long in New York, sir?" Mr Noak asked after a pause.

"A month. Possibly two. Lord George has entrusted me with a commission and I do not know how long it will take."

Mr Noak nodded, as if making a token obeisance to the august name of Lord George Germain, the Secretary of State for the American Department. The truth of my appointment was more prosaic: Mr Rampton, one of the two under secretaries, had decided that I should go to New York. Lord George had signed the necessary order, but I was not perfectly convinced that His Lordship knew who I was.

"Perhaps we may encounter one another there," Noak said.

"Perhaps, sir," I agreed, privately resolving that for my part I would not pursue the acquaintance once we reached America.

"Where will you lodge?"

"At Judge Wintour's. He is an old friend of Mr Rampton, the under secretary."

"Ah yes," he said. "Of course."

"Are you acquainted with the Judge?"

"Only by reputation, sir." Mr Noak paused. "They say his daughter-in-law is a great beauty."

"Indeed."

"And the heiress to Mount George, as well."

"I believe the air is growing chilly. I think I shall go below."

"Once seen," Mr Noak said quietly, "never forgotten. That's what they say. Mrs Arabella Wintour, I mean."

CHAPTER
THREE

At midday, a single cannon boomed from the battery commanding the entrance of the North and East rivers.

"The noon gun, sir," the young officer told me with a knowing air as he took out his watch to adjust the time. "You'll soon be ashore."

Twenty minutes later, we were at last permitted to disembark. We were brought in at Beekman's Slip upriver from the Brooklyn ferry to keep us at a distance from the still-smouldering fire.

The quayside was thronged with soldiers, seamen, officials and porters. It had grown even hotter, with a close, airless warmth. I threaded my way between boxes, barrels and ropes. Men barged into me. Once I tripped and nearly fell. After five weeks aboard a ship, dry land had become alien, even hostile.

Despite my official standing, I was obliged to wait my turn to show my papers and explain my business to three separate individuals. Meanwhile the baggage was brought ashore. A line of glistening negros carried it to the customs shed. The few passengers from the *Earl of Sandwich* joined the queue outside where new arrivals sweltered in the sun.

The south-westerly breeze had dispersed most of the smoke. Beyond the shed the buildings of the shabby little city stretched away to the west, sloping gently up towards the soot-stained tower of a ruined church. Mr Noak had told me that this was Trinity Church, damaged in the first fire two years earlier just after the rebels had evacuated New York, when so many houses and public buildings had been destroyed. He wondered why no one had troubled to repair it.

There was a stir at the guard-post by the entrance to the slip. A moment later a portly gentleman strode towards the customs house with the sergeant of the guard on one side and a harbour official on the other. The latter indicated me with a wave of his hand, and the gentleman surged forward, sweeping off his hat. He was a tall, finely dressed man with an upright carriage and florid face.

"Mr Savill?" he said, waving a crisp lawn handkerchief like a signal flag. "Your servant, sir. I'm Charles Townley, and so very much at your service. A thousand pardons — you should not have to stand about in this heat. I should have been here to greet you two hours ago but my clerk is ill and, to make matters ten times worse, this damned fire has thrown everything awry."

Mr Townley's arrival had an instant effect on my fortunes. A customs official hurried over with two negros carrying my boxes and valises. There was no need, the official said, for the formality of searching them and, at Mr Townley's suggestion, he would have them instantly conveyed to Judge Wintour's house. My pass was countersigned and I was free to go.

As I left, I bowed to Mr Noak, waiting silently in the queue, and said something civilly non-committal about our no doubt meeting again.

"Who was that?" Townley asked as we passed the barrier manned by two sweating sentries.

"A shipboard acquaintance," I said. "No one in particular."

"You will not mind if we walk, I hope? We have not far to go and it will be quicker on a day like this."

For the first few hundred yards, the solid ground felt unyielding and inhospitable beneath my feet. Nor was the city itself more welcoming — it was a veritable anthill, packed with hurrying, wild-eyed people, many of them carrying their belongings on their backs, and with wagons and carriages rumbling over the stones. The streets were paved and tree-lined but narrow. I felt the buildings were closing in on me and yet, after the confined ship, there was also an unsettling sense of limitless space. The air smelled strongly of burning.

"It's busy enough on any other day," Townley observed. "But the fire has made everything ten times worse. The world and his wife are abroad. If they haven't lost their homes then they wish to gawp at those who have."

"Is the damage considerable, sir?"

"Bad enough. Fifty or sixty houses are gone — perhaps more. It began in the middle of the night over there to your left, near Cruger's Wharf and Dock Street. We have fire engines, of course, but our men were overwhelmed by the speed of it, and there were difficulties with the pumps."

"Has there been loss of life?"

"No, we have been spared that, I believe. Through the mercy of God."

"The Captain told us that the fire may have been laid deliberately."

Townley nodded. "It's a strong possibility, in my opinion. The rebels care nothing for their fellow Americans. They endanger the lives of the innocent without a second thought. I believe the Commandant is to post a reward of a hundred and twenty guineas for information about the incendiaries."

He took me first to Headquarters, a short step away, for all newcomers to the city were obliged to register with the authorities.

"You should meet Major Marryot as soon as possible," Townley said, "I had hoped to make you known to him now, but his clerk says he has been called away. You will see a good deal of him, I'm sure, in the course of your duties. He deals with both the Provost Marshal and the city's Superintendent of Police, as well as with the Deputy Adjutant General."

"In that case, sir, would you be good enough to direct me to Judge Wintour's? I should pay my respects to my host."

"Ah." Townley tapped his nose, which reminded me of an axehead bent a few degrees out of true. "I am before you there, sir. I called on the Judge this morning with the news of your arrival. He asked me to convey his compliments to you, of course, and he begs you will

13

do him the favour of calling on him after dinner, when they will have everything in readiness for you. But you must permit me to turn the delay to my own advantage. It would give me immense pleasure if you would dine with me."

I accepted. Townley took my arm. We walked down Broadway to avoid the remains of the fire to the south. In this part of town, the buildings on either side of the road were mostly in a ruinous condition, casualties of the earlier fire in '76. Further eastwards however, the street became pleasant and tree-lined, though a man had to watch where he walked, for it was very dirty.

"I believe Mr Rampton was acquainted with the Wintours when he himself was in America?" Townley said after a moment's silence.

"Yes, sir. Mr Rampton served for a time as Attorney-General of Georgia and he greatly valued the Judge's advice on legal matters."

Townley guided us round the corner into Wall Street. "I am afraid the Wintours are much altered since Mr Rampton knew them." His grip tightened momentarily on my arm. "And for the worse."

CHAPTER
FOUR

Mr Townley had arranged for a room to be set aside at the Merchants Coffee House. The place was on the corner with a fine view of the masts and rigging of ships in the harbour, which lay at the far end of Wall Street. It was a genteel establishment with a balcony running along the tall windows of the principal assembly rooms upstairs.

"They know me pretty well here," Townley said as we went inside. "I think I can promise you a tolerable dinner."

Ceiling fans turned slowly in the big room on the ground floor. It was packed with gentlemen, many of whom seemed acquainted with Mr Townley and anxious to exchange bows with him. But Townley refused to be diverted. He led me through the throng, past a row of booths whose privacy was guarded with green-baize curtains, and up the stairs. On the landing, a negro footman in livery was waiting to show us into a small parlour where a table was laid for three.

"I had hoped that Major Marryot would join us," Townley explained. "No matter. We can talk more confidentially without him."

There was a tap on the door and the servants brought in the dinner. While we ate, Mr Townley asked me for news from London. He was eager to hear what people were thinking and doing, and the more I told him, the more pleased he was.

"You must pardon my appetite for information," he said. "We are starved for it. It's bad enough in peacetime when the mails are better. But nowadays we fasten like leeches on every newcomer and suck him dry as fast as we can."

When the cloth had been withdrawn, Townley pushed back his chair, crossed his legs and passed me the bottle. "And now we can be comfortable, sir. What are they saying about the war in the American Department? I know Lord George has no secrets from Mr Rampton, and Mr Rampton can have no secrets from you." His left eyelid drooped in a wink and he nudged my arm.

I inclined my head but said nothing.

"There's much to be said for keeping these things in the family," Townley went on. "It is a question of loyalty, quite aside from anything else. Whom can one trust but one's own kin and their connections?"

"Indeed," I said, though I rather doubted Mr Rampton trusted anybody at all.

"And — apart from the domestic felicity that no doubt lies in store for you on your return to England — this must mean you are quite the coming man in the Department."

Our conversation turned to the war. Earlier this year, the entry of France on the rebel side had come as a heavy blow. No longer could we take our control of the American seaboard for granted; and there was the constant threat that the French would compel us to divert our resources to the West Indies or even further afield.

"Sir Henry Clinton keeps his own counsel," Townley said. "Between ourselves, sir, there are many Loyalists in this city who cannot understand the General's inactivity."

"But you do not doubt our ability to win, sir?"

"Of course not. Congress will lose this war in the end: it lacks the gold it needs to buy weapons and pay its men and feed its people. None of us can do without money, eh? It's a bitter pill for those damned Whigs to swallow — their soldiers want guineas, for all they carry the King's head on them. The dollar is a laughing stock, barely worth the paper it is printed on. If we Tories but hold our nerve, sir, and prosecute the war with determination, we cannot help but win."

Townley hammered the table in his enthusiasm and proposed that we drink His Majesty's health again. Afterwards, he turned the conversation to Major Marryot.

"It is providential that he could not be here with us," he said. "A word in your private ear before you meet may not come amiss. You may find him — how shall I put it? — a little brusque. He may not be disposed to make your task less burdensome, even if it lies within his power."

"Why, sir? I have no quarrel with the Major."

17

My host fanned himself with his handkerchief, now stained with wine. "You know what soldiers are. Marryot instinctively distrusts any man who doesn't wear a red coat. He was wounded at White Plains, you know, and as a result is quite lame in the left leg, which has not improved a temper already inclined towards the choleric. Add to this the usual prejudices of a true-born Englishman . . ."

"Forgive me, sir," I said, "but I do not understand how this would influence his behaviour towards me."

Townley dabbed with his handkerchief at the moisture on his forehead, which ran in gleaming rivulets through the powder that had fallen from his wig. "He does not have much time for the American Department," he said. "Particularly when it bestirs itself to protect in some small way the interests of the Loyalists." He paused, and then added, "His father was killed at Minden. He served in the Twenty-third."

"Ah," I said. "Yes, I see."

All of us in the Department knew the power of that one word, Minden. Lord George Germain had everything the world could offer — rank, wealth, position, the confidence of his sovereign — but the memory of the battle of Minden was a curse on him he had never contrived to exorcise. Nearly twenty years earlier, he had commanded the British cavalry against the French at the battle. He was widely believed to have disobeyed an order to attack, which had led to many casualties. He had been court-martialled and censured; some said he was lucky to have escaped execution, others that he had been cruelly misjudged. His wealth, connections and ability had enabled him to put the affair behind him. But the army remembered.

"Putting that on one side for a moment, sir," I said quickly. "You implied on our way here that Judge Wintour has had his difficulties."

"Poor man. He has suffered a deal of sorrow in the last few years. He does not go much abroad now, either — so you may find he is not *au courant* with —"

There was a knock at the door. A footman entered with a letter. Murmuring an apology, Mr Townley broke the seal and unfolded the sheet of paper. Breathing heavily, he held it at arm's length and read the contents with a frown deepening on his forehead.

He looked up. "I regret, sir, I'm called away." He tapped the letter. "Talk of the devil, eh? This comes from the Major himself. They have found a body in Canvas Town. So that was why he was not in the way at Headquarters."

"Perhaps I should accompany you, sir? After all . . ."

He nodded, taking my meaning, for his understanding was as quick as any man's. "Indeed — if you are not too fatigued, of course. This is just the sort of affair for you. By the way, Marryot writes that, judging by his dress, the dead man was a gentleman. And I'm afraid there's no doubt about it: the poor fellow met his end by violent means."

CHAPTER
FIVE

The eyes were open, though the orbs were now dull, dry and speckled with dust. The irises were a cloudy blue. The whites were fretted with networks of red veins as delicate as a spider's thread.

"Not much blood," Townley said. "I'd have expected more."

It was very hot. The sweat was pouring off me. I stared at the sightless eyes. It was better than looking at the terrible wound on the neck.

Another dead body, I told myself, that is all. But this body was worse than the first of the day, the decaying merman floating in the harbour. Standing on the deck of the *Earl of Sandwich*, Noak and I had been safely removed from the corpse in the water; and then the kindly tide had borne it away into the ocean, out of sight and out of mind. But this body was so near that, if I had wished, I could have bent down and touched its stockinged feet. This body still looked like someone.

A fly landed on the corpse's left eye but transferred itself almost at once to the dark, dried blood on the neck. My stomach heaved. Hand on mouth, I ducked away from the knot of men around the body and vomited up what I could of our long, luxurious dinner.

One of the soldiers began to laugh but strangled the sound at birth.

"For God's sake," Marryot said, not troubling to lower his voice. "Sergeant, cover the face. It distresses Mr Savill."

"Who is the man?" Townley said, perhaps in a charitable attempt to divert attention from me. "Do you know?"

"No idea. Nothing in the pockets. No rings, though there's the mark of one on his right hand."

"They've picked him clean."

"It would be strange if they hadn't. If he'd been here an hour or two longer, he'd have been as naked as the day he was born. The people here are no better than jackals."

The sergeant stepped back, having arranged a cloth over the corpse's face.

"I think I've seen him before," Townley said. "I'm not perfectly convinced of it, mind you, but I believe he was in church yesterday."

"Newly arrived?"

"Probably. In which case the Commandant will have a note of him."

I straightened up and wiped my mouth. Townley smiled at me. We were standing in a rectangular enclosure of soot-stained bricks, formerly the cellar of a house, one of those destroyed in the great fire of '76. The only traces of it now were the blackened stumps of what had once been the joists supporting the floor above. A ragged canvas sheet, the remains of a patched sail, had been draped across one corner to make a primitive shelter. They had found the body there — not exactly concealed, but not in plain sight from above, either.

Marryot turned to the sergeant. "Have them bring the door. Look sharp."

The body lay in an unnaturally contorted huddle of limbs, one shoulder against the wall. The man was short and thickset, with a yellowy, unhealthy complexion like old wax. He had been stabbed at least twice, once in the neck and once in the back. He wore a grey suit of clothes, the breeches much soiled. He had lost his wig along with his hat, but there were still traces of powder on his face and on the stubble on the scalp. I wondered what had happened to his shoes.

Two soldiers lowered a panelled door into the cellar. The sergeant and another soldier each took a leg of the corpse and dragged it on to the makeshift litter. The jaw of the dead man fell open, revealing the stumps of three blackened teeth. Townley covered his nose with his wine-stained handkerchief.

"Christ," Marryot said. "I swear he's beginning to smell already. This damned heat. The sooner we get him underground the better."

The soldiers heaved the body on to the door. A white speck danced across the earth floor where the body had lain and came to rest against the wall. I bent down and picked it up.

"Mr Savill?" Townley said. "What have you found?"

I held out my hand, palm upwards.

Marryot turned towards us. "What's this?"

"A die," I said. "It was either under the body or lodged in the clothes."

"A gambler, and the game went awry?" The Major addressed his words to Townley. "We'll make enquiries, but I doubt we'll ever know for certain."

"You do not think he might have had something to do with the fire?" Townley asked.

"I don't think anything at all if I can help it," Marryot said. "Not in this goddam heat."

He limped away, dragging his left leg behind him, and led the way up the steps at one end of the cellar into what had once been the yard at the back of the house. I dropped the little die in my pocket and followed with Townley.

The long afternoon had turned into evening. It was still light but the sun was now low in the sky. To the south-west were a few wisps of smoke, the remnants of the fire.

I looked about me. I had never seen a landscape of such utter desolation. According to Townley, this area had been the heart of the first fire, two years earlier, which had broken out near Whitehall Slip and, driven by changing winds, had spread a swathe of destruction through much of the city. The authorities had been ill-prepared for the conflagration and, to make matters worse, many of the buildings had been partly of wood, as dry as tinder from the long summer heat. Reconstruction had been postponed until after the war.

The ruins had long since been looted of anything of value that their owners had left behind. Now, Townley had told me, much of the area was known as Canvas

Town, for it had become home to the worst elements in New York — deserters, vagrants, pickpockets, whores, murderers — in short, all the riff-raff of peace allied to the rogues and vagabonds of war. Temporary sailcloth shelters had sprung up, propped against chimneystacks and ruined walls. Respectable citizens rarely ventured into this piecemeal and provisional quarter of the city, particularly after nightfall.

Three more private soldiers, the rest of Marryot's patrol, were waiting at ground level. One of them was standing on the roadway, holding the head of a broken-down nag that stood between the shafts of a small cart. They were not alone. A score or so of ragged men and women were watching the proceedings from a safe distance. Among them was a gaunt little boy, a tawny-skinned mulatto of ten or eleven years of age, leading a goat by a rope. A sign on the wall said that this was, or had been, Deyes Street.

"Scarcely human, are they?" Townley murmured in my ear. "But what can we do? If we had them thrown into gaol, the charge to the city would be intolerable. Besides, the gaols are full of rebels already. In my view, sir, these knaves should be rounded up and hanged — or be turned loose to fend for themselves in the Debatable Ground. It would be kindness to them and a relief to the respectable class of citizen."

The watchers scattered as the rest of the party appeared from the cellar. The goat had a bell around its neck and it tinkled as it followed the boy. Only one man lingered — a tall negro wearing the faded red coat of a British soldier. He stared with strange hauteur at the

24

men beside the cart, as though he were a person of consequence in this commonwealth of knaves and unfortunates. His dignity was marred by the pink scars that ran from his eyes to his mouth, one on either side of his nose. They twisted the face into the semblance of a smile.

The soldiers brought the body into the street and rolled it into the cart. The sergeant threw a tarpaulin over it. The negro sauntered into the empty doorway of a roofless house.

Marryot gave the slightest of bows and turned smartly away, gesturing to the sergeant to move off.

"A moment, sir, if you please," I said.

The Major stopped and, for the first time, looked directly at me. He was below medium height but made up for his lack of inches in other ways, for he was broad in the chest and decisive in his movements.

"What enquiries will you make in this matter?" I asked.

"That's my business, sir. Mine and the City Commandant's, unless Sir Henry Clinton decides otherwise."

"Mine too, sir. Under the terms of my commission I am obliged to report on the administration of justice in the city in all its aspects — and in particular upon the authority that the military power exercises over the civilian population."

Marryot's colour darkened. "Need I remind you that we are at war?"

"The American Department is well aware of that, sir. And so am I."

The Major glanced at Townley. "Sir, would you have the goodness to explain to Mr Savill that this is a city under martial law? Capital crimes are tried in courts martial, as Lord George Germain knows from personal experience."

Townley smiled impartially and shrugged his shoulders.

"I do not dispute that capital crimes come under military jurisdiction, sir." I spoke in an intentionally quiet voice, purged of emotion. "I do not wish to interfere. Merely to have an oversight."

Marryot's grip tightened around his cane. "If wishes were horses, sir, then beggars would ride."

"If you deny me in this, sir," I said quietly, "I shall complain formally both to Sir Henry here in New York and Lord George Germain in London. My orders are signed by Lord George, and his authority in this matter derives directly from His Majesty."

"I'm damned if —"

"I repeat, sir. I do not wish to interfere with the discharge of your duties in any way. My orders are to observe, nothing more. I have my commission here, if you would like a sight of it."

The Major's forehead was scored with three vertical lines that sprang from the bridge of his nose. When he frowned, the lines deepened. He did not speak for a moment. Then he held out his hand.

"You may show me your wretched scrap of paper."

He read the commission slowly, while Townley paced up and down, fanning himself with his hat and whistling softly. The soldiers clustered around the cart

26

in silence. They must have gathered something of what was going on, for Marryot's voice was naturally loud and harsh, and he had made no attempt to moderate its volume.

He handed back the letter of authorization. "I warn you, sir, it will be a waste of your time and mine. But what can one expect when our affairs in America are at the mercy of a man who hides behind a desk three thousand miles away?"

I had no desire to fight other people's battles. "And how will you proceed in this matter?"

"We'll find out who the man is, if we are lucky. Then at least he can be buried under his own name. As to his murderer: I do not hold out much hope there, sir, unless someone lays information. If a man looks for his pleasures in Canvas Town, he runs the risk of paying heavily for them."

"Thank you, sir," I said. "I'm much obliged."

Townley smiled at us. "I'm rejoiced to see you such good friends, gentlemen." He pulled out his watch. "Mr Savill, I do not wish to hurry you, but we should be on our way. I fancy the Wintours keep early hours."

"Eh?" Marryot said. "You are engaged at Judge Wintour's?"

Townley bowed. "In a manner of speaking. Mr Savill will be lodging there during his stay in New York."

Marryot coloured again. "Pray — ah — pray give my compliments to the Judge and his ladies. Tell them that I hope to do myself the honour of calling on them to see how they do."

The three of us, followed by the soldiers and the cart, walked down to Broadway, where we separated. Townley and I turned left and made our way slowly eastwards in the direction of St Paul's Chapel.

"Well," Townley said, "you are quite the Daniel, I perceive, and have ventured into the lion's den and emerged unscathed. I have seen Major Marryot make grown men quail." He smiled at me. "But have a care, sir. He is a man of some importance in this city and you should mind how you cross him."

We strolled in silence the length of another block. Then Townley added: "Oh — and by the by — they say he has a certain tendresse for young Mrs Wintour."

CHAPTER
SIX

The high-ceilinged room was a place of shadows. Despite the heat, the windows were shut and the curtains closed — because, old Mrs Wintour said, the smell of the great fire had become intolerable and the street below so noisy.

Ten candles burned on brackets attached to the walls but they served mainly to accentuate the surrounding gloom. A heavy moth, drunk with desire, circled one of the flames. I could not drag my eyes away from it. The candle singed first one wing, then the other. At last, and with supernatural strength, the besotted insect reached the fatal flame again. There was a faint sizzling sound. The moth fell to the pier table immediately beneath the bracket and lay there, twitching.

"More tea, sir?" Mrs Wintour asked, pale and indistinct on a sofa.

"Thank you, ma'am, but no."

I rubbed sweating palms on my breeches. The Judge let slip a long, rumbling snore from the recesses of his high-backed armchair. Only his legs were visible.

Having discharged her duties as a hostess, Mrs Wintour sat back and did not speak. I could not tell whether her eyes were open or closed. From somewhere below came a clatter as though a pot had fallen on the floor. The moth gave up its unequal struggle with the world and expired. The air in the room seemed to condense into a dark, swaying liquid, trapping the humans like three curious natural specimens suspended in alcohol.

Would it always be like this, I wondered? Would I sit in silence, night after night, in this smothering subaqueous fog? The memory of the corpse in the harbour drifted into my mind, and I saw again the decaying face of the merman. Perhaps the poor fellow now lay in just such a stifling semi-darkness at the bottom of the ocean.

It was past ten o'clock. In a moment the grandfather clock in the hall must chime the quarter. It seemed as if days or even weeks had passed since it had last chimed the hour. A frugal supper had been served at nine by a manservant out of livery and a maid. I had been here since eight o'clock. Townley had introduced me to the Judge and had then slipped away, promising to call for me in the morning.

The drawing-room door opened. Mrs Wintour twitched in her chair and emitted a little cry as though someone had pinched her. A lady entered.

"Ah, my dear," the Judge said, levering himself up with the help of the tea table. "There you are, Bella, bless my soul. Are you quite restored?"

I rose to my feet. The light was so poor that the woman's face was barely visible. I was aware only that she was small and slim, and she brought with her the smell of otto of roses.

"You startled me," Mrs Wintour said. "Why is everything so loud nowadays?"

"Bella," the Judge went on, "allow me to name Mr Savill of the American Department. And, Mr Savill, here at last is my dear daughter, my son's wife, Mrs Arabella."

I bowed over the lady's hand.

"Mr Savill," she said in a low voice. "I am happy to meet you."

"Come and sit with us, my dear," the Judge said, stretching out his hand to her. "We shall send for fresh tea."

"Would you excuse me this once, sir?" Mrs Arabella took the Judge's hand in both of hers. "My head is still splitting — it is this terrible heat, I think." She stroked her father-in-law's hand as though it were a small animal in need of reassurance. "I came down for a moment to welcome Mr Savill. I would not want him to think us unmannerly."

"Never that, madam," I said. "You are politeness itself. But I am sorry you are indisposed."

"You must take something," the Judge said. "Have Miriam mix you up a James's Powder. I'm sure it will answer."

"Yes, sir, you may be sure I shall."

Mrs Arabella kissed her parents-in-law. She curtsied to me and left the room.

"The dear child should not overdo it," the Judge observed, sinking back into his chair.

The flurry of movement gave me the opportunity to withdraw. I had been up at dawn, I explained, and my first day ashore had been a tiring one.

"Be so good as to ring the bell, sir," the Judge said. "Josiah will bring a candle and take you up to your chamber."

The manservant conducted me up the stairs. My room was at the back of the house on the second floor. Square and low-ceilinged, it was dominated by a high bed with an enormous feather mattress. My bags and boxes had been brought up during the day.

I dismissed the man for the night. It struck me that it was only now, for the first time in over five weeks, that I was alone. Noak had always been there on the *Earl of Sandwich*, usually within arm's reach. Even in the ship's heads, someone else had generally been beside me or at least within sight and sound. Nor had I been alone today. Indeed, my overwhelming impression was that this was a city where it would be almost impossible to be solitary, for the streets and buildings were packed with people — townsfolk, refugees, British and Loyalist soldiers, and the crowds of followers that accumulate around an army.

I undressed, allowing my clothes to lie where they fell. For a moment I stood naked at the foot of the bed, hoping for a draught to cool my skin. But the air was warm and motionless.

I was too tired to read. Leaving the bed-curtains tied back, I climbed into bed. I laid myself on top of the bedclothes. The mattress enveloped me. I pinched out the candle.

The darkness was soft and caressing. I found myself thinking of Mrs Arabella. Because the drawing room had been so dimly lit, and because she had not come close to any of the candles, I had not seen her face clearly — it had been no more than a pale smudge floating above her body.

My impression of her derived from information provided by other senses. First, there had been the scent of otto of roses: but the smell of it had combined with the private odours of Mrs Arabella herself to form something richer and denser. Second, I remembered her voice, which had not been like any other I knew. This was partly because she spoke with an American accent, though it was not the broad twang used by so many people I had heard today. Also, of course, she was a woman, with the soft, insinuating tone that certain women possessed.

There had been no women aboard the *Earl of Sandwich*. To my surprise I felt my naked body responding even to this largely formless memory of Mrs Arabella with a rush of blood that both disconcerted and embarrassed me.

Hastily I directed my attention to my wife, Augusta. I imagined her walking in the park or reading or talking about the clothes and homes of other ladies, as she seemed interminably to do; and by degrees I grew calmer.

In the silence and the darkness, I thought about my daughter. Lizzie had wept when I left her. She was five now, and living with my sister in Shepperton, for her mother had remained in London. I prayed for my daughter's happiness and for her preservation from all harm, as I did every night.

As I lay there, I became aware that the silence was no longer as absolute as it had been. Somewhere in the distance, a barely distinguishable sound rose and fell in volume in a series of irregular ululations.

The wind in the chimney? A bird of the night? An animal in pain? I did not recognize the sound but that was not strange in itself, for I was in a strange house in a strange city on the coast of a strange continent.

A minute or so slipped by. The sound grew fainter and then stopped altogether.

By that time I was sliding into sleep. My last conscious thought was that the sound might have been a weeping child. But, God be thanked, someone had dried her tears.

CHAPTER
SEVEN

My Dear Daughter —

I put down the pen and stared out of the window. How did I find the words that would speak directly to a five-year-old child? How could I assure my Lizzie at a distance of three thousand miles of my paternal care and love for her?

> After a voyage of five weeks I arrived here without any accident and in as good health as when I left you in Shepperton. The conviction that you will derive more benefit from where you are than if still with me has consoled me greatly on my parting from you.

Dull, I thought — dull, dull, dull. But I must write something to let her know I am safe and that she is in my thoughts. Anything was better than nothing.

> Pray give my service to your aunt and ask her to write to me every week to tell me how you all do.

I reminded myself that a father should provide moral guidance to his children. In the rearing of the young, the tender emotions should be, by and large, the province of the tender sex.

> If you love me, strive to be good under every situation and to all living creatures, and to acquire those accomplishments which I have put in your power, and which will go far towards ensuring you the warmest love of your affectionate father,
>   E. Savill

I threw down the pen more violently this time. Ink drops spattered across the table. A moment later, I picked up the pen again, dipped it in the inkpot and wrote in a swift scrawl:

> Postscriptum: It feels strange to be on dry land. It does not wobble like the sea. New York is monstrous hot and busy. It is full of our soldiers, and very brave and gay they look in their fine uniforms. I saw many great ships in the harbour. Last night I slept in a featherbed that was as big as an elephant.

I folded the letter, addressed it, and put it to one side, ready to be sealed. It was still early in the morning and the sun was on the other side of the house. I took a fresh sheet and wrote:

> My dear Augusta — We are safely arrived in New York, after a passage of some five weeks and two days. The —

I paused again. At this moment, I could think of nothing to write after *The*. Augusta would not wish to know that the weather was hot or that my mattress was as big as an elephant. Nor perhaps would she wish to hear that I was lodging in a house with a woman who smelled of otto of roses.

As I waited, three drops of ink fell from the pen and blotted the paper. I swore, crumpled up the sheet and tossed it into the empty fireplace. I set down the pen, propped my head on my hands and stared at the view.

The writing table was drawn up to the room's single window, which looked out on a small garden laid out with bushes and gravelled walks in the old style. To the left was a service yard with a line of outbuildings. On the right, beyond a high wall, was another street, for Judge Wintour's house stood at an intersection.

At the bottom of the garden, in the angle where the rear wall met the long side wall, was a square pavilion built of red bricks, with the quoins and architraves dressed with stone. Beside it was a narrow gate to the street. The little building was raised above the road. A flight of shallow steps led up to a glazed door on the side facing the house, and there was a tall window on at least two of the other sides. It was some sort of summerhouse, I thought, a species of gazebo or belvedere. Lizzie would love to play house there. I would describe it to her in my next letter.

I took up the pen again.

I have not yet seen much of the house where I am to lodge for I did not arrive here until yesterday evening. It is in Warren Street, not far from King's College. Judge Wintour was most welcoming and he was gratified to have intelligence of your Uncle Rampton, for whom he entertains the most cordial regard. Pray believe me to be your most devoted servant in all things, ES.

I rang the bell. A young manservant named Abraham, little more than a boy, showed me down to the parlour where the table was set for breakfast. He said that Mrs Wintour rarely rose before midday, and that the Judge and Mrs Arabella were still in their rooms.

While I was eating, there was a double knock on the street door. Abraham returned to say that a gentleman had called to see me.

"Me? Is it Mr Townley?"

"No, your honour. A Mr Noak."

"Very well. You had better ask him to step in."

Noak bowed from the doorway. "Your servant, sir. I apologize for calling on you so early. I fear necessity has no manners."

I had a sudden, uncomfortable memory of vomiting over a pewter platter containing Mr Noak's dinner, not a fortnight ago. "My dear sir, in that case necessity is a welcome guest. Pray join me — have you breakfasted?"

Noak perched on the edge of a chair. He said he had already had breakfast but would be glad of a cup of coffee.

"I know you must be much engaged at present," he said. "But I did not know whom to turn to."

I guessed that Noak wanted money. People always wanted money. Townley had been right, when he talked at dinner of Congress's lack of gold, its fatal weakness: *None of us can do without money, eh?*

"— so any form of employment commensurate with my skills and small talents, sir."

"What?" I said. "I beg your pardon, I did not quite catch what you said before that."

"I said that unfortunately the position I had been invited to fill no longer exists, sir. The gentleman I was to work for has died, and his son has wound up the business. There it is — I have come all this way for nothing, and now I am in want of a situation."

"I am sorry to hear it. But I'm not sure what I can do to help — except offer you another cup of coffee."

Noak shook his head. "May I hope for your good offices? You will soon, I'm sure, have an extensive acquaintance here. If you should come across a gentleman who is in want of a clerk — with, I may say, the very highest character from his previous employer in London, as well as considerable experience in the management of affairs both in America and in London — then I beg that you might mention my name."

"Nothing would give me greater pleasure," I said. "But . . ."

"I know," Noak interrupted. "I am clutching at straws, sir. But a man in my position must clutch at something."

"Of course." I liked the man's doggedness, his refusal to be cowed. "Leave me your direction, sir — I will send you a line if I hear of a place."

The American took out a pocket book and pencil. "A line addressed to the Charing Cross Tavern will always find me."

A moment later, he pushed back his chair and said abruptly that he would not trouble me any further. It was clear that asking the favour had not come easily to him, and I liked him the better for it.

After I had finished breakfast, I was passing through the hall when I heard another knock at the front door. Abraham opened it. A servant was on the step. I heard him mention my name. Abraham took a letter from him and presented it with a low bow to me. I tore it open.

Mr Savill
I have just this moment received intelligence that our body yesterday has acquired a name: a corporal on the Commandant's staff says he is a Mr Roger Pickett, a gentleman newly arrived in New York, who was lodging at Widow Muller's on Beekman Street (opposite St George's Chapel). Major Marryot suggests we meet him there as soon as is convenient. The bearer of this will conduct you to the house if you are at leisure. If not, I shall do myself the honour of waiting on you later in the day.
   Yours, etc. C. Townley

Judge Wintour came down the stairs, clinging to the rail.

"Mr Savill, good morning. I hope you have passed a satisfactory night. You've breakfasted, I hear. Would you do me the kindness of sitting with me and taking another cup of coffee while I have mine? There is much I should like to ask you about the current state of affairs in London."

"Nothing would give me more pleasure, sir — but perhaps I might defer our conversation until later." I held up the letter. "I have to go out."

The Judge's eyes had strayed to the open door, where the messenger was waiting. "You there," he said, his voice suddenly sharp. "You're Mr Townley's man, aren't you?"

"Yes, your honour. He sent me for Mr Savill."

"Another dreadful crime, I suppose," the Judge said. "I have never known the city like this. We shall soon be murdered in our beds."

"Yes, sir. And murder it is. A gentleman, too — Mr Pickett."

"What?" The Judge clung to the newel post at the foot of the stairs. Abraham moved instantly to his other side and took his arm. "Roger Pickett? But it can't be." The old man turned his faded blue eyes from the servant's face to mine. "Mr Pickett was in this very house, sir — not a week ago."

CHAPTER
EIGHT

"Not a man of substance, as you see," Townley said. "Not now."

The little room was at the back of the house in Beekman Street and on the third floor. The window overlooked a farrier's yard. It was warm and close. I heard a roll of thunder in the distance.

Roger Pickett's possessions were strewn over the bed, the table, the one chair, the chest and the floor. Mingled with them were unwashed glasses, plates, bottles, bowls and cups, many with scraps of rotting food still adhering to them. Widow Muller, the woman who kept the house, was a slattern. Besides, she had told Marryot that Pickett could not pay for the maid's services.

I stood in the doorway, hat in hand. "Had he lived here long?"

"A matter of ten days," the Major said. "Time enough to turn it into a pigsty."

Townley was delving into the papers on the table. He raised his head and smiled at me. "I fancy he would have called on you, if his life had been spared."

"I suppose he desired compensation like the rest of them?" Marryot said, opening the chest. "Dear God, you Americans are like hogs around a trough — not you, of course, sir; there must be exceptions to every rule — but I hold by the general principle."

"No doubt Mr Pickett suffered losses, sir," Townley said coldly. "Most of us have." He held up a sheet of paper. "It appears he came down from Philadelphia."

"After the evacuation?"

"Yes. But he had only been there a matter of weeks. According to this he was originally from North Carolina."

Marryot snorted. "Ha! I wager his loyalty has cost him a fortune. It is curious, is it not? All our refugees claim to have been as rich as Croesus before the war. It's as if gold grew on the very trees here."

I took a step into the room. "It should not be difficult to establish Mr Pickett's situation, sir. Judge Wintour says he was acquainted with his daughter-in-law, Mrs Arabella."

"What?" Marryot said. "What? No one told me that."

Townley frowned. "Acquainted? How?"

"Only slightly, I believe." I looked from one to the other. "It appears that Mrs Arabella's late father met the man when he was in North Carolina before the war."

"Her father? Mr Froude?" Townley rubbed his beak of a nose. "You are full of surprises, sir."

"Why did you not tell me earlier?" Marryot said.

"I've only just found you, sir," I pointed out. "And I did not hear of Mr Pickett's visit to Warren Street until this morning — the Judge was with me when Mr

Townley's billet arrived. In any case, even if I had known about it yesterday evening, I could hardly have known its significance since the corpse had not been identified."

Marryot coloured but did not apologize. "Why did Pickett call on them? And when, precisely?"

"Last Thursday, sir — it was a morning call. He was but recently arrived and he called to renew his acquaintance with them, which I believe was very slight. He did not stay long for both the Judge and Mrs Arabella were obliged to go out."

"What did she say of him?" Townley asked. "Mrs Arabella, I mean?"

"I have not seen her this morning, sir. Indeed, I met her only for a moment last night."

Townley shrugged. "It don't signify — we shall probably find that Pickett called on everyone he had ever scraped an acquaintance with. All the refugees do that when they first come to New York. What else can the poor devils do? It is a form of genteel beggary."

Marryot limped over to the table. "What have we here?"

"I believe this to be a list of debts, sir." Townley handed him a sheet of paper. "Nearly two hundred guineas in all. But we cannot tell who his creditors are. There's only a single initial beside each figure. Large sums. Guineas and pounds, not shillings and pence."

"A gambler," Marryot said. "What did I tell you?"

I slipped two fingers into my waistcoat pocket and took out the die I had found on Pickett's body. It was made of ivory, not of bone or wood. A genteel die for a genteel beggar.

Townley smiled at me. "You have corroboration in the palm of your hand, I fancy. Faro? Backgammon? Fortunes change hands every night in this city at a throw of the dice."

"A man who gambles in Canvas Town is a fool," Marryot said.

"Or desperate for money," Townley said. "Plenty of men go to Canvas Town after nightfall who would not be seen there in the day. Darkness covers a multitude of sins, does it not? And do you not think that if Pickett could not pay his debts . . .?"

"Very likely — but I doubt we'll ever know." Marryot took up another paper. "Depend upon it, if we find the murderer at all, we shall find him in Canvas Town."

"When did the people of the house last see Mr Pickett?" I asked.

"Sunday afternoon," Marryot said. "He dined at the tavern over the way and came back here to change his shirt. He didn't stay long — he went out at about five o'clock. That was the last they saw of him. We must trace the next of kin."

We did not linger in Pickett's chamber. It was stiflingly hot and so small that the three of us made it unpleasantly crowded. Marryot leafed through the rest of the papers. In a satchel, he found an unfinished and undated letter written in a sprawling, untidy hand.

My dear sister, I am safely arrived in New York from
Philadelphia. My design prospers, and I have great hopes
that my fortunes will soon

"His design?" Townley said. "A gambler's new and
quite infallible system, no doubt. The next turn of the
cards, the next throw of the dice, and all will be
changed."

"No indication who the sister is, where she lives,"
Marryot said. "Perhaps Mrs Arabella knows." He
pulled out his watch. "We've done all we can here. I'll
leave a guard at the door and have the room sealed up."

"What other enquiries will you make now, sir?" I
asked.

"I shall make my report to the Commandant and he
will order me to do as he thinks fit. Which may very
well be nothing. That would certainly be my advice. We
are in the middle of a war, sir, and young men are dying
every day. I cannot waste my time on every fool who
pays the price for his folly."

"Very true, sir," Townley put in. "In any case, what
can one do unless a witness comes forward? And I'm
afraid one does not find many public-spirited citizens in
Canvas Town."

"But is this your usual policy with murder, sir?" I
said to Marryot. "You bury the dead and let the
perpetrator go free?"

"May I remind you again, sir? We are at war." He
limped to the door. "The civil population cannot enjoy
the same privileges and the same degree of comfort as
it does in peacetime. New York looks to the army for its

protection, and military objectives are of paramount importance."

Townley stared at the sloping ceiling. "Still," he said, "I hope that the news of Mr Pickett's death does not distress the Judge or Mrs Arabella."

Once again, the blood rushed to Marryot's face. "No, indeed. It is fortunate that the acquaintance was slight."

There, I thought, my anger subsiding, there is the man's weak spot: Mrs Arabella Wintour.

CHAPTER
NINE

Shortly after one o'clock, there was an explosion.

It came without warning, an enormous, reverberating crash that swept over the city like an invisible tidal wave. For an instant, silence fell, an auditory equivalent to the trough following the wave.

Time seemed to elongate itself in defiance of the natural laws regulating the universe. I saw Townley's face in profile beside me, the mouth open, the nose jutting outwards, his features as rigid as if turned to stone. The horses walking and trotting down Broadway stopped moving. Two oxen pulling a wagon not ten yards away might have fallen asleep where they stood. The trees on either side of the avenue were motionless. The leg of a dog lying in the shade of shop doorway was as stiff as a ramrod now though an instant before it had been a blur as the animal scratched its ribcage.

All this dissolved into a flurry of movement. The nearer of the oxen collided with the trunk of a tree. A horse reared and a Hessian officer tumbled from its saddle. The dog scrambled into the darkness of the shop behind him, its tail between its legs. A plump middle-aged woman fainted. Her maid tried to support her but her mistress's weight was too heavy for her, and they both fell to the ground.

The sounds were slower to return. They came in scraps and fragments, muffled at first, and accompanied by a ringing in my ears. Townley yelped, "Christ!" A window shattered across the street. Shouts and screams filled the air. Horses neighed. Oxen bellowed.

Several soldiers stumbled down the road at a trot towards Fort George. The middle-aged woman woke up and went into violent hysterics, pummelling the poor maid without mercy. Townley touched my sleeve and pointed over the roofline of the houses on the other side of the street. A feathery column of black smoke was rising into the sky.

"The French fleet?" I said, and my voice sounded muffled and remote.

"There would have been some warning if they were that close inshore. I think one of the ammunition ships must have blown up."

"By accident?"

"God knows." Townley dabbed his face with a scented handkerchief. "First the fire, now this. Look at that damned smoke — it's like a black plume at a funeral. Either it's cursed ill luck or we have enemies within."

"My windows!" cried the plump woman, suddenly emerging from her hysterics. "Quick, girl, what are you about? Help me up, we must go home."

The Hessian officer scrambled to his feet and stumbled after his bolting horse, leaving a stream of German oaths behind him. The shopkeeper, a perruquier in apron and shirt-sleeves with a face as pale as his own powder, appeared in his doorway with the dog cowering at his heels as though it had been given one whipping and feared another.

Townley and I walked quickly down Broadway toward Fort George. But there was nothing to be learned at Headquarters, either about the explosion or about the unfortunate Pickett.

I scribbled a note to Mr Rampton and enclosed with it the letters I had earlier written to Lizzie and Augusta. Townley showed me to the Post Room and introduced me to the head clerk who guarded the mails. The letters would go out in the lead-weighted Government mailbags by the first packet that sailed for home.

"Though God knows when that will be," the official observed. "What with the rebels within and the French fleet without."

"We might as well have our dinner now," Townley said afterwards. "Nothing else can be done at present until this fuss and bother die down."

As we were leaving, one of Mr Townley's servants approached him with the news that the fever had claimed the life of his clerk in the early hours of the morning.

"The poor fellow," Townley said. "Troubles never come singly, do they? It is this damned heat — it encourages every kind of pestilence. I must send something to his widow."

We walked slowly towards the Common. Townley knew of a little inn in King George Street — nothing to look at from the outside, he told me, but the cook was from Milan and could do quite exceptional things with the meanest materials. I had already learned that Mr Townley thought a great deal about his meals and how they were prepared.

The excitement had ebbed away from the city. The broken glass had been swept up. The shops were as busy as ever.

"It's as if nothing had happened," I said.

"That is the nature of war, sir," Townley said. "Terrors succeed terrors, but one cannot be apprehensive all the time. These exceptional alarms are much less of an inconvenience than something more mundane — like the death of my unfortunate clerk, for example. In life he was sadly imperfect, but in death he will be sorely missed. A mass of tedious business must inevitably fall on my own shoulders."

"I wonder." I hesitated, but only for a moment. "I think I told you, I met an American on the voyage. He worked as a lawyer's clerk in London, and even knows something of the American Department. I believe he is in want of a position."

A happy coincidence. Indeed I even congratulated myself on this turn of events — at a stroke, I thought, I might be able to oblige a new acquaintance while discharging a debt I owed to an older one.

"Really?" Mr Townley said. "How very interesting."

CHAPTER
TEN

After dinner, I returned to Warren Street. I found the ladies of the house in the drawing room. Mrs Arabella was at a table by the window with a copy of the *Royal American Gazette* spread out before her. Old Mrs Wintour was sitting in front of the empty fireplace.

I bowed in turn to them and wished them good afternoon. The old lady nodded graciously to me. But she said nothing and in a moment began to stare fixedly at the fireback as if trying to commit its sooty surface to memory.

Mrs Arabella beckoned me towards her. For the first time I saw her by daylight. Her face was oval, the complexion pale and unblemished, the lips full and the eyes brown. Her hair was partly concealed beneath her cap, but what I could see of it was lustrous and so dark as to be almost black.

"Pray do not mention the explosion or yesterday's fire, sir," she said in low voice. "Nor Mr Pickett's death. Mrs Wintour finds subjects of that nature disagreeable."

I nodded. Major Marryot was a bear in a red coat yet she clearly had him in thrall. Mr Townley spoke of her with a strange mixture of delicacy and wariness. Even

Noak, as dry and dull as a ledger, knew her charms by reputation: "Once seen, never forgotten."

Now, seeing Mrs Arabella in the glare of natural light from the window, I was frankly disappointed. She was well enough but her face lacked the classical proportions and high-bred refinement of Augusta's; her figure would not have been considered *à la mode* in London, and her cotton dress seemed positively dowdy. The Americans, I thought, perhaps judged a lady's personal attractions by lower standards than we did.

I had, on Mr Rampton's advice, brought the Wintours some small presents from London — lace for the ladies, chosen by Augusta, a volume of sermons for the Judge and several pounds of tea for them all. When I presented the gifts, Mrs Wintour became quite animated.

"I'm sure my son will enjoy the sermons too, when he comes home," she said in a voice like rustling paper. "His attention has always been turned towards spiritual matters — even as a little boy. I remember when we went to church: he listened so attentively to the sermons."

Mrs Arabella wiped her fingers, inky from the fresh newsprint, on her handkerchief. She thanked me for the gifts but said she would not examine the lace until her hands were clean.

Mrs Wintour patted the sofa on which she sat. "Come and tell me how dear Mr Rampton does, Mr Savill. It must be nearly twenty years since we saw him. And you are married to his niece, Miss Augusta, I hear?"

"Mr Rampton does very well, thank you, ma'am. Now he is under secretary of the American Department, Lord George Germain entrusts a great deal of business to him."

"And you, sir? My husband tells me that Mr Rampton speaks most highly of you."

"He is kindness itself, ma'am." This was not entirely true. Mr Rampton had opposed Augusta's marriage to me, a mere junior clerk.

"And do you have the consolation of children? You must pardon an old lady's curiosity, Mr Savill."

"A daughter, ma'am — Elizabeth."

"How fortunate you are. I always wished for a daughter. When my son comes home, he and Bella will have one, possibly two. It will be as good as having them myself." She smiled at me. "It will be delightful, will it not? I dare say they will live at Mount George for much of the year — the air is healthier for children."

The mention of Lizzie reminded me of the crying child I had heard — or thought I had heard — as I was going to sleep. I was about to ask whether there was a child in the house when the conversation shifted direction and the old lady began to ask me about which London clergymen were at present esteemed for their preaching.

"Mama," Mrs Arabella said. "You should not plague Mr Savill with questions. I am sure he is weary."

Mrs Wintour looked bewildered. "Ah — yes — do forgive me, Mr Savill, I run on, sometimes. My son tells me I must have been born chattering. Have you met my son John, sir?"

54

"I've not had that pleasure, ma'am."

"You will meet him soon, I'm sure. He will make everything right when he comes home, and then I shall have my little granddaughters."

"You are tired, ma'am," said Mrs Arabella, rising from her chair. "Should you not rest for a while? I shall ring the bell for Miriam."

Miriam came, and the old woman rose obediently and hobbled out of the room, clinging with two thin hands to the servant's arm. The maid looked without hesitation to Mrs Arabella for her orders, though in this case few words passed between them, only a look of intelligence. This situation, I thought, had happened before, and more than once.

Mrs Arabella sat down again. "The Judge tells me that Mr Pickett has been found dead in Canvas Town. Was he murdered?"

That was plain-speaking indeed. "He is certainly dead, ma'am, and in all probability murdered." I tried not to think of the fly settling on the ragged wound in Pickett's neck.

"What was the motive?"

"The affair is still a mystery. I apprehend that Major Marryot thinks Mr Pickett was a gambling man, and that may have had something to do with it. But I hope I do not distress you. I understand he was an acquaintance."

"I did not know him at all well, sir. Besides, we have grown used to hearing of horrors."

"I understand he has a sister. Do you know anything of her?"

"No. I was not aware he had any family at all. I met him only once before and very briefly. I think he had had a few dealings with my father, but purely in the way of business."

She said nothing further on the subject. A silence fell, and it was not altogether comfortable.

"I — I understand your husband, madam, is expected home?" I said. "Do you know when he will come?"

She stared at me with heavy-lidded eyes. "He has been missing since Saratoga. I thought you must know."

"Why yes — Mr Rampton said as much. But from what Mrs Wintour said, I inferred —"

"Mrs Wintour desires his return so strongly that she believes he must come. I am not so sanguine, and nor is the Judge. But we do not contradict her."

"No, indeed."

"You would be doing us all a kindness if you would humour her in this as well."

"Of course."

The Battle of Saratoga had been ten months ago. If there had been no news of Captain Wintour since then, the odds must be against his having survived.

"You have heard nothing at all of him?" I said after a moment.

"No. We fear the worst. We hear so many reports of atrocities."

Anger had brought colour to her face, and she looked almost beautiful. There was a fire about her when her passions were roused. I murmured a platitude about the horrors of war, particularly civil war.

"Why does Lord George not advise the King to bring an end to this folly?" she burst out.

"Madam, I wish I knew, and then I should tell you. But Lord George does not open his mind to me."

"Of course not." Mrs Arabella's eyelids closed, as though she wished to blot out the sight of me. "You are only a clerk."

CHAPTER
ELEVEN

The following day, Wednesday, Mr Townley arrived in Warren Street as I was in the act of leaving the house.

"Mr Savill, sir," he cried from across the street. "This is well met. Have you heard the news?"

"No, sir. What news?"

"I thought the Major might have sent a man over to you. No matter — I am here instead. It appears that someone laid information late last night, and a man has been taken up for poor Mr Pickett's murder."

"On what grounds?"

"Oh, they have plenty of evidence — they have not charged the fellow yet, but I do not think there can be much doubt about it. We must not linger — he is to be interrogated at ten o'clock, and it wants but twenty minutes of that now. They are holding him at Van Cortlandt's Sugar House at the corner of Trinity churchyard. And we are to meet your shipboard acquaintance there — what is his name? Note? Slope? Poke?"

"Noak, sir." I had written to him yesterday afternoon and told him he might call on Mr Townley. "It is good of you to spare the time to see him."

"I have seen him already — he seems capable enough. And there's something to be said for a man who knows a little of the wider world. I have decided to give him a trial for a day or two."

"That's most obliging, sir — I hope he answers."

"We shall soon begin to discover whether he does or not. He can keep a record this morning."

As we walked along, Townley asked if I was perfectly satisfied with my lodging; if not he would look about for somewhere else that might suit me.

I told him not to trouble himself for I liked it very well and added, "By the way, I had some conversation with the Wintour ladies yesterday evening."

"They are in good health, I hope? How did they strike you?"

"I had not realized that Mrs Arabella's husband is missing rather than dead."

"It is most unfortunate," Townley said. "No one has seen Captain Wintour since Saratoga, though there was a report of his being wounded. It leaves them all in a species of limbo — Mrs Arabella in particular. They do not know whether to mourn a son and husband or to pray for his happy return."

"Mrs Wintour seems in no doubt that it should be the latter."

"Alas, sir — as you may already have observed, Mrs Wintour's sufferings have taken their toll on the poor lady's rational faculties." Townley pointed with his stick. "We are nearly there — see? That is Van Cortlandt's."

The main sugar house was situated on a corner where two streets met. It was a big, brick-faced structure five storeys high and as ugly as a barn. An annex stood to one side. The establishment overlooked a yard enclosed by a wall. The building's barred windows were deeply recessed and well above the height of a man. They accentuated rather than relieved the monolithic blankness of the façade.

"This place is for prisoners of war," he murmured in my ear. "Marryot's man shouldn't be here at all, but the Provost is full."

We stood aside to allow a file of soldiers to march down the road to the high wooden gates, which were guarded by two sentries. One leaf of the gates opened at the sentry's double-knock and the file passed through to a yard. We followed them in.

Once inside, the sergeant of the guard told us to wait in the hall. Townley chafed at the delay.

"At least it is cool and pleasant in here," I said.

"The walls are immensely thick, sir. And there are few windows, as you see. The place was built to store sugar in good condition and safe from thieves. But it keeps people in as well as it keeps people out."

A door at the back of the hall opened and Mr Noak came through.

Townley stared at him. "What? You? Here already?"

Noak bobbed his head to us, more like a bird pecking at a worm than a mark of respect. "Yes, sir. I made myself known to Major Marryot and showed him your letter. If you would care to step this way."

60

As soon as we left the hall, the atmosphere changed. Sights and smells assaulted the senses. But I was first aware of the noise: a chaotic concerto of voices, groans, cries, and restless movements, all of them bouncing off the high, barrel-vaulted ceiling and setting off rolling echoes.

On the other side of the door to the hall was a table at which three soldiers were playing cards, apparently oblivious of what was going on around them. They glanced up incuriously and nodded us through.

Noak led us down a long, stone-flagged corridor lined with doors on either side. Along the centre of the passage was a drainage gulley apparently used as a sewer. Both Townley and I covered our noses with handkerchiefs.

A barred opening was set high in each door, and each opening framed a man's face; his hands clung to the bars; and behind him was a multitude of other faces, packed together in one heaving, shouting, stinking mass of humanity.

"For the love of Christ, your honours," a man called to us, "for the love of Christ, I can't stop the bleeding."

We walked faster and faster to a door at the far end. A guard let us into a lobby at the foot of a flight of stairs.

"Dear God," I said. "It's a perfect Bedlam in there. Worse than Bedlam — a foretaste of hell itself."

"They have only themselves to thank, sir," Townley said. "If they take up arms against their lawful government, they must expect to pay the price. The problem is that we have so many rebels to cope with.

61

We are obliged to pack them in the best we can, wherever we find room."

We mounted the stairs first to an anteroom guarded by a sentry and then to an inner apartment. A narrow window looked out across a neatly tended churchyard at the blackened ruins of Trinity Church.

Marryot was sitting at a long oak table, his lame leg resting on a footstool. He was leafing through a pile of papers. "Good morning, sirs," he said, looking up. "Pray sit down, now you are come at last. I was about to start without you." He nodded to Noak. "Tell the man outside to pass the word for the prisoner."

We took chairs on either side of the Major. When he returned, Noak sat at the end nearer the window, with pen, ink and paper set out before him.

"How fortunate that an informer came forward, sir," Townley said.

"Fortunate?" Marryot sniffed. "Fortune has nothing to do with it, sir. The army pays for its information. There are always men in want of gold."

"Can you be sure that the information is accurate, sir?" I asked.

"Little is certain in this world, sir, but the fellow we have in custody is certainly a rogue."

We heard the stamp of marching feet outside. There was a knock on the door. At Marryot's word, two soldiers entered with a small negro between them. He was cuffed at the wrists and swaying from side to side. When the soldiers came smartly to attention in front of the table, he collapsed on the floor in a huddle of limbs and filthy clothes.

62

"Pull him up," Marryot ordered.

The soldiers hooked their arms under the prisoner's shoulders and lifted him back to his feet.

"Master, I didn't do it, I swear on —"

"Hold your tongue," Marryot roared. He turned to Noak. "You may write this down under today's date, the fifth of August. And the place and time, of course. That this is the interrogation of a negro slave, a runaway, name of Virgil, property of the heirs of the late George Selden, esquire, of Queens County."

The man whimpered. His cheeks glistened with tears. He wore filthy canvas breeches, loose at the knee, and a torn shirt. The feet were bare and the toes widely splayed. I wanted to look away but found I could not.

Townley took a silver toothpick from his waistcoat pocket and began to clean his teeth.

"You are a vagabond, are you not?" Marryot demanded. "Don't speak unless I tell you — just nod."

Virgil's head drooped.

"You absconded from your master when he was in Brooklyn the summer before last. And you've been living in Canvas Town with the rest of the rogues and knaves ever since." Marryot glanced down the table. "Have you noted that, Mr Noak?"

"Master, for pity's sake, I never saw —"

"Hold your peace — I didn't tell you to speak to me. You will have your chance later. And for God's sake, stop snivelling or I'll have you whipped."

Noak scribbled.

"Strike those last words out, Mr Noak," Marryot snapped. "They are not part of the record."

Townley leaned back in his chair. "What evidence is against the man?"

"All in good time, sir." Marryot put his elbows on the table and leaned towards the prisoner. "Tell me where you were last Sunday. Tell me what you did, what you saw."

"I was in Canvas Town, your honour. And I walked about the city looking for work. And then I went back to Canvas Town and fell asleep with nothing in my belly."

"Your belly looks plump enough to me," Townley observed, fanning himself with his handkerchief.

Marryot ignored the interruption. "That may be where you were but it's not what you did. You're a thief, a damned pickpocket. There were two empty purses in your bundle. And those shoes you had on your feet — well, they tell their own story, don't they?"

"Eh?" Townley said. "What shoes? Nobody mentioned any shoes."

"Mr Noak," Marryot said. "Have the goodness to open the press and bring us what you find on the third shelf down."

The press was a tall cupboard in an alcove by the empty fireplace. Noak took out a pair of black round-toed shoes with plain steel buckles on the flaps. He set them down on the table. The prisoner moaned softly at the sight of them. Marryot stretched out a hand and removed a small leather bag from one of the shoes.

"So," he said. "When they brought you in last night, these shoes were on your feet."

I picked up one of the shoes. The uppers were scuffed and creased. The sole needed reheeling. But the leather was good.

"We had information that these shoes belonged to Mr Pickett," Marryot said. "I had them sent over to Beekman Street this morning. The kitchen boy who cleans the shoes is sure that these were Pickett's."

"Information?" I said. "From whom, sir?"

"It don't signify, sir. All that signifies is that the information is good. You'll grant me that, I hope?"

Virgil lifted his head and, for the first time, looked directly at me.

"You need not enter Mr Savill's questions into the record either, Noak," Marryot said.

He untied the drawstring that fastened the bag and upended it. A heavy gold ring dropped on the palm of his hand.

"It's a seal ring," he said, holding it up between finger and thumb. "It has a stag incised on it. The woman at the house where he lodges, the Widow Muller, swears it's Pickett's. He wore it on his left hand and she noted it most particularly — he was behind with what he owed, and when he said he could not pay directly, she asked him why he did not turn his ring into guineas and be done with it."

"I never seen it, master, I swear, sir. Hope to die, God's my —"

"But the shoes?" I interrupted. "You've seen those before?"

The prisoner glanced at me again. "Yes, sir."

"Of course he had," Marryot put in. "They were on his damned feet when they arrested him."

"And where did you get them, Virgil?" I said.

"I — I found them, your honour."

"On Mr Pickett's body?"

"Yes, sir. Poor gentleman was lying there, all dead. I thought he didn't need them, so what's the harm? Look, sir." He pointed down at his feet. "I lost a toe to frostbite last winter."

"He was dead because you'd killed him," Marryot said. "That's how you knew, eh? So you helped yourself to his shoes and took the ring off his finger as well."

"No, sir, weren't no ring when I found him."

"Then why was the ring in your bundle?"

Virgil shook his head violently. "Didn't put it there, master, swear by —"

"Hold your tongue, damn you." Marryot looked at the soldiers, who were staring blankly at the wall behind the table. "Take him away. Keep him in irons."

No one spoke until the guards had led out the prisoner. Marryot stood up and went to the window.

"Well, gentlemen," he said, still with his back to the room. "This need not detain us much longer, I think? The evidence points to the knave's guilt."

"No rational man could entertain a doubt about it," Townley said, yawning. "If someone else had killed him, he would not have left the ring on Pickett's finger. Shall Noak write you out a fair copy of the proceedings?"

"I'd be obliged."

Mr Noak dipped his head.

"When you write it up, you should mention that Mr Savill of the American Department was present as an observer," Marryot went on, turning to face us. "But anything he said may be omitted."

"Now what?" I said.

"Why, sir, what do you think?" Marryot said. "We wait and let the law take its course. Martial law, that is."

CHAPTER
TWELVE

On the night of Wednesday, I heard the child crying again. In the morning, I mentioned it to Josiah, the older of the two manservants. It must be one of the neighbour's infants in the slave quarters, he said — he would investigate and have the nuisance abated. I said he should not trouble himself; it did not matter in the least.

The administration had found me an apartment to use as an office in a house it leased at the eastern end of Broad Street, not far from the City Hall. It was a pokey chamber up two pairs of stairs. My first caller was already waiting for me — a clergyman from Connecticut whom the rebels had turned out of his parsonage and parish. His crime had been to preach a sermon whose text had been Luke Chapter 20, verse 25. "And he said unto them, Render therefore unto Caesar the things which be Caesar's, and unto God the things which be God's." Caesar in this case was intended to be taken as George III rather than Congress. The poor man had lost all he owned, including a farm he had inherited from an uncle.

Shortly before dinnertime, Townley swept into the room. "Why, sir," he said without any preamble, "I have just this moment heard from the Major and I clapped on my hat at once and said to myself I should give myself the pleasure of bringing the news to you directly."

I rose to my feet. "What news? A battle?"

"Nothing of that nature. It's the negro — Virgil. He came before the court this morning and they found him guilty of Pickett's murder. Marryot says the fellow is to hang tomorrow morning. Sir Henry Clinton has confirmed the sentence. They say the Commander-in-Chief wishes to make an example of this man to deter other slaves."

"Is justice always so swift in New York?"

Townley shrugged. "Military courts have this to be said for them, at least: they do not drag their heels. Besides, at this time especially, when the city is awash with rumours about rebel incendiarists within our lines, it does no harm to show that we have the city firmly in our control. Will you come, sir?"

"What? To the hanging?"

"Of course — I am obliged to attend for the city and I thought it might interest you to accompany me. It's as well to know how these things are done. Matters have arranged themselves very neatly. It's at eight o'clock, and they will give us breakfast afterwards. They keep a good table." Townley took out his watch. "Talking of which, my dear sir, I believe it is time to dine."

After dining with Townley, I had walked back towards my office, skirting the fringe of Canvas Town. It was very hot and I did not hurry. I was not yet sure of my way, and by chance I found myself passing Van Cortlandt's Sugar House.

I turned into Trinity churchyard. The air seemed a little cooler here. Despite its proximity to the prison, the grassy enclosure was used as a place of resort, and at least a score of people were strolling among the gravestones. Indeed, it was more like a pleasure garden than a churchyard, with a broad, gravelled walk lined with benches, hooks for lanterns on the trees and even a platform for an orchestra amid the ruins. As I came up to the church, a familiar figure ambled round the corner of the tower at the west end.

"Judge!" I uncovered and bowed. "How do you do, sir? It is unconscionably hot, is it not?"

Wintour blinked up at me. "Ah — Mr Savill. Your servant, sir. You took me by surprise."

"Do you come here to take the air?"

"No. In point of fact, I am looking for my goat."

"I beg your pardon, sir. I do not quite —"

"My milch goat. It is the most charming animal imaginable. Mrs Wintour has a particular taste for its milk. Josiah tethered it here on Monday morning. Just there, sir, attached to those railings you see by the path. He swears he only turned his back for a moment, but in that moment it vanished."

"I am sorry to hear it, sir." I felt a memory shifting like shingle in the depths of my mind.

"It is our own family burying ground, too. Which makes the theft somehow worse, as though the perpetrator had committed a sort of burglary. My poor brother is here, you see, and that is why Josiah brought the goat in the first place." Mr Wintour saw the lack of comprehension on my face and smiled at me. "I beg your pardon, sir — I have presented you with an unnecessary enigma."

"Your brother is buried here?"

"Just so. He was as steadfast as any man in his attachment to the Crown." The old man's face crumpled for a moment. "Alas, even as a boy, he was impetuous, and liable to speak his mind without counting the likely cost of it. That was his undoing. The rebels killed him, you know, whatever they say."

"Did he die in the fighting, sir?" I asked.

"No, sir, he did not."

While the Judge was talking, he drifted closer to the railings and stared at the memorials they enclosed. I followed him. One of the inscriptions had been more recently cut than the others:

Erected in Memory
of
Francis de Lancey Wintour, D.D., M.A.
Fellow of King's College, New York
Son of William Wintour, Esqre
Died 21 June 1776
Aged 57 years

"When the rebels occupied this city at the start of the war," Wintour said, "they inflamed the Republican riff-raff and sought out all the prominent Tories they could find. Age and infirmity was no barrier to them. My poor brother Francis spoke his mind to the Whigs, just as he had done before the war. He urged them to lay down their arms and return to their natural allegiance." Wintour gripped one of the spikes of the railings and turned aside. "And then," he continued in a lower voice, "the mob came to his house, and broke down the door, and dragged him in his nightshirt into the street. He cried out, 'God bless King George.' They placed him on a rail and paraded him through the streets with loud huzzas. Yes, and there were soldiers there too, and city militia men who had dined at my own table, though afterwards they denied it. They were laughing, sir — can you credit it? They were laughing while they persecuted an old, infirm scholar in the name of what they call liberty and the rights of man."

I took Mr Wintour's arm. "My dear sir — pray, you must not distress yourself any more. Let us walk home."

"No." He shook off my hand. "No, sir — it is better you should know all. They paraded my unhappy brother outside General Washington's windows, and that gallant officer raised his hat to them and returned their huzzas. They had it in mind to plunge poor Francis in the Fresh Water Pond and then to run him out of the city. But God was merciful to my brother and permitted death to supervene. He suffered a rush of blood to the head and he died instantly of an apoplexy."

"Let us go home, sir," I said. "I am so sorry."

"But I wish I could find the goat." He released the railing and stood straight. "She was my brother's, you see, and a particular favourite. And Josiah too — our father gave him to my brother when he was a boy. After my brother died, they both came to me with what was left of his estate. The man and the goat. And Josiah likes to bring the goat here sometimes to see her old master and his resting place. It is — it is a harmless practice, is it not? I could not find it in myself to forbid it. Perhaps the animal has simply strayed. Josiah is most upset. I shall place an advertisement in the newspaper."

He allowed me to lead him away from the grave. Once we had left the churchyard, he released my arm and stepped out almost briskly in the direction of Warren Street.

"I had some news today, sir," I said, hoping to steer the old man's attention to safer subjects. "The court has tried the man accused of Mr Pickett's killing. They found him guilty."

Wintour stopped abruptly. "Really? So he will hang?"

"Yes, sir. Tomorrow morning."

"God rest his soul. There is no doubt about his guilt, I suppose?"

"I attended the preliminary hearing," I said. "He was wearing Mr Pickett's shoes and had his ring."

"Did he confess?"

"Only to theft, and only of the shoes. He claims that he stumbled across the body."

Mr Wintour shrugged. "Well, the court must go by the evidence, not what an accused man says in his own defence. Though one can hardly call it a court in any proper sense, since the judges sit without a jury and none of them has more than a smattering of the law. Still — poor Pickett — an unhappy end to an unhappy life."

"I thought perhaps that, in view of the acquaintance, Mrs Wintour and Mrs Arabella should be told."

"You may leave that to me, Mr Savill. I take it kindly that you have given us a little warning. I should not have liked them to have come across it in a newspaper or from a friend's gossip." He stopped and shook me warmly by the hand. "I shall trouble you no further, sir. I am quite restored now."

We said goodbye. I resumed my walk back to my office. It was only as I was turning into Broadway that I remembered the goat.

On Monday morning, Josiah had lost his master's goat in Trinity churchyard. In the early evening of the same day, I had seen another goat not far away in the remains of Deyes Street. A mulatto boy had been leading it over a pile of rubble.

The same goat?

CHAPTER
THIRTEEN

That night I did not hear the crying child. I turned this way and that on the overstuffed feather mattress, drifting in and out of a doze. I woke to full consciousness before five o'clock and could not settle to sleep again.

I am going to see a man hanged.

When I rose, I stayed in my chamber. I took a little tea but did not eat anything, feeling that for some obscure but powerful reason one should not attend the death of another man with a full belly. I tried to pray but found that would not answer. I read a chapter or two from the First Epistle to the Corinthians. That was no use either. Next I took up *The Theory of Moral Sentiments*, which Augusta had given me when we parted. She believed it did a man's career no harm if he was known to spend his leisure hours engaged in serious reading of an uplifting nature. But the book irritated me so much and so quickly that I tossed the volume into the empty grate before I had read a couple of sentences.

I contemplated writing to Augusta. But I discovered that I had nothing to write that would be fit for her to read. I would much rather have written a line or two to

Lizzie. But how could one say words like these to a beloved child?

In a moment I shall step out to watch a man be strangled on a string, and I wish to God I could do anything else in the world instead, even being seasick for eternity or having all my teeth pulled.

Why did this agitate me so much? It was almost as if I myself were the condemned man, as if I, not Virgil, had taken the life of another and deserved to die.

By seven o'clock I could no longer stand the confinement of my chamber. I left the house and walked down to the North River, where the air was somewhat cooler. By a quarter to eight, I was in front of the Upper Barracks.

Despite the short notice of the hanging, a crowd had gathered on the level ground outside the wall of the barracks. People of all conditions were talking, laughing, eating, drinking, buying, selling, shuffling to and fro or simply standing in silence. There was nothing sombre or discontented about them. They were merely waiting and they were perfectly good-humoured about it.

As I pushed my way through the throng I glimpsed a familiar face: the negro with the scars on his cheeks, the man whom I had seen in Canvas Town. He was wearing the faded red coat he had worn on Monday when the soldiers had carried Pickett's body away. He was playing a jig on a penny whistle with his hat on the

76

ground before him. Beside him was a boy with a tray of raw meat at his feet. Flies buzzed above the meat.

"Mr Savill! This way, sir."

Major Marryot was standing by the wicket set in the main gate of the barrack yard, waving his cane to attract my attention.

"Cutlets and fricassees, chops and casseroles," shrieked the boy, his high voice cutting through the noise of the crowd. "Fresh goat, tender and sweet."

I glanced in the lad's direction. He was a mulatto with skin the colour of dark honey. The crowd shifted and the boy vanished.

"We are pressed for time, Mr Savill," Marryot called, and he rapped the gate with his cane.

The sergeant of the guard ticked off my name on a list pinned to the guardroom door. Marryot took me through to a little parlour with a view of the gallows behind the barracks. The noise of the crowd was still audible.

"They won't see anything, you know," Marryot said testily as we were walking along, slapping his boot with his cane. It was as if he took the crowd as a personal insult. "This is a military hanging — an entirely private affair. But still those damnable jackals gather outside the gates."

The Provost Marshal, a red-faced Irishman, was already standing at the open window and calling instructions to his subordinates. The scaffold had been built out from the main building, to which it was linked at first-floor level by a wooden bridge. He acknowledged us with the most cursory of bows.

"He won't need that long a drop," he shouted to the sergeant who was arranging matters on the scaffold.

No one spoke after that. The Provost Marshal stayed by the window. Even at this hour there was a sour tang of brandy about him. Marryot sucked his teeth and scowled at the floor. I put my hands in my pockets and leaned against the wall, pretending an ease I did not feel.

My fingers felt the outlines of something small and hard-edged in the right-hand pocket. It was the ivory die I had found on Pickett's body. A gentleman's die on a gentleman's corpse. I took it out and rolled it on my palm. A three.

Townley entered, with Noak like a terrier at his heels. "Good day to you all, gentlemen — we are not come too late, I hope?"

"Damned incompetent fools," the Provost Marshal said to the world at large. "They cannot even manage to hang a rogue without assistance."

Somewhere a bell chimed the hour. Townley pulled out his watch and compared it with the clock on the wall.

"They're late," Marryot said. "Devilish unkind to the prisoner."

The miserable, waiting silence embraced us once again. Noak consulted his pocketbook, turning the pages rapidly. Townley massaged his nose, applying pressure to the left side as if trying to push it so it would stand at a right angle to the rest of his face rather than a few degrees out of true.

I stared out of the window at the gallows. It consisted of a crossbeam supported by an upright post at either end. Three black chains hung from the crossbeam.

At last, at eight minutes past eight, the door re-opened. One by one, half a dozen men emerged on to the scaffold. First came the Provost Marshal's sergeant, strutting like a cock in his own barnyard. He was followed by two soldiers with the condemned man shuffling between them. Next came a youthful parson, whose limbs seemed too long for his body and not entirely under their owner's control. Another soldier brought up the rear with a canvas bag swinging from his hand.

Marryot removed his hat. The other gentlemen followed suit.

"It is quite a military affair, as you see," Townley observed to me in a low voice, fanning himself with his hat. "The army usually handles this unpleasant necessity for us — the Commandant prefers it so. Of course, the Provost Marshal has everything to hand here, so it is convenient for everyone. He is unhappily obliged to oversee a great many executions — he is responsible for our rebel prisoners of war, you apprehend."

Virgil's arms were bound together in front of him and his ankles were shackled with a chain. Once they reached the scaffold, his escort pushed him directly under the cross-beam. The soldiers released his arms, though they stayed close to him.

The little slave looked about him, his head turning this way and that. His eyes found the window of the room where the gentlemen were waiting for him to die so that they might have their breakfast. His head became still. He flexed his wrists. His hands flapped and twitched. His lips moved but no sound came from them.

"Come along, come along," the Provost Marshal cried. "We don't have all day."

Virgil stared at the window.

No one else spoke. I prayed silently, wordlessly and surely meaninglessly: for how could God be here?

The soldier with the bag came forward. The men in the room became still, watching the soldier take out a nightcap from his bag, which he placed on Virgil's head. With surprising gentleness he drew it down over the negro's face and patted him on his shoulder as a man touches a nervous horse to reassure him.

No one spoke, either on the scaffold or in the room that overlooked it. The nightcap had transformed Virgil from a person into something not quite human. It stripped the individuality from him. All that was left was a bundle of rags trembling like a shrivelled leaf in a breeze.

The soldier took the rope from the same bag and looped it through the end of the chain. He tied a knot to secure it. He lifted the noose at the other end of the rope, glanced at the Provost Marshal, and then placed the noose on the shoulders of the condemned man. He tightened it and stood to one side.

As if the touch of the noose had been a signal, Virgil cried out "God, God, God." His voice was muffled and not loud but it scraped against the surface of my mind like a rusty nail. He would not stop. "God, God, God."

The sergeant stepped forward and checked the knots. The clergyman opened his prayer book and began to speak, though his voice was too low to hear what he was saying through the open window. But I knew what the words must be: *I am the resurrection and the life.*

The slave's legs gave way. He would have collapsed if the soldiers had not seized him under the arms. *The Lord giveth and the Lord taketh away.* The parson stood back.

All this time, Virgil was crying, "God, God, God."

The sergeant turned towards the window. The Provost Marshal raised his arm and let it fall. The sergeant stamped twice. An assistant beneath the scaffold released the trap.

"God, God, God —"

The planks on which Virgil was standing gave way. He vanished into the darkness under the scaffold with a violent clatter. There was an instant of silence, broken by the beat of an invisible drum.

Virgil dangled in the air, his feet kicking. His hands fluttered and then the fingers clenched into fists. He was dancing and twisting on the rope. He tried to raise his hands towards his neck but his arms were bound to his sides at the elbows.

The Provost Marshal leaned on the windowsill. "Goddamn it. I told you to make this quick. I have not had my breakfast yet."

Two hands appeared from the darkness under the scaffold. They gripped the ankles of the hanging man and pulled sharply downwards. A spasm of movement rippled through Virgil's body. And then at last he was still.

CHAPTER
FOURTEEN

"The air is a little cooler, I find," Mrs Arabella said. "But we rarely sit here in the evening because Mrs Wintour finds it fatiguing to walk so far."

"I distinctly felt a draught on my cheek, madam," I said. "Indeed, it is very pleasant with all the windows open."

I could hardly believe the banality of my own conversation. For a moment my remark seemed to have stunned the others into silence. Mrs Arabella must have thought me the most pompous fool in creation.

We were sitting in the summerhouse at the bottom of the Wintours' garden. Mrs Wintour had been too tired to come down for supper. Afterwards, the Judge had suggested that the three of us take our tea in the belvedere.

"There is a charming westerly prospect of Vauxhall Garden and the grounds of King's College," Mr Wintour had said. "One can glimpse the North River beyond. Though of course it will be almost dark by the time we are settled. Still, it will be agreeable to know that the prospect is there, will it not?"

The twilight was already far advanced, though we had not had the candles lit because of the flying insects their flames would attract. The air smelled faintly of lemon juice and vinegar, an agreeable contrast to the stink that pervaded so much of the city.

I turned towards Mr Wintour. "I had meant to enquire sooner, sir: is there any news of the goat?"

"No. I fear the worst. But I have placed an advertisement in the *Gazette. Nil desperandum* must be our motto in this matter, as well as in our larger concerns."

I wondered whether to mention the boy who had been selling goat meat outside the barracks before the hanging. It was impossible to be sure, but he might have been the boy whom I had seen with a living goat and the scar-faced negro on the day we had inspected Roger Pickett's body. But even if it had been —

"Her milk is much missed, sir," Mrs Arabella said, picking up the teapot and breaking my train of thought. "If we have lost her, I fear it will be nigh impossible to find another milch goat."

She was wearing a pale gown that in the fading light made her almost luminous. She refilled my cup. I rose to take it and, in doing so, I felt the warmth radiating from her body and smelled the perfume I remembered from that first evening: otto of roses, mingled with her own peculiar fragrance. As I took the cup and saucer, her finger brushed my hand.

"No more tea for me, my dear," Mr Wintour said, struggling to his feet. "I must see how Mrs Wintour does and then I shall retire for the night."

For a moment we watched the old man picking his way down the path towards the garden door of the house.

Mrs Arabella stirred in her chair, and the wicker creaked beneath her body. "Miriam tells me you went to see that man hanged this morning."

"Yes, ma'am, I did. A melancholy duty."

"Did he confess to the murder in the end?"

"I believe not."

"You would think a man would speak the truth if he knew he was to go before his maker in a few moments."

"He may have desired to confess, ma'am. But he was not given an opportunity as far as I know. But forgive me — the subject must be painful to you."

The wicker creaked again. "Yes, of course. Though I barely knew Mr Pickett — but his murder is a terrible thing. Tell me, sir — was it — was it a hard death?"

I stared at her in the gathering dusk. "Mr Pickett's?"

"No, no — I mean the man who was hanged for the murder."

"How can it not have been?" I said, more sharply than I intended.

"I spoke without thinking." She sounded upset, though there was not enough light for me to read her expression. "But — but there must be degrees in these matters, must there not?"

"It cannot have been easy." I remembered Virgil's clenched fists, the kicking feet and, most vividly of all, the hands that had risen from beneath the scaffold to give the sharp, fatal tug at the slave's ankles. "But it did not take long."

She sighed. "I am glad of that, at least. Of course they do not have feelings as we do."

"Who do not?"

"Negros. They are made of coarser clay. Indeed, many of them are little better than beasts of the field. Most negros have no more idea of true religion or morality than the man in the moon."

"I cannot believe that to be true, madam," I said. "Their situation may be inferior to ours, their education neglected, but one cannot blame them for that. Indeed, if we blame anyone, surely we must blame ourselves for their shortcomings."

She threw back her head and laughed with such spontaneous merriment that I found myself smiling in sympathy. "Oh, you would not say that if you knew them as I do, sir."

"But I have encountered many negros in London, freed men, who —"

"I do not mean all negros, of course," she interrupted, "or even all slaves, for that matter — for example, I except those like Josiah and Miriam and Abraham — they have lived so long among us as almost to be like us, as far as God permits them to be and allowing for the difference between our station in life and theirs."

"They are slaves, then? I did not know."

"They are perfectly content in their condition and give us faithful service. Their loyalty is beyond question. Believe me, sir, Josiah would not have his freedom if Mr Wintour offered it him on a silver platter."

A silence fell between us.

"Let us talk to something more agreeable," she said at length. "Your family, perhaps — I'm sure Mrs Savill is counting the days towards your happy return." She spoke seriously but there was an edge of mockery to her words that irritated me. "And the other evening you told us that you have a daughter, I think?"

"Yes, ma'am — Elizabeth; she is five years old."

There was another silence. Then Mrs Arabella said, in a voice barely above a whisper, "It cannot have been easy to leave her and to come all this way. And even worse for her, of course, to lose her papa."

The twilight had grown darker. I heard her breathing. How strange, I thought, that she talked of Lizzie missing me, but not Augusta; how strange, and how oddly near the mark.

A door slammed. Both of us sat up sharply. It was as if, I thought later, we had been on the verge of being discovered in some shameful assignation. Miriam was coming down the garden with a lantern in her hand.

"Good girl," Mrs Arabella said. "I was about to ring for candles."

Miriam made her obedience in the doorway. "No, ma'am, it's master. He begs you to join him in the library."

"But I thought he had retired."

"He came down again, ma'am. Major Marryot's called."

"So late? And why should they want me?"

"I'm sure I don't know."

Mrs Arabella rose to her feet. "I suppose I must find out what they want. But do not disturb yourself, Mr Savill. Shall we play backgammon when I come back? I need diversion — I do not feel at all sleepy yet."

I said that nothing would give me more pleasure.

"Then that is settled. Miriam — light me into the house and then bring candles for Mr Savill directly. You will find the backgammon board under that seat in the corner, sir. Or Miriam will fetch it out for you."

The two women set off for the house. After a moment I went over to the corner and put my hand into the darkness under the seat. The smell of lemon juice and vinegar was stronger here. The Wintour ladies were good housekeepers. I felt the outlines of the backgammon box and drew it out. I laid it on the table and opened it. It was too dark to see the counters clearly.

I did not have long to wait. Miriam came down the path with a candelabra, its candles unlit, a taper and the lantern. She put them on the table beside the backgammon board but made no move to light the candles. Her hands were shaking.

"If it please your honour," she said, "I think mistress will stay in the house now."

"It doesn't matter. I shall come in myself in that case." I rose to my feet and, as I did so, the woman clutched the edge of the table. "Is something wrong, Miriam?"

"Oh, sir, it's the Captain."

"But I thought you said Major Marryot had called."

"Yes, sir," Miriam said, stumbling over her words. "He brought the news. Mr John, sir. Captain Wintour."

It took me a moment to realize what she meant. "Oh, I'm so sorry. Such distressing —"

"No, sir, it's not that. Mr John ain't dead. He's alive."

CHAPTER
FIFTEEN

The first week in New York stretched into a month and then to another. I found myself imperceptibly adjusting to my situation until it appeared almost unremarkable.

The war coloured everything and nothing. Perhaps it had been like this in Troy for most of the ten years that city had been invested by the Greeks. Perhaps in Troy, as in New York, life had continued much as usual in the long intervals between battles. It almost made a man wonder whether the battles were necessary in the first place.

In October, Mr Rampton wrote with what he said was good news. Lord George Germain had been pleased to say with the kindest condescension imaginable that he had glanced over a memorandum I had composed before leaving for New York, and thought it a model of its kind. The Department would benefit greatly from a man of Mr Savill's proven abilities as its eyes and ears in New York.

This being so, His Lordship desires me to communicate to you his wish that you should remain in New York for a few months more. Since a winter passage would not be at all agreeable for you, I took the liberty of suggesting that we should therefore extend your commission until the March or April. Who knows, by that time the rebels may have capitulated. We hear on every side that the Continental troops are deserting in droves because Congress cannot pay them except in their own worthless dollars.

My dear Savill, what a feather in your cap is this! Matters are turning out just as I had hoped. In haste, for the messenger is about to post to Falmouth to catch the packet before it sails with the August mail, believe me

Truly yours, HR.

At first I could not but be pleased that my abilities had earned such approval — not only from Mr Rampton but from Lord George himself. Then my mind swung to the other extreme. I had been sentenced to pass another five or six months in this uncomfortable provincial backwater. I should be obliged to deal, week in, week out, with ever-swelling numbers of unfortunate Loyalists, with the rudeness of Major Marryot and with an array of criminal cases.

And what of Augusta? My wife and I did not agree in many respects but she had never denied me a husband's rights. Indeed, she showed a surprising enthusiasm for granting them to me when the candle was out and the curtains were drawn. To be absent from her was to have an itch one could not scratch. As a prudent and rational man, I should no doubt have told myself that the gratifications of marriage would prove all the sweeter if I continued longer in New York.

But prudent and rational considerations seemed to have no noticeable effect on this particular itch.

In this reckoning of potential profit and probable loss, where did Lizzie figure on my balance sheet? For a child of five, a single month was an eternity, and I had already been separated from her for three. I knew she would be well looked after in Shepperton, and that my sister would ensure that she had no material wants. But she must miss her papa. Her mother had never cared much for Lizzie, perhaps because hers had been a difficult birth, and disliked having the child about her. But I had loved her from the first. I felt my daughter's absence as a man must feel the lack of an amputated limb.

Still, there was no help for it. If I were to make a new home for the three of us and provide Augusta and Lizzie with the necessities of life and even a few luxuries, I must remain in New York for the time being.

I asked Mr Wintour whether I might extend my stay in Warren Street.

"Nothing would give me greater pleasure," the Judge said, staring at me over the top of the glasses he wore for reading. "Before you came I was entirely surrounded by a monstrous regiment of women." He smiled to show that the words were intended as a pleasantry. "Besides, I do not find it agreeable to drink His Majesty's health by myself. Toasts should be made in company, and another gentleman is indispensable for that. And of course it means I shall have the pleasure of making my son known to you when he returns. It may be any week now, you know — he writes that he is almost restored."

"I would not wish to inconvenience Captain Wintour, sir," I said. "If you would prefer me to remove —"

"No, no, my dear sir. I would not hear of it. And nor would Mrs Wintour, and nor Bella. It is Bella who counts most particularly, you know, for this is her house. As for John, he will enjoy having a man his own age to talk to. Otherwise I fear he will find us very dull."

Mrs Arabella came into the library, and he told her the news. She was looking remarkably handsome today, I thought — this fine autumn weather must suit her. Indeed, I could not understand how I had so readily dismissed her claims to beauty on our first acquaintance. "Once seen," Mr Noak had said of her, "never forgotten." Perhaps he had been right all along. I had not been a very good judge of anything after the discomforts of our passage from England and the horrors that had confronted me on my arrival in New York.

"I hope your staying longer will not grieve Mrs Savill and your daughter, sir," she said. "Your daughter is called Elizabeth, is she not?"

"Yes, ma'am." I was touched that she had remembered the name. "It will certainly grieve me not to see her."

"And yet you stay?"

"Bella, Bella," the Judge said. "A man must go where he is ordered. You know that, as a soldier's wife."

"Yes, sir," she said. "Of course I know it. But a child cannot understand the bitterness of parting in the way a wife can."

Mr Wintour patted her hand. "You are too tender-hearted, my dear."

"Five years old is very young."

"It cannot be helped," I said. "Though I wish with all my heart that it could."

CHAPTER
SIXTEEN

Mr Townley lived very comfortably with his family in a commodious and most respectable house in Hanover Square, next door to an admiral. Most of the ground floor was given over to business.

I had gradually learned that Townley was a man with his fingers in many pies. As well as superintending the city's police, he sat on several boards, one to do with the execution of port regulations and another to do with the issuing of licences to the cartmen who transported goods about the city and its environs. He had a warehouse on Long Island and also leased Norman's Slip, out on the Greenwich Road, which enabled him to trade on his own account.

"My dear sir," he said, when I brought the news that my mission in New York had been extended, "how very agreeable — for us, at least. And for you too, I hope. Now pray sit down. Another five or six months, eh? Nothing could be better."

We were in his private room, a back parlour. There was an autumnal chill in the air, and a fire burned brightly in the grate.

"Will you look for an establishment of your own now?" Townley asked, leaning forward in his chair.

"You would be so much more comfortable. I believe I could find you most respectable lodgings in Queen Street if you liked: three chambers, a spacious parlour, a kitchen and wine cellar there. With use of the hall, of course, and the coachhouse and the stables. The widow who owns the house — a most delightful lady — is a friend of my wife's. I'm sure I could obtain a six-month lease for — let me see — forty-five guineas." He raised a long, languid hand as if I had objected. "The American Department has a position in the world, after all. Mr Rampton would wish you to live in a style that befits it."

"I shall remain at Judge Wintour's, sir, for the time being at any rate. It is very convenient in all respects."

"Ah." He looked up. "Well, no doubt Mrs Arabella is an excellent housekeeper. It is in fact her house, you know — it was her father's residence in the city — though she has lent it to her parents-in-law for the duration of the war. But in any case, I am sure the family is happy to have you there."

Neither of us mentioned money, but I knew my two guineas a week must be a welcome addition to the Wintours' income. The Judge needed ready money. Everywhere in the house were signs of past affluence and present shortages, from Josiah's livery with its frayed cuffs and stained armpits, to the carefully rationed tea leaves which were re-used at least once above stairs and probably two or three times more in the kitchen and the slave quarters.

"Still," Townley continued, after a pause, "I wonder how you will find Warren Street when Captain Wintour returns."

"Equally convenient, I hope."

"That remains to be seen. Captain Wintour is not the easiest of men. Of course he has reason enough for that."

"Because of Saratoga?"

"Yes, indeed." Townley glanced at me, his face bland but oddly attentive. "But there are other reasons, too. He had great expectations from his father-in-law, Mr Froude, but this war has put paid to those, at least until we have peace again." He paused. "When does he come home?"

"In a few weeks. He is well enough to travel now, I apprehend, and is in Quebec. His father has sent money for his passage home."

There was a tap on the door, and Mr Noak brought in a letter for Townley to sign.

"Ah — the incomparable Noak," Townley said with a smile. "I cannot imagine how I managed without you."

Mr Noak bowed but did not return the smile. He was now permanently employed by Mr Townley, who entrusted him with the management of more and more business. His unobtrusive efficiency was matched by his kindness of heart, as I had learned from his care of me at sea. So I was not altogether surprised when, one Sunday afternoon in September, I had found him in the drawing room at Warren Street reading the Bible to old Mrs Wintour, whose eyes were failing. These Sunday visits had settled into what was almost a routine; Mrs

Wintour became quite agitated if Mr Noak happened not to be at leisure.

"There was one other matter, sir," Noak said as he took back the letter from Townley. He hesitated, waving the letter to and fro to dry the ink.

"You may speak, man — we need have no secrets from Mr Savill."

"Yes, sir. It is only the docket for Major Marryot."

"What of it?"

"The list includes the boy found drowned by the Paulus Hook ferry. I believe he may be the Government informer who goes by the name of Benjamin Taggart."

Townley straightened his long spine. "Oh yes — well, was he murdered?"

"I cannot say for certain, sir, either way — he drowned, that is all; I saw no sign of violence on his body. They are keeping it at King's Wharf for the time being. But what shall I say your recommendation is?"

"To let sleeping dogs die. Or, rather, drowned dogs in this case." He chuckled in appreciation of his own wit. "Unless there are reasons why Major Marryot should enquire further into it?"

"Not that I am aware of, sir. And, even if there were, the boy's body can tell him nothing more than it already has."

"Well, then. I think we need waste no further time on a slave's by-blow, do you? And I'm sure Major Marryot will agree."

Noak bowed.

"Mind you," Townley said, "Taggart did us one good service, did he not?" He turned to me. "It was he who tipped us the wink about poor Pickett's murderer. You remember? The runaway, Virgil. We'd not have been able to hang the rogue without Taggart."

CHAPTER
SEVENTEEN

There could be no harm in it, surely?

On the other hand, a prudent man knew when to leave well alone. Especially a man with his way to make in the world.

As the day went on, I found myself thinking more and more about the Pickett affair. I could not avoid the fact that I felt not only curious about his murder but also in some strange way responsible for the runaway slave they had hanged for it.

It was as if I had failed him.

But was not the man a convicted murderer? Who was I to set my judgement against that of the officers who had made up the court martial? They were vastly experienced; they had been cognizant of all the facts — whereas I was but newly arrived in this city and a positive babe in arms in such matters. Most important of all, my duty was merely to observe the administration of justice: apart from that, I had no legal standing in the affair; nor was I under any moral obligation to go beyond the terms of my commission.

And yet — these were a civil servant's arguments, perfectly adequate for a departmental inquiry or Mr Rampton or even a court of law. But they did not quite convince me as a man. Now Taggart, the informer, was dead too.

The decision hung in the balance for the rest of the morning, and later at the coffee house where I dined alone and frugally on an elderly mutton chop and a pint of sherry. At the end of the meal, I decided to let chance take a hand in the matter. I felt in my waistcoat pocket for the ivory die I had found under Pickett's body. I pushed aside the plate and brushed the crumbs away with the napkin.

If it came up with an odd number, I should go back to the office and forget all about the drowned informer, the hanged slave and Pickett's murder. If the number were even, I should refresh myself with a stroll to the river in the mild afternoon sunshine.

I rolled the die. It danced across the stained linen cloth, ricocheted off the base of the wine glass and came to rest beside the fork. It was a four.

There could be no harm in it, I repeated to myself again and again like a Papist with his rosary, as if repetition could somehow make it true. There could be no harm in it, none in the world.

The Paulus Hook ferry was at the north-west end of Cortland Street, by King's Wharf. My choice of route proved to be a mistake, for Cortland Street took me through the desolate heart of Canvas Town, not far from the cellar where they had found the body of Roger Pickett.

The roadway itself was an illicit market place. As I passed along it, three whores solicited me, a negro offered me a Pembroke table with three legs and two unmatched chairs, a one-armed soldier tried to sell me a pair of boots, a variety of entertainers sought to distract me, and beggars haunted my every step. A woman showed me the baby at her breast. "For the love of God," she said, "for the love of God."

This was the other New York, the shadow town, the dark simulacrum of the prosperous shops and stalls that lined Broadway.

At the end of the street, a breeze was coming off the water. Near the shore the river was dense with small craft bobbing on the swell. Further out lay a scattering of merchant ships with a line of men-of-war beyond them. The sea shifted and glittered in the sunshine. A mile or so away was the Jersey coast.

To the south, towards Fort George at the tip of the island, a party of prisoners of war were working with picks and shovels, strengthening the embankment along the shore. A small detachment of Hessians watched over them, though without much interest. There was nowhere for the prisoners to run to and, besides, most of them were in no condition to run anywhere.

At the wharf were more guards, part-time Provincials drunk with their petty authority. I showed the sergeant in charge my passes, one from Headquarters, the other from Townley, and his arrogance modulated swiftly to something approaching servility.

"Where do you keep the bodies you take from the water?" I asked. "I want to see one of them."

He laughed. "A body, sir? We can show you a fair few of those. We keep them for a day or two, and if no one claims them they go with the others."

"What others?"

The sergeant pointed his staff at the prisoners at work on the embankment. "They pack the rebel dead into the foundations. Saves all of us a deal of work."

"You mean they put dead prisoners there? Under the new embankment?"

"Yes, sir — and the ones from the water, like I said, assuming they're not claimed. Might as well do something useful with them, eh?"

"I wish to inspect the body of a boy," I said. "His name's Taggart. Mr Townley's man has already looked at him."

"Ah, yes — that little negro. Over here, sir." He led the way towards a warehouse built into the gently sloping ground away from the water. "We keep them down the end," he said over his shoulder. "It's cooler."

He unbolted a heavy door and stood aside to allow me to enter first. I found myself in a narrow chamber with a vaulted ceiling stretching across the width of the building. The room was lit by two arched openings, barred but unglazed, placed high in the walls. Below them was a bank of broad, slatted shelves.

The first thing I noticed was the smell — an unlovely compound of salt water, seaweed and decaying flesh. My gorge rose. I covered my mouth and nose with a handkerchief.

"A man grows used to the stink," the sergeant said. "I hardly notice it now."

I glanced about me at the shapes stacked on the shelves. The bodies had been hunched together to save space. Some were naked; others wore a ragged shirt or breeches. I knew that anything worth taking would have been plundered before they were brought here.

"It's that one." The sergeant poked a mottled arm with his staff. "Came in the day before yesterday."

The small body lay on its side with its back to us.

"I want to see the face," I said.

The sergeant seized the upper arm by the wrist. He tugged it. The body did not move. He grinned at me, spat on his hands and braced his leg against the brick support of the shelves.

"He's being a little contrary, sir. But not for long."

He took the corpse's arm with both hands and wrenched it violently towards him. There was a sucking, squelching sound. The upper part of the body twisted. The corpse was now on its back, though its legs were still angled away from us. The smell worsened.

The head faced upwards. The sergeant took hold of it by the nearer ear and pulled it closer to the edge of the shelf.

"That suffice, sir? I can stretch him out if you want."

"No need, thank you." I forced myself to look at the face. The eyes had gone. I swallowed hard.

"The one you're looking for?" the sergeant asked.

"Yes."

There was no doubt about it. It was the mulatto boy I had encountered twice before. He was smaller than I remembered, and perhaps younger — no more than nine or ten. He was very thin, the ribs as clearly defined as the ridges on a fluted column; and there were faded weals on his side where he had been beaten, probably with a rope's end, but not recently.

"How long had he been in the water?"

"A day or two, sir, maybe less. Don't take long for the fish to get the eyes. Minutes, sometimes."

Here was the informer who, according to Noak, had brought about Virgil's death on the gallows. I had seen him twice before, though I had not known his name. On the first occasion, the day of my arrival, the boy had been leading a goat close to the spot where they had found Pickett's body. The second time, he had been selling goat meat outside the barracks on the morning when they hanged a man for Pickett's murder.

I straightened up. "Have you had any other bodies lately?"

"A rebel prisoner on Sunday. He'd been in the water for a week or two."

"What about a big negro with a long scar on either side of his nose?"

"No one like that, sir, not to my recollection." The sergeant gestured at the boy on the shelf. "Seen enough?"

"Yes. I'm obliged to you."

"Do you want me to hold him here for Major Marryot to see?"

I shook my head. What was the point, after all? Marryot would laugh at me.

The sergeant pushed the body back on to its side and rubbed his hands on his coat. "Runaway, was he?"

"I don't know," I said. "Perhaps he was running from something."

"And then it caught up with him," the sergeant said.

CHAPTER
EIGHTEEN

Early in November, I saw the little girl for the first and last time.

I had just dined with the Commandant and a considerable company of gentlemen, most of them in uniform. There had been much food and many toasts. I was a little drunk, and therefore disposed to be emotional.

As I strolled along, Lizzie was in my mind, which was perhaps why I noticed the child in the first place. The thought of my daughter aroused a host of feelings in me — love, of course, and a sort of hunger for her company, and also anxiety: suppose she fell ill? Suppose her mother or her aunt treated her cruelly? Suppose I were to die, leaving her penniless and unprotected in this harsh and unforgiving world? Suppose the unthinkable, that Lizzie herself should die?

It was still early in the evening and Broadway was crowded. It was dark. There were a few streetlights, and the lighted windows and shop doorways. But these emphasized the gloom rather than dispelled it. That was when I saw the child.

The girl was younger than Lizzie and was in leading strings. She was with a woman. The two of them had emerged from a haberdasher's shop about twenty or thirty yards in front of me. Both were muffled against the weather in long cloaks with hoods over their heads. The woman tugged the girl along, almost pulling her off her feet. The child had not yet learned how to walk quickly without falling over. She strained against the harness that held her as if bursting to escape.

In a moment they passed a pastry-cook's shop — a large and brightly lit establishment with two big windows. The child was distracted by the smells and the warmth. She pulled her reins free from the woman's hand and darted towards the open door.

The woman caught her in an instant. She hooked her arm around the girl's waist and spun her, legs kicking, into the air. The movement dislodged the hoods from their heads.

The scene was as brightly lit as a stage. I saw the child in profile, her arms outstretched towards the pastry-cook's, her mouth open in a howl of frustration. She was a negro, as was the woman who had charge of her.

In that same moment, alerted by my footsteps, the woman looked in my direction. To my surprise, I recognized Miriam, Mrs Arabella's maid.

The scene dissolved. Miriam walked rapidly away, almost at a run, still with the kicking, wailing child in her arms. I called out. She did not turn round. A porter staggered out of the furniture shop next door with his arms wrapped around a large wing armchair, which stopped me dead in my tracks and blocked my view.

By the time I reached the pastry-cook's, there was no sign of the woman and the girl. I could no longer hear the child's cries. Either the two of them were obscured by the throng of passers-by or they had turned into another shop or down one of the narrow alleys that punctuated the line of buildings.

Why such apparently furtive behaviour? Was Miriam outside the house on some unlicensed errand? Was it possible that she was married? Could the child be hers? I began to doubt it had been Miriam — after all, I had barely glimpsed the young woman and the light had been poor.

I returned to Warren Street. Josiah answered my knock on the street door. The old man helped me remove my hat and greatcoat, murmuring gently that the ladies were in the drawing room and Judge Wintour was at work in his library. He turned aside to dispose of my coat.

"Josiah?"

"Sir?"

"I saw Miriam this evening. At least I believe I did."

Josiah hung my coat without undue haste. He faced me and bowed, his face expressionless.

"She was with a child — a negro girl, an infant. Has Miriam a daughter?"

"No, sir."

Josiah bowed again and retreated into the shadows at the back of the hall.

It cannot have been more than a week later that Captain John Wintour came home. I have a note of the date: it was on Thursday, 12 November. He had been badly wounded at Saratoga and, by his own account, had spent many months on the borders of life and death. An old and feeble-witted woman stumbled across him half dead in a wood when she was gathering kindling near her cottage. She had nursed him back to health.

Eventually he had reached Canada and found his way to Kingstown, where there were cousins of his mother who were able to shelter him; but his health had broken down again. Fortunately he had, in his own words, the constitution of a horse and had recovered sufficiently to be able to undertake the voyage home.

He arrived in Warren Street in the evening. It was the dead hour before supper. As chance would have it, when he knocked at the door I was descending the stairs on my way to the parlour.

The younger manservant, Abraham, let him in, trying to say a few words of welcome. Wintour pushed past him and stood in the middle of the hall, legs apart and hands in the pockets of his patched greatcoat, which had clearly been made for someone much smaller. He was a spare man of about thirty, with flushed, bony features and deep-set eyes, which were an unusually bright blue. He stared at me.

"And who the devil are you?" he demanded, swaying as he spoke.

"My name is Savill, sir. Have I the honour of meeting Captain Wintour?"

"Indeed, sir. The honour is entirely mine." Wintour attempted a bow, staggered forward and righted himself. "You must be the gentleman from the American Department. My father told me."

"Yes, sir. You have —"

The parlour door opened and Mrs Wintour almost ran to her son, an extraordinary exhibition of physical energy from the old lady. She embraced him. The Captain closed his eyes and patted her shoulder. With his other hand he scratched his nose.

Next came the Judge, more slowly. He looked his son up and down.

"I am happy to see you home, John," he said.

"Yes, sir. And — and I to be here."

"You are — you are fatigued?"

"It has been a long day, sir, and my health is not yet quite restored."

"Then perhaps you should rest — after you have seen Bella, of course. Let Abraham take your coat."

Mr Wintour took his wife's arm and drew her from her son. The Captain held out his arms and let the slave ease the coat away from him.

No one looked in my direction. I thought they had forgotten me.

There were footsteps on the stairs. I turned. Mrs Arabella was rounding the bend at the half-landing. She paused at the top of the last flight down to the hall.

First she must have seen me. She let her eyes drift past me to the group in the hall below. I could not see her expression because the light was dim and the flame of the candle she held was below the level of her chin.

But the candlelight revealed two things about Mrs Arabella. It showed her slim white neck. It showed that she was swallowing repeatedly, as if trying to force down an unpalatable morsel. And the flame also picked out her hand holding the top of the newel post, and how the fingers gripped it so tightly that the skin wrinkled.

The Captain looked up. "Ah — there you are, madam. My pretty, witty wife."

CHAPTER
NINETEEN

Townley was a hospitable man, who talked easily to anyone, and perhaps let his tongue wag more freely than a gentleman should. But I enjoyed his company because he was almost always cheerful and had a pleasant wit.

I would sometimes sup with him, either alone or with two or three of his friends. On those occasions I saw another side of New York, for the gentlemen around the table were Loyalists of course but, unlike those who came up to my office in Broad Street, they were on the whole content with their lives.

"I bless the day," Townley confided to me in a fit of drunken confidence, "when those damned Yankees dumped the tea in Boston Harbour. Indeed, sir, it has been the making of us here."

We were sitting at table in a small private room in the King's Arms. The shutters were up and a fire of unseasoned wood crackled and spluttered in the grate. Two other men, a contractor and a commissioner for the harbour administration, made up the party. But they were oblivious to our conversation for they were engaged in an animated discussion about the need to bring in professional actresses at the John Street Theatre.

"Surely it must be difficult for you," I said to Townley. "Since so many goods are in short supply, there must be a constant —"

"Supply and demand, sir," Townley interrupted. "That's what the students of political economy call it. It is a beautiful thing, for the supplier at least. If the available stock diminishes, you raise the price of what you have. Or, if demand remains keen when the supply is exhausted, you simply sell promises instead, which is like selling air. No, for a man with his wits about him, this war has been a blessing."

He hesitated, frowning. I ran my finger round the rim of my glass and tried not to smile.

"Of course, sir, I do not mean to suggest that the war is — well, in any way, even in the slightest, a desirable thing, but — taken, as a whole, you understand, considered in the round — there is no harm in a man looking to his own interests." Townley wagged his forefinger in front of my face. "Always with the proviso, my dear sir, that His Majesty's interests must be served, first and foremost, without fear or favour, in any —"

"Sir," I said gently, "I believe I understand you perfectly. Should we drink a toast to His Majesty?"

"Indeed." Townley seized the bottle and burst out laughing from sheer animal spirits. "And damnation to his enemies. Good God, I had not realized it was so early. Shall we call for the punchbowl?"

By the time the party broke up it was nearly midnight. As we went outside, I almost recoiled from the cold. November was well advanced now, and so was winter.

Townley and one of the other men had servants to light them home. The third man took a waiting hackney chair. I decided to walk back to Warren Street. It was only a step away and the exercise would clear my head. Despite the lateness of the hour, the streets were still busy, for the city came alive at night with theatre parties, musical entertainments, suppers and dances. I knew my way perfectly and I believed, if a man was cautious, there could be no danger.

On the other side of the road, facing the fields, I saw the silhouettes of the prison and the poorhouse looming square and black against the sky. As I drew level with them, I turned up towards King's College.

It was darker here and there were fewer people about. Someone ahead was whistling. A dog barked in the distance, somewhere near Freshwater Pond. The ferrule of my stick tapped against the paving stones. The change of direction brought me into the wind, which was blowing hard from the north. I felt its chilly bite on my neck above the collar of the greatcoat, and it cut through the thin silk of my stockings.

It was the wind that saved me. It was the wind that made me slacken my pace to adjust my muffler, which had worked loose.

Directly ahead, a man shot out from a dark entry between two buildings. But for my change of pace, he would have collided with me. Simultaneously, I heard footsteps behind me, whose presence I had already registered, footsteps that now were speeding up.

114

"It's him," said a man's voice behind me.

I'm trapped.

I raised the stick above my head and turned sharply to the right, which brought my back to the blank wall of the building beside me.

The man in front leapt at me. I slashed the stick down in a diagonal arc. I heard a cry of pain. Metal chinked on stone.

I reversed the direction of the stick and swung it blindly backwards. I shouted, a wordless cry. The stick landed on something soft. It twisted like a live thing. I lost hold of it and swore at my assailant.

As suddenly as it had begun, it was over. There were more running footsteps. My two attackers darted into the alley. A couple of men gave chase, whooping and hallooing as if they were chasing hares.

"Run, boyo, run," someone cried in great excitement, his voice bouncing against the walls of the alley.

I leaned back against the wall, hunched over and drawing breath in great shuddering gasps. As the danger subsided, my mind filled with all the stories I had heard of assault and robbery on the streets of New York, of the brutish attacks by drunken soldiers and vulgar criminals which the military authorities so rarely troubled to check.

"Sir?" It was an English voice, a gentleman's. "Are you hurt?"

I looked up. "Thank you, no."

"Good God, this town is a perfect nursery of crime."

Another man came running up to us, this one bearing a lantern. By its light I made out that my rescuer was a middle-aged naval lieutenant, with a footman to light his way.

"Your arrival was providential, sir." I paused, for I still found it hard to breathe. "I cannot thank you enough."

"I can't take the credit, sir — a pair of soldiers chased the villains away."

His servant picked up my stick and handed it to me.

"Footpads," my rescuer said, gripping the hilt of his dress sword. "Sprang on you like — like a pair of tigers on a goat. Saw that happen once, sir, in the East Indies. Not a pretty sight, believe me."

"Did you see the rogues, sir?" I asked.

"No, sir. Too dark to see more than the shape of them. Tell you what, though: I'd lay ten to one they were negros. You know that musty smell their clothes have, sir?" The lieutenant sniffed, as if to illustrate his point. "I've often remarked it. Thieving magpies, the whole pack of them. They'd steal their grandmother's teeth if they could."

I shifted position and one of my shoes kicked against something that scraped on the pavement. I bent down and picked up the object, holding it so the light from the lantern fell upon it.

For a moment no one spoke. In my hand was a knife with a crude horn handle. The blade was about eight inches long and sharpened to a tapering point.

The lieutenant touched the blade with a fingertip. "After your purse and your rings, I suppose," he said. "But if need be, I dare say they would not have scrupled to murder you while they were at it."

116

CHAPTER
TWENTY

Fear has a terrible habit of breeding fear; it spreads like maggots through rotting meat.

Once the danger was past I began to tremble. My rescuer kindly ignored my shameful weakness and escorted me to Warren Street. No one was about, except for servants. The lieutenant would not stay — his ship sailed at dawn tomorrow. I would have welcomed the company of anyone, even Captain Wintour, whose conversation, I had discovered, was not always agreeable. Instead I drank rum and water alone in the parlour, huddled over the banked-up fire, and the alcohol seemed to have no effect on me whatsoever.

My mind raced to and fro. It was as if it were under the influence of a powerful stimulant. When at last I retired to bed, I could not sleep.

Time and again, I ran over what had happened and what might have happened. The memory of my own unheroic conduct made me toss and turn in the smothering embrace of the featherbed.

Time and again, I returned to that terrible moment when the man had bounded out from the alley in front of me, and the footsteps behind had speeded up.

It's him. That's what the man behind me had said. *It's him.*

After a sleepless night, I walked through the rain-slicked streets to Headquarters and asked to see Marryot. His servant ushered me into the Major's private room. A masked white figure was sitting by the window. Two blue eyes, gleaming bright as if illuminated from within, stared out of the blank white face. For an instant I believed my mind had given way under the strain.

The moment dissolved and reformed itself: Marryot was swathed in a sheet, with his scalp and face lathered white. A regimental barber stood to one side, sharpening his razor on a strop. The blade slapped to and fro, glinting as it passed through a shaft of weak sunshine from the window.

I bowed.

"Good morning to you, sir," the Major said, revealing the vivid pink of his mouth and an irregular palisade of blackened teeth. "You'll forgive me if I don't stand."

"Of course. I'm obliged to you for seeing me at such short notice."

"And how may I serve you?"

I glanced at the barber. "I wished to speak privately. Shall I wait until you are at leisure?"

"You could wait all day for that and most of tomorrow as well. The General is to inspect the fortifications at King's Bridge, and I am ordered to accompany him." Marryot looked up at the barber. "Wait outside. Send for more hot water."

We waited in silence until the man had withdrawn, closing the door behind him.

Marryot did not ask me to sit. "Well, sir? What is it?"

"I was set upon last night. It was about midnight — I was walking back to Warren Street after supping with Mr Townley at the King's Arms."

"Were you robbed?"

"No. Two soldiers came to my aid and chased the villains off."

"Were you hurt?"

"No."

"All in all, a happy escape," he said. "I congratulate you, sir. And now, if that is —"

"Sir, I am not altogether easy in my mind about this. There was something . . . something contrived about the attack. It was as if they had been lying in wait."

"What are you saying?"

"I felt as if I had walked into a trap, sir. There was a man in front and a man behind."

"But perhaps you *had* walked into a trap. Robbers work in pairs often enough."

"They had been waiting for me." I paused. "For *me*. Not for any passer-by that might have had a purse in his pocket. *It's him.* That's what one of them said."

"Well? All that means is that they had picked you out earlier as a likely mark."

"No, sir, I do not think so. Or they would not have made their attempt with so many witnesses about."

Marryot sighed. "In my experience a robber can be as foolish as any man alive."

"Would you assist me in one thing at least? It would greatly set my mind at rest if I might talk to the two soldiers who chased them off. They may be able to tell me more about the men who attacked me. Besides, I should like to reward them. They may well have saved my life."

"Did you see their facings?"

"No, sir. To all intents and purposes it was dark."

"So for all you know, they might have been from Provincial or militia —"

"I heard them shouting, sir," I said, thinking, *Run, boyo, run.* "I believe I detected that one of them had a Welsh accent. Of course they may have come from a Loyalist regiment, but it is more probable that they did not."

"Very well." The lather on Marryot's face was drying: cracks appeared, revealing the pink skin beneath. "I shall have enquiries made. And I suppose Mr Townley may learn something from his own informants."

There was nothing to be gained by prolonging the meeting. I took my leave. But as I reached the door —

"One other thing, sir," Marryot said. "How do they do in Warren Street?"

"Very well, thank you, sir."

"And Captain Wintour? Pray, how is he?"

"He improves every day, I believe," I said. "But his wound and the privations he endured have left their mark."

"His family must rejoice to have him restored to them. How are his parents? And — and Mrs Arabella, of course?"

"Quite well, thank you."

"Pray pass on my compliments to them all, Mr Savill. I have not thought it proper to call in person to congratulate them on Captain Wintour's happy return. In case his health still caused anxiety, you understand."

"I am sure that they are always happy to receive you, sir."

"You think so?"

I knew that when he spoke of the Wintours he meant Mrs Arabella and I pitied him for his doglike devotion. "I am perfectly convinced of it."

"Then I'm obliged to you, sir." The eyes blazed in the cracked white mask. "And I wish you good day."

CHAPTER
TWENTY-ONE

Shortly before Christmas, I had occasion to become better acquainted with Captain Wintour. We found ourselves alone at supper one day; the ladies had not come down and the Judge was suffering from a head-cold and had kept to his room. It was chilly, and afterwards we drew up our chairs to the parlour fire.

"It is so confoundedly dull here," he said, prodding the logs with a poker. "My father should entertain more. And we should be seen out and about in the world, where we belong. We are one of the first families of the province. Besides, a man cannot spend all his time at home with his wife, can he?"

I nodded, acknowledging the remark but not answering it.

"Mark you, sir, Mrs Arabella is an adornment to any assembly or private party. She is wasted in Warren Street, shut up where nobody sees her. The Wintour diamonds are the best in New York, you know, and she looks charming in them. They were my grandmother's. After the war is over I shall take Mrs Arabella to London and she shall wear them at court."

"You have visited London before, sir?"

"As a young man, I passed several months there." Wintour clicked his fingers. "But let us have a game. What shall it be, sir? Cards? Backgammon? We can play by the fire — they will bring us up another bottle and we shall be famously snug."

We were drinking an old madeira, pale and golden like watery sunlight. Mr Wintour had put aside a few bottles until the end of the war, so he would have a fitting wine with which to drink the King's health when victory was declared. But his son argued that if they left the wine much longer, it would be spoiled; it would be better to drink it now.

"Let us make this more interesting," he suggested as we were waiting for Josiah to bring up another bottle, and a second one too in case it should be needed. "Let us put a trifle on the outcome. I find that a stake concentrates the faculties wonderfully."

Josiah brought the wine and Captain Wintour shouted at him for forgetting to bring the cards and the backgammon as well. The old man bowed low and said nothing, though I knew as well as he did that he could not have forgotten because he had not been ordered to bring them in the first place.

When the slave returned, Wintour had him set up a little table between us. It had flaps that drew out at either end, and we placed a candle on each of them. The Captain opened the backgammon board and laid out the ebony and ivory counters with trembling fingers. The arrows had been painted a delicate shade of green and they rested on a black ground. The board made a pretty sight in flickering light. It was a handsome set, as good as anything I had seen in London apart from the dice, which were clearly of colonial manufacture, being made of bone and crudely painted.

"They say this is a game of chance, sir," Wintour said, taking up his glass. "But that is all stuff and nonsense, is it not? Chance may dictate the fall of the dice but, taken all in all, it's skill that counts. When I waited for my ship in Quebec, I paid for my dinners with backgammon."

A counter slipped from his hand. His wine glass tilted. Madeira splashed on to the board and formed a small, glistening puddle in one of its corners.

"Goddamn it!" He stared at the board and slowly shook his head.

"It don't signify, sir." I took out a handkerchief and dabbed at the wine. "It is only a drop or two. See — it is gone."

Wintour stared at the handkerchief. "You've cut yourself."

"What? Where?"

"Your hand, I apprehend — look at the handkerchief."

I held the square of cloth to the light of the nearer candle. He was right: the cambric had a reddish tinge resembling blood in one corner. I examined my hand. The skin was unbroken.

"It must be paint, sir, not blood," I said.

"Very likely," Wintour said, losing interest in the matter as swiftly as he had gained it.

I frowned. The ground of the board looked black in the candlelight but it was possible that it was really a very dark red.

He reached for the bottle. "Shall we put a guinea on the first game, sir?"

"Or there might have been blood," I said slowly. "A spot of blood on the board."

As I spoke I imagined someone — Mrs Arabella, perhaps — pricking her finger by accident while she was sewing, with the board open before her. Or even suffering an unexpected nosebleed, such as one sometimes had as a result of a heavy cold. A few drops of blood might so easily have fallen on the board and lain there, drying in a moment, and invisible against the dark paint, particularly if the bloodletting had happened in poor light. The madeira had reliquefied the blood, bringing it back to a watery half-life.

"Well, sir — guinea?" said Wintour, sharply. "I find a little wager lends spice to a game, any game at all. Playing for love is so confoundedly dull."

I had not played backgammon since my arrival in America. To begin with I found it difficult to concentrate. I lost the first game quite unnecessarily, allowing Wintour to gammon me.

"We play according to Hoyle's rules, do we not?" he said, almost crowing with triumph. "If I remember rightly that means we double the stake. And therefore we triple it for a backgammon."

I nodded, though I could not recall that the chapter on backgammon in Mr Hoyle's book said anything about wagers at all, only a great deal on the mathematical probabilities of chance in relation to two six-sided dice.

Wintour paused to drink a toast to Dea Fortuna. He refilled his glass while I set the thirty men back on the board. By the time the first bottle of madeira was empty, he owed me eleven guineas.

"Double or quits?" he cried, as he set the pieces for the next game. "What do you say?" He placed his bets with a sort of wild enthusiasm that rode roughshod over mere calculation.

There was a tap on the door and Miriam slipped into the room. She walked almost silently towards Wintour and stood by his chair, her head bowed and her hands clasped tightly together in front of her as if holding a secret.

"Well, sir? Double or quits?"

"If you wish, sir." I made up my mind that, if I lost, this must be the last game.

I smelled a hint of Mrs Arabella's perfume in the air, clinging to the maid's dress or her hands. I looked up at Miriam and saw the whites of her eyes flickering in the shadows behind her master's chair. She was a comely young woman, in her way. She turned her head away from me.

Wintour set down the last of the counters and sat back. "What is it, girl?"

"If it please your honour, mistress begs the favour of a word with you."

"Can't you see I'm engaged? Tell her I'll wait on her when I'm at leisure."

"Yes, sir."

Her head still bowed, Miriam glided away.

My fingers slipped as if of their own accord into my waistcoat pocket. I touched the die I had found with Pickett's body. The practice was on the verge of becoming habitual with me: like touching a rabbit's foot for luck.

"They pester me at all hours," Wintour complained as the door closed. His consonants were blurring now; the vowels slopped to and fro like water in a pail. "My father, my wife, my mother. Can they not understand that I need tranquillity above all if I am ever to recover my health? Your glass, sir — let us have a toast before we play: to the absence of women."

He drank his glass in one and seemed not to notice that I did not do the same. We played the game, and he lost; so we played another, and another, and a fourth; and each time he lost.

I proposed that we call a halt, but Wintour demanded a chance to make good his losses.

"I'm a little fatigued, sir. Besides, should we not cast our accounts?"

"You sound like a damned clerk, man." He laughed. "But I suppose that's what you are, sir — no offence, none in the world: I suppose a gentleman may hold a pen in an office, if he wishes, rather than a sword on a battlefield."

He had kept a note of what he lost, scrawling the figures in pencil. He screwed up his face and blinked rapidly, holding the paper up to the candle. His lips moved silently as he totted up the figures.

"Seventy guineas or thereabouts," he said at last. "Good God, how it creeps up on a man. Oblige me, sir — cast your eye over it. I never had much skill at reckoning."

I glanced at the paper, reading the figures with difficulty. I already knew it must be nearer eighty guineas. "Let us call it seventy, sir," I said. "I prefer round numbers."

"Very well," he said with a gracious wave of his hand. "I'd give you the money this instant, if I could, sir, if it weren't for those damned tight-purses. Damn them, eh? Let's drink to their damnation."

He lifted the bottle, but it was empty.

"Who?" I asked. "Whose damnation?"

Wintour set down the bottle and picked up the other, which was also empty. "Who? Eh? Oh yes — all of them — they're all tight-purses in this city — you would not believe it, sir, these petty tradesmen, they would not have behaved like this before the war. Why should you wait for your money?"

"It's of no consequence to me in the least, sir —"

"But it is. My dear — dear Savill, of course it is. I know you would take my note of hand. But when a debt of honour is involved, a gentleman feels it here." He laid his hand on his heart. "A tradesman's bill can wait until the Last Trump for all I care, but a debt of honour is a very different thing. Besides, why should you wait? You're my friend. And anyone in this city will tell you: Jack Wintour is a man of his word. Ask anyone, anyone at all. If any man says otherwise, I'll blow out his brains, do you hear?"

"Really, sir, you are too kind, but I am in no hurry for the money."

He hammered his fist on the table, making the counters twitch on the board. "Nothing could be more absurd than the situation I'm in, sir. Is it not perfectly ludicrous that a man of my expectations should have to suffer from a shortage of ready money? Does Mount George mean nothing? God damn it, what's credit for, sir, if not to ease a temporary embarrassment of this nature? And I insist — you shall not wait. There is no need, either. I have a scheme that will settle the matter at once. Pray have the goodness to ring the bell."

I leaned across from my chair to the bell-pull to the left of the fireplace. "I believe I have had enough wine for this evening."

"No, no — it's not for that; though come to think of it, we might as well have them bring up another bottle."

Josiah came into the room and made his reverence.

"Tell Miriam to step this way," Wintour said.

The old man looked up. "Miriam, sir?"

"Yes, you old fool — Miriam. Are you going deaf? And then bring up another bottle."

Josiah bowed again and withdrew. A moment later, the maidservant entered the room. She curtsied and waited for Wintour to speak.

"Step forward, woman — there: stand in the light by the fire."

She obeyed him. Her face was blank, like a house with the shutters up.

"Turn round," he ordered, raising one of the candles so it shone more on her. "No, not like that — slowly. So we may study you at all points." He glanced at me. "What do you think, sir?"

"I do not think it proper for me to have an opinion about another man's servant."

Wintour laughed. "But that's the point, sir. Don't you see? She's not a servant. She's a slave."

"Yes, but the principle —"

"The principle is the same as if she was my horse. Or my dog. Or my house, for that matter. She's mine. That is to say, she's mine to sell."

He turned back to Miriam, who was no longer revolving. Her face was averted from the light.

"What would you say? Ninety guineas at auction? A hundred? Trained ladies' maids don't grow on trees. Prime of life, too, fine figure." His voice roughened. "Look at me, girl, and open your mouth."

Miriam stared down at him. She opened her mouth. I glimpsed her pink, wet tongue.

"There! I knew it!" he cried. "See? She's got her own teeth, or most of them. They like that in a house slave, you know. Damned if I know why, but they do. I'll put her in for auction tomorrow. You won't have to wait long, I assure you. She'll be snapped up in a trice."

"But Miriam is Mrs Arabella's maid, sir — wouldn't the sale inconvenience her? I would not do that for the world."

Wintour laughed. "You won't do that, I assure you. My wife does not need a maid all the time — she can share my mother's if she wants one — and anyway she shall have any number of maids when the war's over."

"But Miriam serves Mrs Wintour, too, I believe."

He sat up very straight in his chair. "This is a matter of honour with me, sir."

At this moment there was a distraction in the form of Josiah and another bottle of madeira. The old man opened and poured the wine. I took a glass to be companionable. Josiah did not withdraw but stood back in the shadows near the door.

"I wonder, sir, would you oblige me in this?" I said, holding my wine up to the candle flame.

"If I could, sir, I would oblige you in anything you care to name but a debt of honour is —"

"You see," I interrupted, "it does not suit me to have so large a sum of ready money about me at present, with the city in such a lawless state. And these days one cannot trust a bank or a merchant to negotiate a bill without cheating a man, or defaulting, or going bankrupt."

"True, sir." Wintour frowned. "Bankers are the worst of criminals. Greed blinds them to all morality as well as to common sense. I have often remarked upon it."

"It follows, sir, as a simple matter of logic, that it would be far more secure and indeed more convenient for me to accept your note of hand for the money instead. I know it will be safer with you than with the Bank of England itself."

I held my breath, wondering if the absurdity of discussing the security of non-existent money would strike my host. But it did not.

Instead he sipped his wine and contemplated with evident enjoyment the idea that money, whether real or not, was safer with him than with the Bank of England.

He set down the empty glass. "I cannot bear to deny a friend's request," he said. His chin sank to his chest. After a moment he stirred and his eyelids fluttered. "Besides, my dear sir, I shall soon have my box of curiosities and all our troubles will be over."

His eyes closed. His breathing became heavy and regular. A log shifted in the grate. Miriam and Josiah stood waiting like dark statues in the shadows.

CHAPTER
TWENTY-TWO

The following morning, I slept late. I awoke when Josiah drew back the bed-curtains and a current of cold air swirled over my face. My throat was dry and my head ached from the madeira.

I struggled up to a sitting position.

Something was different. Something had changed. The very air was charged with brightness.

The old man was standing by the window with his back to the room.

"What is it?" I said. "What are you looking at?"

"The snow, your honour." Josiah turned. He was smiling broadly. "It came in the night. Just an inch or two. But everything is white."

I breakfasted by myself in the parlour; I rarely saw any of the family before I left for the office. As Josiah was bringing me my hat and coat, however, Mrs Arabella came down the stairs with Miriam behind her. The women were dressed for going out.

"You are going to your office, I collect?" Mrs Arabella said, when we had wished each other good morning. For the first time that winter she was wearing furs, which brought out the extraordinary lustre of her dark eyes and the creamy pallor of her complexion.

"Yes, ma'am. Unless I may have the honour of escorting you somewhere first?"

Mrs Arabella inclined her head. "Perhaps you would be good enough to give me your arm as far as Little Queen Street. I promised to meet a friend there this morning."

"With pleasure."

I offered her my arm and we left the house with Miriam following five paces behind. Under the winter sun, we trudged towards Broadway. Icicles clung to window sills and gutters. Smoke rose in lazy spirals from the chimneys and smudged the hard blue sky. Warren Street had seen little traffic at this hour and the snow lay largely undisturbed.

Neither of us spoke. I was conscious of Mrs Arabella's proximity, of the weight of her arm on mine, and the way her hand tightened its grip when the going was at all treacherous. Her touch gave me a disproportionate pleasure. I had not been so intimately close to a woman since I had said goodbye to Augusta.

We turned into Broadway. The street was already busy and here the snow was turning to slush. Prisoners of war, working in groups of two or three, were shovelling it into piles along the roadway.

"It is always like this in New York," Mrs Arabella said.

"What is, madam?"

"The snow. Charming at first and then, as soon as people come along, ugly and inconvenient. People ruin everything, don't they?"

She glanced up at me as she spoke. I glimpsed her profile framed in fur, her cheeks now tinged a delicate pink with the cold; and I marvelled that I had ever thought her anything less than beautiful.

"I'm in your debt, sir," she said, in a lower voice.

I thought I had misheard. "I beg your pardon, ma'am?"

"Miriam told me what you did last night."

"It is not worth mentioning, ma'am. A trifle."

"It was not a trifle to me, sir." She hesitated. "You cannot know how important it was."

"I beg you not to think of it again. It was nothing."

"Seventy guineas, Miriam said. That is not nothing."

"But I have no need of the money, ma'am." I felt myself colouring. "Not at present. Whereas I'm sure I should miss Miriam's contribution to our domestic economy. Why, my shirts have never been as white as they have been here, nor my stockings so neatly darned. So you see my motives are entirely selfish and as such I deserve your censure, not your praise."

She burst out laughing, turned her head and smiled up at me, exposing white, regular teeth. "That was a pretty speech, sir. And you argue like a Jesuit."

A cavalry officer trotted past us. He glanced first at Mrs Arabella, and then at me. He touched his hat and smiled down at me with good-humoured envy.

Mrs Arabella did not notice, for she was still looking at me and her expression had grown serious. "It is not easy at present," she said in a low voice. "Captain Wintour has been away so long and endured so much that he does not find it easy to — to live as his circumstances now require."

"It is not to be wondered at, ma'am."

"But you must forgive me, sir — I chatter on about my own concerns, which can be of no interest to you — I'm afraid it's a poor return to you for your kindness."

She turned away and we walked on. I could not help pitying her — and the Captain too. When riches dwindle to a mere competence, then even a competence becomes a form of poverty.

The winter of 1778–79 was hard and bitter. In fact all the wartime winters were exceptionally long and cold. In some quarters New Yorkers murmured that this was a sign of divine displeasure. If so, Mr Townley remarked to me, God was displeased with the rebels as well, for the harsh weather fell on them and they too suffered from the shortages of food and fuel that made matters so much worse. But the rebels had a continent with all its resources at their backs. We had only the sea.

In the winter, during the cruel months of the year, we longed with an almost mystical hunger for the arrival of the Cork Fleet. It sailed across three thousand miles of ocean in a great convoy protected by our warships from the menace of the French navy and, near the end of the voyage, from the impudent attacks of American privateers. It brought flour and wine, tea and cloth, candles and crockery, furnishings and books — and, best of all, news from home. It was a marvellous sight to behold the Narrows choked with white sails that then burst like an exploding firework into the waters of New York Bay.

The fleet came much later than expected that year. The stock of flour held in the public stores was quite exhausted and there were rumours that the oatmeal used as a substitute for making bread would soon be gone. And what then? If the city and its soldiers starved, Washington could march in at the head of his men without firing a single shot.

Our household in Warren Street was better off than most. For this we had to thank Mr Townley and Major Marryot. Indeed, if it had not been for their influence, I doubt the Wintours would have been permitted to retain their house or at least to avoid the annoyance of having soldiers billeted on them.

Mr Townley was on cordial terms with many of the contractors. He seemed always to know when a shipment was due or when a consignment of vegetables arrived from Brooklyn. More mysteriously, he found ways of sending Mr Noak with small presents of meat, usually tough and salted. When I asked him once where it came from, Mr Townley tapped his great nose and murmured that heaven helps those who help themselves.

Hunger blunts moral niceties as well as the finer sensations of taste. I ate whatever food there was without troubling myself overmuch about where it came from; and everyone else did the same.

Major Marryot was peculiarly well placed to provide wood for the fires. As more and more trees were cut down beyond the city boundary and on Brooklyn, prices shot up as availability diminished. But the army never went short. The Major was conveniently based at Headquarters and was something of a favourite with the Commandant. It was due to his good offices that a wagon carrying a cord or two of firewood would sometimes rumble down Warren Street and stop outside our door.

During that winter, I often found Marryot or Townley at the house, chatting with the ladies in the parlour or discussing the state of the war with Judge Wintour or playing cards with his son. Townley was always affable, always obliging; he seemed drawn to Warren Street from simple good nature, perhaps mingled with decorous admiration for Mrs Arabella and a general respect for the family, for he himself came from humbler stock than the Wintours. It was only odd that such a busy, thrusting man could find the time to cultivate a family which at present had so little influence or wealth at its command.

As for the Major, his motive was easy enough to discern, though he tried to conceal it: he made calf's eyes at Mrs Arabella when he thought no one was observing him and coloured when she talked to him.

Noak was often in the house too, making himself useful in the Judge's library, which was in a sad state, or running errands that could not be entrusted to a servant.

"I do believe you spend more time here than at Hanover Square with Mr Townley," I said one afternoon in January when I found him sharpening Mr Wintour's pens.

138

"Mr Townley offered my services, sir," Noak said without looking up, and the blade of his penknife continued to scrape to and fro at the tip of the pen. "And of course I am happy to oblige the old gentleman."

As January turned to February, there came by degrees a change in the household. Mrs Wintour was particularly susceptible to the cold. They took care to build up great fires in the parlour, and she would sit almost on top of it, swathed in elderly furs, holding mittened hands out to the flames. Her husband fussed over her, chafing her hands with his, sending Miriam for tea or broth or a rum toddy flavoured with nutmeg or indeed anything that might warm her. But she allowed the drinks to go cold and barely touched the food they brought.

Winter invaded the old lady's mind as well as her body. It was as if her mental faculties had been gripped with an iron frost and her perceptions masked by an invisible blanket of snow. The surgeon came to bleed her, which merely made her weaker, whiter and colder than before.

Sometimes, the only parts of the poor lady that seemed to move for hours on end were her narrow chest, rising and falling almost imperceptibly, and her lips, which parted and closed as a stream of mumbled words emerged from some remote part of her brain that remained unfrozen. Her eyes watered chronically and the tears trickled through the crooked channels of her wrinkled cheeks. It was a miracle, I thought, that these salty rivulets did not turn to ice.

"Oh, my dear," the Judge would say when he took her hands or stooped to salute her gently on the cheek, "you must not trouble yourself, indeed you must not. Hush, my dear, hush."

If you listened to Mrs Wintour for long enough, there were fragments of sense, or not quite nonsense, among the words that tumbled out of her like fragments of nursery rhymes. As in a concerto, there were themes that came and went, sometimes in different guises. "Chilly willy chilly willy." Or "Dinner now, now." Or "Hetty-Petty. Hetty-Petty." I noticed that "Hetty-Petty" was often accompanied with tears.

"There was a daughter," Mrs Arabella explained in a low voice when I mentioned it to her. "Henrietta — she was their first child, before my husband was born."

"She died?"

"On her first birthday. I fear that Mrs Wintour's mind wanders in the past."

"But there is sense, of a sort, in what she says."

"Sense, sir?" Mrs Arabella gave a short laugh. "Who knows what the sense of it is?"

"If a child dies," I said, thinking of Lizzie as much as Hetty-Petty, "then . . ."

I hesitated, as that unbearable prospect opened before me: *if Lizzie were to die.*

"Then what, sir?" she said, and her voice was as soft as the wood ash that spilled out beneath the grate.

"Then I believe it would drive me to nonsense too."

"Or worse, I fancy." It was her turn to hesitate. She looked at me for a moment, her eyes wide and beautiful, her expression unreadable. I turned away, fearing that my staring at her would seem ill bred. She added in an even lower voice than before, "Much worse."

There was a tap on the door, and Josiah came in with a letter on a salver. Bowing low, he held it out to me. He coughed gently.

"By your leave, sir, Miriam said to say that she's turned the cuffs and collar of your shirt and left it in your press."

"Thank you." I broke the seal on the letter.

Josiah coughed again. "And the boots are back from the cobbler's."

I looked up. "That's quick work. I only gave them you this morning."

"I took them down myself, sir, and waited until they were done."

"I'm obliged."

Josiah bowed again, including Mrs Arabella within the range of his reverence, and withdrew.

I glanced at her and smiled. "They treat me with a mother's tender care, ma'am. It's quite extraordinary."

"It's because of Miriam."

"I beg your pardon?"

Mrs Arabella rose to her feet. She looked coldly on me, as if I had somehow presumed too far on our enforced intimacy in this house. These sudden reversals in her demeanour were not uncommon in her intercourse with me; they pained me; and yet they also exerted a strange fascination on me, which I attributed to the charm of the unpredictable.

"Slaves are like dogs or horses, you see." She spoke slowly and deliberately. "They don't forget a kindness. If you hadn't chosen otherwise, Miriam would have been sold to a stranger by now."

She curtseyed. I opened the door for her. When she had gone I went back to my chair, the letter still in my hand. I unfolded it, my mind still on Mrs Arabella and what she had said.

The letter contained only a few words scribbled in pencil.

Sir, I believe I have one of the soldiers who were of service to you in November. Pray send me word if you still desire to speak to him. I am, sir, etc. R. Marryot.

CHAPTER
TWENTY-THREE

The man that Marryot had found was a corporal from the 23rd, the Royal Welch Fusiliers. On the strength of one word — *boyo* — that I had heard a soldier say I had been expecting a Welshman, a small dark fellow called Lewis or Jones, perhaps; and the name of his regiment reinforced my preconception.

But the corporal's name was Grantford; he was well over six feet in height and as thin as a musket. Judging by the stubble on his chin, he had red hair; and judging by his voice when he snapped to attention and announced his name and rank, he came from Yorkshire.

"Make yourself easy," I said. "You are not on parade."

Still in coat and hat, I was sitting at the table in my private office in Broad Street with the chair drawn close to the small stove and a muffler around my neck. The windowpanes were rimmed with ice on the inside.

Grantford remained at attention.

"I'm in your debt, Corporal," I said. "You and your comrade saved my purse and possibly my life."

"Sir," said Grantford, as if acknowledging an order.

"Warm yourself at the stove. Why did it take you so long to come forward? Major Marryot said he made enquiries in November."

Grantford moved a step nearer the warmth. "We were up in the Debatable Ground on patrol, your honour, and then I fell ill. Pleurisy, they called it."

"In all events, it's better late than never. You are quite restored, I hope?"

"Yes, your honour. Can't say as much for poor Ifor, though, God rest his soul."

Run, boyo, run? "Your comrade? He had pleurisy too?"

"No, sir. One of their Skinners shot him in the back when we were up in Westchester County." Grantford's mouth worked, as if he would have liked to spit. "The cowards pretended to surrender then shot him in the back. I'd hang the lot of them if I could, so help me God. They're no better than savages up there."

The Skinners were the irregulars who haunted the Debatable Ground searching for livestock to provision the Continental Army, and for whatever else took their fancy. We had our own Cowboys who did the same for our side.

"It was because of him I found you, you know," I said. "I heard him call out as you chased my attackers away. I heard the Welshness in his voice."

"He was the one who first went after them, your honour. Always up for a fight or a bit of fun. Like a terrier in a barn full of rats."

"Tell me what happened. And tell me how you chanced to be there."

144

Grantford scratched his chin, considering. "We'd been at sea all autumn with the navy, sir, and then we moved into quarters on Staten Island with the rest of the army. Our company came up for guard duty in Brooklyn, and at the end of that they gave us a furlough in the city on the way back to barracks. We made a night of it, if you take my meaning."

"So you were merry?" I said, smiling.

"In a manner of speaking, your honour. And for Ifor, the drink always brought out his fighting spirit. So when we heard an Englishman shouting for help, he was off like a ball from a musket. With me at his heels to try to stop him."

"The street was ill lit."

"Aye, sir, but we could see enough to know a pair of negros had set upon a gentleman. When we came running, they went off like all the devils in hell were after them. Which in a manner of speaking they were, because when Ifor's blood was up there's no saying what he'd do."

Grantford was beginning to relax, and he provided more and more detail and needed less and less prompting. The two negros had zigzagged through alleys linking the streets. The Fusiliers had caught up with them on the fringes of Canvas Town. After a running fight, they cornered their quarry in the shell of an outhouse.

"I was trying to get Ifor away, your honour," Grantford said. "You never know what's going to come at you in Canvas Town. But it was like trying to stop a fighting cock that's tasted blood."

145

In the near darkness, the negros had come at them with knives. The bigger of the two had a stick of some sort. But the soldiers were capable fellows. Grantford thought it probable that Ifor had wounded, perhaps even killed, the smaller negro before being himself knocked insensible by the other one.

"Then the big fellow made a run for it. But I had to get Ifor out of there in one piece. I put him over my shoulder and by the grace of God I met a patrol before I'd gone far, or they'd have had me for sure."

"Did you get a clear view of them?" I asked. "Did you see their faces?"

"All look the same to me, them black heathens." He paused. "That's why Ifor noticed the scars."

I rubbed at a spot of grease on my breeches. "What scars, pray?"

"The negros were just ahead of us, sir, and they went by the door of a tavern. And the big one looked back, just as the door opened. Ifor said he'd know him again because he had a scar on each cheek. Like this" — Grantford traced a line from the outer corner of his eye to the corner of his lips — "on both sides. It was a devil's face, Ifor said. Fit to give you nightmares."

"A tall man, you said, I think? And well built?"

"Aye, sir, and ugly as sin."

I continued to question him for a few minutes longer but learned nothing more of significance. I sent Grantford on his way with a guinea in his pocket for his trouble.

146

For half an hour afterwards, I sat shivering, huddled over the stove, much to the annoyance of the people waiting in the outer office to see me.

The big negro with the scarred face seemed to haunt me like a malevolent spirit. He had been there on my very first day in New York, along with the mulatto boy, Benjamin Taggart, and the milch goat that might have been stolen from the Wintours. The negro had been watching when the soldiers loaded Pickett's body on to the cart.

The negro had been there again, a few days later, playing the penny whistle for the crowd outside the Upper Barracks on the morning when Virgil, the little runaway, had been hanged for Pickett's murder. The lad had been with him again on that occasion, with a tray of fresh goat meat. Was that the remains of the Wintours' milch goat?

According to Townley, the mulatto, Taggart, was the Government informer who had led Marryot to Virgil as Pickett's murderer. In October, Taggart had been found drowned near the Paulus Hook ferry.

Finally, a big negro with a scarred face had been one of the men who assaulted me in November. But I could not be sure of this, I reminded myself, for the identification rested on Grantford's report of what his comrade claimed to have glimpsed, and on a dark night, too.

Thoughts swirled in my mind. There must surely be an underlying design to this. Was all this to do with Pickett's murder? But why should a negro from Canvas Town turn his murderous thoughts towards a harmless

English official like me, who had not even been in New York when Pickett had been killed?

That was the worst feature of this business. Somehow, I had contrived to earn the animosity of the scar-faced negro. I knew nothing about him for certain. All I had were suspicions: that he might already be a double murderer and that, quite possibly, he had tried to murder me.

If I was right, did it not follow as night follows day that he would try again?

CHAPTER
TWENTY-FOUR

After my interview with Corporal Grantford, I took precautions when I went abroad. I was at pains to avoid walking alone at night; if I could not go in company, I took a coach or a chair. Even in the day, I was wary of secluded places and of crowds where the press of people might allow a man to wield a knife or pick a pocket in perfect tranquillity.

Wild speculations circled and swooped in my mind like predatory crows about a sheep's carcass. I felt as if I had wandered into the borders of madness and, like many a lunatic, would soon imagine every man's hand to be against me.

My best course of action, I decided in the end, was the obvious one. I saw Grantford on a Wednesday. As it happened, the Judge had invited both Marryot and Townley to dine at Warren Street on the following Friday. Mrs Townley had been invited too, as a matter of course, but she had declined, pleading ill health.

"Ill fiddlesticks," Captain Wintour said to me in a loud whisper while his mother and his wife were greeting the guests. "He's ashamed of her. It's as plain as the nose on my face. They say he only married her for the dowry and she's about as genteel as a mule.

Twenty thousand pounds he got by her, and he had the worse of the bargain."

So there were seven of us at table — the four Wintours, Marryot, Townley and me. The Wintours rarely entertained now, but the Judge felt that his family had received so many kindnesses from Mr Townley and the Major that a show of hospitality was long overdue. The shutters were up and candles made pools of warm, yellow light among the shadows. The flames were reflected in old silver, in waxed mahogany and in the rippling, tarnished glass of the great mirror above the mantelshelf.

The food was plain and indifferent but the wine was good, for which Mr Townley was largely responsible. Mrs Wintour murmured to herself while Miriam cut up her food and helped her eat. The Judge held forth about the iniquities of the rebels and the pusillanimity of the Peace Commissioners who were trying ineffectually to negotiate a settlement between the two sides. When these subjects palled, he turned to the incompetence of the administration and the self-seeking behaviour of certain members of the New York judiciary, whose loyalty to the King was clearly tempered by their loyalty to themselves.

Captain Wintour talked, as usual, about Captain Wintour, though his eyes flickered constantly between his wife and his guests. He often addressed his conversation to me; since our backgammon party before Christmas he had conceived a kindness for me and considered me a friend, though not, I fear, an equal. Marryot and Townley played a lesser part in the conversation while the ladies were with us but their attention was never far from Mrs Arabella.

It was curious how she dominated the room. She ate sparingly and said little, though what she did say was to the point. Townley and Marryot vied with each other to monopolize her. Indeed, she looked very fine that evening for she was dressed for company and candles are always kind to the ladies; so I suppose it was not to be wondered at.

While playing the hostess with her guests, she ensured that Miriam did everything necessary for Mrs Wintour's comfort and that Josiah and Abraham kept up an uninterrupted flow of dishes and wine. She addressed none of her remarks to Captain Wintour.

Nor did she speak to me. A large silver-gilt candlestick stood between us on the table, which made it difficult to talk directly to each other without awkwardness. Perhaps she did not wish to. Once, however, I caught her looking at me with a cold, calculating expression on her face as though I were a set of household accounts which would not balance quite as they should. As soon as our eyes met, she looked away.

After the meal, the cloth was withdrawn and the ladies withdrew. "Hetty-Petty," Mrs Wintour murmured to me with a gracious inclination of her head as I held open the door for them. Then again, with an interrogatory inflection: "Hetty-Petty?"

"Hush, Mother," Mrs Arabella said, and her eyes met mine. Then the ladies were gone, leaving only a hint of otto of roses in the air to mark their passage.

151

At the Judge's suggestion, the gentlemen drew up their chairs around the fire. Now the ladies had left us, I intended to raise the subject of Grantford's visit, but Marryot was there before me.

"Was the fusilier I sent you of service, sir?" he asked, loudly enough for the others to hear.

"Yes, indeed. I was glad to have the opportunity to show my gratitude to him." I turned to the Wintours and Townley. "The Major was able to discover one of the soldiers who came to my rescue when I was set upon in the street before Christmas."

"Disgraceful," said Mr Wintour. "These attacks have become a daily occurrence. There is no respect for the law."

"Did you learn anything from him?" Townley asked.

I set down my glass. "Yes. Though I do not know quite how much weight to put upon it. He and his comrade chased the rogues into Canvas Town but they did not get a good view of them."

"Negros, I think you said, sir?"

"I believe so. And the soldier confirmed it — his comrade caught a glimpse of one of them in the light. He noted one feature in particular: the man had a scarred face — one scar on each cheek, running down from the eye to the mouth."

Captain Wintour reached for the bottle. "Send a patrol into Canvas Town, sir," he said to Marryot. "That's what I'd do. You'd soon flush the devil out."

"Easier said than done, sir." Marryot's face was dark red, perhaps from the wine or the fire, perhaps from

152

irritation. "There are twenty or thirty thousand people in the city now, and half of them have gone to roost in Canvas Town."

"I have seen a negro with a scarred face before," I said. I did not add that I saw him sometimes in my dreams. "On several occasions. He watched us take away the body of poor Mr Pickett from Canvas Town. And again, he was outside the Upper Barracks when the runaway was hanged for the murder."

"Very probably the same man," Townley said. "They are attracted to trouble like bedbugs to blood."

"But is it not strange?"

Townley smiled; he looked rather bored. "One might almost argue it would have been stranger if the rogue had not been there."

"Mr Savill, sir," Captain Wintour cried. "The honour of a glass of wine with you. We shall drink damnation to the knaves who set upon you."

The conversation became general and moved away to the war. I sat in silence, wondering whether I had made a fool of myself by allowing my fears to overmaster my reason. But soon, I reassured myself, the matter would resolve itself. It was already February. In a month or so — eight or ten weeks at the outside, I would sail for home and enjoy the fruits of my labours in this unhappy city: I would have a home of my own with Augusta and Lizzie, and a career that, with Mr Rampton's benevolent assistance, would flourish in London.

153

The others were now talking about the increasing difficulty in obtaining fresh food, both meat and vegetables.

"It is our one weakness," Mr Wintour said, "though not, I hope, a fatal one."

His son looked up from his glass. "Surely our forays into the Debatable Ground should be able to fill that need, sir? And the smugglers, of course."

"Up to a point," Townley said. "But the supply is diminishing all the time, and the longer the war drags on . . ."

Captain Wintour turned to Marryot. "The army sends regular patrols into Westchester County, I believe?"

"Naturally. And so do the rebels. And the irregulars, on both sides." The Major smiled, without humour. "Hence the name, of course: we debate the point all the time. But there's not much livestock left up there now."

"I've a fancy to go there myself," Captain Wintour said.

There was a sudden silence.

"When my wound is better, of course," he went on. "And when winter is over."

"I should not advise it, sir," Marryot said. "You know it is not safe to visit the Debatable Ground."

"Not by myself. I thought I might attach myself to a patrol. Or even a band of irregulars."

"Nonsense, John," Mr Wintour said. "There would be considerable danger and no possible benefit."

"I don't agree, sir. If a man knows where to look, I am sure there are many benefits to be found. Besides, I

154

find that I have a great yearning to see Mount George again."

"Mount George? Why?"

"Because it's mine now, sir, is it not? Mount George and all it contains. Is that not enough of a reason?"

CHAPTER
TWENTY-FIVE

A painting hung above the fireplace in the drawing room. It was a view of a shallow valley laid out as a gentleman's park. The land sloped upwards to a long, white mansion on a low eminence. It had a porch or verandah running along its front and a pediment supported by eight columns. Further up the valley, cattle and sheep grazed under a blue sky adorned with fluffy white clouds.

In the foreground, to the left, was a group of figures: a gentleman with a plan or chart in his hand and a brass telescope protruding from his pocket; an elegant young lady clinging to his arm; a little girl, equally elegant, clinging to the young lady; and a small golden spaniel sitting at the girl's feet. The gentleman was gesturing at the mansion with his other hand, as though pointing out its admirable features. The spaniel was looking the other way.

I had not paid the painting much attention before. But the conversation at dinner had aroused my curiosity. A couple of days later, after church on Sunday, I examined it more closely. Mr Wintour and his son were in the library. But I was not alone, for the ladies were in the drawing room too. We were drinking tea and trying to warm ourselves, for St Paul's Chapel had been particularly cold that morning despite the size of the congregation.

"Is this Mount George?" I asked.

"Yes, sir," Mrs Arabella said, without looking up from the tea tray.

"And that is yourself, my dear," Mrs Wintour said. "As a little girl. It is truly charming."

"I never cared for that dress," Mrs Arabella said.

"And the lady and gentleman are your parents, ma'am?"

"Yes."

"Mr Froude was a fine-looking man, was he not?" Mrs Wintour said. By and large, the old lady was more lucid in the mornings. "But he was never much of a sportsman, was he, my dear? His interests were scientific. Nothing delighted him more than dissecting a dead bird or tapping at a piece of rock with a hammer. Why, I once came upon him mounting a butterfly on a pin, and very pretty it looked."

I turned to Mrs Arabella. "Mr Froude's pursuits were scholarly?"

"Yes, sir. Natural philosophy in the main. He corresponded with the Royal Society on a variety of subjects."

"Gentlemen entertain themselves in such curious ways," Mrs Wintour said in a tone of wonder. "Perhaps it's as well your poor mother died young, Bella. I'm sure she cannot have liked it above half."

"It is a handsome property," I said, hoping to divert the conversation from a line that could only be increasingly uncomfortable to Mrs Arabella.

"The artist exaggerated everything," she said. "As artists always do. In England, I am sure that gentlemen's residences are much finer, and their demesnes more extensive."

"Not at all, madam," I said. "Or rather, not all of them. But in any event, you must long for the day when this war is over and you will return to Mount George."

"But not in winter," Mrs Wintour said. "There's no society then. We always winter in New York. Except the one year we went to London instead."

Mrs Arabella looked up at the painting. "Mount George does not look like that now," she said in a low voice. "In any case, I would not want to see it."

"Perhaps, ma'am." I smiled at her. "But after this sad business has been concluded, we shall all return to our former lives. No doubt the effects of any damage or neglect will soon be made good —"

"You misunderstand me, sir," she interrupted. "I never wish to see the place again in any condition."

"Indeed, the country is terribly cold in the winter," Mrs Wintour said, nodding vigorously as if agreeing with her daughter-in-law; and then she added a footnote: "Cold at heart."

On 19 February, a few days after this conversation, the packet *Mercury* brought the December mail from Falmouth. My letters were waiting at Headquarters when I called there on my way to the office.

158

I did not open them until I had reached an apartment at the back of the building, a room rarely used so early in the day. I sat on a window-seat set in a deep embrasure, which gave me a view out to sea. The water was grey, flecked with restless streaks of white. A military transport was sailing across the bay in the direction of Staten Island. A ragged cloud of seagulls trailed in its wake.

Home, I thought. *Pray God: let me go home.*

The letters had come under two covers. I broke the seal of the smaller first, the one with my sister's handwriting on the outside; Mr Rampton had obligingly had it franked at the Department. Inside was a scrap of paper, folded once. As I opened it, a lock of fair hair slid out. It would have fallen to the floor if I had not clapped the palm of my hand on it and caught it against my breeches.

The hair curled like a tiny golden bow. It was secured with a blue ribbon, frayed at one end. At the foot of the paper was a pencil drawing of a ship with two masts floating on a jagged fragment of sea. A stick-like figure stood behind the larger mast. Below the drawing were two lines of blotchy, irregular writing:

Dearest Papa, Thank you for the doll. This is your boat comming home and you on it. I send you my best love and duty, Elizabeth

Most of the sheet was given over to my sister's letter. She wrote that Lizzie was well, and that she adored the

159

doll which at my request her aunt had presented to her in my name on her birthday. The child had been sickly but they had purged her and her uncle had bled her; she was much better now. She had fallen asleep during the sermon last Sunday and had been chastised for it.

After a moment, I folded the paper and its enclosure and slipped it into the waistcoat pocket that also contained the die I had found on Pickett's body. My mouth was strangely dry. I felt a pulse throbbing at my temple. I looked out of the window. The transport was still wallowing on the water but the seagulls had gone.

Rampton's letter lay on the seat beside me. I tore it open. His small and very regular script filled the page, crept around the margins and then passed vertically across the lines already written. Frugality, as Mr Rampton was fond of saying to the junior clerks of the American Department, must be our watchword; and neither he nor His Majesty possessed an inexhaustible supply of paper. In an instant, my eyes seized on the passage in the letter that affected me most.

Only last week, Lord George was good enough to intimate that having our own source of intelligence in New York itself was invaluable. That being so, he wishes you to remain there for a few more months, perhaps until the autumn, by which time this unhappy rebellion may well be no more than a memory.

I swore. I kicked at the wall behind me with my heel.

You will recall the murder of the Loyalist gentleman, Mr Pickett, last August, which you reported to us in your very first letter from New York. I see that you made reference to a sister of the deceased, whom the authorities did not trouble to trace. It appears that this lady is in England, the wife of a Bristol merchant named Dornford, and that she received a letter from her brother, written shortly before his murder. In it, Mr Pickett wrote that he feared for his life as a result of some information he had about him concerning a Box of Curiosities whose contents, he added, would make him rich beyond the dreams of avarice and might change the course of the War.

I kicked the wall again.

This is very strange and we might well dismiss it as a mere freak or, more probably, as a ploy by a desperate man designed to cozen a loan from his sister. But there remains the possibility that Mr Pickett spoke no more than sober truth, and that he was murdered by rebels for possession of a large sum of money.

Nevertheless, none of this might have concerned us, had it not been that this lady's husband has a brother who is Lord North's man of business in Somerset and who has made interest to His Lordship about it, on Mrs Dornford's behalf. His Lordship has now been pleased to raise the matter with Lord George. At his request I

161

prepared a memorandum based on the information about the affair which you had given me.

To put it in plain language, Mr Rampton had taken care to distance himself as far as possible from the inquiry into the circumstances of Pickett's death. Lord North, the premier himself, was behind the renewal of interest, and Mr Rampton would not wish to have himself associated with an investigation that might prove to have been incomplete or even, perhaps, fatally flawed. There was worse to come:

> Their lordships have now considered this, and have decided that the matter merits further investigation; and Lord George believes that you are the man best suited for the commission. However, he commands me to urge you to employ the utmost discretion. For, if the murder was not after all the spontaneous act of a runaway slave, it may well have been part of a rebel plot; and we do not wish to alarm the perpetrators.

The rolling periods of Mr Rampton's prose drew to a stately conclusion. He added a perfunctory postscript after his signature, saying that he understood his niece Augusta to be in the best of health. I realized that Augusta herself had not troubled to write to me; and I also realized that this omission did not cause me much distress.

I heard dragging footsteps enter the lobby from the anteroom beyond. I looked up. Marryot was limping towards me, his face flushed.

162

"They told me I'd find you down here, Mr Savill. What are you doing — hiding away?"

"I wished to be alone, sir." I lost my temper. "I still do."

"You won't find solitude in this damned town. You should know that by now. Anyway, what the devil is all this about?"

"Is what about?"

He came to a halt in front of me. "This nonsense about a box of curiosities."

CHAPTER
TWENTY-SIX

"There he is!" Marryot shouted, pushing me out of his way to obtain a better view. "There's the black devil! Aim for the legs! In your own time, fire!"

There was a ragged volley of shots. None of them reached their target. The big negro in his faded red coat continued to duck and weave among the ruins. For all his bulk he was fast and agile.

"You damned numskulls. After him."

It was only mid-afternoon but the February day was already fading and it was growing very cold. The soldiers, weighed down by their equipment, ran deeper into Canvas Town. They had not had time to reload but they had been issued with naval cutlasses, which Marryot said were shorter and therefore better suited to close-quarters work than standard military swords. There were seven of them, six privates and a corporal from the Royal Americans, part of a company on detachment in the city that week.

"He's making for the road! Quick!"

The negro was now invisible, concealed from us by the gable wall of what had once been a stable. The corporal yelled at his men, trying to divide his party into two. His voice was cut off when he slipped and fell.

"Idiots," Marryot muttered. "Blockheads."

The ground was uneven and treacherous, puddled with icy water and a few drifts of muddy, frozen snow. The sky was a monotonous grey. There was no one else in sight. When the soldiers had come marching up the road, Canvas Town had been crawling with people; but already they had been moving away, for someone must have alerted them. They were still out there somewhere. I felt their eyes on me.

"That devil's making fools of them."

Three days after the arrival of the December mail, Marryot had had a tip-off from an informer. In Canvas Town, the negro was known by the name of Scarface. It was almost as if he was proud of his disfigurement. I had picked him out at once among a knot of men clustered around a fire; he was easily recognizable even at a distance because of his coat and his height. The soldiers had gone after him like a pack of hounds.

"They've botched it," Marryot said, drawing his pistol and limping down the muddy lane towards the intersection.

He must have calculated that the negro was hoping to reach Broadway, where the crowds and the maze of streets beyond would give a better chance of escape. At the junction the Major would have a clear line of sight in two directions.

I followed more slowly, picking my way between heaps of refuse and fragments of brick, glass and slate. My heart was beating faster than usual. I wished this unpleasant business was over. A manhunt was a dreary, dangerous affair and I had no stomach for it.

In their haste to flee, the inhabitants of this place had abandoned their possessions — among them, a coarse blanket, a knife with a broken blade, a small fire whose embers had been made into a nest for a blackened pot containing brown, watery liquid and a selection of bones. I had seen a little of the slums of Whitefriars and St Giles in London, but the poverty of Canvas Town was of a different order. Here, in the heart of this crowded city, the poor lived like wild animals, without rights, without shelter and, worst of all, without hope.

From the ruins to the right came the sounds of shouting and running footsteps. Marryot was now twenty or thirty yards in front, his head swinging from side to side. As well as his pistol, he carried a stick weighted with lead.

Suddenly, with a great cry and clatter, Scarface leapt from a gap in the brickwork overlooking the lane. Marryot staggered and fell beneath the negro's weight.

I broke into a run. Afterwards I could not understand why I had not run in the other direction. It was as if someone else were controlling me. I had no more ability to choose which way to move than a horse does with an experienced rider tugging at his reins.

I ran clumsily down the road, waving my stick and shouting. Marryot was on his front, pinned down by the negro's body. He was heaving like a landed fish and bellowing with rage.

Scarface wrenched the pistol away from him. He struck Marryot on the head with its butt, a powerful backhanded blow that elicited a howl of pain. The Major slumped into the ground and lay still. Scarface swung the pistol up and cocked it with the heel of his free hand.

The muzzle was pointing at me. I was now no more than a couple of paces from the two men on the ground. For the first time I saw the negro at close quarters. His face was impassive. His features were European as much as African. The pink weals on his cheeks curved up from the lips like a gigantic, joyless smile.

I hit out with the stick in a blind, sweeping arc. Scarface's finger tightened on the trigger. The hammer cracked down. The pistol went off. All these things in the same instant.

The shot came so close to me that I felt the wind of it on my cheek. But I saw nothing for — shamefully but with a child's absurd logic — I had shut my eyes so that I would encounter Death in the dark, and perhaps he might not see me and therefore pass me by.

A jolt ran up my arm. Someone cried out. I tripped and fell. I lost my hold on the stick. Someone groaned. There were more footsteps, more shouts.

At last I opened my eyes. Marryot was beside me. He was on his hands and knees, swaying and moaning. His hat and wig had fallen off. Blood dripped from his face. The wig lay in a muddy puddle of water and ice with splashes of red dropping into it and dissolving.

Scarface had gone.

"How I loathe New York," Marryot said. "How I wish this abominable town was at the bottom of the sea."

We were sitting opposite one another in a booth at the Bunch of Grapes. We had the curtain drawn across to discourage intruders and a bottle of brandy on the table. Marryot had refused to have his wound dressed by an army surgeon: it was only a damned scratch, he said, and if that negro hadn't run off he'd have made the cowardly fellow suffer for it.

The butt of the pistol was ornamented with chased steel. It was this that had caught Marryot's cheek, gouging out a graze along the cheekbone. The broken skin was already scabbing over. But the wound must be painful, judging by the swelling it had caused. The bruise was growing darker and angrier by the moment.

He set down his glass and cleared his throat. "I have to thank you, sir," he said in a voice better suited to making an accusation.

"It was nothing, sir."

"Indeed it was something. That scoundrel could have killed me. But now what are we to do?"

He stared into the flame of the solitary candle on the table as if looking for the answer there. I leaned against the padded back of the booth. On the other side of the blue curtain, in the body of the room, men were talking and laughing, spitting and smoking, reading newspapers and playing games. The air was hazy with smoke from pipes, cigars, lamps and candles. But here in the booth we might have been alone on the surface of the moon. There was nothing to distract us from the difficulty we faced.

"This is a damnable business, is it not?" Marryot went on, splashing more brandy into the glasses and a few drops on the table between them. "Nothing for a man to get hold of. It's like chasing . . . chasing clouds."

"At least a man can see a cloud," I said.

"Eh?" Marryot glared at me. Then the meaning hit him and he gave a harsh laugh. "Yes, very droll, I am sure. And what about this box of curiosities? What's a man to make of that? What the devil has it to do with Scarface?"

For a moment we drank in silence. I kept to myself the knowledge that Captain Wintour had mentioned a box of curiosities too, when we played backgammon two months ago. For him, as for Roger Pickett, a box of curiosities had promised some great reward.

All our troubles will be over.

But Wintour had been drunk at the time and I myself had been a long way from sober. There was no possible link between him and Pickett's murder — why, the Captain had been in Canada at the time, and his family had not known if he was alive or dead. It was a coincidence, nothing more, but I made a mental note to discover whether the two men had been acquainted.

We knew one thing for certain: Lord George Germain was taking this matter seriously. He had not only ordered Mr Rampton to commission me to look into it, but he had also added a postscript on the subject in his letter to General Clinton, the Commander-in-Chief in North America himself. Clinton had sent down the word to General Jones, the Commandant of the city, who had naturally delegated the task to Marryot as the officer who had originally been charged with the investigation of Pickett's murder.

Did that imply that Germain knew something about Pickett's claim? Or was he merely trying to oblige Lord North as a dog will do his best for his master, however unreasonable his demands?

"Do you think you'll find him, sir?" I asked, breaking the long, despondent silence.

"Scarface? Maybe." The Major dabbed his wound with the corner of his handkerchief soaked in a little brandy. He winced. "But New York has more leaks than a colander. Ten to one he'll slip away to Long Island or the Debatable Ground. Still, perhaps it don't matter one way or the other."

"It's true that we don't know that he can assist us," I said. "And we have nothing to tie him directly to Mr Pickett. But he's put himself about too much in this matter for us to ignore him. We need to talk to him."

"That's all very well, sir," Marryot said, "but I doubt he'll grant us the opportunity."

"There are other lines of approach. Mr Pickett was in Philadelphia for a few weeks before coming here. He may have confided in someone there. We should also call at his lodging in Beekman Street. And of course we must ask the Wintours about him again."

"I don't believe it's necessary to trouble the Wintours. It would distress them."

"They are the only people we know that he called on," I said.

"They barely exchanged half a dozen words."

170

I noticed a ripple running through the curtain at the end of the booth. "Are you hungry, sir? I believe I should like a biscuit or a slice of pie."

"Food?" Marryot slammed down his glass on the table. "We haven't time for —"

I reached out a hand and pulled back the curtain. There, not a yard away, was Mr Townley, smiling pleasantly and with his hand raised and balled into a fist, as if the curtain had been a door and he had been about to knock on it.

"Ah — I am rejoiced to see you!" he said. "Noak told me I should find you in the Bunch of Grapes, and it is most convenient because I wanted particularly to speak to you both."

Marryot blinked at him. He half-rose and bowed. His bruised cheek was on the side away from Townley, towards the back of the booth. "Your servant, sir. But —"

"You will not mind if I join you?"

Townley waved to a waiter and slid on to the bench beside the Major. I wondered how long he had been standing on the other side of the curtain and how audible our conversation had been.

"But why do you wish to speak to me?" the Major said, slurring his words.

"To you both, to be precise." Townley smiled at me. "I am come to invite you to the theatre."

"What? Why?"

"I have taken a box for Friday. The Wintours are coming — well, the Judge is and the Captain, and Mrs Arabella, of course. I fear Mrs Wintour may not find it convenient. It's a small return for their kindness the other evening and Mrs Arabella happened to mention to me that she had seen nothing at the theatre since *Venice Preserv'd* last year. And I thought — naturally I cannot leave out Major Marryot and Mr Savill from our little party. Afterwards we shall go on to supper at Fraunces's."

"How delightful," I said. "And what's the play we are to see?"

"*Othello*. One cannot outdo Shakespeare for elevated sentiments, though sometimes the language is not as genteel as one would wish, and the construction not as polished." Townley smiled and gave a shrug, as if inviting us to join with him in mocking his essay at dramatic criticism. He turned to Marryot. "Will you join us, sir? I know the Wintours will be as glad to see you as myself."

"Yes, sir. Thank you — I — I'm obliged."

The waiter arrived. We ordered more brandy, another glass and a plate of biscuits.

"Well — this is very agreeable," Townley said when the waiter had withdrawn. "I do not usually drink spirits until later in the evening. But the weather is so raw outside that one needs a little fire in the stomach." He peered at us. "But why so serious, gentlemen? You look as if you had been plotting something."

Marryot had turned his head. The flame of the candle flickered over his discoloured cheek.

"Good God, sir," Townley blurted. "What the devil have you done to your face?"

172

CHAPTER
TWENTY-SEVEN

I was not quite sober when I returned to Warren Street before supper, which had a bearing on what happened. Alcohol unleashes the tongue. I was not drunk, though — unlike Marryot, whom Townley and I had been obliged to manhandle into a coach when we left the Bunch of Grapes.

I found Mr Wintour studying a map. He had unrolled it on the big table in the middle of the library and was examining it by the light of a candle in his hand. The only other illumination in the room came from the small fire and from a second candle. This was guttering in the socket of the candlestick that stood in lieu of a paperweight on one corner of the map.

"Ah — good," he said. "I shall have a gentleman to take a glass of wine with at supper. My son is abroad and will not be back until late."

I glanced down at the map and saw the name written at the top. "So this is Mount George, sir?"

"Yes — this was Mr Froude's plan of the estate. Or rather of the house and its desmesne. The estate as a whole is much larger. John mentioned it the other day, and Noak, too. I said I would look it out for them."

"Noak?"

"Yes — my books and papers are in a sad pickle and he is helping me sort them out. It seems to be taking an age but Noak believes that the map may clarify some aspects of his classificatory system for the Froude estate."

The Judge lifted the candle. The light was too poor to see the details clearly. The house, the stable block and the farm buildings were over to the right. There was what looked like a large patch of woodland behind it. Otherwise the estate consisted of a patchwork of enclosures, of pastures, fields, paddocks and gardens. Unlike the painting in the drawing room, this was a purely practical representation of Mount George, something for farmers and lawyers and agents to pore over.

"Mrs Wintour and I passed several months there, the summer that John and Bella became betrothed," the Judge said. "It is a most agreeable spot, and the land is extraordinarily fertile. Poor Froude. I remember at the time I thought him the luckiest of men."

"He died soon afterwards?"

"Early in the war. A sad business." Mr Wintour moved away from the table. "Was there something you wanted?"

"I had a letter from Mr Rampton this morning, sir. My commission has been extended, probably until the autumn."

"And will you continue here with us, Mr Savill? I'm sure you would be very welcome."

The business was arranged in a moment, though the Judge said that, as a matter of form, he should consult the ladies about it.

"Bella says I must treat this house quite as my own," he said. "But I do not like to take advantage of her good nature. There's no time like the present — I believe we shall find them both in the drawing room."

"First, sir, may I mention something else? I regret to say that Mr Rampton has desired me to look into Mr Pickett's death again. It appears he had a sister in England."

"Pickett?" Mr Wintour picked up the second candle and the map instantly constricted itself into an untidy scroll. "That poor young man who was killed last summer?"

"Yes, sir."

"Yes — Roger Pickett, was it not? They hanged a runaway for it."

I nodded. "You know what government departments are, sir. They move like snails and they want everything five times over."

"I fear I cannot help you — I met Mr Pickett only once — in this house. We never had these dreadful murders before the war, you know."

"No, sir. Did you have much conversation with him?"

"Hardly any. I was obliged to go out, you see — if I remember right, Judge Jones and I were meeting to talk over what we might do to urge the re-establishment of New York's courts. The Government will achieve nothing if they do not allow us that."

I bowed, unwilling to be drawn into this familiar discussion. "Can you remember what you talked about with Mr Pickett? How he seemed?"

"It's so long ago now . . . He tried to make himself agreeable enough, I fancy — though I believe he was not comfortably situated, but that is true of so many of us nowadays. But I hardly had time to say 'how do you do' to him. You must ask Mrs Arabella. She was still there when I left, and of course she knew him a little beforehand, which I did not." He lowered his voice. "I'm afraid you may think me unchristian, but I remember wondering if he was come to ask for a loan."

"One more thing, sir — I suppose he did not mention a box of curiosities?"

"A box of curiosities?" Mr Wintour frowned. "No. Why do you ask?"

"I gather that his sister believes he may have had one."

"Very likely he did — many gentlemen do. It was all the rage before the war. My poor brother had one, I remember — when he was in Europe he collected miniature antiquities — seals and coins and the like — and he had a case made for them in London. I wonder where it is now. Was Mr Pickett's box valuable?"

"Perhaps. But I do not even know what he collected or whether his box ever existed."

There was nothing more to be said on the subject. We went along the hall to the drawing room. The ladies were sitting over the fire. Mrs Arabella was reading aloud to her mother-in-law, who appeared to be asleep.

It took only a moment to settle my extended stay in Warren Street. The Judge wandered away, pleading a need to tidy his papers before supper; otherwise Noak

176

would have something to say to him when he next called.

"Your daughter will be sad," Mrs Arabella said to me.

"Hetty-Petty," Mrs Wintour murmured, addressing the fire.

"Yes, poor Lizzie," I said. "She will be disappointed, and so am I."

"Have you considered bringing her here? And your wife, of course."

"The child is very young, ma'am, and she and her mother are comfortably settled where they are. If I sent for them, they would not arrive for at least three or four months. And Mrs Savill does not find sea voyages agree with her and she dislikes to leave London at the best of times. Besides, where would they live?"

"They could stay with us."

"You are very kind, but New York is not the best place to bring a child. Not at present."

Mrs Arabella looked down at her lap. "That is true, sir. Forgive me. I allowed the heart to outweigh the reason."

"There's no shame in that, ma'am."

She raised her head. The firelight flickered in her eyes. "There may be," she said.

"That has not been my experience."

I spoke more bitterly than I had intended. I turned away, holding my hands to the fire. Mrs Wintour's chin drooped to her chest. Her mouth fell open and she emitted a gentle snore. Dear God, I thought, what a fool I have made of myself in marrying Augusta.

177

"I am heartily sorry for it," she said.

"Sorry?" My voice rose. "Sorry?" I knew I should not direct my foolish anger with Augusta and Rampton at Mrs Arabella, and I tried to moderate my tone. "I beg your pardon, ma'am. In any case, I wished to speak to you of something quite different, if I may. Mr Pickett."

"Mr Pickett?" she echoed. "Why?"

"I have been commanded to look at the circumstances of his murder again." I glanced at her, but she had turned away to put her book on the table beside her. "I believe Mr Pickett's sister has petitioned Lord North about it."

"I know nothing of that, sir."

"He called here a few days before his death."

"Yes, but he was only here for a few minutes, and I hardly knew him to begin with. That was the long and the short of it."

"Forgive me, ma'am, I do not wish to pry but it is my duty to ask for particulars of your conversation. What did you talk about?"

"It was months ago," she said with a touch of anger, which was hardly to be wondered at since I was coming it so high and mighty with her. "There was nothing of importance. Oh, I believe he said he had been in Philadelphia before he came here, and everything was in confusion there because of the evacuation."

"Did he ask for anything?"

"What do you mean?"

"A loan, perhaps," I suggested.

She shook her head.

"Or talk of his plans? Or of his friends in the city?"

178

Another shake of the head. "He said nothing of consequence, sir. To own the truth, I did not much like him and I was glad to get rid of him. I thought it impertinent that he should call on so slight an acquaintance. As I told you, my father was acquainted with him over some small matter of business, nothing more. He had no conversation except about himself and no breeding. I dislike men like that and would rather not talk to them."

I felt the blood rushing to my face, for the words were aimed at me as much as Mr Pickett.

"I beg your pardon, ma'am. One more question and I am done. Did he say anything of a box of curiosities?"

"No, nothing at all," she said, raising her voice; Mrs Wintour whimpered in her sleep. "Pray have the goodness to ring the bell, sir. I cannot think what they are doing downstairs. They should have announced supper by now."

CHAPTER
TWENTY-EIGHT

Two days later, on Wednesday Morning, Marryot and I revisited the house in Beekman Street where Pickett had briefly lodged in the last days of his life. Our shared commission engendered a fragile intimacy between us.

The woman who kept the house, Mrs Muller, was a blowsy wide-bodied widow with thick forearms, a large chin and a forehead like an ape's.

"Pickett?" she said. "The man got himself killed by the negro?"

"Yes, ma'am," I said. "We came to search his room if you remember."

"I know you did, but you didn't pay his reckoning, did you?"

"This is not to the point," Marryot said. "Did he have any callers while he was here?"

"I don't know, and I don't much care."

Marryot said, "If you don't keep a civil tongue in your head and answer our questions, I'll have your licence to keep a lodging house revoked."

"I told you, I don't know if he had any callers."

"What about your servants?" I asked.

"There's only the girl. But she did hardly nothing for him because his pockets were to let, and my gentlemen have to pay if they want to be served. Besides, she's sixpence short of a shilling and —"

"We'll talk to her," Marryot interrupted. "Call her."

Mrs Muller grumbled but shouted down the stairs until the maid came, wiping her hands on a filthy rag. She was a mulatto, as broad as her mistress, barefooted despite the cold and with eyes like sloes. She dropped a token curtsey when she saw us. Then, quite unafraid, she stared first at Marryot, then at me.

"Do you recall Mr Pickett who was here in the summer?" I asked.

She nodded.

"No money," Widow Muller prompted, keeping to the essentials of the matter. "Got himself killed in Canvas Town."

"Hold your peace, ma'am," Marryot said.

"Did you talk to him?"

The girl stared boldly at me. "He wanted me to do his linen, your honour. Mistress said no, so I didn't."

"Quite right too," said the widow.

"Did he have any callers while he was here?"

"No, sir."

"Did anyone ask for him or bring him anything? Try to think."

"No, sir. Well — only that beggar."

Marryot loomed over her. "What? Eh? What's that?"

I pushed between them. "What did the beggar want?"

"Just asked if Mr Pickett lived here, your honour, and then he give me the letter."

"A letter for Mr Pickett, you mean? What was this man like?"

"Big negro," she said. "Red coat. Someone had carved up his face like a leg of mutton."

We got no more out of the girl or her mistress. They knew nothing of Pickett's sister, nothing of a box of curiosities.

"The fool might as well not have existed for all the trace he left behind him," Marryot said as we walked back to Fort George. "What the devil do they expect us to do?"

"What about the negro with the letter?"

The Major didn't answer. The negro in the red coat must have been Scarface. But why should he have called at Beekman Street? Who had the letter been from? If he had killed Pickett, why call on him beforehand as if to announce a connection between them?

In the next few days we found answers to none of the questions. Nor did our enquiries throw any light on the whereabouts of the scar-faced negro. He had — almost literally — slipped through our fingers.

Both Marryot and I talked to gentlemen who had encountered Pickett during his brief stay in Philadelphia; but their acquaintance had been superficial; and in any case the withdrawal of the British from the city had been on everyone's mind to the exclusion of anything else. The town had been full of strangers.

We were hampered at every turn by the need to pursue the investigation with discretion. We could not have bills posted about Pickett offering rewards for information or advertise in the newspapers. We discussed whether we should enlist Mr Townley as an ally but decided, in the end, that even with him we would risk more than we might gain.

"A man never quite knows where he is with Townley," the Major said in an uncharacteristic burst of frankness. "I — well, I sometimes wonder if he's laughing in his sleeve at us. He's an odd fish, even though he drinks the King's health as cheerfully as a man could wish. To be candid, I do not altogether trust him."

"Perhaps it's because he's American," I said. "At home people think the colonists are a species of inferior Englishmen who labour under the misfortune of living among savages on the other side of the world. But I believe they are in the wrong of it. An American may call himself a Whig or a Tory but in this respect at least a man's loyalty to His Majesty is neither here nor there. The point is, sir, however loyal an American may be, he is not a Englishman any more. He is become quite a different animal."

CHAPTER
TWENTY-NINE

New York had only one theatre, which was in John Street. Sometimes in an access of loyal enthusiasm it was referred to as the Theatre Royal, a misleading grand name for an ugly red building little better than a barn. It stood twenty yards back from the road; a covered way led from the street to its double doors. This was a ramshackle, wooden affair, and in wet weather the roof leaked. Indeed, there was something provisional about the entire establishment.

But I soon discovered that the very act of patronizing the theatre was in itself considered meritorious, a token of one's loyalty to the Crown. The dramatic entertainments were put on by the gentlemen of the army and the navy for the impeccably charitable purpose of relieving the widows and orphans of those who had fallen during the war. The ladies of New York were particularly happy to support a theatrical enterprise in which the dramatic roles, both male and female, were acted to such perfection by our brave soldiers, many of whom were young, handsome, well connected and unmarried.

On Friday, 26 February, Mr Townley sent his carriage to collect us from Warren Street. It would have been faster to walk for the distance was not great and the crush of carriages was such that we were obliged to queue for a quarter of an hour before we could enter John Street from Broadway.

Mr Townley and Major Marryot had made their own way to the theatre and were there to greet us when we arrived. We pushed our way through the lobby towards the stairs to the boxes. Mr Townley said that at least eight hundred tickets had already been sold, and more people were pressing to get in.

There were two rows of boxes. Mr Townley had taken one of the larger ones, which were on the lower tier. The box contained two rows of spindly gilt-legged chairs and afforded a splendid view of both stage and the pit. In theory these boxes could seat eight, but in practice ours felt crowded even with six of us.

The interior of the theatre was ablaze with lights and very warm. People came here to see and to be seen. Townley waved to his acquaintances as we settled ourselves. He placed himself at Mrs Arabella's right hand. Major Marryot was on her left, with the Judge beside him.

Captain Wintour and I sat behind. He chatted to me with hectic animation. This evening, he had dined well and was not, as he whispered to me, looking forward to seeing this fanciful piece of nonsense. He believed it to be about a woman who should have known better and an upstart negro who should have been whipped and sent to the galleys, or whatever they did to them in those days.

When the play began, however, nature came to the Captain's rescue: he nodded off. By the start of Act II, he had begun to snore. Mrs Arabella turned in her seat and nudged him in the ribs with her fan, which made him splutter and then breathe a little more quietly.

She caught my eye as she did so and we exchanged a smile. I was glad of it, for there had been a coolness between us since I had quizzed her so clumsily about Roger Pickett.

I confess that I did not pay a great deal of attention to the play after that. I was distracted by Mrs Arabella's nearness in the relative gloom of the box. My eyes were drawn towards the back of her head, the curve of her neck, the line of her shoulders.

I was shocked to find myself playing in a small way the part of a Peeping Tom. I was married to Augusta, who (as she often reminded me) was a lady of refinement and firm Christian principles who tried unceasingly to further my career; and who was, more to the point, the mother of my child. And now I was sitting in a theatre and ogling a married woman whose husband was snuffling and grunting on the seat beside mine. My behaviour distressed me. But I did not turn my eyes away. Sometimes a man does not cut a very admirable figure, even to himself.

All this while the tragedy of *Othello* unfolded beneath our noses on the stage below. The management had hired a professional actress from London to take the part of Desdemona, a break with tradition that irritated Major Marryot for the other actors were officers in His Majesty's service.

"Gentlemen who hold the King's commission should not tread the boards with women of that sort," I heard him say to Judge Wintour in a whisper so loud it must have been audible on the stage. "It flies in the face of the spirit of the thing."

"It is hard to quarrel too harshly with it, sir, if it helps to raise money for our widows and orphans," Mr Wintour said. "But I would not wish to do it myself. And I do not think Mrs Wintour would find it an agreeable spectacle."

I heard a tap on the door behind me. It opened, and Miriam put her head inside the box. She grimaced and made a token reverence. She edged past me and handed her mistress a note.

Mrs Arabella turned her head. I was watching her closely and I saw her face — and saw how it changed when she caught sight of her maid: a look of mild curiosity gave way first to one of alarm, so swift as to be almost imperceptible, and then to a studiously blank expression as though she had willed herself in an instant to purge all trace of emotion from her face.

Captain Wintour slept on.

She tore open the note and leaned forward to read it by the light cast up from the blaze of candles on the stage below. I caught a glimpse of the paper — enough to gain an impression that there was only a line or two of writing; but of course I was too far away to read any of the words.

The next moment, Mrs Arabella was rising to her feet. The rest of us, with the exception of Captain Wintour, automatically followed suit. Othello, strutting

187

and declaiming on the stage below, paused in mid flow and raised his face to see what the commotion was, the whites of his eyes unnaturally bright in his blackened face.

"Forgive me, sir," Mrs Arabella murmured to the Judge, "I must leave you. Pray do not disturb yourself. There is a difficulty in the slave quarters, and I do not wish Mrs Wintour to be troubled with it."

"But, my dear, you cannot very well go alone with only Miriam to look after you, it —"

"Abraham is below, sir, with a hired carriage."

Major Marryot, Mr Townley and I each offered to escort her, but Mrs Arabella rejected us and was out of the box before the Judge had time to raise further objections.

"Well, well," Mr Wintour said, sinking back on his chair, "I cannot say I like it at all — why she would not wait a moment, I —"

"Hush!" hissed a voice from the stage below.

Captain Wintour stirred, snorted and fell silent. Several members of Othello's entourage glanced up at our box, their expressions a mixture of disapproval and curiosity.

After that it was difficult to concentrate on the play. During the last act, one of the footmen attached to the theatre came up to the box with a note from Mrs Arabella. She wrote that there was no reason for concern but that she would remain at Warren Street now because she had a headache. She regretted that she would have to cry off Mr Townley's supper and begged that the entertainment would continue in her absence.

188

Captain Wintour woke up as the play was drawing to a close. He rubbed his eyes. "Is the Moor not dead yet?" he whispered to me.

"He has not long in this world, sir."

"Good. Then we shall soon have supper. Where's my wife?"

I explained the circumstances of Mrs Arabella's departure.

Captain Wintour yawned. "Perhaps it's as well — we shall be without the Fair Sex at supper entirely. And sometimes that's more agreeable." He dug his elbow into my ribs. "Eh? Or does a sly dog like you prefer the company of the ladies?"

"I kissed thee ere I killed thee," cried Othello in a hoarse voice, plucking a large dagger from the bosom of his velvet doublet.

He fell upon the corpse of Desdemona, which was lying at his feet. The corpse emitted a gasp, for Othello was a well-built gentleman.

"Killing myself to die upon a kiss," he roared, jabbing the dagger into his side.

He reared up in a rictus of agony and gave Desdemona a smacking kiss on the cheek. She twitched as she tried to avoid the thrashing limbs of her dying husband. Othello at last collapsed beside her and rolled on to his back. The dagger fell from his lifeless hand and landed with a dull, wooden clunk on the stage.

"Thank God for that," Captain Wintour said; and he smiled at me.

CHAPTER
THIRTY

Townley had hired a private room at Fraunces's Tavern on Pearl Street. The parlour was snug, our supper well chosen and the wine, as ever when Townley was at table, flowed generously.

Afterwards our host called for the punchbowl. He turned to me. "Have you been introduced to rumbo, sir?"

"I believe not," I said. "What is it?"

"It is something of a speciality of ours in New York. A punch based on rum."

"Principally rum," said Captain Wintour, pronouncing the consonants with enthusiasm. "Pray sit by me, Mr Savill, and I will show you how we prepare it."

It looked as if the evening would stretch without apparent effort into the further reaches of Saturday morning. Captain Wintour, waving the silver porringer used to strain the punch as a conductor waves his baton, broke into song; but the rest of us declined to join him and at length he returned to drinking and talking.

It did not surprise me that the Captain and Townley were happy to make an evening of it, for I had rarely seen either of them very far away from a glass and a bottle after midday. Marryot seemed disposed to join them on this occasion; he was no toper but, as I had noticed on Monday in the Bunch of Grapes, when he had a mind for it he was capable of drinking deeply and quickly.

However, I had not expected Judge Wintour to join them with such enthusiasm. Hitherto I had seen only the sober side of the old gentleman. This evening, I glimpsed the ghost of another, younger man. Perhaps it was because he was away from the cares of home and family and untrammelled by the society of ladies. Or perhaps he drank to drown his sorrows, for God knows the poor man had enough of them, with more sorrows in store.

Rumbo was so strong that a man could drown any amount of sorrows in the shortest possible time. Mr Wintour drank so hard and so fast that his constitution revolted, and he was forced to withdraw behind the screen for some time. When he returned, pale but nothing daunted, he drank more.

"A toast, sir," cried his son. "To the restoration of what is ours. Come, Mr Savill, I know you will join us."

They drank and we drank. The Judge drank more but not for long. His constitution had grown unaccustomed to excess. This time sleep was his enemy. His head sank slowly down his waistcoat until it came to rest on the table, dislodging his wig. He fell into a deep slumber among the crumbs and nutshells scattered across the mahogany.

"The old gentleman had better go to his bed," Townley said, enunciating his words with care. "A man needs his rest."

"But the night is young," Captain Wintour said. "My father will do well enough where he is for the time being. Let us have another bowl."

Marryot grunted and ladled more punch into his glass. "In my opinion he'd do better in his own bed."

I pushed back my chair. "Certainly I believe I should. I must be up in good time in the morning."

"You've time for another glass, sir," Townley said. "They will need a moment to bring the carriage round. Then you will be home directly and in perfect safety."

"Thank you. And, in that case, shall I take Mr Wintour with me?"

"A capital plan, sir," the Captain said. "And I'm sure my father will thank you for it in the morning. I'm obliged to you, Savill, truly I am — it's the act of a true friend. I'd expect no less of you, of course."

"It's nothing, sir."

He laid his hand on my arm. "But Townley's in the right of it — you must wet your whistle before you go. A toast to friendship, eh?"

I took another glass with them for fellowship's sake. When the carriage was at the door, Mr Townley's footman and two of the tavern's manservants bundled the old man downstairs. He stirred but did not wake. They settled him in a corner and he snored all the way home.

The cold night air invigorated me. I had drunk less than the others and now I felt misleadingly sober — I knew this must in fact be an illusion for the fumes of rumbo were still rising in my brain and no doubt clinging to my person.

192

It was true that I had to be up early in the morning, for a deputation of disgruntled Loyalists from North Carolina were due to call on me at the office. But I had another reason to leave, though I did not acknowledge it to myself at the time. In the back of my mind there lurked the possibility that Mrs Arabella might not have retired to bed and that perhaps I might have a few words with her. I did not altogether believe in the existence of her headache.

When we reached Warren Street, it took an age for Josiah to unlock and unbar the front door. He and Abraham helped their master into the house. They set Mr Wintour in a chair and he fell into a doze. Josiah secured the door and Abraham knelt to unbuckle the old man's shoes.

"Is Mrs Arabella still about?" I asked.

"No, your honour," Abraham said, glancing up at me. "She retired an hour or so ago. But Mr Noak is in the library."

"Why on earth is he here?"

"I understand he had some work to do for Master, sir."

Josiah and Abraham draped the Judge's arms across their shoulders and took him upstairs. His stockinged feet bumped against the treads. I went down the hall to the library door, which was shut. There was a faint glow beneath it. I turned the handle and threw open the door.

Quill in hand, Samuel Noak was standing by the big table where earlier in the week the Judge had sat with Mr Froude's estate map of Mount George. His face was turned towards the door and was lit from below by the flame of a single candle. His mouth was open, with his lips pursed into a perfect O, as if he were on the verge of whistling.

He looked up. The candle flame created a flickering globe of light over the table and threw his misshapen shadow on to the bookcases lining the wall behind him. The shadow shifted in an ungainly dance, mocking every movement of his small, neat body. The fire had burned out. He wore a muffler and mittens against the cold.

"Good evening, sir," he said. He laid down the quill and bowed.

"What are you doing here?"

"Mr Wintour desired me to sort his correspondence." His voice was mild and he appeared unaware of my rudeness. "I am compiling an index to it."

"At this hour?"

"Mr Townley sometimes finds it inconvenient to spare me during the day, sir. I understand he arranged with the Judge for me to come this evening."

"Neither of them said anything about it."

Noak waited long enough for me to reflect that there was no particular reason why either man should have mentioned the circumstance to me. "Has Mr Wintour returned, sir?"

"Yes."

"Then perhaps I should lock up his secretary now and return his key to him."

It was only then that I realized that the flap of the desk was down. This was part of the secretary, a large piece of furniture made of cherrywood with drawers beneath and bookcase with glazed doors above. At the back of the desk itself was a complicated array of pigeonholes and miniature drawers.

"The Judge has retired to bed," I said. "As have the ladies. Captain Wintour has not yet returned. I think you had better give the key to me."

He allowed another pause to develop. "Very good, sir." He fell to tidying the papers on the table.

I could not let this go. "Mr Wintour usually keeps the key of his secretary on his person. Did he entrust it to you?"

Noak continued to tie a red ribbon around one of the bundles. "No, sir," he said. "He did not. He had already laid out the papers on the table." He looked up. "But when I arrived this evening, I found the secretary standing open, as you see it now, with the key in the lock. I did not like to close it."

He asked permission to write a note for the Judge. It occurred to me that he must have heard Townley's servant knocking on the street door ten minutes earlier; and he must have heard the sounds of voices in the hall and therefore deduced that at least some of the party had returned. His conduct had been that of an innocent man going about his duties, who had nothing to fear from discovery. On the other hand, he would have had ample time to conceal anything that needed concealment.

He left the note he had written unfolded on one of the piles of loose papers. He set a paperweight on top of it and capped the inkpot. Carrying the candle, he went to the desk, closed the flap and locked it.

"I have finished here, sir," he said to me. As always, his tone was civil but not in the least deferential. He handed me the key. "Will there be anything more?"

I shook my head and stood aside to allow him to leave the room.

"How will you get home?" I asked. I knew that he now lodged at Townley's house in Hanover Square.

"Abraham will light me there, sir. It is all arranged."

Noak gave me the candle and bid me goodnight. I watched as he went through the door leading to the servants' part of the house. Indeed he was such a frequent visitor that he had become almost one of the family.

CHAPTER
THIRTY-ONE

Something was wrong.

I knew I was tired and perhaps a little drunk. I knew that Mr Noak's explanations for his presence in the library were perfectly reasonable. Indeed, I could not put my finger on anything that could truly be called suspicious. But instead a cumulative uneasiness about him had crept over me. This evening's encounter had brought it to a point where I could not quite ignore it — though not to a point where I could quite justify it, even to myself.

Lit by the single candle, the library seemed larger than by day. I had never been in here by myself. It was a square and high-ceilinged room with bookcases on two walls, the fireplace on the third and the secretary beside the window on the fourth.

I went first to the table in the middle and looked at the papers lying on it in their neat piles and bundles. Most of them had to do with Mr Wintour's activities before the war. Some concerned cases he had presided over in the province's courts. Others related to the Governor's Council, for he had been a member of this body in the early years of the decade.

Here, too, was the index that Mr Noak was compiling for him. It classified the correspondence by date and then by subject. The Judge contemplated the composition of a great work to be called *The History of New York in Recent Times*, and his own papers would provide an important source of materials for it. Looked at from one angle, the enterprise was a form of vain if harmless drudgery; but, from another, it amounted to an old man's forlorn attempt to make sense of a world gone mad. There was something of folly to it, something of sense, and something of honour too.

My own actions, I fear, had nothing of the honourable about them. I carried the candle to the secretary and unlocked the flap of its desk. A man's bureau is his sanctum, his private place, and I did not wish to pry into Mr Wintour's. The proper course would have been to inform the Judge that I had found Mr Noak alone in the room with the open secretary and to leave him to pursue the matter however seemed best to him. Instead I opened the flap and held up the candle so that I might see what lay within.

More papers lay scattered on the horizontal surface of the desk, together with a red ribbon that had probably held them in a bundle. One of them was a sort of docket indicating that the papers related to Mount George and the Froude Estate.

At the back of the secretary was a rack of pigeonholes resting on two tiers of drawers. One of the drawers was slightly open and I pulled it further out, taking care not to let the candlewax drip on the papers.

The drawer was empty. The anticlimax shocked me back to a sense of what I was doing: I had allowed my curiosity to overpower every principle of good sense and right conduct. Shame crept over me. I stepped back, closed the flap and turned the key in the lock again.

My change of heart had an unexpected sequel. As I moved away, I glanced down to see if I had left any trace of my prying. My eye caught a glimpse of something on the floor by the side of the secretary: a small, pale triangle that stood out against the dark wood of the furniture and the floorboards.

I bent down to examine it. A sheet of paper had slid under the secretary, leaving only a corner of it visible. I picked it up and, as I did so, the light fell on the lines of writing that crossed the paper. A single word sprang out at me: *Arabella*.

In an instant my rectitude was put to one side, if not absolutely forgotten. In that same instant I remembered the sounds of rustling and hurried movement as I had opened the library door: had Noak been examining this paper and, in his haste, had he dropped it as he tried to return it to the secretary before he was discovered with it in his hand?

I could not resist the temptation. I sat down at the table with the candle. If Noak was a spy, then so was I. I was looking at a letter addressed to Judge Wintour at Warren Street. I glanced at the signature and made it out as *H. Froude*. To the left of this was the place and date of writing: Mount George, 28 November, 1776.

My Dear Sir — It is with a heavy heart that I must inform you that my Daughter was brought to bed and delivered of a stillborn Baby, a girl. Her Waters broke sooner than expected in the early hours of yesterday morning, and we were unable to find a Midwife; and of course there is no Physician to be had. As a Consequence she had only her Maid to attend her, though I believe the Fatality was inevitable for the Cord was wrapped about the Child's neck in the Womb. We do not know where Captain Wintour is at present and I should be obliged if you would communicate the unhappy News of his Child's Death to him.

We despaired of Arabella's life for several hours after the Birth but her condition has improved and with God's help she will recover. The roads are in a sad Condition but, despite the time of year, we shall leave for New York as soon as we are able. I am, sir, etc. H. Froude

P.S. I send this letter by the hand of a Farrier who says he is going to New York to find Work now the Rebels have been put to Flight. Also, pray inform the Captain that his slave Juvenal has absconded, for our troubles do not come singly. But we pray God we shall reach New York in Safety.

So that explained it, I thought: that was why Mrs Arabella hated Mount George so much that she wished never to see the place again.

CHAPTER
THIRTY-TWO

I might have learned nothing more about this unhappy affair if it hadn't been for Mrs Ann Frobisher.

She was a stout, vigorous lady from North Carolina, where her husband had a substantial estate. She arrived in my office on Wednesday, 3 March, took as if by right the chair nearest the stove and handed me her papers with the air of one conferring a favour. I judged from her appearance that she had already taken the opportunity of her visit to patronize New York's shops, as did most Whig ladies when they had occasion to cross the lines and visit the city.

During this strange and unnecessary war, both military and civil visitors came and went continuously in New York. Some, like Mrs Frobisher, had passes and arrived under a flag of truce. Others travelled without the benefit of permission from either side or both, slipping through the lines as if they simply didn't exist.

Mrs Frobisher's pass was signed by Governor Livingston on the rebel side and by General Pattison on ours; so her papers were entirely in order.

"I came over on the flag-boat from Elizabethtown," she said. "It was a terrible crossing — I was quite prostrated, sir, believe me — but the dear general was so obliging as to send his coach for me."

I knew from this that I would be wise to take the lady seriously and begged her to tell me how I might be of service to her. It transpired that her husband was an incorrigible Whig, and was linked by blood, interest and friendship with many other rebels in North Carolina and in neighbouring Virginia. He had declared for Congress early in the war.

But, as was so often the case in this strange conflict, there were divided loyalties in the bosom of the family and perhaps in the majestic bosom of Mrs Frobisher herself. One of her three sons had joined a Loyalist regiment and had died at the Battle of Harlem Heights. A daughter had married a British officer, whose regiment was at present quartered on Staten Island.

The daughter was the ostensible reason for Mrs Frobisher's visit to New York. The young lady had suffered a difficult pregnancy; there were already young children in the house; and it was felt that a mother's tender care for a few weeks would be of inexpressible value to the little family.

All this Mrs Frobisher explained to me at length. There was nothing exceptional about her story: many American families had a foot in both camps — in most cases not so much from calculation, I believe, as from necessity: for that is the nature of civil war.

Now, like so many American ladies and gentlemen of my acquaintance, she was convinced that King George owed her compensation for the inconveniences he had caused her. She wished to place in my hands a petition from her husband to His Majesty for instant transmission to London.

"Madam," I said gently, "if I understand you aright, your husband is of the Whig persuasion and has given his support to the King's enemies. I do not think it probable that His Majesty will desire to compensate him for any losses he may have sustained."

"Ah — but you labour under a misapprehension, sir." Mrs Frobisher's heavy eyebrows drew together in a frown, and her small eyes shrank back into the folds of skin that enveloped them. "These losses were not my husband's. They were my son's. And, God rest his soul, he was as loyal a subject of the King as ever lived."

I bowed my head, choosing not to dispute the fact.

Mrs Frobisher leaned forward in her chair as if about to pounce on me. "And, as I have already told you, sir, he laid down his life for King George."

"I applaud your son's valour, ma'am," I said. "But did he leave a widow or children?"

She shook her head.

"Then who is his heir?"

"Why, his father, of course."

"And what does his estate consist of?"

"It's a plantation my son got from his godfather, sir. The terms of the bequest are that, in the event of his death without heirs, it should pass to my husband." She thrust her hand into the pocket of her dress. "I have all the papers here, including affidavits from Loyalist gentlemen in the neighbourhood and the colonel of my poor son's regiment. He is a great friend of General Pattison's, as it happens."

At this point the lady placed a plump packet of papers on the table between us. Next, she resorted to a piece of theatre: she gave out a great sigh and dabbed at her eyes with a handkerchief, all the while observing me closely.

I looked over the papers. Now and then Mrs Frobisher sniffed loudly, perhaps to remind me of her grief over her son's death.

The estate in question was near Charlotte. It consisted of a small tobacco plantation together with about forty slaves. According to Mrs Frobisher, the place had been worth in the region of £120 per annum. There had been a house for the owner and a smaller dwelling for the overseer and his family. British troops had passed through the country and had burned the building, plundered everything of value and ravaged the land. They had also freed the slaves, some of whom had not been recaptured.

"Those wicked soldiers believed it was my husband's plantation," Mrs Frobisher said, lowering her handkerchief for a moment. "They did not realize it belonged to my poor dear boy."

The claim was supported by a copy of the godfather's will and the letter from the son's colonel. There was a letter from the Governor of North Carolina, no less, confirming the loyalty of Ensign Frobisher and his gallant death in action. Finally there were two depositions from neighbouring gentlemen, both Loyalists and both intimate with the Frobishers, confirming the material facts of their claim.

204

As far as I was concerned, the matter was straightforward: I would accept Mrs Frobisher's petition and assure her of my best offices. I would forward it to Mr Rampton at the American Department with all the other claims. And that would probably be the last I should hear of the matter.

But — as I was folding the papers and considering how best to send the lady on her way without trampling on her tender feelings — a detail struck me.

I looked up at Mrs Frobisher. "I see your son's estate is near Charlotte, madam."

"Yes, sir." She made a play with her handkerchief. "Such a convenient location adds inestimably to its value."

"Indeed. I wonder — were you by any chance acquainted with a gentleman named Pickett? I believe he lived near Charlotte."

"Jonathan Pickett? Slightly, yes. He died before the war."

"I meant Roger Pickett."

"That is his son."

I sat forward in my chair. "Did you know him, ma'am?"

"Only by reputation." She stared at me. "Why do you ask?"

"I regret to say the young man was murdered last year."

"Good God. Here in New York? How very strange — what happened?"

"He was robbed. A runaway slave was hanged for the crime."

Mrs Frobisher folded her hands on her lap. "Well —
I confess I'm not surprised."

"Why not, pray?"

"People always said that Roger Pickett would come
to a bad end, one way or another. When his father died,
he sold the estate before the poor man's body was cold
in his grave. Then he set about sowing as many wild
oats as he could. That's what they say, in any case. He
ran through all his money within the year and was
obliged to enlist in the army to escape his creditors."

"Do you remember if he had any family, any
connections?"

"There was a sister, too, but she married and went to
live in England when her papa was still alive." Mrs
Frobisher must have sensed my eagerness, and
fortunately she wished to please me. "But I tell you
what you should do, sir, if you wish to know about the
Picketts: you should talk to Dr Slype."

"Who is Dr Slype, ma'am?"

"A clergyman who lived in Charlotte before the war.
He and his wife removed to New York. They are very
amiable people and they knew everybody. If they are
still here, my daughter will know their direction."

"I should like to talk to him, ma'am."

"Then, if you desire it, I shall find out where they are
living. If I could, I would call on dear Mrs Slype myself.
But at present I cannot call my time my own."

Five minutes later, I showed Mrs Frobisher to the
door in a perfect shower of mutual compliments. She
paused in the doorway, turning back and smiling at me

in a manner that could almost be described as flirtatious.

"I wonder what he was doing here," she said.

"Who, ma'am? Mr Pickett?"

"Yes." She tapped my arm with her gloved hand. "For surely, my dear sir, New York is the last place you would expect to find him. Unless of course he was one of our poor prisoners of war in those dreadful hulks of yours."

CHAPTER
THIRTY-THREE

A contagious distemper had broken out in the slave quarters at Warren Street. This had been the reason for Mrs Arabella's premature return from the theatre the other night, for Josiah had feared that the symptoms might signal the onset of smallpox.

But we were spared smallpox, at least for the time being, though the lesser distemper showed little sign of abating. Some of the servants went down with it. Both Mrs Wintour and I caught it as well. I spent several days confined to bed and feeling wretchedly miserable.

When at last I returned to the office I found a mass of work awaiting me, together with a scented billet from Mrs Frobisher. She thanked me profusely for my kindness in being so obliging and hinted at the great pleasure it would give her to renew our acquaintance when she next had the happiness of being in New York. Almost as an afterthought, she enclosed the address of the Reverend Dr Slype.

I was not able to find time to call on the gentleman for about a fortnight. In the meantime, Josiah's fears proved well founded. Nearly a week after my interview with Mrs Frobisher, I was dining at Warren Street when

Abraham came into the room and whispered something in the Judge's ear.

Mr Wintour looked very grave. He waved the young servant away and tapped the blade of his knife against a wine glass. The rest of us fell silent.

"Bad news, I'm afraid. They have a case of confluent smallpox further down the street — at the Morleys'. There is no doubt about it."

"The smallpox?" said the Captain. "Is it an epidemic, sir?"

His father massaged his forehead. "If it is, it is unusually early in the year." He turned to me. "Summer is our worst season, of course, sir — the disease thrives in the heat. But the city is so crowded nowadays that there is no longer any pattern to it. Our situation is most unhealthy and grows worse by the day. Indeed, nothing is certain any more. We shall have snow in August before we are done."

"Snow?" Mrs Wintour dropped her spoon on the plate. "I do hope not, sir. I cannot abide the cold."

"No, no, no," Mr Wintour said, flapping his napkin with each negative as if to shake away the very possibility of it. "It was a mere figure of speech, my dear. You must not disturb yourself in the slightest."

"No need for long faces, eh?" The Captain motioned to Josiah to refill his glass. "At least we ourselves shan't fall sick with it."

Mr Wintour turned back to me. "Have you had the smallpox yourself, sir?"

"I was inoculated against it as a child, sir."

"I am glad to hear it."

"We have our own methods of inoculation here, sir," the Captain put in, waving his knife at me. "Rough and ready by London standards, no doubt, but perfectly serviceable. We take infected matter from someone who already has the disease; we push it under the fingernails: so —" he mimed the action with the knife, and a spot of gravy fell from the blade to the cloth "— and remove ourselves to an isolated place. And we suffer a mild dose of the disease with little discomfort. Some friends and I made up a party for it when I was a young man, and we spent a most agreeable week or so amusing ourselves on one of our farms."

"I shall make sure that everyone in the household has been inoculated," Mrs Arabella said, staring out of the window at the strip of garden and the belvedere at the end.

Captain Wintour helped himself to a dish of pickled cabbage. "Yes. Damned inconvenient if it runs through the servants."

"Sir," said the Judge. "There are ladies present."

"Eh? Oh — I beg your pardon, Mother."

"What is it, Johnny my love?" she said. "Do you need more cabbage, dear?"

Mrs Arabella was a woman of decision. Having made up her mind to do something, she did not postpone it and did not permit half-measures. The inoculation of the household was arranged on the following day and put into practice on the day after.

The domestics who had been with the family for some time had either had the disease or been inoculated already. But there remained the youthful footman, Abraham, a maid who helped Miriam above stairs, the kitchen maid and the scullery boy, as well as others I had never met. Some of these were not sure whether they had had smallpox or not, for there was sometimes an element of doubt in the milder cases. Mrs Arabella made up her mind that it would be better not to take chances in the matter. They would all be inoculated.

In peacetime, the usual practice was to isolate the patients in some rural retreat. But a Hessian general had been given the Wintours' country house for his summer residence; farms, cottages and even barns were at a premium, such was the overcrowding in the British-held territory near the city.

Mrs Arabella decided that it would be both simpler and cheaper to set aside our own slave quarters as a hospital isolated from the house, and to keep the patients there. She talked to other residents in the street and found that some of them were in the same situation as ourselves. In a few hours she had more than doubled the numbers in our hospital and halved the cost for the Wintours.

With so many of the servants unable to fulfil their duties in their usual way, the house was a cheerless place for a week or two, with dust gathering in corners and inadequate meals served at odd times. Captain Wintour grumbled about the inconvenience. Mrs Arabella apologized to me and offered to remit some of the cost of my board and lodging. I said that would not be necessary and she did not press me further.

Mrs Arabella insisted on nursing the sufferers herself and provided them with a diet suitable for invalids. Both the Judge and her husband suggested that she send Miriam instead to avoid exposure to the noxious humours of the sickroom. She refused. My admiration for her increased considerably. Her desire to care for the household's slaves might be no more than domestic prudence. But this devotion to duty was something else, which I could only attribute to selfless benevolence.

Once, late at night, I chanced to look down from my bedroom window and I saw Mrs Arabella's cloaked figure moving swiftly across the yard. She had not covered her head with a hood and, for a moment as a door opened to receive her, I glimpsed her face in the muddy yellow light cast by the rushlights within.

I thought I heard a child crying. But my window was sealed tight and perhaps I heard only the wind in the chimney.

CHAPTER
THIRTY-FOUR

The address Mrs Frobisher had given me was in King George Street, convenient for the Fresh Water Pond and the pump at the bottom of Orange Street, but too close for comfort to the stench of the tan-yards.

The Reverend Dr Slype lived in a tall, thin house. At first I thought I had been given the wrong address for my knock of the door was answered by a Hessian private wearing a long apron over his regimentals. When I asked for Dr Slype, however, he directed me upstairs.

"Up and up, sir," he said in low, thickly accented voice. "Higher and higher. To the top, eh?"

I passed a smart young German officer on the first-floor landing who saluted me civilly as he went by but said nothing. I climbed flight after flight of stairs that became progressively narrower until I came at last to a heavy leather curtain blocking my way. On the step at its foot was a handbell.

I rang the bell and almost immediately a negro maid pulled aside the curtain. When I asked for Dr Slype and gave her Mrs Frobisher's letter of introduction, she showed me into a tiny parlour with a sloping ceiling.

The day was sunny and, even at this time of the year, it had grown warm under the roof. The room was furnished comfortably enough, though it was unpleasantly crowded because the pieces had been made for larger rooms.

In a moment I heard a heavy step outside, and a tall, very fat gentleman eased himself sideways through the doorway. He was attired decently in black though his waistcoat was unbuttoned and his neckcloth hung loose. He wore an ancient tie-wig, somewhat askew and tied with a frayed black ribbon.

"Mr Savill, sir." He bowed slowly. "I am honoured to make your acquaintance."

I bowed in my turn. "Your servant, sir."

"You have found us in our eyrie, sir." His voice was soft and rumbling, like the purr of a great contented cat. "I congratulate you."

"The soldier who answered the door told me where to come."

"You were fortunate." He spoke slowly, sucking air between groups of words. "You chanced on one of the more civil of the cuckoos we have in our nest."

"You have lodgers, I collect?"

"Four officers and their servants. They come and go. Some of them are rowdier than others. One can never tell. At least the Hessians we have at present are gentlemen, though sometimes you would not think it." He wiped his forehead with a large handkerchief. "It is very close today, do you not find?"

"Indeed, sir. I hope my visit does not fatigue you."

"Not in the least. You may consider yourself a welcome diversion. I do not enjoy climbing stairs so I value it when society comes to me." He eased his neckcloth further away from his neck. "Shall we sit outside? It is infinitely cooler."

For a moment I thought my host had taken leave of his senses. He reversed slowly through the doorway. I followed him on to the landing. The maid hurried forward and opened another door immediately opposite. It led directly out to a large balcony bordered by a low iron rail. Beyond it was the great sweep of the sunlit sky above and the glittering waters of the bay below.

"Good God," I said. Here, high above the stench and hubbub of the streets, I understood why New York was sometimes accounted a beautiful city.

"Indeed, sir." Dr Slype smiled at me. "If faith and reason were not enough, then this prospect alone would incline me to believe in the existence of a benevolent deity."

In an alcove sheltered from the wind were two chairs of wicker and a daybed arranged around a table laden with books. We settled ourselves in the chairs. Without being bidden, the maid brought a tray with two glasses, a bottle of hock and a flask of selzer water.

"My Hessians sometimes bring me selzer water," Dr Slype told me, leaning forward to mix the drinks. "They know I have a taste for it. You will join me, I hope? I generally take a glass or two at this time of the morning. It cools the brain most wonderfully."

My host sipped his hock and selzer and set down the glass. "And now, sir. Mrs Frobisher tells me you are a very charming gentleman." He held up his face to the sun. "And that you are a high government official sent from London."

"I come from London and I have a position at the American Department. But it is not a particularly lofty one, I'm afraid."

"I am sure you are modest."

"I deal with Loyalist claims for compensation, sir. I do not mean that I assess them in any way: I act merely as a conduit for them and ensure they take the best form and go to the most suitable place."

"The bonfire?" he said, not unkindly.

"I hope not. God knows, there are deserving cases among them."

"Yes. It is a terrible business, this war. You would think that rational beings should be able to manage their disagreements in a way that would not damage all parties concerned. There is really only one explanation: that man is not a rational being at all."

"I find you are a philosopher, sir," I said.

"You flatter me, sir. I am a fat old fool." He took up the wine. "Come, let me refill your glass and you shall tell me how I may be of service. Mrs Frobisher tells me you have been enquiring about Roger Pickett."

"Did you know him well?"

"Forgive me, sir, but why do you need to know? And are you acting for yourself or for the Government?"

216

"There is a claim for compensation in train. I have been instructed to assemble any details that may be material to the case."

Dr Slype raised his eyebrows. "So you must know he was found murdered last year?"

"Yes."

The chair creaked beneath him as he sat back and considered me. "Poor fellow. I did not hear about it until after he was dead and buried — my wife and I were on Long Island with her sister at the time, and I did not see the newspapers. They hanged the man who did it. A runaway, was it not?"

"A runaway was hanged for it, certainly," I said. "But that is another matter. I —"

He pounced. "Ah! I apprehend you have some doubt that the right man was executed."

I hesitated only a moment. "Yes, sir. Though I do not know for sure, and there is much else that is mysterious about the business."

"But why do you wish to enquire into it now, so long afterwards?"

"It is possible that agents of Congress may have had a hand in the matter."

"This business grows murkier by the moment, sir." Dr Slype chuckled quietly, and his whole body vibrated in sympathy. "But I really do not understand how I can assist you."

"We have very little information about Roger Pickett and his family, sir. I hoped you might be able to help us."

"I would not say I knew him well. I doubt if I exchanged more than two or three words with him, and that must have been five or six years ago. I knew his father slightly better — Jonathan Pickett — he had an estate near Charlotte. But the family was Presbyterian so we did not see them in church or meet them much in society. I'm afraid Mr Pickett's son was a sad disappointment to him. I do know that."

"In what way?"

"The father was a sober, God-fearing man. Young Roger sowed his wild oats and they quarrelled. They say the father died of an apoplexy when he discovered the extent of his son's debts, but I cannot vouch for the truth of that." Dr Slype picked up his wine and stared placidly out to sea. "And so the son inherited," he went on. "He sold the estate as soon as his father was in his grave. I heard that he went down to Charleston and spent his inheritance as quickly as he could."

"Mrs Frobisher thought he had enlisted in the Continental Army," I said.

"Yes, I know. The father would have approved of that, at least. As I said, the family was Presbyterian and Mr Jonathan Pickett was stuffed to the gills with Whig principles."

"And the son?"

"I'm not sure he had any principles." Dr Slype smiled at me. "I know it is uncharitable of me, but I fear that Mr Roger followed where expediency led. Which in his case was New York. As a matter of fact, I saw him walking down Broadway but —"

"I thought you said you hadn't spoken —"

He held up a plump white hand and stopped me in mid-sentence. "I beg your pardon, sir — I did not mean to mislead you. I saw him in Broadway in the spring of seventy-six, when General Washington held the city for Congress. But we did not speak. Mr Roger was wearing regimentals of some sort. I believe he was a sergeant."

"Did he see you?"

Dr Slype shook his head. "It would not have been desirable. I did not like to be recognized in those days — not that I am retiring by nature, you understand. But I am a Fellow of King's College and I found that my principles were not altogether fashionable when the Continentals occupied the city."

I remembered the Judge's brother, whose memorial was in Trinity churchyard. "Then you must have known the late Dr Wintour? I believe he was a Fellow of King's."

A shadow passed over Dr Slype's face. "The poor gentleman. He was more Tory than His Majesty himself and quite unable to dissemble it. And he paid the price for that. You will understand my desire to be discreet."

"As it happens, I lodge at his brother's house."

"The Judge? I have met him once or twice in company with Dr Wintour but I never had the honour of being on intimate terms with the family."

"Do you happen to know if they were acquainted with the Picketts?"

Dr Slype looked surprised. "Not as far as I know. Why?"

"No particular reason, sir."

"I believe the Wintours were not in the city when the rebels seized it. Apart from Dr Wintour, that is. So they cannot have met Roger Pickett then."

I drained my glass and began to think of leaving. Dr Slype gestured to the bottle. I shook my head with a smile and stood up.

"I suppose there was a connection of sorts," he said suddenly. "Between the Picketts and Wintours, that is. But a very indirect one."

The sun was in my eyes. Dr Slype was reduced to a dark shadow overflowing from his chair.

"If I remember right," he said, "Dr Wintour's nephew married a lady named Miss Froude."

"Yes, sir — indeed he did."

"I'm almost sure — I cannot be quite certain, mind — that it must have been the young lady's father who bought the Pickett estate in North Carolina. Mr Henry Froude. That was his name."

CHAPTER
THIRTY-FIVE

When I returned to Warren Street after my visit to Dr Slype, I could not help overhearing Captain Wintour's raised voice in the parlour as I passed through the hall.

"Dinner was cold again," he was saying. "I swear that's the third time they've served up that ham. It's rotting on the bone. Are you trying to kill us all? And I could not even find a clean shirt this morning."

Mrs Arabella said something I did not catch.

"It won't do, madam, I tell you — you spend too much time looking after those mewling negros and not enough on your duties, do you hear?"

I passed on. On the evening of the same day, after supper, in a tone that did not brook argument the Captain desired Mrs Arabella to read to us. When she asked what he would like her to read, he looked about the room and his eyes fell on a volume of *The Rambler* that lay on a side table.

"There — that will do very well."

She began to read aloud an essay on the evils of idleness. Within a moment or two her parents-in-law were asleep. I was turning over the pages of the *Royal Gazette*, for I had nothing to take me out of the house that evening. Captain Wintour twitched and fidgeted in his chair.

"Let us take a turn in the garden," he said suddenly, interrupting his wife's reading in mid-sentence.

"What, now, sir?"

"Yes, now. It is so close in here I cannot breathe. Put on your cloak, madam, you will not come to any harm."

Mrs Arabella turned to me. "Will you join us, sir?"

The Captain scowled.

"I think not," I said.

They were gone above twenty minutes. I sat yawning over the paper, while Mr and Mrs Wintour snored and snuffled in their armchairs on either side of the small fire. At one point I heard a noise — a distant cry or yelp, instantly extinguished. I read on.

I decided to go up to my room and write to Augusta and to Lizzie. As I went out of the drawing room, the garden door burst open. Mrs Arabella came into the house, kicking off her pattens. Her left hand obscured her face on the side nearer me. She must have seen me standing in the doorway but she did not falter or greet me in any way.

Then her husband appeared behind her, his arm raised. For a moment the three of us stood there as still as waxworks in an exhibition.

There are no third parties in a marriage. What a man and his wife say to each other is no concern of anyone else. What a man does to his wife is their business alone.

I knew all this. I knew what Captain Wintour must have done as surely as if I had seen it happen. And I knew that any court in America or England would say that, strictly speaking, he had the law on his side.

Despite that, I stepped forward. Mrs Arabella ran past me. Wintour lunged towards me. He was a big man, no taller than me but rather heavier; he was in that dangerous stage of drunkenness when caution is thrown to the wind but the body retains at least some of its ability to execute the mind's concerns.

"No, sir," I said.

I smelled his hot, liquorish breath. His face was contorted with passion. I heard the gentle snores of the Judge and the sound of Mrs Arabella's feet pattering up the stairs.

"You dare, sir?" He raised his fist.

I did not move or speak.

"Damnation, I —"

"Johnny, dear?" his mother called. "Is that you?"

Wintour wheeled about and marched down the hall into the garden.

I went back into the drawing room. "No, ma'am — it is I. Captain Wintour is taking a turn in the garden. I'm come to bid you goodnight."

The old lady nodded, frowning slightly as if trying to reconcile my face with her son's. "And my daughter?"

"I believe I heard Mrs Arabella going upstairs."

The Judge's snoring changed in tempo. Mrs Wintour and I glanced at him. His head had rolled against the wing of his armchair. His wig was now askew and his mouth was open. He looked old and foolish.

"Mr Savill?" Mrs Wintour was staring at me again. "Take care."

"I beg your pardon, madam?"

"Very great care. I am an old woman, sir, and you will permit me to speak frankly."

I realized with surprise that she was perfectly lucid, which was unusual at this time of day and, increasingly, at any time.

"It would be easy for a gentleman in your position to allow an attachment to develop — almost without his knowing. An attachment which was quite impossible and which could only bring pain to all concerned."

"I'm afraid I do not catch your —"

"It would distress my husband inexpressibly," she went on, "— it would distress us all, I believe — if you were obliged to leave us before your visit to New York was finished. We consider you quite one of the family now."

I bowed. "You are very kind."

"But it is growing late." She smiled graciously at me. "I must not keep you from your bed any longer."

Bowing again, I left the drawing room, closing the door behind me.

I stood in the hall, attempting to digest what had just happened. The garden door was still ajar. It was dark outside. There was a half-moon veiled in clouds that streamed across a night sky the colour of slate. Captain Wintour was nowhere to be seen.

I heard the faintest sound above me. I looked up. The light was dim — an oil lamp burned on the landing and a single candle on the hall table below.

A person was leaning over the rail and looking down at me. I glimpsed, if that is not too definite a word, a shadow with flashes of white for eyes and teeth.

Slippered feet scampered across the landing. A door closed.

CHAPTER
THIRTY-SIX

During the next ten days or so it was perhaps as well that I spent few of my waking hours in Warren Street. Mrs Wintour did not refer to our conversation again. She retreated across the borders of old age to a place where she seemed only partly aware of what was going on around her. A day or two later, she fell victim to a putrid sore throat and was confined to bed, which I confess came as a relief to me.

I could not ignore the fact that Mrs Wintour had, without saying as much, warned me of the danger of nursing adulterous desires for Mrs Arabella. If these desires, which I barely acknowledged even to myself, had been evident to Mrs Wintour, who else might have noticed the tell-tale signs?

The mood in the city at this time was buoyant, for our forces had had considerable success in Georgia, so much so that the province had been declared in the King's Peace and civil government re-established. But the mood at the Wintours' house was quite the reverse.

Our domestic economy was still at sixes and sevens because of the inoculations. On top of everything else, the necessity of nursing Mrs Wintour placed another strain on the straitened household.

I hardly saw Mrs Arabella. I encountered her in the stairs on the day after she had run in from the garden. The flesh around her left eye was a deep purple in colour, so dark it was almost black like the skin of a plum.

Later that day, at supper, in answer to Judge Wintour's questions, she explained that she had collided with an open door when she went to her closet in the night. She spoke of it in a mechanical, uninterested way, as if the accident had happened to someone else, someone she did not care for very much. The Judge was concerned for her health — he believed the misfortune could be attributed to her overtaxing herself with her patients. He seemed to suspect nothing of the truth.

There were only the three of us at table that evening, for Mrs Wintour was upstairs and the Captain was out. As a general rule, he returned late, slept late and went out early. On the few occasions that he and I met during those ten days, he was perfectly amiable. We exchanged bows and the occasional commonplace as if nothing had happened between us. Had he been too drunk to remember the incident? Or did he simply believe that there was no profit in quarrelling with me?

As for Miriam, she avoided me. It supported my suspicion that it had been she who had witnessed my confrontation with Captain Wintour in the hall and who had scampered across the landing afterwards. Clearly she did not want to run the risk of my questioning her.

The bond between a woman and her maid can be almost as intimate as that between a man and his wife — in this case perhaps more so. I fancied that there was a sullenness in her demeanour when she met me, a disapproving look in her eye. Did she condemn me in her heart for failing either to protect or to avenge her mistress? Or did she condemn me merely for knowing of Mrs Arabella's unhappiness?

But I did not blame her for that. Indeed, I condemned myself.

Duty pointed one way, inclination another.

Though I was much occupied with the routine business of the office, I could not forget the Pickett affair. I knew I must come to a decision. Put bluntly, should I share all that I knew with Marryot and Rampton, and therefore with our masters in the Government — or should I let Roger Pickett rest in his grave, and spare both myself and the Wintours, especially Mrs Arabella, the inconvenience and unpleasantness of an investigation into the family's connections with a rebel?

Towards the end of March, the *Romulus* man-of-war brought in a fleet of twenty storeships and merchantmen which had sailed from Torbay at the beginning of January. At this time of year the weather made communication between New York and England even slower and riskier than usual.

Mr Rampton had forwarded a bag of mail. His letter to me, written a fortnight after his last, concerned itself solely with the business of the Department; there was not the slightest hint of the private connection between us. I was beginning to suspect that he had selected me for the New York mission not to advance my career but to condemn me to a form of exile.

I found one small compensation: Mr Rampton made no mention of Mr Pickett and his supposed box of curiosities. I interpreted this omission to signify that he believed he had done all he might reasonably be expected to do: therefore he did not propose to exert himself any further in the matter.

If I was right, then it followed that neither Lord George nor Lord North had wished to do more than appear obliging — the former to his prime minister, the latter to his agent, Mr Pickett's brother-in-law. I had not yet composed my memorandum on the renewed investigation, but nothing it would contain was likely materially to affect Mr Rampton's opinion.

A day or two later, I was at Fort George for a meeting with the Deputy Adjutant General, the Provost and Major Marryot. Afterwards, Marryot caught my eye and gave me an almost imperceptible nod. We strolled out as if by chance to the parade ground. In this crowded city, a public space offered the most privacy.

"Well?" he said, coming to a halt and wheeling round to face me. "This Pickett affair."

I said nothing.

He frowned. "Have you fresh intelligence?"

I shrugged and blew out a sigh. "What do you suppose, sir?"

"I suppose it's a damned wild-goose chase." The Major rubbed his left leg, the lame one. He often massaged it without, I think, knowing that he did so. "I've had no reports of Scarface in the city."

"Could he be within the lines somewhere? Long Island, perhaps?"

"Of course he could if he had someone to shelter him. He could be here in the city for all we know."

"If so, I cannot think he goes abroad very much," I said. "Or only at night. He stands out in a crowd."

Marryot nodded. "Ten to one he slipped through the lines and he's somewhere in the Debatable Ground."

"Nothing from Philadelphia, either," I said, "nor from Pickett's lodgings here. Not a whisper of this box of curiosities or of a design against Pickett's life."

"It's like wrestling with shadows," Marryot said.

I looked sharply at him. For a plain soldier, Marryot had a strange tendency to produce these queer, poetical metaphors. He had once described the Pickett affair as "chasing clouds". Now he was "wrestling shadows". But I wasn't tempted to smile at them. His metaphorical fancies fitted this strange investigation as much as any words could.

His colour rose. "That's to say, it's a devil of business. Nothing for a man to get hold of. And I hate running other men's errands to no purpose."

"Then perhaps we shouldn't try."

"Eh? But I thought Lord George —"

"We have done as much as we can, sir," I said. "After all, what man can do more? This is what I propose: that I write a digest of what we have discovered — and in

230

some detail too — and that we both fix our signatures to it. We send it to the Department and, God willing, we shall hear no more about it."

"You really think it would answer?"

"I believe so. If they want more, they will tell us. Of course, if we stumble on anything pertinent in the meantime, we shall report it to them."

Marryot looked from side to side, as if fearing eavesdroppers. "Are you sure this is wise, sir? It will not harm our prospects?"

"Why should it?" I spoke with some confidence, for this was my world not the Major's: I knew the workings of Mr Rampton's mind; I understood the words he employed and the words he did not. "We have nothing to lose except a deal of tedious distraction."

He rubbed the stubble on his chin. "Very well, sir. It shall be as you say. And — and, well, I'm obliged to you."

CHAPTER
THIRTY-SEVEN

That night I met Townley by arrangement at the assembly that was held every fortnight or so in the big upper room at Roubalet's Tavern. He and I were subscribers at two guineas apiece.

"I'm happy to see you in such good spirits, sir," he said when I laughed immoderately at a foolish joke told by an elderly naval lieutenant. "Did the *Romulus* bring news of your recall?"

"No, sir." I was instantly sober again.

"Of course, for selfish reasons, I'm rejoiced to hear it." He gestured around the room, at the gaily dressed figures that moved in and out, following the music. "You have a silver lining at least," he went on, smiling all the while. "You will be obliged to prolong your stay at Warren Street. You will continue to enjoy the society of your charming hostess. The younger of the two, that is."

There was no mistaking his insinuation. After Mrs Wintour's veiled warning, it alarmed me, though I hoped it was merely the sort of loose talk that Townley so often indulged in. I bowed coldly.

"Talking of which," he went on, seemingly unabashed, "how is the gallant captain? I saw him the other evening at Governor Franklin's but I was not able to enter into conversation with him. Does he still cherish his project of making an expedition to Mount George?"

The change of subject was smoothly done but I did not altogether like it. As so often with Townley, his manner was confiding but, under the surface, I sensed a restless, prying intelligence pursuing a subterranean course towards a hidden end.

"I cannot say, sir," I said. "Captain Wintour has not mentioned it recently. Or not to me."

"It's curious that he should want to go at all," Townley said, staring at the dancers. "He is not in the best of health. The expedition would be uncomfortable and dangerous. And to what end? I believe the house was burned down and the estate has been raided many times. I should have thought that there was nothing to be gained by going there until the war is over."

"You know as much as I do, sir."

"And of course the place must have unhappy memories for Mrs Arabella."

"Indeed?" I looked sharply at him, wondering if the stillbirth at Mount George was public knowledge. "Why?"

"Didn't you know? Her father died there in late seventy-six. A sad business."

"Why — what happened?"

Townley lowered his voice. "It was a month or two after we'd recaptured New York and the Continental troops were retreating north. A party of their irregulars attacked the place and Mr Froude was killed."

"Was Mrs Arabella there?" I said.

"Yes — but by the grace of God she and some of the servants got away." He smiled at me. "So you understand my curiosity about the projected expedition, sir — Captain Wintour seems quite the man of mystery."

"If there's a mystery, I'm afraid I cannot solve it." I glanced towards the door to the anteroom where the card tables had been set up. "Would you care for a rubber of whist? Shall we see if we can make up a four?"

Townley accepted the distraction and we whiled away an hour or two in the card room. It was after two in the morning by the time the party broke up. Mr Townley gave me a lift to Warren Street in his coach. He dropped me off at the door.

Usually at this hour the house was in darkness and the inhabitants were asleep. Abraham, the young footman, would be dozing on his chair in the hall, ready to unbar the door when a late-comer arrived. Tonight, though, even before the door opened, I knew something was different. There were cracks of light around the parlour shutters and a lantern still burned above the fanlight of the front door.

I was obliged to wait for longer than I liked. I listened to the sounds of Townley's coach diminishing and the distant catcalls and shouts from merrymakers on Broadway. At length it was Josiah who opened the door, and without the habitual fumbling with bolts and bars. The old man looked dismayed to see me.

234

"Has he come?" Judge Wintour called from the parlour. "Show him in here at once."

"What is it?" I said, thrusting my hat at Josiah.

He took it automatically and reached for my cloak.

"Quickly!" Mr Wintour cried, his voice cracking.

Josiah stood back, gesturing for me to enter the parlour.

A moment later, I saw Captain Wintour stretched out on the parlour sofa. One arm trailed to the ground. His coat and waistcoat lay on the floor.

Mrs Arabella knelt beside him. Mr Wintour paced up and down behind the sofa. He glanced at me and his features contorted with disappointment.

Still on her knees, Mrs Arabella turned her head. In the poor light the bruise on her face was like an eyepatch. Her wrapper had fallen open, revealing a linen shift beneath. Across its white bosom was a smear of blood.

CHAPTER
THIRTY-EIGHT

The Judge rushed towards me and seized my arm. "John has been attacked, sir! And on our very doorstep! How will I tell his poor mother if he is murdered?"

Mrs Arabella rose to her feet and drew her wrapper tightly across her body. "By the mercy of God, Abraham heard him shouting and got the door open. It must have frightened the villain off."

"Is he badly hurt?"

"He's been stabbed. And there is a wound on his head, too. I sent Abraham for the doctor. You missed him by a moment or two."

Mr Wintour resumed his pacing. He moaned softly as he walked. His nightcap was awry and he had lost one of his slippers.

The room was lit by three candles, one on the mantelshelf and the others on the tables at either end of the sofa. The fire was out and the air was very cold.

Abraham would be lucky to rouse a doctor at this hour, I thought, and even luckier to find one who was willing to venture into the streets at night without an armed guard. It was a thousand pities that Townley and I had not arrived in the coach a little earlier.

"Pray bring me a light, madam," I said. "Would you hold it for me while I examine him?"

Mrs Arabella took up a candle. I bent over Captain Wintour. He lay on his back, propped against the arm of the sofa and breathing heavily. His mouth was open and his breath smelled powerfully of rumbo. For all the world he looked as if he were sleeping off a debauch.

The front of his shirt was saturated with blood on the left side. His neckcloth had been removed and used as a pad on the wound. I peeled back the bloodstained cloth to expose the skin beneath. There was a wound just below the collarbone. It was about half an inch wide and shaped like a narrowed eye. A blade then, probably, not a bullet. I judged by the tears in the skin that it had entered at an angle, driving upwards. The wound was still weeping blood but it was beginning to coagulate.

"We must do something," Mrs Arabella said in my ear. "And we must do it quickly or he will die."

"Be quiet, ma'am," I said. "Hold the candle so I can see."

The fingers of the Captain's right hand were touching the ground. The fingertips rested in a puddle of blood. The surrounding carpet was spotted with more blood. I lifted the hand and turned it over. The palm and the lower parts of the fingers were a mass of blood. Wintour must have seized the blade and tried to wrest the knife from his assailant's grasp. Otherwise, perhaps it would have found his heart, not his shoulder.

I released the hand. "Where's the other wound?"

"Here."

Mrs Arabella set down the candle and gently turned her husband's head, which was resting on the arm of the sofa. He had lost his wig and hat. The scalp was covered with coarse stubble which, I was surprised to see, was already turning grey.

There was an ugly graze on the left temple, which in places had broken the skin. I probed it gently with my fingertips. The bone beneath seemed firm and smooth: I could not detect a fracture.

I heard footsteps outside and Miriam came into the room with a candle. She too was in her night-clothing.

Arabella looked up. "How's your mistress?"

"I've settled her in bed again, ma'am, and given her some drops — I think she'll sleep now." The maid saw me and bobbed a curtsey. "I didn't tell her it was the Captain."

"Where in God's name is the doctor?" Mr Wintour said.

"Pray do not distress yourself, sir." I straightened up and turned to Mrs Arabella. "We should not wait, ma'am. We should lay the Captain on a door and get him to his bed."

"Moving him upstairs might re-open the wound. And the disturbance would wake his mother."

"Then let us have a mattress brought down here and laid on the floor by the sofa. We can lift him on to that and do what we can to make him easy."

"Very well."

For a moment, I had the strangest sense that her mind was elsewhere, that this scene in the parlour was

238

merely a sideshow. But then she turned briskly and told Josiah to have the flockbed in her closet brought down.

"Put water on to boil," I added. "And bring clean cloths and more candles. Light the fire, too — there's a chill in the air. Have you a jar of basilicon in your store cupboard, ma'am? And some lint? We should dress the wounds."

Within an hour, matters had a more cheerful aspect. Captain Wintour had been washed, bandaged and made comfortable. The room was much brighter, partly because there were more candles and partly because the fire was now well established, the flames climbing into the chimney and the damp logs cracking and popping as they burned.

Abraham returned but without the doctor. I was relieved to see him. I had feared for his safety in those lawless streets.

"This is too bad," the Judge grumbled. "Does the Hippocratic Oath mean nothing to these men? Is venality their only guide?"

"Perhaps it is for the best, sir," I said. I knew from Townley that few if any of the doctors left in the city were trained physicians, whatever they claimed. "I shall write a note for our friend Major Marryot and ask him to send one of the army surgeons. They know what they are about. Abraham shall take the note as soon as it is light."

Mrs Arabella and I persuaded him to go to bed on the understanding that we would at once arouse him if Captain Wintour's condition worsened. We sent Josiah away too, for the old man was clearly exhausted.

"Abraham," I said to the footman. "Did you see Captain Wintour's attacker?"

"No, sir." The young man was swaying on his feet with weariness. "Heard him running away, though."

"Just the one?"

"Yes, sir."

"Where was he going?"

"Down past the college, your honour."

Mrs Arabella told him to snatch a couple of hours' sleep while he could.

"And you, sir?" she asked. "Will you retire now?"

"I believe I shall stay in case I can be of service. If the Captain awakes, for example."

"Some refreshment then? Something to eat?"

"Tea would be more than welcome, ma'am."

She sent Miriam down to the kitchen to prepare it. For the first time Mrs Arabella and I were alone — apart from her husband, of course, an unconscious chaperone. She and I sat like an old married couple on either side of the fireplace. Captain Wintour's mattress was in the shadows by the sofa. He lay on his back, snoring — a long, growling rumble as he took in air, followed by a profound silence pregnant with undesired anticipation before the next rumble began.

"I cannot begin to thank you, sir," Mrs Arabella said in one of these silences. "You have done us a kindness this evening."

"It's nothing of consequence, ma'am." I was obliged to raise my voice to be heard above the rumble of the next snore. "You and the servants would have managed it just as well if I had not been here."

240

"I think not. You were very prompt in our emergency." She hesitated. "The situation did not seem altogether strange to you, if I may say so. You knew at once what was needed."

"My brother-in-law is a surgeon and I accompanied him on his rounds for a month or two when I was a young man. Much of the craft seems little more than the application of common sense."

The rhythm of Captain Wintour's breathing changed. We turned to look at him. When the snore resumed, it had changed its character, becoming less of a rumble and more of a rustle like dead leaves shifting on a pavement.

"Is that his purse over there?" I asked suddenly. "On the sofa table — there, by the candle."

"Yes. And his pocketbook."

"So the robber ran off empty-handed?"

"Yes," she said. "Thanks to Abraham."

There was a tap on the door and Miriam returned with the tea things. Mrs Arabella rose to her feet.

"Would you excuse me, sir? I must pay a visit to my hospital. Some of my patients are wakeful tonight. Miriam will make the tea for you and I will return in a moment or two."

She was gone for longer than that. Miriam gave me my tea and set a cup for her mistress. When that was done she made her reverence and begged permission to withdraw.

I threw another log on the fire. I was not at all easy in my mind. A man had attacked Captain Wintour on his own doorstep. There had been no robbery. I thought it probable that the assailant had knocked the Captain down with a blow to the head and then stabbed him. If robbery had been the sole motive, why not either stun him with the bludgeon or threaten him with the knife? The Captain had fought back; otherwise the knife wound might well have been fatal. The rogue had run off in the direction of Canvas Town as soon as his work was interrupted.

There was an uncomfortable familiarity to this. I remembered only too well the attack I had suffered in November. True, this was a lawless city, especially at night, and full of thieves with knives. On the face of it, there was no reason why this attack on Captain Wintour should have been the work of the negro Scarface. For a start, it would entail the enormous coincidence of his striking a random victim on the very doorstep of the house where I happened to lodge.

Unless — and here I wished for something stronger than the cup of tea in my hand — it was no coincidence.

Perhaps Wintour had not been the target at all. He and I were of much the same build and the light was poor. Had Scarface mistaken Wintour for me? Had he simply returned, knife in one hand and bludgeon in the other, to finish off what he had begun four months before?

CHAPTER
THIRTY-NINE

The sound of the opening door woke me from a shallow sleep. Mrs Arabella had returned. Her candle shone full on her face. She looked tired and unwell, as if it were she who were ill and in need of the doctor.

She apologized for leaving me here on my own with her husband, who was still snoring away on the mattress. There was, she said, some crisis among her patients in the slave quarters that necessitated her presence and that of Miriam as her deputy. I asked what it was and whether there was anything in my power that might assist her.

"Thank you, no. These inoculations do not always agree with patients, you know, and in the end the only thing is to let the infection run its course."

At another point, I awoke to find Mrs Arabella sitting near me in old Mrs Wintour's chair, her head and shoulders wrapped in a shawl. I stared at her in confusion. I had been dreaming of a great white mansion with many rooms. I knew in the dream that this house must be Mount George. I was searching with desperate urgency for someone or something. I ran from one huge, echoing room to another; there was no discernible plan or shape to the place, and the rooms went on and on; sometimes I seemed to enter rooms that I had already searched but by a different door, though I could not be sure of this. Now, caught for an instant between waking and sleeping, I knew that I had been looking for Mrs Arabella.

I sat up sharply. The fire had reduced itself to embers that gave off a dull red light. All the candles had burned out except one on the sofa table. I found I had a blanket draped across my legs. The Captain was still snoring.

"Madam, I —"

"Pray do not disturb yourself, sir. You were so soundly asleep, I hoped not to wake you."

"This blanket?"

"It's growing cold. My husband has more than enough."

"Is all well in your hospital?"

For a moment she did not reply. "I do not know." Her breathing had become irregular. "Not yet."

"You should rest," I said bluntly. "Can you not retire and leave Miriam to watch over your patients?"

"I am quite rested now. It is you who should retire, sir."

She leaned forward and threw fuel on the fire. I pushed the blanket aside, took up the poker and stirred the embers. Soon the flames were licking around the new log.

I added more wood and went to look at Captain Wintour. The snores had modulated from andante to adagio.

"He's smiling in his sleep," I said.

244

She did not turn her head. "He will have a better night than any of us."

"No doubt."

This time she looked at me. "That is the way of things, is it not? But I must return to my patients."

She stood up abruptly, wished me goodnight in the same, sour tone and left the room. I wondered if I had somehow offended her. Or was her bitterness directed at her husband or even at something deeper and broader whose shape was entirely mysterious to me?

I was now quite awake. I walked about the room, for my limbs had grown stiff in the chair. Mrs Arabella had taken her candle but there was still the one on the sofa table. I carried it to the fireplace and set it on the mantelshelf. I held out my hands to the blaze and glanced up at the candle to see if the wick needed trimming.

I discovered that the painting above the fire had acquired a sort of half-life. The varnished ridges and grooves of the oil paint sometimes reflected and sometimes absorbed the light of the candle flame. As the draught made the flame flicker, so the light it cast made the painting ripple and sway as though it lay under clear, shallow water whose surface had been agitated by a breeze.

There was the white house of my dream with its eight pillars and its porch. There were the grazing sheep and the plump cattle. There was the prosperous little family group in the foreground, together with the spaniel who was not paying attention.

Mount George. I raised the candle and studied the painting more closely. As Mrs Arabella had pointed out, the artists who produce such works play with perspective to magnify what they see. I tried to make allowances for this, to see the place for what it really was — or, rather, for what it had been.

By the same token I tried to imagine what the family had truly been like — Mr Froude in the prime of life with his chart and his telescope; Mrs Froude as a young and perhaps desirable woman; and the infant Arabella, implausibly poised and genteel. Mr and Mrs Froude were dead now, and so was the bored spaniel. I suspected that the dog had been truer to life than anything else, the artist's solitary concession to what he actually saw before his eyes.

There was something about Mount George that eluded me. Why the devil should Captain Wintour wish to go there now? How could it profit him in its present state? He was not a man of much sensibility but Townley had surely been right this evening: Wintour must know of his wife's dislike of the place where her father and her daughter had died in such distressing circumstances.

I sat down again and pulled the blanket over me. In the semi-darkness, Captain Wintour snuffled like a dozing hound in his basket. There had to be something at Mount George, I thought, something that he wanted or something he needed to do.

I fell asleep. This time oblivion rolled over me. If there were dreams, I do not remember them.

246

The next thing I knew was that I had been jerked into full consciousness. Lines of daylight showed around the shutters. I was very cold. The fire was nearly out. Wintour breathed steadily, more quietly than before.

I heard footsteps hurrying to and fro in the hall.

I threw aside the blanket, stood up and stumbled to the door. My limbs were stiff and still half asleep.

In the hall, Mrs Arabella and Miriam were clinging together at the foot of the stairs. Mrs Arabella was holding on to the newel post. They looked old beyond their time, older than Mrs Wintour.

"Madam?" I said. "Madam? What is it?"

Mrs Arabella did not reply.

But Miriam looked at me. The tears were running down her face. "We lost a child."

"A child?" I echoed, not understanding.

"A slave's child," Miriam said harshly.

"Is there anything I can do?"

"No, sir. Nothing that anyone can do."

CHAPTER
FORTY

Major Marryot arrived on the doorstep before eight o'clock in the morning with a regimental surgeon in tow. The Judge was roused by their knocking and came down the stairs in his dressing gown.

"You must not alarm yourself, sir," I said. "Captain Wintour has had a comfortable night. I have just been talking to him and he seems quite his old self."

Mr Wintour took my hand and pressed it. Then he almost pushed the surgeon into the drawing room. I lingered in the hall with the Major.

"A blow to the head and a flesh-wound in the shoulder," I said. "Wintour fought back and his hand is cut badly. Fortunately his attacker was interrupted when the servant unbolted the door."

"And Mrs Arabella?"

"She's asleep now — she's been to and fro between here and the slave quarters. One of the slaves died last night."

"The poor lady. Pray let me know if there is anything I can do, sir, anything at all. I would esteem it a favour."

"Of course." I nodded towards the drawing-room doorway. "You have already done a great deal, and done it sooner than any of us could have hoped."

I sent Abraham downstairs to fetch a pot of coffee. Marryot and I stood just inside the room and watched the surgeon examining his patient. Wintour was awake. His face was paler than usual but he seemed in remarkably good spirits. He swore at the surgeon when the man probed at the wound in his shoulder.

"There was no robbery, sir," I said softly to Marryot. "Abraham says the Captain's assailant ran off towards Canvas Town. I can't help wondering if there's more to this than meets the eye."

"I doubt it. Why make it more complicated than it is? Man like Wintour — coming home at night, drunk as a lord —"

The surgeon straightened up and wiped his hands on a towel. "I see no reason for concern, sir," he said to the Judge.

"Are you sure?"

"As sure as a man can be. The wound is clean, no sign of inflammation. The blow to the head did no more than stun the gentleman. I'll bandage him and return this evening. But sleep will be the best medicine, I believe."

Marryot compressed his lips and looked sourly at the patient. Perhaps he would not have been unduly distressed to hear that the wounds might prove fatal. At that moment Abraham returned with a tray of coffee. Josiah was in the hall. I went outside to speak to him.

"Mrs Arabella told me there was a death in the slave quarters last night."

The old man's eyes were red-rimmed. "Yes, sir."

"I'm heartily sorry — one of ours?"

"No, sir. A neighbour's."

"A child, I apprehend."

He said nothing.

"Your master is distracted at present," I continued in a low voice. "And Mrs Arabella is asleep, and has other responsibilities besides. If anything is needed, you must come to me, and I will do my best to help."

He bowed. As he straightened up, a shaft of sunshine from the fanlight over the door shone full on his face. Tears glittered on his cheeks. Even a slave may be a creature of sentiment.

The surgeon was oversanguine. Later in the day the servants carried Captain Wintour on a makeshift litter to his room. The exertion tired him. He took a little broth and a little wine during the day and grew steadily more petulant.

He demanded amusement. I played a game of backgammon with him but he was unable to concentrate on the board for long. There was a hectic flush on his cheek. His mind flitted from one subject to another. Next, he demanded the latest news. His father read the *Gazette* to him but after a few minutes the Captain discovered that the news was too tedious for words.

He asked for Mrs Arabella but, when at last she came, he found that she had no conversation worth hearing and a face like a month of Sundays.

By the evening, he was running a fever. The surgeon came again and declared the wound might be infected. He returned again in the morning, found the fever worse and ordered the patient to be cupped. But bloodletting merely made the Captain weaker and his fever continued unabated.

I ate supper alone in the parlour. Josiah served me.

"How are matters in the slave quarters?" I asked.

He did not look at me. "Better, sir."

"And the child?"

He said nothing.

"Do you need funds for the funeral? Will the child's owners pay? If there is a difficulty, you must apply to me."

He bowed. "Thank you, sir, but everything has been seen to."

By the following morning, it was clear that Captain Wintour was very ill. The surgeon brought in two professional nurses. He ordered that the patient should not be disturbed and excluded all visitors from the sickroom including his immediate family.

Somehow the news was kept from his mother, but the Judge drifted about the house like a ghost.

Major Marryot called to enquire after the patient. So did Mr Townley, who also sent Noak over with presents intended to help restore health: but redcurrant jelly, port wine and the small, boiled chicken did not find favour with the sick man.

The fever continued to mount. On the evening of its second day, Wintour's temperature was higher still. I was preparing for bed when there was a tap on the door. Josiah came into the room, stumbling from weariness.

"The Captain's asking for you, sir."

"For me?"

"Yes, sir. The doctor sent me to fetch you."

"And the Judge? Mrs Arabella?"

"Already there, sir. But he asks for you in particular. He is — he is talking wildly, sir."

I pulled on a dressing gown and allowed Josiah to escort me downstairs. Captain Wintour's chamber was directly beneath my own, though it was a larger, higher room. The doctor and the nurse stood by the bed. The Judge and Mrs Arabella sat in the relative gloom nearer the fire. They acknowledged my entry but neither spoke.

The doctor, a swarthy man with only one arm, beckoned me to approach the bed. The Captain was propped up on three pillows.

"Pray talk to him, sir," the doctor murmured. "But try not to cause agitation. The crisis has come and I really do not wish to bleed him any more."

"Who's that?" Captain Wintour cried. "Who's there? Juvenal?"

"It is Mr Savill, sir," the doctor said. "He has come to see how you do."

252

"Savill — is it you? I do not like this darkness. Why is it so dark this morning?"

"It is quite all right, sir," I said. "It is the evening now. We have candles."

"Let me see you then."

I took up the nearest candle and held it high so the light fell on my face. The same light shone on Wintour. His nightgown was open at the neck and was damp with sweat. His head was bare and his face was rough with stubble.

He frowned and screwed up his face. "My eyes hurt," he said. "I do not like it."

"It will soon pass," I said. "You must not disturb yourself about it."

"I dreamed we were there, you know. We were playing backgammon on the terrace."

"Where?"

"At Mount George, of course. You shall have your own apartments there, Savill, and you shall come and go just as you please."

"That's most kind," I said, glancing at the doctor, who shook his head.

The Captain ran his tongue over his lips, which were chapped. He lowered his voice to a whisper. "Did you bring the box?"

"Which box?"

"The box of curiosities."

"No. Would you like some water?"

"What?" He looked about him. "Yes, I believe I should."

I took a glass from the night table. I supported his head and held the water to his lips. The neck of his nightgown fell open, revealing the bulky dressing on the wound and the ribs poking at the skin. I had not realized he was so terribly thin.

He moistened his lips with water, spilling some on to his chest, and then took a few sips. He sank back, exhausted.

The doctor brought a chair for me and set it by the bedside. I sat down. For a moment neither of us spoke.

"A whole wing," he said at last. "All to yourself."

"To eat?" I asked, imagining he was thinking of chicken or some other bird.

"No, no. Savill, my dear man, you are a dunderhead. A wing." His mouth dropped open in a rictus that was in fact a smile. "How — how very droll."

"What sort of wing?"

"A whole wing."

"Indeed — you said that before, I believe."

"And I meant it, sir, as sure as my name's Jack Wintour. A gentleman's word is his bond." He looked fiercely at me, and the doctor stirred by my side. "And I dare any man to tell me otherwise."

"I know. I never doubted it for a moment."

He nodded, smiling. "There's a good fellow. I knew I could rely on you. That's why you shall have a wing to yourself. It is no more than you deserve."

"Thank you," I said. "You are most obliging."

"There's plenty of room to build, you see." His head rocked slowly from side to side on the pillow. "I can't see why old Froude didn't improve the place himself.

Too busy with his hammers and spades, eh, and chasing his confounded bugs and sweating like a negro. So you shall have a whole wing, with a suite of splendid apartments, all fitted up just as you like. And we shall get Bella to find you a wife and we shall rub along very nicely. Shan't we?"

"It will be delightful."

"We shall be like those men in Cicero."

"I'm not quite sure —"

"You know the story I mean," he burst out. "Of course you do. You always do." He hesitated, frowning, and squinted at me. "Juvenal? Is that you? Juvenal? I thought you was dead."

"No, sir — I'm Savill, you know, I am —"

"To be sure, my friend Savill, to be sure. But you sounded like Juvenal, and for a moment I thought you was him — and he would know, I'm certain of it. He minds his lessons, you see, and I never do."

"What would he know?"

"Who those men in the story were. Was one called David? No — but it was a name like that. There was a tyrant too."

Suddenly I saw whom Wintour might mean. I dredged up scraps of knowledge from my schooldays. "Damon and Pythias? The friends who fell foul of Dionysius, the Tyrant of Syracuse?"

"Of course. But they were true to each other through thick and thin and all ended well. Just as it will for us. And you shall have your wing. And a wife to put in it."

"That is excellent news," I said. "And now, perhaps it is time for sleep."

255

He ignored what I had said and raised his forefinger as if summoning a waiter in a tavern. "So let us see it."

"I beg your pardon — the wing?"

Again, he lowered his voice. "The box." His arm swung outwards and nudged my shoulder. "The box! We shall need it if you are to have your wing, shan't we? We shall need it for . . . for everything."

"I told you — I don't have it."

"Ah — of course. I forgot. It's still there."

I hazarded a guess. "At Mount George?"

"Will it take long to get there?"

"Not long, I dare say, when you are better. Would you like another sip of water?"

He did not refuse, so I raised his head again and gave him more to drink. Afterwards, he lay back with his eyes closed, breathing heavily.

Slowly I rose to my feet and moved away. I looked at the doctor, who nodded and smiled. I was aware of Mrs Arabella and the Judge, their faces turned towards me. The light was too poor for me to be able to read their expressions.

A movement on the bed made me swing round. Wintour had turned his head on the pillow. His eyes were open. They glowed with fire, reflecting the flames of the candelabra on the night table.

"Savill?" he whispered. "Are you there?"

I crouched beside the bed so my head was on a level with his. "Yes — I'm here."

"Not a dream?"

"No." I stretched out an arm and touched his shoulder. "See? You are awake, and so am I."

256

"Yes." He drew in his breath slowly. "You will come with me, won't you? To Mount George? I don't want to go alone."

The room was silent, as if everyone and everything between these four walls were holding their breath, waiting for my answer.

"Yes, of course I will," I said. "Now, go to sleep."

CHAPTER
FORTY-ONE

That night, Captain Wintour slept peacefully for six hours. By morning, the fever had diminished. He accepted a mouthful of broth and a small glass of wine.

The crisis had passed. I spent the day at the office. When I returned to Warren Street in the evening, I supped alone with the Judge. The Captain had eaten more broth and was now sleeping again. Mrs Wintour was still convalescing from her putrid cold and Mrs Arabella was lying down with the migraine.

Mr Wintour was convinced that his son's recovery was due in large measure to me and nothing I could say would dissuade him from this opinion.

"He listens to you, my dear sir," he said, pressing my hand. "He trusts you. I believe you made him feel that all was well. Then he could sleep at last and let nature be his physician."

We sat for nearly an hour over our wine. Towards the end the Judge grew confidential.

"I cannot understand my son's desire to see Mount George," he said. "It is the height of folly."

"It was the fever speaking, surely?"

"I think not — he's cherished the scheme for some time now, has he not? And what is this box he talked of?"

"Did you not tell me your brother had a box of curiosities?" I said.

"Yes, but that was never at Mount George."

I smiled. "Then perhaps the fever made it so."

"I remember now." The Judge wrinkled his forehead. "I remember how I came to tell you of my brother's cabinet of antiquities. You had asked me whether poor Mr Pickett had mentioned a box of curiosities when he paid his visit to us."

"It can hardly be the same box," I said. "Anyway, the Captain talked a deal of nonsense last night, did he not? You remember my projected suite of apartments at Mount George. And he called me Juvenal at one moment. Why should he do that?"

"That at least I can explain, sir." He turned his head toward the dark shape standing behind his chair. "See — here is Josiah. You recall I told you that he grew up with my brother Francis? Well, Juvenal was John's slave. I gave him the lad as a playmate on his sixth birthday." He leaned closer to me and lowered his voice. "But — to go back to this mad freak of John's about Mount George. Will you try to dissuade him from it if he mentions it to you again? There is no possible advantage in his going there until the whole province has been restored to the King's Peace."

I promised to do my best, and our conversation turned to other things. Three-quarters of an hour later, however, when we said goodnight, Mr Wintour gave me his hand, which he did not usually do.

"I know one thing," he said. "That my son considers you his friend. You have not seen him at his best since his return from Canada, but he is an affectionate boy — a good boy at heart — I should say man, I suppose. He does not bestow his friendship lightly."

I gently disengaged my hand. "I'm honoured that he should think of me as a friend, sir."

"Damon and Pythias," he said, smiling. "Those dear comrades of antiquity. John compared your friendship to theirs. It would give me much joy if he spoke no more than sober truth."

The following morning, at my office, I barred my door to all callers and settled down to write my memorandum about Mr Pickett's murder. For the benefit of Mr Rampton and his masters, I outlined the facts of the case again and listed in some detail the measures that Major Marryot and I had taken to enquire into the crime, both in August last year and more recently.

I concluded that we had found nothing new of any consequence but added that we would of course keep the case open and put out a general warrant for the arrest of the scar-faced negro who might have had some connection with the murder.

I sanded the last sheet of paper and read it over. Marryot and I would sign it in the afternoon and it would go out with the mail on the next packet home.

I told myself that I did not wish to confuse matters with gossip, speculation and irrelevant information. Therefore, I did not mention the two items of information I had learned from the Reverend Dr Slype — that Pickett had been a rebel soldier in New York in 1776, and that, some time earlier, he might have sold his land in North Carolina to Mr Froude of Mount George. Nor did I mention that Captain Wintour, Froude's son-in-law, attached a curious importance to a box of curiosities. I also omitted the facts that Mr Froude had been killed at Mount George and that I was now lodging at his daughter's house in New York.

For the same reasons, I decided that it would be unwise to confide in Major Marryot when I saw him. I could not rely on his discretion. Besides, any civil servant knows that, when in doubt, one should if at all possible let sleeping dogs lie.

All this was true. Indeed, it was more than true — it was prudent as well. But all this was also a cloak concealing another, deeper truth: that there was some intrigue afoot involving the Wintours; and I did not want to commit myself to any irrevocable action until I knew more about its nature.

I was a civil servant, loyal to my office and to the Crown. But I was also a man of flesh and blood and heart. I had grown attached to the Wintours, to all four of them, though in very different ways. I did not wish to cause them unnecessary pain or difficulty, for they had enough of both to contend with as it was.

It amounted, I supposed, to a question of loyalties; and I tried scrupulously to weigh out the portions, so that each loyalty I owed received its due measure.

Despite his wounds, despite the privations he had suffered after Saratoga, despite his consumption of rumbo, Captain Wintour recovered with a rapidity that amazed his doctor and his nurses. Within three days the fever had subsided and the wound in his shoulder was no longer oozing pus. He was very weak, however, and spent much of the time sleeping.

His mother was allowed to see him. She brought him arrowroot jelly and, perching like a little bird on his bed, fed it to him with her own hand. I had never seen her look so happy or act so vigorously. It was as if she gained strength from his weakness.

As he grew better, Wintour's temper soured. I understood him better now. I knew that inaction wearied him. He had no taste for reading. He fretted at his confinement.

I fell into the habit of looking in on him — after dinner if I dined at Warren Street or sometimes in the evening. He wanted to hear what they were saying in Headquarters, what the gossip was in the coffee houses, what people were doing on the street, who had come and gone in the city. Strange to say, an unexpected intimacy developed between us.

Sometimes we played at cards, draughts or backgammon. After the evening before Christmas, I had made a private vow never to play with him again. But Wintour was different now, and perhaps I was too.

We played for pennies instead of guineas. The regimen of the sickroom prevented him from drinking more than a few glasses of wine a day. As a result, his head was clearer and he revealed himself to have a fine talent for calculating the odds. I lost more than I won.

For a week or so of his convalescence, Wintour remained in his own chamber. For the first time I saw the room by daylight. To the right of the fireplace hung a small and clumsily executed portrait of two boys, one in a green coat and the other wearing blue. I suspected it was the work of a colonial artist. The lads were about ten years old. Behind them was a backdrop painted to resemble a rather cluttered ruin from classical antiquity, complete with broken pillars, crumbling walls and headless marble statues. The boy in green was of European descent. His eyes were strikingly large and he gazed out of the past with a winning smile. But the boy in blue had a face with a dusky African hue, though his features were regular, even handsome. He stared at his companion but he was not smiling. Around his neck was a silver collar.

Wintour noticed me looking at the picture. He paused in shuffling the cards. "Do you find me much changed?"

"I beg your pardon — ah, I see. That is you in the green coat, I apprehend?"

"Yes. My mother commissioned it. It was a tiresome business indeed, being painted. My best suit of clothes, and having to stand still for hours."

"And the negro?"

"My slave Juvenal. We did everything together for a while — he shared my lessons and my sports. I believe he was a better scholar than my tutor by the end of it."

"You mentioned his name when you were ill," I said.

"Did I?" Wintour slid card after card across the table. "I talked a deal of nonsense, I'm sure."

"What happened to him?"

"Juvenal? He died. Now pick up your hand, sir, and I shall give you your revenge."

We played out another game of picquet, which he won.

"By the way, sir," he said afterwards. "How is my wife?"

The question startled me. For an instant I even wondered if it was an oblique accusation of some improper intimacy on my behalf.

"I have seen very little of her in the last week, sir," I said. "I believe she has the headache and keeps to her room."

Wintour gathered the cards together. "She is never well nowadays," he said.

As I came out of Wintour's chamber that afternoon, I found Noak on the landing. He was emerging from the sitting room set aside for the ladies, though Mrs Arabella was the only person who used it much.

I was surprised to see him there. He was a familiar figure in the library and I sometimes encountered him in the drawing room reading to Mrs Wintour. But I had never seen him on this floor of the house, which was frequented only by the family and myself.

He bowed to me. I wished him good-day.

"The Judge sent me to fetch a book from Mrs Arabella." He spread his hands wide, showing they were empty. "But she is nowhere to be seen."

"Perhaps I have seen it — what is the book?"

"A volume of *The Spectator*, sir."

"I will mention it to Mrs Arabella when I see her. Which one?"

"The third."

Noak thanked me and followed me downstairs.

At supper that night, I turned the conversation to Mr Noak.

"He is so obliging," Judge Wintour said. "I was saying this afternoon that I wanted diversion and nothing would satisfy him but I should have a particular volume of *The Spectator* with a most diverting specimen on clubs. He turned the house upside down for it and was mortified he could not find it."

The fact remained, I thought, that Noak had been in the ladies' sitting room when it was empty. And now it seemed that the reason he had given for being there had been manufactured by himself.

I took a walnut from the bowl before me. "Captain Wintour showed me the portrait of himself as a boy, sir."

"The one in his chamber?" The Judge passed me the nutcrackers. "A man from Philadelphia did it. A considerable expense, but Mrs Wintour wanted the best. John insisted that Juvenal be in it too."

"The slave boy?"

"Yes — they were never out of each other's company in those days. Always up to some mischief or another."

The nut exploded, and fragments of shell scattered across the table. "What happened to him?"

"Juvenal?" The cheerfulness ebbed from Mr Wintour's face. "It was a sad business. John left him at Mount George with Bella and Mr Froude when he went away to the war. And he went to the bad. Infected by the poisonous spirit of these revolutionary times? Bad blood coming out? I don't know. You never know what is passing in their heads, do you? Negros, I mean. Even the best of them."

He motioned to Josiah with his finger. The old servant leaned forward and refilled my glass.

"Yes," the Judge went on. "First he decamped, taking money — and this in a most dangerous time of the war, mark you, leaving his mistress and her old father quite alone with only a few servants, and the country around them full of disaffected rebel soldiers. And Bella was in poor health at the time as well."

He drank more wine.

"And that wasn't the worst of it, sir. To compound his disloyalty, the rogue came back in the dead of night. He had robbery in mind, no doubt, and perhaps revenge for some fancied slight. God knows what — he had nothing but kindness from us. And then —"

He broke off, his face working with emotion.

"Sir, you must not distress yourself. I —"

"And then the black devil murdered poor Froude. I believe he would have murdered poor Bella herself, given half a chance. But thank God! Miriam shot him."

266

"Forgive me, sir — I should not have touched on so painful a memory. I had no idea."

He waved away my apologies. "How could you know? We must be grateful that Bella at least was saved. We live in terrible times, do we not? But pray keep this to yourself, sir — we do not care to have the details widely known."

When I went upstairs to bed that night, I heard movement in the ladies' sitting room. It was too late for me to enquire about the volume of *The Spectator*, which I was minded to do to test the truth of Noak's story. Nevertheless, I paused for a moment on the landing.

A woman was weeping on the other side of the door.

CHAPTER
FORTY-TWO

Towards the end of May, Mr Townley took a pleasure party to Long Island for the races and invited me to join them. We crossed the river by the ferry to Brooklyn, where hired horses were waiting for us.

A stream of coaches, riders and foot-passengers travelled eastwards to the extensive heathlands where the race meeting was held. Everyone was in a holiday mood that day. Sedan chairs bobbed among the throng. There were half a dozen in our party, and we were more than a little merry, like boys released from school.

It was curious to think that a few miles to the north the prison hulks with their grim cargo below decks rotted in Wallabout Bay, while the eastern section of Long Island was a great stretch of ravaged territory constantly harried by the raids of rebel whaleboats from Connecticut. But God knows it was often like this in New York — the gayest diversions and the luxurious habits of peace lived side by side with the darkest consequences of war.

A great crowd had assembled on an area of the heath called Ascot after its rather better-established English equivalent. A temporary town of tents, booths and stalls had mushroomed around the racetrack. All ranks of society rubbed shoulders in the throng.

As we were riding along the lane to the concourse, I heard the raucous screech of a trumpet intermingled with the beating of a drum. Gradually we drew closer to the source of the sounds — a little man in a blue coat encrusted with tarnished gold lace. He had lost his left leg below the knee and wore a wooden substitute. Despite this handicap, he moved with ungainly speed among the press with the help of a crutch that served as much a weapon to clear the way as a support. A small drum was attached to his neck with a leather strap. When he was not blowing the trumpet, he used the instrument as a stick to beat the drum.

Beside him strode an enormous figure swathed in a super-structure with canvas curtains that swayed from side to side as they moved along the road. At some point in its history the canvas had been daubed with stripes, approximately red and approximately vertical, by someone with inadequate supplies of both paint and skill. The curtains hung down almost to the ground. Apart from his bare, pale calves and shoes, the man within was entirely concealed from view.

As our party overtook them, the man in the blue coat tucked his trumpet under his arm and doffed his broad-brimmed hat.

"At your service, your honours," he cried. "The finest dramatic entertainment you'll see outside Drury Lane."

Townley bared his teeth. "If you don't get out of our way, I'll have you thrown in the Provost for obstructing the King's highway."

The man cackled as if Townley had made a joke. But he and his companion flattened themselves against the hedge at the side of the road. As we passed, I glimpsed the white, sweating face of the second man, framed by the rectangle of the theatre he carried on his shoulders. He stared open-mouthed at us with melancholy brown eyes as if we were the spectacle and he the audience.

We reached the racetrack shortly after ten o'clock. Townley guided us towards a refreshment tent with a striped awning. His servant took our horses. We found a table and sat down to quench our thirst.

The conversation was almost exclusively about the relative merits of the horses that would be racing that day. I did not play much part in this, for I was not a gambling man and had little knowledge of the sport. But there was plenty to occupy my attention in the holiday crowd that ebbed and flowed about our tent.

It so happened that the showmen we had encountered on the road settled themselves within sight of us. The man inside the tent set it down on the ground and mopped his brow. His broad face glistened like a harvest moon. He was no taller than his colleague but almost twice as broad. As well as the travelling booth, he had carried a large box attached to his shoulder, which he now set carefully on the ground. He tied up the top flap at the front. Soon the complete puppet theatre was revealed. He opened the box and, one by one, laid out the marionettes on the grass.

An audience gathered in front of them. But the one-legged man made sure to keep a clear avenue between the miniature stage and the refreshment tent where we sat.

All the while, he beat his drum and blew his trumpet. "The tragic history of Punch and Joan," he shouted when he tired of the trumpet. "Complete with the Devil and the Executioner!"

Townley glanced irritably in their direction. "Why do they make such a damned racket?" He summoned the waiter and indicated the puppet theatre. "Move them away, would you. I can't hear myself think."

The waiter began to demur but the manager of the establishment, who knew Townley's identity, hurried over and soon arranged matters to his patron's satisfaction. The puppeteers moved away.

We did not have long to wait. The races began at eleven o'clock. There were four that day, all of which consisted of gentlemen riding their own horses. I am no judge of horseflesh but I put ten shillings to win on a horse in the third race. I chose a bay with a blaze on his nose for no better reason than that my father had had a horse with similar markings when I was a boy.

It was not the favourite — the odds quoted to me were seven to one. There were twelve horses in the race, with a purse of thirty guineas and an elegant saddle worth another twenty for the winner. Fool's luck was with me and the horse romped home by a length and a half. I was the only one of our party to win anything.

We dined at the racetrack and then rode back to Brooklyn. Near the ferry stood a big tavern built of stone, which was an uncommon material in this locality. The establishment's fish suppers were famous and Townley's servant had commanded a table for us.

It was the middle of the evening by the time we had finished. The ferry back to the city was not due to leave for another three-quarters of an hour. It had grown intolerably stuffy in the parlour. I left my companions drinking toasts and went out to take the air.

The village was packed with holiday-makers returning from the heath. Many were drunk, some to the point of insensibility, and the merriment had grown wilder and in some cases more vicious in character.

Among the throng was the booth of the puppet theatre. The marionettes were engaged in a frenzy of activity. The one-legged man was encouraging his audience to give generously and promising them a rare jest in return. A tall, thin man was lying on the ground immediately below the booth. He was snoring loudly. I wandered closer.

"Trouble with Mrs Joan," the one-legged man was saying in a hoarse, confidential tone, "is that she needs to piss at the most inconvenient moments." His voice rose to a squeak that was intended to pass as ladylike. "It's not very genteel, is it? Mr Punch ain't pleased."

On the tiny stage, Punch was belabouring Joan with his stick and saying, in his peculiar voice, that he hoped the devil would take her away to the place where she belonged for her shameful impudence. Joan pleaded necessity and at last turned her back on the audience, bent over and lifted her skirts. I glimpsed part of a small leather pipe. A thin stream of water spurted out with surprising force, some of it spattering the leg of the sleeping man. The closest spectators jumped back to avoid being splashed, some holding their noses. A howl of mirth arose. The drunk stirred for a moment and then lay still.

The one-legged man hopped up and down in excitement.

"I do hope that Mrs Joan can control her bowels!" cried the concealed performer, still in his confidential character. "Otherwise I may be obliged to faint!"

At that moment the crowd shifted in front of me and, for the first time, I had a clear view of the victim's face. He had lost his hat and wig. He had a week's growth of beard. It was the colour of rust with a few streaks of grey.

The snoring stopped. The man opened his eyes. He stared up at the booth towering over him and at the ring of faces staring down at him.

In that instant, I recognized him.

"Stop," I shouted. I stepped forward and laid my hand on the shoulder of the one-legged man. "That's enough. Move away."

He stared up at me, baring his teeth. "Why should I?"

The spectators hissed and one of them pushed me. The drunk wriggled away from the booth and into a sitting position.

"Because if you do I shall make it more than worth your while," I said. "And if you don't I shall summon my friend Mr Townley, the Deputy Superintendent of Police, and have you committed to the Provost. I've just been supping with him in the tavern. You know Mr Townley. He's already had cause to send you about your business today."

The hissing was quieter now. The drunk tried to stand but fell back with a groan and rubbed his right arm.

The one-legged man's eyes moved to and fro. "Worth our while?" he said.

I lowered my voice so he alone could hear. "Five shillings. Or the police and the Provost. Which is it to be?"

"Let's see your money, sir."

I took out a handful of silver. He made as if to take it. I closed my fingers over the coins.

"Well?" I said.

He nodded. "Well enough."

The crowd was dissolving. I dropped the coins into the showman's hand. He looked up at me and shrugged, his scorn no less obvious for being mute. His companion was already laying the puppets in their box.

I turned back to the man on the ground. He and I were alone now. Frowning, he stared at me.

"Get up, Corporal Grantford," I said.

Grantford was waiting for me when I arrived at my office the following morning.

He was a very different man from the one I had encountered yesterday evening in Brooklyn. He was dressed in a suit of black clothes — faded and shiny with age, but neat and clean. He wore a scruffy wig, a little too small for him. He was freshly shaved, and the smooth skin of his cheeks showed the angry burn of the razor. He stood just inside the door of the anteroom, upright as a post and not much fatter. His right arm was in a sling.

I unlocked the door of the private room and beckoned him to follow me inside. I sat down at the table and looked up at him. Despite his debauches yesterday he appeared perfectly sober. His countenance did not betray the marks of a habitual drinker.

"I wasn't sure you would come," I said.

He did not speak. Yesterday evening I had given him a few shillings and told him to come to my office in the morning. But I thought it possible that he would drink the money away.

"The last time you were in this room, you were a corporal in the Twenty-third," I said. "Now it seems you are not. What happened?"

"Invalided out, your honour." He touched his right arm. "Honourable discharge."

"A wound, I apprehend?"

"Musket ball in the arm, sir. Not long after I saw you here."

"Why were you discharged?" I asked. "Hasn't it healed?"

"Yes, sir, but it's not right. The arm don't have the movement any more." He demonstrated his inability to raise the arm above his shoulder or to flex it rapidly or to swivel from side to side. "I can fire a musket as straight as the next man but I can't do the arms drill. Can't salute an officer."

The story emerged in fits and starts, with much prodding from me, for Grantford was a Northerner and did not talk easily to strangers, even to well-disposed ones. In March he had been on patrol in the Debatable Ground and had been hit by rebel snipers as they were withdrawing towards King's Bridge.

When the nature of Grantford's wound became apparent, his colonel had discharged him from the service and given him a testimonial. Grantford had also received a gratuity, he told me, but he had drunk half of it away and then tried to repair his fortunes at the races yesterday. This plan had ended in disaster so he had comforted himself with rum. He had been robbed of the money was left to him while he lay insensible in Brooklyn. The thief had also taken the other contents of his pockets, including his pocket knife and his testimonial.

"What will you do now?" I said.

Grantford said nothing, though his shoulders moved in the merest suspicion of a shrug. I knew as well as he that New York was full of penniless men without futures — refugees without resources, tradesmen without trades, apprentices without masters and soldiers whose wounds had cost them their livelihoods; immediately beneath this unfortunate class lay a waiting quagmire of rogues, vagabonds and beggars.

"I am in want of a porter," I said. "A trustworthy man to mind the door and run messages. Do you wish to apply for the situation?"

CHAPTER
FORTY-THREE

By the middle of June, Captain Wintour had recovered from his wound. Indeed, in some ways he was in better health than he had been before the attack on him. His convalescence forced him into something approaching sobriety, a condition that allowed the natural vigour of the man to flourish.

Once he was able to leave his bed, he took regular exercise. He and I would often walk together.

"Do you ride much in England?" he asked one day as we strolled beside the East River.

"A great deal when I was younger."

"Then let us do it tomorrow. It is excellent for the health."

So we hired hacks, former cavalry mounts a little too good to be slaughtered for their hide and hoofs, and rode north from the city. The Captain showed me the rural neighbourhoods of Manhattan. The war had left its scars on the landscape: much of the timber had been cut down for fuel; the better houses were commandeered for military use; and the countryside had been disfigured with fortifications thrown up by the army's engineers.

Nevertheless, there was much to enjoy — the pretty farms and lanes, the elegant demesnes of the gentry, the orchards, the great tidal rivers and the clean, fresh air. For the first time I understood why its inhabitants were attached to this country, despite its remoteness from civilization and the savages on its borders, despite the primitive conditions and the extremes of temperature in summer and winter: so attached that they would fight for it.

I enjoyed the exercise and I found that the better I knew my companion, the more I liked him. When I first made Jack Wintour's acquaintance, his wounds had made him peevish; and excessive drinking had coarsened his sensibilities and even brought out a streak of viciousness. Now I glimpsed the man as nature intended him — no scholar, certainly, but manly and affectionate. He was honest, too — he had not forgotten the seventy guineas he owed me after our disastrous encounter at backgammon. At the time I had privately mocked his willingness to think himself as safe as the Bank of England. I did not mock him now. I might not get my money in the end but it would not be the fault of his intentions if that were the case.

One day, as we were riding down Bowery Lane back to the city, Wintour asked if I remembered when he had a fever. I said yes, I did.

"Do you recall what I talked about?"

"You said a great deal about Mount George, I remember."

"Yes — I thought I had. I had such strange dreams about the place." He fell silent for twenty yards or so.

Then he burst out: "I shall go there, you know. I have talked to Governor Franklin again. He has networks of informers in the Debatable Ground and knows everything that happens."

"Will it not be dangerous?"

He glanced at me. "I shall take precautions. But pray don't mention this to my father yet. I don't wish to agitate him before it is necessary."

We rode on in silence. I foresaw difficulties ahead if Wintour allied his interests too closely to those of William Franklin. Franklin, the Governor of New Jersey, had suffered much for his loyalty. He and his father, the notorious Benjamin, were now bitter enemies. The son had become the *de facto* leader of the refugees in New York. Suffering had made him implacable in his hatreds. Mr Rampton thought him a dangerous man because he would never compromise with the rebels.

But Wintour would take no guidance from me. A shock to the body sometimes brings a shock to the mind in its train, jolting it from one habit of thought to another. Or perhaps the long hours in bed had given him time for reflection. Whatever the reason, he was now a man who knew what he wanted to do.

In all our walks and rides, in all our conversations, Wintour did not once mention either the slave Juvenal or the box of curiosities.

At the beginning of July, Major Marryot called my office. This was unusual — in the general way of things I visited him at Headquarters. Grantford announced him with what in a more demonstrative man would have amounted to a flourish.

Marryot sat down in the chair I offered and fanned himself with his hat. He did not speak.

"It's always a pleasure to see you, sir," I said. "But is there a particular reason for your honouring me with a visit?"

He jerked his thumb towards the outer office. "Isn't that the corporal in the Twenty-third? The one I sent to see you?"

"Yes. He was discharged in March — honourably, with a wound — and I took him on as my porter."

"How long's he been here?"

"Nearly two months." I explained something of the circumstances that had led to his employment.

"And he gives satisfaction?"

"Entirely. He has become a sort of clerk as well as my porter."

This was no more than the truth. Grantford had some education — he had attended the grammar school in Wakefield for a year or two. He wrote letters for me on occasion and reckoned up figures.

He also guarded the door — by day and night, for he slept in the outer office. Some of the refugees who visited me became angry and even violent when their hopes were frustrated. Once when he came to my rescue, he was obliged to fell my attacker to the ground. The corporal kept a weighted stick beside his chair by day. By night it lay on the floor beside his mattress.

280

Marryot grunted. He sounded censorious. But I had the measure of the man now and I sensed that he approved of what I had done.

"Wintour," he said abruptly. "Our Captain Jack. That's why I came to see you."

"What about him?"

"He's applying for a pass to go to Mount George. I thought you'd care to know if you didn't already."

"I'm obliged, sir. Does he go alone?"

"Not sure. He's a fool if he does. But he may get an attachment to one of Franklin's militia patrols. He's saying he needs to assess the damage done to his estate. But he also claims that his tenants will give him useful intelligence so he can assess the loyalty of the neighbourhood."

"Will the pass be granted?" I asked.

"Probably. No reason not." Marryot hesitated. "There's a feeling abroad that Judge Wintour has been a little hard done by, and that granting the son's request would be an easy way of making some slight recompense."

"Denying the request would be a kinder one, perhaps."

"We shall see." He hesitated again. "I thought you should know. I — I assume that Mrs Arabella is in her husband's confidence."

He and I exchanged a glance that assumed quite the contrary. I understood that he believed Mrs Arabella should know and, if she didn't, that he wanted me to give her the hint.

CHAPTER
FORTY-FOUR

The following Monday, three days after my visit from Marryot, I looked in at Warren Street after dinner and found Mrs Arabella and Mrs Wintour in the drawing room. Mrs Wintour was fast asleep in her usual chair near the fireplace.

Mrs Arabella glanced up from her sewing at the table in the window. "My husband is out," she said quietly. "And so is the Judge."

"It doesn't matter. It's so warm and close, isn't it? My only desire at present is for some tea."

She desired me to ring the bell and, a moment later, told Miriam to bring the tea things. I stood by the open window, hoping for a current of cooling air.

Mrs Arabella still looked pale and weary — she had not fully recovered from the events of March and April — from the strain of the Captain's wound, old Mrs Wintour's illness and the smallpox inoculations. I had told her that her husband had applied for a pass to go into the Debatable Ground, and I wondered whether this too was preying on her mind.

As I stood there, waiting for her to speak, an intense tenderness swept over me. Mrs Arabella was so desolate, so vulnerable, that I wanted above all things to protect her. I wanted to protect my little Lizzie too, but that was not the same: all men who are not monsters have a natural desire to keep the young from harm even if they come from a different species from their own; and a father has a special care for his own child. What I felt for Mrs Arabella was a darker emotion altogether. To call it pity is misleading. In the alchemy of the soul, pity may be closely allied with other passions and they take sustenance from one another.

"I apprehend that Mr Townley and Mr Noak will call on Wednesday evening," she said quietly. "To discuss this projected expedition to Mount George."

For the life of me I could not understand what Townley could have to do with Captain Wintour's plan, let alone Noak.

"I'm sure they have no secrets from you, sir," she went on. "And I believe my husband will not object if I have a word with you on the subject beforehand. If you are agreeable, that is?"

"Of course, madam."

She glanced at Mrs Wintour and made a motion with her head that told me that the word was to be a private one. I stood facing her with my back to the room. She laid down her sewing.

"I'm afraid I have no right to draw you into this," she said. "It's a family matter. If it weren't so urgent I wouldn't trouble you about it."

"I hope you believe me when I say I have your best interests at heart."

She looked at her hands on her lap.

"The best interests of you all," I said hurriedly, realizing she might have read more than I intended into my words. Or, rather, more than I intended her to understand by them.

She raised her head. "My husband is set on going to Mount George."

"I know."

"But his father believes it is too dangerous and wants him to stay."

"Now he is recovered, Captain Wintour is growing restless. I believe he craves activity."

"Do you think he would go against his father's wishes?" Mrs Arabella said. "And indeed against his mother's, if she were well enough to be told what is in the wind?"

"He is very taken with the scheme."

She would not let me escape so easily. "What does that mean exactly, sir? Has he intimated to you that he definitely intends to go whatever the Judge says?"

I did not reply.

"So I infer that he has, sir," she said after a pause. "Though whether he would be able to go or not is quite another matter. The truth of it is that my husband may go to Mount George without his father's consent but he cannot go without his father's money."

This was plain speaking indeed. I knew Wintour's expedition into the Debatable Ground would lead to considerable expense. Nothing was free in New York. Everything cost money or its equivalent in kind or services — provisions, horses and of course bribes; and because of the war all prices were inflated beyond reason or need. Governor Franklin might help Captain Wintour obtain the passes and with information. But that was the limit of what he would do.

"I must be frank, I'm afraid," Mrs Arabella said. "My husband's own resources are quite exhausted at present. He is dependent on his father's generosity. But the matter is finely balanced because this is my house, and therefore my husband's, and also because the Judge loves his son and does not want to create discord between them." Her voice dropped to a whisper. "That would wound Mrs Wintour more than anything."

"The difficulty seems insoluble."

"I understand that Mr Townley has proposed a compromise. That is what he is coming to discuss."

Mrs Arabella paused. The light was behind her. I could not read her expression. For all the emotion in her voice, she might have been describing the weather or a book she had been reading.

"He has volunteered the services of his clerk," she said abruptly.

"Noak? But what can he do to help?"

"He can travel to Mount George with my husband."

"Noak?" I repeated like an idiot. "You mean Noak is to go with him?"

"Hush."

On the other side of the room, the rhythm of Mrs Wintour's breathing altered. In a moment it settled again.

"Yes," Mrs Arabella said. "Mr Townley has pointed out that Mr Noak is a prudent man — he knows something of the country for he was there as a young man; it seems his mother came from Bedford. He is a man of business, too — Mr Townley believes he would be invaluable as a secretary — he could record any intelligence they pick up on the way and also what my husband finds at Mount George. Thanks to his work with Mr Townley, he is perfectly accustomed to questioning people and weighing up what they say. And of course he would be a companion, too."

"And a nursemaid?" I said with a touch of asperity in my voice, for I felt sorry for Captain Wintour. "A keeper?"

Mrs Arabella gazed at me. Then she gave a most unlady-like snort. An instant later I understood that she was laughing at me.

"I do not think it will answer." I was mortified. "I'm surprised Mr Townley ever suggested it. For a start, the arrangement would surely inconvenience him."

"Yes, it's strange, I agree." She hesitated again. "But he has been a good friend to us lately and, besides, the plan has its merits."

"How so?"

"It would soothe at least some of the Judge's fears. And my husband might indeed benefit from a companion."

"If that's true, ma'am, I think he will choose his own."

"Exactly so, sir. How well you know him." She leaned forward and actually touched my arm with her hand. "Which is why it is you who should go with him if anyone does. Would you do it, sir? For my sake if not for his?"

CHAPTER
FORTY-FIVE

The next day, Tuesday, I went for a walk. I left the office shortly after the firing of the noon gun at the Battery. I told Grantford I would be back the following day at my usual time. I took a small pack with me and equipped myself with biscuits, a piece of cheese and a flask of water.

When I set out I did not have a particular destination in view. I merely wanted an opportunity to think. Even as a boy, I found that the gentle monotony of walking not only calmed my mind but also lent at least the illusion of clarity to my thoughts.

It was another uncomfortably warm day. I had no very clear idea where I was going, apart from the fact that I did not want to breathe the fetid air of the city for any longer than necessary. New York's situation should have been pleasant enough. Perhaps it had been so before the war. Now, however, it was a place of noisome smells. Some arose from the mud and silt exposed at low water in the docks and slips. Others came from sewage, human and animal, that besmirched so many streets and public spaces. Cesspits and rubbish dumps overflowed. Even by the waterside, where the air was better, one never escaped the scurrying crowds and the spectacles of human misery played out in public.

I toyed with the idea of catching the ferry to Brooklyn. But this would have taken too long. Instead I walked north-west up the Bowery Lane and through the unlovely suburbs of the city, a dreary progression of low alehouses, squalid manufactories and the crowded cabins of the poor. The road was familiar to me from my rides with Captain Wintour. After a while, beyond Bunker Hill, I struck off to my right and walked down to the salt meadows sloping to the Sound north of Corlear's Hook. I had hoped that I should find a breeze from the East River here. But the meadows were full of flies and stinging insects. Two unkempt dogs chased me out of one enclosure, necessitating an undignified scramble through a drainage cut and over a paling.

I turned my footsteps inland and rambled for some miles across farmland — a prosperous and pleasing landscape, though scarred with military fortifications, old and new. I stopped to eat and drink but did not rest for long. I rarely encountered anyone, though on two occasions I was accosted by militia patrols and obliged to show my papers.

By this time my thoughts had settled and I addressed my mind to the problems before it. Should I or should I not offer to accompany Captain Wintour to Mount George?

The arguments against were powerful. It would be dangerous. Did I not owe it to Augusta and Lizzie to stay in the safety of New York? The journey would be uncomfortable and arduous. I would have to share the expenses of the expedition. Wintour could be unpredictable, and his gentlemanly notions could lead us into all sorts of unnecessary scrapes. I would also be obliged to shut up the office for at least a fortnight. What would Mr Rampton say about that?

On the other hand, I was desperate to escape the city and breathe the purer air of the country. I was jaded and needed a change. The flow of refugees up the stairs to my office had slackened of late. I had more than enough leave due to me and ample funds. Mr Rampton had often urged on me the importance of gathering first-hand intelligence, and here was a perfect way to do it. There was no reason why I should not draw on the budget of the American Department to defray at least some of the expenses. I was confident that Wintour and I would rub along well enough for a week or two. As for the dangers, I would find ways to lessen the risks. I would also demonstrate to myself that fear had not prevented me from going.

I owed something to the Wintours, I told myself, for they had made me very welcome in New York. It would be pleasant to be able to resolve the little difficulty between the Judge and his son. I even allowed myself to think that it would be pleasant to earn Mrs Arabella's gratitude. I remembered how she had touched my arm the day before. With it came the memory of the intoxicating pity I had felt for her — the pity that was so strangely like desire.

The next moment, my mind swung the other way again. The danger, I told myself, the folly of it — the proposal was absurd.

The sun was beginning to sink into the west. It was slightly cooler now. The waters of the Hudson glittered before me. I had swung north in a great loop that had taken me across the island.

With some reluctance I set off towards the city. The quickest way would have been to strike down to the Greenwich road along the shore. But I remained inland.

By and by I came to the outskirts of the city again, but by a different route from the way I had left it. This part of the town was unfamiliar to me and appeared to be inhabited by the poorer classes.

I followed a rutted lane bounded on one side by a fence in poor repair and on the other by a row of hovels. The fence ended in a gateway. Gathered in front of it, about fifty yards away from me, was a crowd of negro children. They were looking at something on the ground that was giving them a great deal of merriment.

I came closer and saw what was attracting their attention: a man had slipped and fallen into a heap of horse droppings just inside the gateway. As I watched, he scrambled to his feet and tried to frighten off his jeering tormentors, who had taken to kicking his hat about. He was a squat fellow, sallow skinned and meanly dressed, and I felt almost sorry for him. He seized the boy who had his hat and gave him a tremendous blow on the head that sent him reeling against the gatepost.

The crowd fell back. The man saw me approaching. Hat in hand, he stared open-mouthed. He had a smear of excrement on his cheek. For an instant, something passed between us, a spark of recognition. I knew I had seen him before, though I could not for the life of me think where. I could have sworn the recognition was mutual.

It was over in a flash. The man turned and ran, scattering the children.

I stared after him. The negro children sauntered away, whistling and calling. I walked up to the gateway. It led into a burying ground. On a whim, I went inside and looked about me.

The graves huddled together for company. The majority of the markers were of wood in various stages of decay. I realized from the inscriptions that most, if not all, of the occupants of the graves were negros. A few of the graves were dignified with headstones, usually provided by the slaves' owners. I wondered whether death liberated a slave at last or, even in death, he remained his master's property, just as a cow or a pig did. On the whole, I thought that flesh must remain a possession whether living or dead. Judge Wintour would know.

An elderly negro was raking the gravelled walk that bisected the cemetery. I beckoned him over. He came at once, his face anxious as if he feared a blow from my stick. He swept off his hat and, head bowed, stood before me.

"You saw that man?" I said. "The one who fell over by the gate?"

He knuckled his forehead and nodded.

"He came in here?"

The old negro nodded again.

"What was he doing?"

"Come to see a grave, master."

"Which one?"

He pointed to a spot near the fence along the lane. "New one hard by that tree."

I walked over to it. I knew at once that a child lay here. The small mound of dusty earth was barely a yard long. Someone had laid a fresh nosegay on top of it. The wooden marker was newer than its immediate neighbours but it was already beginning to weather. It bore a crude inscription burned in black, wavering characters, probably with a nail or the tip of a knife heated in the fire:

Henrietta Maria Barville

There were neither dates nor an indication of ownership. Merely the name and the nosegay.

A child's grave is not a happy place, for it implies something that runs contrary to the laws of God and the hopes of man. A child should not die before its parent: it is as if time itself has run backward.

The old negro was in his hut by the gateway. He had been watching me all the time but he pretended to be engaged in sharpening his shears on a grindstone. For the sake of politeness, I rapped on the side of the shed to attract his attention.

"That grave for Henrietta Barville. Who put the flowers on it?"

He looked at me, and I saw fear in his eyes. "Don't know, master."

292

"Was it that man? The one who fell over?"

"Maybe so."

"Did he ask you where the grave was? By name?"

He looked from side to side, as if for rescue. "Yes, sir."

"Who was this Barville girl?"

He shrugged.

"You must have a record of who lies here. Show it to me."

He shuffled over to a shelf at the back of the hut and took up a foolscap-sized volume that lay there. He brought it over to me. The covers were dusty and stained; the spine was broken.

"Show me the entry," I said.

He shook his head and shrugged his shoulders.

I understood he could not read. I took the register from him and opened it, flicking through the pages until I reached the later entries. Each entry was numbered. It contained the name of the deceased, the name of the clergyman who had read the funeral service and the name of the next of kin. Sometimes there was a note to indicate the owner of the dead slave or the address where they had died; but there was no method about this, and it was not always clear who had been a slave and who had been free. All the entries were signed by a man I presumed to be a clerk or sexton who overlooked the work of the burial ground.

In recent months there had been many deaths among the negros, for hot weather breeds disease. I found Henrietta Barville at last. She had been interred on 30 March with one of the usual clergymen in attendance.

It was the name of next of kin that caught my attention: Miriam Barville.

But the child's Christian name also set off an echo in my memory. Henrietta. That had been the name of Captain Wintour's long-dead sister, the girl who had died on her first birthday and who was still so keenly mourned by her mother.

Henrietta. Hetty-Petty.

CHAPTER
FORTY-SIX

When I returned to Warren Street in the evening of the following day, Josiah told me that his master begged me to join him and the other gentlemen in the library if I was at leisure.

I found the Judge sitting at the table with Townley beside him. The Captain stood on the hearthrug with his back to an imaginary fire. Noak stood, hands clasped in front of him, near the door. He bowed slightly as I entered and closed the door for me.

"The very man," Mr Wintour said, flexing his fingers as if the joints were aching. "Pray sit down, sir, and give us the benefit of your advice."

"Ah yes," cried Townley, smiling at me. "We may depend on you, Mr Savill, for sound sense. I'm sure Captain Wintour values your opinion too."

The Captain said nothing but he bowed to me.

"My son is determined to go to Mount George," the Judge went on. "I confess I am not entirely happy about it in my own mind. But Mr Townley has come up with a most excellent notion, that Mr Noak should accompany him. Is it not a good plan, sir? Looking at it in the round, I cannot see a single flaw to it."

"I can't deprive Mr Townley of Noak's services, sir," the Captain said, grim-faced. "Besides the journey may be uncomfortable, perhaps even hazardous at times."

"Exactly so! That's why Mr Noak should accompany you." Mr Wintour beamed at the clerk. "I know Mr Noak will prove equal to everything."

I coughed. "This is a remarkable coincidence," I said to the room at large.

The four of them looked at me.

"How so?" Townley said.

"Because I had made up my mind to talk to Captain Wintour about this myself. About his projected journey."

The Captain said to no one in particular, "I am capable of managing my own affairs, I think." He stopped. For a moment I thought he would fly into a passion. But then he added, quite calmly, "I'm going. There's nothing more to be said about the matter."

"All I wanted, sir, was to ask whether you would permit me to accompany you for at least some of the way."

"You?" said the Judge, the Captain and Townley in a ragged chorus. Only Noak was silent.

Townley took a step towards me. "Surely your position as a civilian, sir, as an official of His Majesty's Government —?"

"Permit me to explain." I turned to the Judge. "I've a great deal of leave accrued to me. I find the summer heat of the city uncomfortable, sir, and I'm persuaded that going to the country for a week or two would do me the world of good. It would be a tonic. And there's the additional advantage that it would enable me to mix business with pleasure."

"Business, sir?" Townley interrupted. "What business?"

I said nothing for a moment, time enough for him to realize that both his question and his manner were impertinent.

"I beg your pardon, sir," he went on. "I spoke out of turn."

"There's no particular secret about it," I said, addressing Mr Wintour. "My instructions from London are that I use all available means to acquire intelligence regarding the Debatable Ground."

"But we have plenty of that from any number of people," Townley said.

"Mr Rampton desires my observations to be founded where possible on direct observation." I tried to assume a grave expression, as befitting a man privy to the most profound secrets of the American Department. "And there are other reasons. But I am afraid I'm not permitted to be more explicit."

The Judge wrinkled his forehead. "My dear sir, you must realize that you would put your life in peril."

"Yes, sir, but I believe I may be able to lessen the risks if I take precautions."

Mr Wintour's frown vanished. "A military escort, perhaps?"

"I don't know the details yet." I glanced at the Captain. "I thought it best to ask your opinion of the idea first. Captain Wintour may not find my company quite convenient — pray tell me if that's the case."

He stared at me for a moment. Then: "I think it would answer very well." A smile broke across his face. "Indeed, I should like it, sir. Though you may not get much pleasure from it, I'm afraid."

Townley shook his head. "I cannot advise it. It would double the danger and —"

"You may let me decide that, sir," the Captain said. He crossed the room to his father and laid his hand on the old man's shoulder. "You'll give us your blessing, sir, I hope?"

Mr Wintour placed his own hand on top on his son's. "You always have that, my dear."

When Townley and Noak had gone, Mr Wintour sent Josiah for the last of the madeira he had laid down to celebrate the restoration of the King's authority in his American dominions.

It was another warm night and the three of us sat in the belvedere at the end of the garden. The door and the windows were open to catch the least breath of air.

The Judge's hand trembled when he raised his glass to drink His Majesty's health. Next we drank to the success of our expedition. Afterwards Mr Wintour rose unsteadily and said goodnight. He picked his way down the path to the garden door of the house.

"He is grown so old," the Captain said in an undertone. "I wish you had seen him as he was before — he has aged ten or twenty years since this damnable war began."

298

Both of us were melancholy that evening, though we strove not to show it. By now I was cursing the folly that had led me to volunteer for this excursion.

Wintour proposed a game of piquet. In one corner of the belvedere was a wicker basket containing a jumble of games. Rather than summon a servant, he drew it out himself and upended it. The contents spread over the floor — counters, boards, cards, spillikins and even a few battered toys, the relics of a distant childhood. He pawed through them.

"I passed a negro burial ground yesterday," I said in as casual a voice as I could manage. "I had not realized they generally took a surname as well. How do they get a surname if they are slaves? Do they take their owners'?"

"Sometimes, yes."

"So your house slaves have surnames?"

"Damn it, why is there not a complete pack?" He took up the handbell and rang it vigorously to summon a servant. "Yes — surnames: I suppose some of them do."

"Does Miriam?"

"I've no idea." He looked up. "Why so curious?"

I shrugged. "No reason. There's still so much I don't know about this country."

"At least you acknowledge it. There are many Englishmen who don't. I believe they have little interest in us at all. Let me give you an example. Have you ever looked up the entry for New York in the *Encyclopaedia Britannica?*"

"No."

"Then you may save yourself the trouble, sir. There isn't one. That tells us more than a thousand words, does it not?" He rose to his feet. "Where's the servant? Pray excuse me — I'll rouse them up."

He went down the steps and took the path to the house. I removed Mr Pickett's ivory die from my pocket and shook it in my hand.

An even number means we shall have a happy return; an odd number means we shall not.

I rolled the die on to the wine table. I tossed it harder than intended. It chinked against the rim of my glass and ricocheted over the edge.

Swearing under my breath, I took the candle and looked for the die. It had tumbled among the heap of games and toys. But I saw it almost at once. It had wedged itself between two spillikins. One of its edges was touching the floor. None of its faces was uppermost.

Neither odd nor even.

I stretched out my hand to pick it up. My fingers nudged the spillikins and they rolled apart. Then the miracle occurred.

One die became two dice.

I blinked. For an instant I thought that I had taken more madeira than was wise, that I was seeing double. But I was not drunk. Nor was I dizzy, despite the bending down. I picked up both dice and held them close to the candle's flame. The same size — both ivory, with delicate dots, both faded from age and use. They might have been twins.

300

Nothing strange about it, I told myself — one die is much the same as another after all; this was no more than a chance resemblance.

I heard footsteps. I dropped the dice in my pocket. Wintour walked down the path brandishing a pack of cards in triumph. Behind him came Josiah, almost at a run, bringing another bottle.

"There!" he said, entering the belvedere and dropping the cards on the table. "And I remembered pencil and paper as well." He glanced at Josiah. "Open the wine and tidy away this mess." He threw himself into his chair. "It's Barville, by the way."

"I beg your pardon?"

He laughed at my confusion. "Had you forgotten already? You were asking about slaves' surnames. Josiah says Miriam's is Barville."

CHAPTER
FORTY-SEVEN

Three weeks later to the day our party clattered across King's Bridge and entered the Debatable Ground. Governor Franklin had arranged for us to ride with a party of irregulars. I never knew Franklin's precise connection with them, though clearly they provided him with intelligence in return for his assistance with our military authorities; his reputation and connections lent a tincture of legitimacy to their operations.

Their leader was a man of about thirty named Piercefield. When we met him beforehand at Mr Franklin's, he had told us that the rebels had turned him out of an estate near Morristown. His mother had starved to death. His younger brother had died in prison. Some of the men he led were no more than schoolboys; others were greybeards; but all of them had claimed similar losses to their leader's and all of them burned with a desire for vengeance or perhaps profit.

"They're a wild, ill-disciplined crew," Wintour said before he introduced me to them. "But they know what they are about and, unless we meet a considerable force of enemy militia, we should be able to go where we please."

He and I had each brought a servant. The Captain had his father's footman, Abraham, a sturdy young man who could ride and handle a gun. His loyalty, Wintour said, was beyond question.

My servant was Corporal Grantford, who had offered to accompany me as soon as he heard of the projected expedition. Indeed, I think he would never have forgiven me if I had not agreed to take him. His wound might incapacitate him on a parade ground or in a line of battle, but it would make little odds to us now. He was not only an experienced soldier but he knew at least something of the terrain through which we must pass.

Once King's Bridge, Harlem Creek and the guns of Fort Charles lay behind us, the mood of our companions became sombre. Until now, on the fifteen-mile ride from New York to King's Bridge, they had behaved almost as a party of holiday-makers and insisted that we stop at every wayside tavern.

As we rode north, the country soon became less densely settled than on Manhattan island. It seemed wild and neglected to my untutored eyes. We saw few of its inhabitants, and those we saw gave us a wide berth.

The highway was in poor repair. The forest encroached on the road. My companions glanced from left to right, trying in vain to penetrate those green depths. After the racket of the city, it was strange and uncomfortable to hear only the sound of our horses' hooves and the jingle of harness. Occasionally an invisible bird would burst into song but then the deadening silence would shut its mouth.

Piercefield pulled up on the verge and waited until we came to him. He was a short, stout man who sprayed spittle at you when he talked.

"Nothing hereabouts for us, gentlemen," he said in his unnervingly high-pitched voice. "The country's picked clean for miles around. But give us a day or two and we'll find something worth having."

"How much further today?" Wintour asked him.

"Ten or twelve miles. There's a farm I know west of White Plains." He grinned at us. "Used to belong to a good Tory but they forced him to flee and turned his wife and children out of doors. There's one of the Upper Party there now."

That's what they called them in the Debatable Ground — the Loyalists formed the Lower Party, the rebel Americans were the Upper.

We soon left the high road. Sometimes we rode along lanes, sometimes across country. We passed within sight of several farms and other isolated homesteads. By the time we reached our destination, it was early evening. Piercefield led us to a clearing in a nearby wood, sheltered with rocks on three sides. He and his men left our party here with instructions not to light a fire until their return.

Nearly four hours passed. The heat and the insects oppressed us terribly. Once we heard shots. We sent Abraham to the edge of the wood to investigate. He brought back the news that there was a fire two or three miles away on the other side of the low hill.

It was dark by the time that Piercefield and his men returned. They said they had met with less profit and more resistance at the farm than expected. They lit a fire. We ate an unsatisfactory supper of biscuit and salted meat. Wintour, Grantford, Abraham and I settled down to sleep at some distance from the main party.

During that first night I slept badly on the hard ground, finding myself constantly scratching. My limbs ached from the unaccustomed exercise. I dropped in and out of a light doze.

At some point I returned to full consciousness. My bladder was bursting. I turned my head and saw that the fire was still burning and that several men were sitting around it, drinking and talking in low voices.

I rose up quietly and made my way slowly into the bushes to relieve myself. There was a moon, though its light was partly obscured by shreds of clouds and by the branches of trees. I stumbled over an object on the ground and almost fell.

I heard a moan at my feet. I bent down. Something pale and insubstantial moved in the gloom, reminding me quite inconsequentially of the merman I had seen in the grey-green waters of New York harbour on my first morning.

But it wasn't a merman. It hadn't been a merman in the water and it wasn't a merman now.

The moon slipped out of the shadows. I saw a man lying spreadeagled on his back. His arms and legs had been lashed to saplings. I saw the twitching whites of his eyes. The lower part of his face was obscured by a rag or cloth. He moaned again. I guessed that the cloth had been used to secure a gag.

There were footsteps behind me. I turned sharply.

Piercefield giggled. "'Tis the fortunes of war, sir," he said. "In the Debatable Ground we must take our profit where we can."

"Who is he?"

"A damned Whig and a snivelling Presbyterian as well. He has a farm on the other side of the ridge. I know he has gold hidden." Piercefield nudged the man on the ground with his boot and added hastily: "As well as useful intelligence on the enemy's movements hereabouts. He will tell us all, by and by."

The following morning I took Grantford into my confidence as we rode along and asked him what he thought of our travelling companions. He turned his head away from me and spat out a mouthful of tobacco juice.

"Is that your answer?" I said.

He lowered his voice. "No better than brigands, your honour. I heard them talking last night. You know that farm?"

"The one they attacked?"

"They trapped a couple of labourers in a barn and set fire to it."

"They killed them?"

Grantford nodded. "They believed so. Don't even know who the farm belongs to."

"Mr Piercefield said it used to be a Tory's but there's a Whig there now."

"That's all gammon, sir. They don't know who the man was. They don't much care, neither."

"And the man they held prisoner last night?"

"He was dead this morning. If I was your honour I'd —"

"You're not me," I said.

We dined on the road in a tavern that no longer had a sign, to avoid the taxes. To judge by the size of it, it must have been a prosperous establishment before the war. The landlord scurried back and forth white-faced, bringing us whatever he could. There were women and children about the place — a sewing basket with a shawl over it stood in the corner of the parlour and a doll lay under a chair — but we saw nothing of them. Piercefield did not offer payment and the landlord did not ask for it.

Afterwards I rode with Wintour. He had drunk too much brandy the previous evening and had been morose all day.

"I don't trust these men," I murmured. "I think we should separate from them."

"What? Why?"

"They are thieves and rogues." I told him what I had observed and what Grantford had said.

"My head aches." He looked at me and rubbed his red-rimmed eyes. "I don't deny they're a little rough and ready, sir, but we're safer with them than without them."

"I disagree. Could you find our way to Mount George without them?"

"Of course I could," he said. "I know this country as well as my own chamber."

"We would travel faster by ourselves. And more safely. These men will cheat us if they can."

"They wouldn't dare. When we got back to New York, we'd —"

"That is my point," I said. "If we stay with Piercefield, I'm not at all convinced we shall get back to New York."

CHAPTER
FORTY-EIGHT

I believe that Piercefield was almost relieved to see us go. We hampered him, I think. Since we did not ask him to return the money we had given him for escorting us, he lost nothing by our departure.

The four of us travelled on towards Mount George. We had a difficult journey, crossing thick woods and craggy hills. I was surprised how wild and desolate the country was. Despite the fact that we were so close to New York, there was often little sign of inhabitants, whether European, Negro or Indian.

We were obliged to walk as much as ride for we avoided even the smallest road if we could. Once we were shot at as we skirted a farm somewhere north of White Plains. Twice we were forced to make extensive detours to avoid detachments of rebel militia. For the first time in my life I understood what it was to be hunted. In the Debatable Ground, I learned to feel what a fox or a deer must feel with a pack of hounds on its heels.

Wintour led us without hesitation through what often seemed to me to be a trackless waste. Our expedition had invigorated him. Despite the danger and the discomfort, he was in the best of spirits.

"How I loathe and abominate a city!" he said to me one afternoon. "Give me the country any day. A man should have fresh air in his lungs."

"No doubt," I said. "And a man should also have a comfortable bed, food on his table and a complete absence of blood-sucking insects."

He roared with laughter and said that I was as droll as Mr Goldsmith, and had I ever thought of writing plays? At the time, we were leading our horses through an evil-smelling swamp where plants wrapped themselves around our ankles and the mud tried to suck the boots from our feet.

That night, which was our third since we had left New York, we camped in a derelict cabin made of logs. Once night had fallen we risked a small fire, for the place was in a hollow and sheltered by rocks. We ate as heartily as our dwindling supplies would permit.

Afterwards we sat for a while over rum and water. We toasted the King, and then each other. There was almost an air of celebration for we were, Wintour thought, within ten miles of Mount George.

The only light in the hut came from a rushlight on the earth floor between us. We were quite alone — Grantford and Abraham were lying outside, near the horses. We were tired but neither of us was sleepy. We talked idly in spurts, as men do when they are comfortable with each other.

After a silence of several minutes, Wintour said, "I suppose we are friends?"

"Indeed we are." I could make out his shape in the gloom but I could not see his face.

310

"Then I wish you'd call me Jack," he said. "We Americans are freer in such matters. All my friends call me Jack."

"Then I shall do so with pleasure. And you must call me Edward."

There was another silence. I suppose he and I had been friends of a sort hitherto. But shared danger turns men into comrades. Either that, or it makes them mortal enemies instead.

Then he surprised me. "Do you miss her?" he said. "Your wife, I mean. It must be above a year since you saw her."

"Yes," I said without enthusiasm. "I suppose it is."

"You sound as though you don't much care for her."

It was as if we were a pair of Papists in the confessional. Rum and tiredness, danger and darkness, had combined to dissolve my habitual discretion.

"She's the mother of our daughter," I said. "That's a great deal."

"Yes, but did you ever love her?"

"Yes — well, in a manner of speaking. I wanted a wife. And she . . . she was suitable in every way."

"Suitable." Wintour passed me the rum. "Ah — old Rampton's niece?"

"Just so." I hesitated. "Mr Rampton has no children of his own." I drank. "But she married me without his permission. And afterwards I discovered that he never liked her above half. I cannot altogether blame him, either — my wife is a foolish woman and not easy to live with."

311

There: the truth was out, a truth I had barely admitted even to myself. I had married Augusta because a man must have a wife and because I had believed the match would advance my career in the American Department. She had married me because she had thought me agreeable and ambitious, a man whom she could mould to the shape of her desires with the help of her family connections. She had seen a glittering future for me as an under secretary in the administration and for herself as my wife. She had dreamed of a salon where she would entertain the rich and powerful who would flock to admire her. She had even dreamed of a knighthood for me and seen herself as Lady Savill.

They had been the worst of reasons for marriage and they had rebounded on our own heads. As a result, here I was in the Debatable Ground in the middle of a war on the other side of the world. I had a wife in name but not in fact and a daughter I had not seen for more than a year. And now, as my posting was extended again and again, I had become convinced that Mr Rampton had sent me to New York to get rid of me, and perhaps to punish me for my temerity. If anyone was a fool, it was I.

"Forgive me," Wintour said. "I didn't mean to pry. I wonder you haven't found consolation. There are plenty of fine women in New York who —"

"No," I said. "I don't wish for that. You must think me a sad prig."

"No. Merely mysterious. Like the Sphinx."

The rushlight flickered and died. The warm darkness smothered us.

"We all make mistakes," he went on in a rush, as if anxious to get the words out before he could change his mind. "I married Bella because she was Froude's heir. But it hasn't answered, has it, not for either of us. I didn't realize that finally until I came back from Canada."

I said nothing. I wondered what Wintour meant. Was it that he did not love his wife, or was it that he was disappointed in her fortune, because of the war? I remembered the violence he had offered her in March, just before the attack on him that had led to his fever: I believed he had hit her at least once in the garden; and he had been in such a drunken passion that he would have hit her again, had I not been on hand to prevent it.

"I know men desire her," he said in a voice so quiet I could hardly make out the words. "I see it in their eyes. Townley. Marryot." He paused, and I sensed he had turned his head towards me. I held my breath, waiting for him to add my name to the list. "They are like hounds with their tongues hanging out. But she's my wife. She would never be unfaithful. And who knows? The game's not over. It all depends what happens at Mount George."

I waited but he did not explain his meaning. Was it something to do with the box of curiosities, whatever and wherever that was? Would it somehow mend his marriage? I opened my mouth to put the question direct. Before I could speak, I heard him yawn in the

313

warm darkness and a rustling as though he were changing his position.

"I believe I shall sleep now," he said. "Goodnight, Edward."

"Goodnight, Jack," I said.

CHAPTER
FORTY-NINE

Next morning, we left our refuge shortly before dawn. We followed the slope of the land down to a small river which, Wintour told me, eventually found its way into the Hudson. We journeyed upstream for several hours.

Most of the time we were on foot, leading the unwilling horses. It was difficult going, for the river ran through a ravine, a place of green shadows between steep, densely wooded slopes where a regiment of marksmen could have lain in ambush without any danger of our noticing them.

Suddenly the ravine bellied out into a broad bowl of land that had been cleared of most of its trees. The river swelled into a pond thick with reeds. On the far side of the water, the land stretched away to the north.

There, half a mile away, where the ground began to rise, was an irregular line of what looked like blackened stumps.

"Mount George," Wintour said. And then he laughed.

The words were hardly out of his mouth when Grantford dropped his horse's reins and plunged into the bushes. In a moment he was out of sight.

Wintour wheeled round, snatching his pistol from the saddle holster. There was a flurry of violent movement and snapping branches. Grantford swore. I heard a high shriek. The corporal reappeared, pushing in front of him a girl in a ragged brown gown. He had gripped her by the forearms and was holding her as far away from him as he could.

"Little vixen, your honours," he said to us. "She bit me."

The child was about twelve years of age and painfully thin. Her dark hair was loose and as ragged as her gown. She twisted violently in Grantford's grasp. He lifted her an inch off the ground and shook her as if to shake the nonsense out of her.

"Well?" Wintour demanded. "What are you doing here?"

The girl said nothing.

"Fishing, I reckon," Grantford said. "There's a basket in the bushes and a couple of lines."

"Fishing? A girl?"

"Why not?" she said suddenly. "There's no one else to do it."

"What's your name?" I asked.

She glanced with a frown in my direction, as if surprised by the sound of an English accent. "Mehitabel," she said. "Mehitabel Tippet."

"Tippet?" Wintour said. "There was a tenant of that name at Grove Farm before the war."

"My father, sir."

"Where is he now?"

The child swallowed. "Dead, sir."

"How, child?"

"The militia men shot him when he tried to leave for New York. One of the patrols fired on him."

"And your mother?"

"Over there." She pointed into the bushes. "On the other side of the road from Squire Froude's. There's a bit of King's land. Except they say it's Congress's now."

"So you're not at Grove Farm?"

"Oh no, sir, not for over a twelve-month. They turned us out of there."

Wintour drew me aside. He wanted to see Mrs Tippet and asked whether I thought it would be prudent.

"She may have information," I said. "But can you trust her?"

"Of course I can," he said imperiously. "She's one of our people."

"Not one of mine," Grantford muttered, the words hardly audible because he was sucking his wound to stop the bleeding.

"Hold your tongue," Wintour said. "And put the girl up on your horse. Abraham, fetch her basket. We'll go and see her mother."

We led our horses through the scrubby copse to the road, which was scarcely more than a track of rutted, sun-dried mud. The wasteland stretched for a mile or so on the other side, a place of bushes, long, coarse grass, stones and brackish pools. The ground was lower here and poorly drained.

The Tippets' cabin was even meaner than the hut where we had spent the previous night. It was windowless and built of untrimmed logs.

The mother had clearly been watching for her daughter. She came out of the cabin when we were still fifty yards away. She gathered up her gown and ran towards us. I saw her anxious face and knew she feared the worse.

"Madam," I said, raising my hat. "We mean you and your daughter no harm."

"Dear God." Wintour stared at her. "Mrs Tippet. I remember you now."

She frowned at him. "Do I know you, sir?" Her voice was cultivated, unlike her appearance.

"Of course. Mr Froude brought me to Grove Farm on several occasions. I'm Miss Bella's husband — Captain Wintour. Look here, ma'am, I'm truly sorry to hear about Mr Tippet."

She burst into tears. Mehitabel clung to her mother, half comforting her and half desiring comfort herself. Mrs Tippet patted her and began to cough and sway on her feet.

"Madam, pray take my arm," Wintour said. "I'm afraid we have startled you by coming upon you so suddenly. And allow me to name my friend, Mr Savill of the American Department in London."

When she had recovered a little we walked slowly towards the hut. I told Grantford and Abraham to wait outside with the horses. Wintour and I took the mother and daughter into their home.

318

There was but a single room, no more than eight feet square. Wintour and I lingered in the doorway. The place was as clean as it was possible for it to be. Here the mother and daughter ate, sat, worked at their spinning wheels and slept together on the narrow straw mattress against one wall. They had a table, a pair of stools and a crudely made deal box of the sort that maidservants use for their possessions.

By and by, Mrs Tippet calmed herself and begged our pardon for her display of weakness. Wintour and I gradually drew out the family's story. Mr Tippet, always a staunch Tory and a churchwarden as well, would not abjure his loyalty to the King. He was fined and otherwise persecuted for his refusal to take up arms for Congress. At last he could bear it no longer. He determined to go to New York and leave the farm in the possession of his wife and son. The local militia, who took a malign pleasure in hunting Tories, intercepted him as he set off by night and found some excuse to open fire.

"They made a sport of it, sir," Mrs Tippet said. "Like boys that drown a cat to watch it squirm."

Her dead husband was considered a traitor and his possessions were therefore declared forfeit to Congress. In practice, the local Committee found ways and means to help themselves and members of their families to whatever they fancied first, from the wines in their cellar and the clothes in their presses to the best of the negros and the contents of the barns. The farm itself was assessed by the Committee at less than a tenth of its value and sold on behalf of Congress to one of the Committee members.

The Tippets' son had been forced to enlist in the army; it was either that or be imprisoned without a trial; and they had last heard of him with General Moultrie in South Carolina; but that was six months ago, and they did not know whether he was alive or dead. Since their eviction from the farm, mother and daughter had struggled to exist on their earnings from spinning and from the occasional gifts of friends, who were themselves subject to persecution if their generosity was discovered.

It was a common enough tale — I had heard variants of it from the Loyalists who came to my office with their sad histories and their impossible demands. This foolish conflict had so many victims and so few victors. Sometimes I think the Tippets and their kind, on both sides of the argument, were most to be pitied. They were the detritus of this war, perhaps of all wars.

Jack Wintour was moved to anger and almost to tears by this recital. I saw a side of him that day that I had never seen before. He had been bred to own land — the Wintours' estate on Manhattan and, after his marriage, Mount George as well. The Tippets were, or would have been, his tenants. He had an old-fashioned and almost feudal notion of his responsibilities to them which would not have seemed out of place to a country squire in Queen Anne's time.

"I never dreamed," Mrs Tippet said, "I never thought I'd see the day."

320

She fell to coughing again. Wintour glanced at me and bit his lip, his habit when he was perplexed. The girl stood in the shadows near the back of the hut and watched us all.

"We shall not be here long, ma'am," Wintour said. "It's of the utmost importance that neither you nor your daughter mention to anyone at all that you have seen us."

Still coughing, Mrs Tippet nodded.

"But when we leave we can take you and your daughter to New York with us, if you like."

I said nothing. The offer was a credit to Wintour's humanity if not to his common sense.

"Thank you, sir, and bless you," she said. "But no. We must stay here so my son can find us when he comes home." She touched her narrow chest. "And I am not well. I do not think I should be able to travel."

"We shall see you before we go. You may change your mind. And when this war is over and the country returns to its senses, we shall see you back in Grove Farm. You have my word on it, ma'am."

She shrugged almost imperceptibly as she thanked him. I think she believed there was no one this side of the grave who had it in his power to help her.

But we did share a simple meal of our biscuits and cheese with her, washed down with water from the nearby stream. The four of us sat around the table with the child and her mother perching together on the box that contained their remaining possessions. Wintour insisted that Mrs Tippet take a tot of rum afterwards, which brought a hectic colour to her cheeks.

"Why are you and Mr Savill here, sir?" she asked suddenly. "Is it not dangerous?"

"Yes," he said. "Which is why we shall not linger. We came because I desire to see Mount George. I must know what we shall face when Mrs Wintour and I return."

"Poor Miss Bella," Mrs Tippet said. "I remember when she was a girl and she would come and help us in the dairy. She would find this desolation so terrible, sir, indeed she would. And the memories too — would they not distress her? Seeing Mr Froude murdered before her eyes and the house going up in flames? Losing her baby, too." Her eyes filled with tears again. "Pray forgive me, sir. It was your child, too."

Wintour looked away. For a moment no one spoke. Mehitabel darted glances at each of us and I realized from her expression the strain the girl was under, constantly on her guard, constantly watching for danger from those around her. I picked up the flask and offered Mrs Tippet another dram. She refused.

"I suppose they took what they could from the house?" Wintour said abruptly. "Whatever the fire had left."

"Yes. There's only rubbish now, I fear."

"Is anyone still living there?"

She shook her head. "No one will go near the place." She licked thin, chapped lips. "They say it's haunted, sir, that Mr Froude walks there, looking for that slave. The one that killed him. And some people say he's there, too — that negro, I mean — he's all covered in blood, and he's still looking for Mr Froude."

Wintour stood up and went to the doorway. He looked out over the waste ground in the direction of Mount George.

He glanced over his shoulder at Mrs Tippet. "That reminds me," he said. "Where's the grave?"

"He's buried in the peach orchard, sir. Poor gentleman. My husband and son were among the ones who went back. They said a prayer over the squire but there was no clergyman, I'm afraid."

"No," Wintour said. "Not Mr Froude's grave. I mean the baby's."

CHAPTER
FIFTY

Before we rode away, I pressed three guineas into Mrs Tippet's hand. The poor woman would have to be careful how she spent them to avoid arousing the suspicion or cupidity of her neighbours.

We also left her biscuits and cheese, as well as all our little store of rum. It was the rum that gave me an indication of the strength of the obligation that Jack Wintour felt towards the family's former tenants. He was not a man who would lightly forgo the relief that spirits offered him; but in this case he did not hesitate.

We made for the ruins of Mount George itself. We reasoned that its reputation for being haunted would be some protection for us.

"But it's madness, Jack," I said quietly as we went along. "They'll raise the country against us if we're seen. Must we really go up to the house? You can see for yourself that there's no point. We should leave now."

"Tomorrow. I promise you." He looked at me and nodded, as if he saw something he was expecting in my face. "It quickens the apprehension, does it not? The plight of those poor people — the war makes animals of us all."

I nodded but said nothing. Mrs Tippet and her daughter had also quickened my apprehension of the danger we were in. I felt sick with fear, which formed a cold, hard knot in my bowels. I would have given everything I had to be back in the safety of New York.

We crossed the road and passed through a patch of dense woodland. After a mile or so we came to the other side. We had returned to the shallow valley which served as a sort of home park for the mansion itself, though we entered it at some distance beyond the pond where we had found Mehitabel Tippet.

Mount George was visible on the far slope. From this angle, a huddle of smaller buildings could be seen in a dip in the ground to one side of the house. They seemed to have escaped the worst of the fire. Some of them retained at least part of their roofs.

We did not go there directly but rode along the fringe of the wood to make the most of what cover there was. Over a similar tract of ground in England we would have been observed; but in America, even in a vicinity that had been settled for several generations, the inhabitants were still scattered very thinly over the immensity of this wild land.

Wintour led us to a stream that ran down the slope beside the house. We followed its course toward the ruins, for much of it ran through a defile that offered a modicum of cover to our approach. I could not shake off the idea that invisible eyes were watching us from the surrounding country.

I was not the only one to wish himself elsewhere. Grantford muttered to himself as we rode along, a stream of mumbled oaths I judged it best to ignore. Abraham was silent. He had a sheen of perspiration on his black face and his eyes were never still.

The defile with the stream took us along what had been the garden front of the mansion. The land was terraced here, and a sunken fence rose up on our right, making a sort of ha-ha. On the other side was a level acre or so of wasteland which must once have been the pleasure ground immediately outside the principal apartments of the house.

The picture of Mount George that hung in the drawing room at Warren Street had given me a misleading impression of both the size and solidity of the mansion. In life it was smaller than art had made it seem; and it had been built mainly of wood rather than of stone, which was why the fire had wrought such terrible damage.

Wintour glanced at it as we rode past. "It doesn't much matter," he said over his shoulder to me. "I never liked the house in any case. And it was too small as well. So this is a blessing in disguise, perhaps. God willing, we shall build it anew after the war. It shall be far more elegant and done up entirely in the modern taste."

I remembered his ramblings while the fever had been upon him, how he had promised me a suite of splendid apartments at Mount George. But he did not mention my apartments on this occasion, or the box of curiosities which, at the time of his feverish ramblings, had somehow been necessary to the fulfilment of this scheme.

We continued to follow the course of the stream. The sunken fence diminished and at last vanished. We had reached a spot beyond the ruins where, higher up the slope and partly concealed in a shallow depression, the cluster of outbuildings lay.

This, I guessed, had been the farmstead of the original settlers. The yard formed an enclosure bounded by two roofless barns, an irregular line of byres, stables and pigsties and a sturdy building with crude stone walls, stained by fire. The latter had small square windows and a central chimney of brick. There was still a tiled roof over one end.

Wintour dismounted and hitched the reins of his horse to a gatepost. He looked up at me.

"That's the house the old patroon built," he said.

"It's in better condition than the mansion."

"They knew what they were about, those Dutchmen. They built to last."

I dismounted and followed him into the building by the one central doorway, which was wide and low. The door itself lay abandoned on the ground, ripped from its hinges. It was made of oak, black with age and at least two inches thick.

On the ground floor there were two rooms, each with a fireplace served by the central chimney and each with a surround of old Delft tiles, the blues and whites still strangely vivid, though many were cracked and some were missing. Originally there had been windows and a doorway on the other side of the house, which faced the mansion itself; but the openings had been sealed with bricks, perhaps when the big house was built, so its occupants would have the comfort of not being overlooked by their farmworkers. Narrow wooden stairs, almost a ladder, led up from the kitchen to the attic where the bedchambers had been. Though the joists remained, the partitions and many of the floorboards had gone, either torn out or burned where they were.

But the most striking feature of the place was the litter of objects that covered almost every inch of the floor. It was as if a malicious angel had swept through the little house, destroying all that lay in his path with a great hammer. Wintour picked his way through the rooms, staring down at the mess beneath his feet.

Everything was broken. There was splintered glass, scraps of varnished wood and rags of cloth that might have been silk or velvet. Books lay here and there, their spines ripped apart and their yellowing pages rustling like dead leaves in the draught from the doorway. A small cast-iron furnace lay undamaged but on its side. The flue-pipe that once connected it to the chimney had been torn away and thrown to the other end of the kitchen. Fragments of brass gleamed among the debris. I saw the dial of a grandfather clock lying on the ruins of its case and its machinery. A smiling sun looked up at me.

"Dear God," I murmured. "Is this the work of looters?"

Wintour glanced at me. "It wasn't plunder they wanted, Edward. It was revenge."

"On whom?"

"Mr Froude, of course. This place was his study and his laboratory. It was his passion. He doted on it like a child." Wintour gave a harsh bark of laughter. "No — it was something dearer to him than any child ever was."

CHAPTER
FIFTY-ONE

We could not find the baby's grave.

The air was heavy with warmth and laden with the sweet, decaying stench of rotting fruit. We did not even know for certain whether we were in the right orchard — there had been three enclosures at Mount George, each for different kinds of fruit.

But Wintour thought it must have been this one, the smallest orchard, for he remembered that Arabella had loved the taste of peaches and apricots; sometimes she would order the slaves to set up an awning here against the south wall and bring out chairs, a table and even a carpet, so she might sit and read or dream with the smell of fruit in her nostrils.

We found Mr Froude easily enough. He lay in what had once been a herb bed at the base of one of the walls. Tendrils of rosemary had spread a vigorous grey web over the grave, feeding on his corruption. There was still a low mound, seven or eight feet long, to show precisely where his body lay. Someone had fashioned a crude cross from two planks nailed together and pushed it into the earth at the head of the grave. They had burned the initials HF at one end of the crosspiece and the date 1776 at the other. But over the years the nail had rusted, the wood had rotted and the planks now lay separately on the earth beneath the rosemary.

This land was so fertile that the trees were not espaliered but stood unsupported as standards. They were lank and ragged, overgrown and misshapen, for no one had troubled to prune them for two or three years. But still their branches bowed and sometimes snapped under the weight of the fruit they bore.

"Why does no one pick the fruit?" I said. "You could feed an army with it."

"Because of the ghosts, your honour," whispered Abraham, his eyelids twitching.

"Hold your tongue."

"But Mistress Tippet —"

"Superstition," I said. "Rank superstition."

The young footman shook his head, as unshakeable in his fear as I was in mine. "They eat your soul, master. My mama told me."

I took pity on him and told him to stand at the gateway to the orchard and keep watch. Corporal Grantford, unperturbed by the ghosts, was strolling among the trees and gathering fruit in his hat. Wintour was still looking for the baby's grave. I joined him, and we walked methodically over the ground, examining every square foot of it.

"November seventy-six," he said. "Damn it, that's nearly three years ago now. And a baby's body don't take much more room than a cat's, does it?" He kicked savagely at a tussock of grass. "But you'd think they'd have left a marker, wouldn't you?"

"They might have done," I said. "It could have rotted away."

We took another turn, examining the ground in silence. Mrs Tippet believed that they had buried the baby here a few days before its grandfather. But she hadn't been there herself. She had no idea where the body might lie.

"God's death, why the orchard?" Wintour burst out suddenly. "I can see why they put old Froude here after the place was sacked. But the baby died before that. So why not in the churchyard in the village? After all, my daughter was a Wintour. Half a Froude, too."

"Conditions were unsettled," I pointed out. "And the roads were probably bad at that time of year. No doubt they intended to re-inter the child later."

I wondered whether the explanation had in fact been simpler and sadder, though I said nothing of this to Jack Wintour: perhaps poor Mrs Arabella had wished to keep her child as close to her as possible.

He said no more, but paced on. When we reached the far wall of the orchard, he stopped and rested his head on the brickwork. He rapped his forehead against it, three times.

"Jack —"

He turned. I saw that tears were streaming down his cheeks.

"Pray calm yourself, my friend," I said.

I looked behind us. Abraham was in the gateway at the other end of the orchard and he had his back to us. Grantford was nearer, though he appeared to be absorbed in gathering fruit.

Wintour wiped his face with the sleeve of his coat. "What else can a man do but weep?" he said thickly. "I'm not like my father. Or even old Froude."

"What do you mean?"

"My father would talk of God's providence and the certainty of heaven — ay, and he believes it all too. And he would quote all the philosophical gentry at you, from old Socrates onwards. As for Froude, he was as cold as charity: he'd have said at least it was only a girl, and what we needed was a son and heir. But me —" He hit his chest with sudden violence. "I'm no good at thinking or talking or praying, Edward." He straightened up and added, in a much quieter voice: "I merely thought — I hoped — that there would be something of her left. Something of my daughter."

We walked a turn or two in silence.

"Come," I said after a while. "I'm hungry. And we need to decide what we are to do."

He looked at me and blinked. He was like a man waking from a dream. "Yes. I want to see what's left in the patroon's house."

"Why? Have you not seen enough already?"

He ignored the question. "And we haven't looked at the mansion yet, either."

"When are we leaving?" I asked. "Why not tonight? It would be safer, would it not? We could put ten miles between us and Mount George by dawn."

"I wonder if those thieving Whigs found the wine cellar." Wintour's voice had a rasp in it. "Froude knew what he was about in that direction at least."

"Jack, we cannot linger here."

"Why not?" He gave a shout of laughter, so loud and reckless that Grantford stared at us and even Abraham turned to see what was happening. "No one will disturb us, Edward. They're all cowards, you know. They are afraid of the ghosts."

CHAPTER
FIFTY-TWO

The mansion was barely more than a memory. The fire had gutted it, destroying most of its contents. The storms of three winters had ravaged what was left. The heat of two summers had baked the remains.

Fragments of wall rose fifteen or twenty feet into the air. Doorways linked one vacancy to another. Chimneystacks of blackened brick and stone served rooms that no longer existed. Weeds, shrubs and saplings sprouted from every cranny they could find. In a year or two, there would be no trace at all of the great house at Mount George.

We left Abraham and Grantford to mount sentry outside — indeed, I doubt we could have found any inducement to persuade Abraham to enter the place. Wintour and I picked our way through the ruins. Under our feet was a blackened litter of broken glass, china and a multitude of other objects that I could not begin to identify.

"This must be the hall, I apprehend." Wintour scraped at the rubbish with the toe of his boot. "Yes, it had a flagged floor. So here was the great parlour, with the dining room beyond, and then the library."

"Jack — we dare not spend too long here. We should go."

"Soon. A few hours, that's all."

"But there's nothing left. And it's too dangerous to stay."

He scowled at me. "I shall do as I please, sir. I'm my own master here, I think."

He led the way out of the ruin and turned towards the farmstead. After a few yards, however, he turned back.

"Forgive me," he said. "I should not have spoken like that to you."

"It doesn't matter. But we cannot stay. It is not only our own lives we put at risk. It is Grantford's and Abraham's as well."

"I know. I'm truly sorry for it but there are reasons." The argument had touched him, as I had known it would. "Give me a little more time. I beg of you."

"Why?"

He stared at me for a long moment. Then he sighed. "Soon you will know everything, Edward. I swear it. But for now will you trust me?"

We turned the horses out to graze in a small, grassy enclosure beside the larger barn. Abraham and Grantford took turn and turn about mounting guard. There was the remains of a dovecote in one corner of the yard, the top of which commanded a view not only of the immediate approach to the farmyard and the garden front of the house but also of much of the desmesne below.

By this time it was almost three o'clock in the afternoon. Wintour went back to the patroon's house and began to examine the rubbish on the floor more carefully. Meanwhile, I walked about the yard and wandered through the barns, sheds and enclosures.

Hard by the Dutchman's dwelling was another, smaller building constructed of similar materials and retaining its roof. It had only one storey. Inside was a single chamber with a brick floor sloping down to a central drain. In one corner was a wooden cover that concealed the head of a well. There were also two stone sinks and several ovens built into the side of the massive chimney. Clearly it had once been a scullery and bakehouse, built apart from the dwelling-place to lessen the risk from fire.

It was equally obvious that the building had not been used for this purpose for many years. But I noticed a number of rings had been let into the walls, some of them nearly at the level of the floor. Dusty ropes were attached to them. They caught my attention because there was little else in the room — and that in itself was unusual, for the other buildings were crowded with rubbish. Near the drain in the centre of the floor was a great iron plate. A heavy hammer had been discarded beside it, along with a pair of pincers. I speculated that a blacksmith might have worked here, though there was no evidence of that in the form of rusting horseshoes or nails.

This conundrum occupied me for several minutes. In truth I was so worried about our dangerous situation — and about Jack Wintour's erratic behaviour — that I would have seized with fervour on any distraction, however trivial.

The floor was covered with a fine, gritty dust that had probably lain undisturbed for years. It was perfectly dry for the roof was sound. An irregular patch of the dust, some of it on the iron plate, some of it immediately to one side, was slightly darker than the rest. I bent to examine it.

At that moment — and on such small events, whole countries may rise and fall, let alone the life of one man — a fly entered my mouth. Instinctively I spat it out. Along with the fly came a silver drop of my spittle, which landed on the darker section of the iron plate.

On a whim, I touched it with my forefinger and rubbed at it to expose the metal beneath the encrusted layer of dust. But the iron held no secrets. I learned only that it was free from rust and slightly indented, as though it had been hit many times by a hammer.

I straightened up and went to the doorway. I took out my handkerchief. I was about to clean my finger when I realized that, though the iron had no secrets, perhaps the dust did. My fingertip was tinted rusty-red.

Suddenly I remembered my games of backgammon with Jack Wintour in Warren Street. I remembered the splash of madeira on the board and the colour it revealed.

Blood, I thought. More blood. Always blood in this damned country, ever since I had seen Roger Pickett's body with the bloody gash in his neck.

I chided myself for allowing my imagination to run riot. No doubt it was the trace of rust on my finger.

338

Even if it were blood, there was nothing strange in that. This was a farm, after all, a place where animals lived and died.

My reason should have calmed my heart. But still my own blood thudded through my veins. I told myself my nerves were overwrought. There was nothing strange in that.

I heard running footsteps in the yard. My panic surged back. I swung to face the door, my hand groping for the pistol in my belt.

Grantford's figure filled the doorway, which was so low he had to duck.

"Sir. It's Abraham. I can't find him."

Jack Wintour was on his hands and knees, picking through the trash scattered over the floor of what must once have been the patroon's parlour.

"I shall search the barns after this," he announced, glancing towards us. "And then —"

"Abraham's gone," I interrupted.

"What?"

"He was meant to be up in the dovecote keeping watch. But when Grantford went to relieve him he wasn't there."

Grantford coughed. "Begging your pardon, your honours, but his satchel's still over there in the corner."

"But where would he go?" Wintour said.

"Perhaps he didn't want to go anywhere," I said. "Perhaps it was more that he didn't want to stay here. He was terrified of the ghosts. But if he's picked up and questioned by the enemy —"

"He'll hold his tongue," Wintour said. "He'd never betray us. Why, he's never known any other family than us."

"He's a slave," I said, suddenly angry. "Why should he owe you any loyalty, Jack? He never had any choice in the matter before. But now he has."

Wintour blinked. "Are you sure he's not somewhere about? He — he could have fallen asleep in a corner. Depend on it, that's what happened, or something like that."

"We should search for him," I said. "And if we don't find him we'll know he's gone."

Grantford suggested we look outside first. If Abraham had run away, he could not have gone far; and we might be able to see him in the relatively open terrain of the parkland surrounding the mansion.

By unspoken agreement, the three of us kept together. Once outside the farmyard we walked in the direction of the orchards. The path led us beside the outer wall of one of the yard's barns. This was supported by brick buttresses. We found Abraham between two of them.

He was lying on his side with his breeches about his ankles. It was clear that he had been interrupted in the urgent business of evacuating his bowels. The body stank for the process of evacuation had begun in life and finished in death.

I could no longer afford to be squeamish. I crouched beside him and felt for a pulse that I knew I would not find. His face was suffused with blood. I could see a single, staring eye. Around his neck was a circular contusion. There was no sign of his cutlass.

I straightened up. Grantford was scanning the countryside. Wintour looked at me without speaking.

"Strangled," I said. "With a cord, I think."

CHAPTER
FIFTY-THREE

The horses were restless. They knew something was wrong.

We carried Abraham back to the yard and laid him in a byre with a piece of sacking to cover his face. I said a short prayer for I thought no one else would do it and we owed it to him that someone should. Wintour and Grantford stood bareheaded beside me. All of us were alert for movement outside.

Afterwards the three of us lingered in the sunlit yard.

"Why should someone strangle him?" Wintour said with a touch of petulance as if he took the action as a personal affront.

"I agree — it makes no sense." I turned slightly, to include Grantford in the conversation. "Soldiers would attack us or call on us to surrender. So would militia. But this?"

"Skinners, sir?" Grantford said.

It was possible. The stealth and brutality of the attack certainly suited those predatory irregulars who infested the Debatable Ground on behalf of Congress.

"Unlikely," Wintour said. "It's not as if he can have surprised them. The killer took him unawares."

"True. It's almost as if he wanted to kill Abraham and he seized the chance when it was offered. It's as if —"

I broke off. But in my mind I followed the thought to its conclusion: it was as if the strangler desired to kill us all for some unknown reason, and was content to pick us off one by one as the opportunity arose. So now all three of us who remained had another reason to be afraid.

"We must leave," I said to Wintour. "I insist, Jack. Now."

"I need more time."

"Safer by night, your honours," Grantford said.

"Exactly!" Wintour turned towards him, delighted to have an ally of sorts. "The corporal's in the right of it. We shall —"

Three things happened at once.

Grantford grunted and flung himself on the caked earth of the farmyard.

Wintour swore.

The sound of a shot bounced to and fro among the farm buildings.

And I did nothing.

Wintour shouted: "Take his other arm."

His words broke into my stillness. We seized Grantford and dragged him towards the doorway of the patroon's house. He left behind a trail of blood pooling and puddling in the ruts.

We gained the shelter of the house and laid the corporal on the flagstone floor. His face was the colour of old wax. I knew by the amount of blood he had already lost that the bullet had probably hit an artery. He tried to speak but no words came out, only a spray of blood shot through with bubbles.

The wound was in the neck. I tore off my neckcloth and tried to stop the bleeding. It was fruitless even to try. I pressed his hand and told him he had been a good and faithful friend. I don't know whether he heard me.

It took him a minute or two to die, though it felt like as many centuries. After his soul had left his body. I stood up slowly, feeling like an old man.

Wintour had positioned himself so he could not be seen from the doorway or the windows. He was laying out his weapons. "Is he dead?" he said without looking at me.

"Yes."

"The bullet was meant for me. If I hadn't moved —"

"They mean to kill us all, I think."

We were both whispering as if our enemies were among us, invisible sprites bent on our destruction. I stared at Grantford's face, already skull-like and strangely fragile. This was my fault, I thought, I brought the man to his death.

I said, "Remember Abraham. There was no need to kill him unless they wanted to. Which suggests they mean to kill us all."

"But why?"

I ignored the question. "We must get to the horses. It's our only chance."

He let out his breath in a long sigh. "We need to divert their attention, then." He glanced at the stairs.

344

"Go up and fire a shot or two from an upper window. That'll make them keep their heads down. I'll fetch the horses."

"What if I throw something, rather than fire a shot, to see if it flushes them out? It might fool them into thinking there are others of us concealed about the yard. Then we can fire if they show themselves."

Wintour nodded. I cast around for a moment and gathered a hatful of small pieces of rubble and metal scraps from the wreckage of Froude's laboratory. I carried my missiles and my pistols up the stairs. The treads groaned under my weight and one gave way altogether. I contrived to save myself only by throwing myself forward. The hat tipped, and at least half the missiles fell to the floor below.

When I reached the upper storey, I crossed to the window embrasure on the front, walking gingerly on the joists. The opening had once been glazed but the glass was gone. Nothing was moving in the farmyard below. I had a view of the range of outbuildings facing me, and also of the dovecote and part of the scullery. But I could not see the enclosure where we had left the horses, nor the gateway that led out of the yard.

I looked down between the joists. Wintour's face was below, turned up towards me. I raised a piece of rubble to show I was ready. He nodded and lifted a pistol in a sort of salute.

Drawing a deep breath, I lobbed my missile towards the roof of an open shelter directly opposite. It smacked against the shingles near the ridge and clattered down the sloping roof. I heard it land on the caked mud of the yard.

Nothing happened. Wintour was waiting just inside the doorway. I picked up a second missile, this one a delicate tangle of brass clockwork twisted out of shape.

Before I could throw it, there was another shot and a loud hallooing, followed by the sound of hooves. I watched in horror as all four of our horses passed in a panic-stricken canter below me and disappeared in the direction of the parkland beyond the house.

The sound of hooves diminished and died away. I listened to the silence. Beneath me I heard Wintour swearing monotonously as he sifted the debris on the floor. While the horses were fleeing, he had contrived to manoeuvre the old door in front of the doorway. Now he was assembling a miniature arsenal of missiles and other makeshift weapons.

I clambered across the remains of the floor to the head of the narrow stairs. There I stopped abruptly. For the first time, as I faced down the stairs, I saw past the tapering column of the chimneystack to the attic space over the former parlour. Beyond it was the gable wall of the old farmhouse. Piercing it, directly opposite where I stood, was a window.

As I have said, the door and window openings facing the mansion had been blocked up, and by a bricklayer who knew what he was about. But this window in the gable had been left as it was; even its glass was intact.

I walked down to it and rubbed at the dusty pane of the single casement. The window looked over the roof of a former milking parlour that abutted on the parlour end of the house. It did not have a view of the mansion or indeed of anything very much except the blank wall of the byre beyond the milking parlour, which was presumably the reason that nobody had bothered to block it.

The window was large enough to permit an agile man to climb through it. The roof was little more than a yard below the level of the sill. It sloped down towards the overgrown paddock that lay between the farmyard and the kitchen wing of the house.

I scrambled back to the stairs and descended. Wintour had stopped assembling ammunition. He was standing in a brown study near the old fireplace, staring down at an object in his hand.

"Jack," I whispered. "Quickly — I believe there is another way to escape."

He looked up. "Eh? What?"

I crossed the floor, took him by the arm and pushed him back so the chimney breast afforded us some cover.

"There's an unblocked window upstairs. We can get through it and out of this house on the side away from the yard. Towards the mansion."

He blinked. "Oh — yes."

His eyes dropped back to the object in his hand. It was a piece of rubble the size of an apple. It was irregularly shaped and brownish in colour.

"What is it?" I said.

He put it in my hand. My first impression was that it was surprisingly heavy. I thought it was probably a piece of bog iron or something of that nature.

"Turn it over," he said. "Look at it."

"We have no time for —"

"Do it, Edward."

I obeyed him. The object looked much the same on the other side, apart from a small, freshly gouged scratch. I wondered whether it had been one of the missiles I had dropped from my hat when I stumbled on the stairs. Beneath the patina of grime was a faint metallic sheen. I turned it in my hand to allow the light to play upon it.

"Well?" I said.

He smiled at me and for an instant the years dropped away from his face and he looked as young and as carefree as the boy in the double portrait of himself and his slave.

"It's gold," he said.

CHAPTER
FIFTY-FOUR

Fortune smiled on us, though not for long enough.

I had achieved more than I had known with my desperate rummaging. While I was filling my hat with impromptu missiles, I had been close to a sort of alcove beyond the kitchen fireplace. This was where the iron stove had stood with its flue pipe running into the main chimney. The stove was still there, as I have said, but lying askew and on its side. In its fall, it had crushed a small wooden chest made of mahogany reinforced with brass. The wreckage had been either beneath the stove or concealed between it and the wall behind.

There was no time for questions or explanations. Wintour desired me to help him prise the stove away from what was left of the chest. With two of us and the assistance of a broken rafter as a lever, it was the work of a moment. That done, I kept watch while he picked through the remains. The chest had contained a number of drawers, some of which were lined with velvet, which he examined with particular attention.

All this time, I waited for our enemies to attack. But nothing happened. I knew they must be readying their forces. My senses were so overwrought that I fancied I heard sounds when perhaps there were none. While I listened and watched I tried to assemble a few items that might be useful to us in our flight, though I was too distracted to achieve as much as I should have done.

In another part of my mind, which the stress of the moment had goaded to a furious activity, a thought formed: *So that's Jack's box of curiosities.* A jumble of broken wood, metal and stone. Was that all? Was it for this that Abraham and Grantford had lost their lives?

At last he was done. We climbed the stairs, our eyes constantly on the doorway to the yard, and made our way down the length of the attic to the window in the gable wall. Wintour had a foolish great grin on his face. He carried a leather satchel on a strap over his shoulder.

He kept a pistol trained on the barricaded doorway below while I tried to open the window. The wood had warped and at first the casement was immovable. But it yielded to gentle pressure and opened with a screech that set my nerves fluttering like a nervous girl's.

We scrambled through it and on to the sloping roof below. From our new vantage point, we saw the blackened ruins of the mansion less than a hundred yards distant. As we moved down the roof, a lizard slid away from us with incredible speed and slipped into a crack under a shingle.

Neither of us spoke. Near the end of the roof slope, Wintour turned on his belly, wriggled over the edge and dropped feet first to the ground beneath. I imitated him but landed clumsily: off-balance, I sprawled on the ground. He pulled me to my feet. In a moment we were running across the paddock, forcing our way through the waist-high tangle of weeds and long grass.

We reached the ruins. From here we had a view across the shallow valley to the woods on the further slope. I gripped Wintour's arm and pointed. To the left — at the opposite end of the valley from the lake — a party of horsemen moved steadily towards the house. There were at least a dozen of them but they were too far away for us to see them clearly. I guessed that they were following the line of the carriage drive to the mansion. The wind was behind us so we could not hear the sound of their hooves.

"Reinforcements," I said. "Militia?"

"Or even regulars. If only we had a glass. Quick — over here."

We took temporary cover in a building beyond the servants' privies and the laundry. It faced away from the house and into a small yard of its own, which opened on to an overgrown vegetable patch. The fire had done little damage here, though the roof was tarred clapperboard and the walls no more than roughly trimmed logs with the chinks between them plugged with mud. Wintour wrinkled his nose as we went in, a tiny, unthinking expression of distaste.

It was the first time I had been inside the quarters set aside for slaves. We lingered only long enough to catch our breath and decide on our next step. It was fortunate that Wintour knew the ground so well. He took me through a back door and led me by a path that zigzagged up the slope behind the ruins. Trees and overgrown hedgerows gave us a modicum of cover. The slope grew steadily steeper and became almost a cliff. The pasture gave way to a hanger of trees and bushes just beneath the ridge of the valley.

This was a tract of virgin forest. The path petered out entirely. The trees grew closely together, many of them to a great height, their branches and roots entwining. A variety of stones, coated with lichens and mosses, were dotted among them.

Even for men on foot, the going was difficult. It would have been impossible with a horse for the woods were so cramped and crowded, and the gradient so steep. It was very quiet and gloomy. The dense green canopy of branches dropped over us like a cloak.

A terrible weariness came over me. For days on end, my faculties had been strung up to an unnatural pitch. Now, though our peril was as great as ever, they were in desperate need of rest.

"Should we not hide and wait for nightfall?" I asked.

Wintour looked back at me. "We cannot stop for a moment," he said.

"But surely, under cover of darkness —?"

"No. Soon they will have the dogs out."

We struggled on. Still in the wood, we passed over the ridge and followed the course of a stream to the bed of another valley. We crossed and recrossed the stream to confuse the scent; sometimes we waded through the water for a hundred yards or more. As we travelled up the valley, the forest gradually diminished. Our route now took us across rough pastureland studded with bushes and stunted trees.

352

We were walking towards the east. I felt the sun on my back and saw our long black shadows gliding ahead of us.

As time went on, my weariness changed its form and became a dull ache. I followed where Jack Wintour led; it was as though an invisible thread attached me to him and drew me along in his wake. I moved as if in a dream, planting one foot in front of the other while my mind floated free, as powerless to control its destiny as a clump of thistledown in a breeze.

We saw no one. When at last Wintour called a halt, we quenched our thirst in a pool at the foot of rocky outcrop. I had thrown into my bag several of the peaches that poor Grantford had picked in the orchard where Froude and his grandchild lay. We shared them one by one as the shadows of evening were falling. We had no other food.

"We shall reach the road soon," Wintour said.

"Which road?"

"The one we crossed this morning. Then we shall come to another stream and then to the wasteland."

"You think we should return by the way we came?" I asked.

"For some of the way at least."

"Do you trust the Tippets?"

He stared blankly at me. "Of course. They're our people."

"We need food, Jack. And intelligence — they may know something of the enemy's movements."

He drew himself up, very much the high-and-mighty gentleman, and stared down his long nose at me. "We cannot put their lives at risk."

I burst out laughing, which was ill-mannered of me. But he looked so ridiculous, a veritable Don Quixote. His clothes were filthy and disreputable; he had not been shaved for over a week. We were a pair of vagabonds, he and I, and he was talking to me as if he were a peer of the realm with a rent roll of six thousand a year.

"I beg your pardon," I said. "I'm so weary that I scarcely know what I'm doing or saying."

His face remained stern. "I accept your apology, Edward."

I forced back another laugh. "Thank you. But my point remains: we must approach the Tippets."

"No," he said. "Not now, especially — the whole country is roused up against us."

"Yes," I said.

CHAPTER
FIFTY-FIVE

It was the last day of July so the evenings were still long and light. It hardly seemed possible that it had been only that morning when our party had left the abandoned cabin where we had spent the night. So much had happened. And two of us were now dead.

When we reached the Tippets' hut there was a wavering tendril of smoke rising from their cooking fire. We took our time and lay at a distance in the shelter of some bushes, watching and waiting. Occasionally we saw the woman or the child moving between the doorway of the hut and the fire, which was at the side of the cabin under a lean-to roof. We saw no one else.

They appeared to be quite unaware that they were being watched. We were too far away to make out their faces. But it seemed to me that their weariness was obvious in every movement they made.

After about half an hour, Wintour whispered that he would make a slow circuit of the hut and, if there were no sign of danger, approach the Tippets. I was to remain where I was and be ready to intervene in case of trouble.

Before he left, he unslung the leather satchel he carried over his shoulder. "Keep this safe for me, will you?" he said with an air of indifference that would not have deceived a child.

I waited as the light slowly faded. Hunger gnawed at my belly. My body ached with weariness. The satchel was heavy and, by the feel of it, I guessed it contained several pieces of ore. I had no temptation to open it, not then: our present danger smothered my curiosity.

Sometimes I fancied I saw Wintour or traces of his movements but I was rarely sure. He once told me that he had spent much of his youth stalking game of one sort or another; and, now that he had become the quarry, the same skills served him well.

At last I saw him plainly, walking quickly across the open ground towards the Tippets' hut. He reached it, glanced over his shoulder and slipped through the doorway into the darkness within.

As I was watching him, however, I glimpsed a flicker of movement in a clump of saplings and bushes that lay some seventy or eighty yards beyond the cabin.

Something white moved among the branches, a foot or two above the ground. An animal? A spy? A trick of the light? I stared at the spot for another five minutes or so, straining my eyes to catch the slightest movement.

But there was nothing. The evening was still. Even the branches were motionless.

Not five minutes later, Wintour came out with a small bundle in his hand. When he rejoined me, we wasted no time but set out directly for the pond where we had found Mehitabel.

By the time it was dark, we had reached the ravine below Mount George. The moon had risen, and

356

although its light was often obscured by wisps of cloud, it helped us find our way. After three or four miles we stopped to rest and to make a belated supper. Mrs Tippet had given Wintour a portion of our own cheese and biscuits.

"We cast our bread upon the waters," I said, "and now we're rejoiced to receive even a quarter of it in return."

Our benefactress had contrived to change one of the guineas we had given her, which allowed her to provide us with some food of her own as well. There were a few slices of bacon, not in the first blush of youth, a sort of hard bread made of maize, and three cold potatoes. We rationed what we had. We might find little more to eat between here and King's Bridge.

"You were in and out of the Tippets' house like a fox in a chicken coop," I said.

"I could not in all conscience stay. Poor woman. She was cowed before but this evening she was terrified."

"Why the alteration?"

"A detachment of militia called on her this afternoon. Their colonel was a man called Varden — he's a Presbyterian deacon in the village. I remember him from before the war, a weaselly, snivelling rogue who quotes Scripture as he cheats you."

"What was he after?"

"Us. They knew we were in the neighbourhood. Mrs Tippet swore she did not betray us. But now she fears every shadow and bitterly repents having changed that guinea."

"They knew that 'we' were here — what does 'we' mean?"

"Four treacherous Tories, they said — myself by name, for of course old Varden was aware Mrs Tippet was acquainted with me, you as an English spy in the pay of General Clinton, and our servants — a negro slave, they said, and a damned lobster out of uniform."

"Their intelligence was precise." I removed a shred of bacon from between my teeth. "Perhaps we have a spy somewhere."

"She gathered that Piercefield and his men ran into a party of Continental dragoons after we left them. Half of them were killed but the rest are talking in the hope of saving their dirty skins. It's a cursed piece of luck for us."

"Luck?" I said. "Is that what it was?"

We said nothing for a moment. What had Continental regulars been doing so near King's Bridge? It was unusual, as I knew from my conversations with Major Marryot, though not impossible.

"The riders we saw on the drive — might they have been the dragoons, or at least some of them?" I asked. "In which case it must have been Varden and his militia who attacked us at the farm."

We considered this in silence. I wondered whether the curious fact that our attackers had been invisible to us had struck Wintour as it had myself. We had heard them and seen their fatal handiwork. But we had not actually seen them.

His mind moved to another subject. "Perhaps it's as well we lost the horses. We can go where horses can't."

"But it will take much longer to get back to King's Bridge." I did not attempt to disguise my distaste at the prospect of such a long and difficult walk. "And they will hunt us like —"

"Hush." Wintour laid his hand on my arm. "What's that?"

"What?"

"Hush. Listen."

Now I heard it too. This wooded landscape was full of sounds, which carried easily in the dark. We had grown accustomed to the repertoire of the night, from the chattering of leaves to the lumbering movements of large animals.

But this sound was different. Though it was so faint it must come from some distance away, it was clear that it was not one sound but a series. There was a regularity about the series and a sense of purpose. It sounded like slow, stealthy footsteps.

That was when I told Wintour about the movement I might have seen in the bushes near the Tippets' hut. Or the trick of the light.

Whatever it was. Whoever it was.

CHAPTER
FIFTY-SIX

There was no more rest for us that night. We made our way along the course of the river. By the time we reached the deserted cabin where we had passed the previous night, it was well after dawn.

We did not stop there. Instead we walked on two or three miles to the south, playing our old trick of using streams in the hope of confusing the scent we left behind. Insects plagued us but at least the itches they caused were temporary distractions from our wretched plight.

At last tiredness made me beg that we stop for a while.

"God be thanked," Wintour said with unusual piety. "I made myself swear an oath that I would only stop when you did."

We spent that day, a Sunday, on a low hillock looking towards the west. The grey gleam of the Hudson was visible in the distance. We settled in a cleft between two rocks. We snatched a mouthful of food and then fell into the deep sleep of complete exhaustion.

I woke with a start. At first I did not know where I was. Then, equally abruptly, the memory of the last few

360

days flooded back into my mind. I sat up and looked wildly about me.

Wintour was still sleeping, his hat over his face, snoring gently. A fly made a slow circuit of his head and settled to feed on his filthy collar.

The world was silent apart from the cries of seagulls and the softer conversations of lesser birds. To judge by the sun, it was long past midday, perhaps three or four o'clock in the afternoon. Though we had lain in the shade, it was uncomfortably warm. My leg muscles ached. I was very thirsty. Above all — and this may seem strange but it is the truth and I must record it — I felt profoundly glad to be alive: so much so that for an instant I was intoxicated with joy.

Sobriety returned almost at once with a sense of the danger we were in. I rose as quietly as I could and scratched myself, desperate for relief from the stings and bites I had acquired in the night. There was a stream nearby. I went over to it and drank deeply. I washed my face and hands. By degrees I felt more myself again.

Wintour was stirring when I returned. After we had broken our fast, there was nothing to occupy us till nightfall. We had determined that it would be safer to wait here until we could trust in the concealment offered by the dark.

We spent the day between those rocks. At one point we heard dogs barking in the distance and prepared for flight. But the barking diminished and at last stopped altogether.

"What are we to do?" Wintour said, for he hated to be idle; I believe that was why he drank so much during periods of inactivity.

"Well, Jack — this is the perfect opportunity."

"For what, pray?"

"For you to tell me about your box of curiosities."

His eyes dropped to the satchel by his side. He had lain on it as he slept and kept the strap across his body. He rubbed the buckle between finger and thumb.

"And about the gold," I said. "For that's the reason we're here. That's the reason you made such a to-do about coming to Mount George in the first place."

I did not say the words that really mattered but Wintour heard them in my tone, which had a sharp, impatient edge to it. He flinched as though I had hit him.

At last he raised his head. "Aye," he said. "I know. And that's the reason Grantford and Abraham are dead. Pray do not look at me like that, Edward. I'm wretched enough already."

I did not know what to say. Grantford had come for my sake. His death lay on my conscience too.

"Old Froude," Wintour said slowly. "I never liked him above half, you know. And Bella hated him. He blighted everything he touched. I almost fancy he still does — I've half a mind to throw away this damned bag."

But he stroked the leather as he spoke, quite unconscious of what he was doing, and I knew he would not.

362

"That piece of ore you showed me," I said. "You said it was gold. Is there more of it?"

"I found two other fragments."

"I mean, is there a source for it? Where did it come from?"

He massaged his head as if the questions had made it ache. "Froude discovered a vein of it on some land he owned. It could be worked, he said, and he believed there was a fortune to be extracted if one went about it the right way."

"Where? Near Mount George?"

He shook his head. "It's miles away. Froude had parcels of land here, there and everywhere. But it's behind the enemy lines now."

"Then what had you to gain by coming here? And how did you know about the gold in the first place?"

"You should have been a lawyer," Wintour said. "My father could not do this better."

I did not apologize but pressed him harder instead. "You were looking for the box of curiosities. You knew about that from the first. You expected to find it in what had been Mr Froude's laboratory. And you knew it would contain those pieces of ore. Either Mr Froude told you or your wife did."

"Bella knows nothing," Wintour said in a rush. "Froude would not have trusted her with something like this. He took me aside just before I went to join my regiment in seventy-six. That's when he told me about the gold. As times were so troubled, he said, I should know about the mine in case something happened to him. I should know where to look."

"He must have trusted you," I said.

Wintour laughed. "He had no one else to confide in. He had more enemies than friends. Indeed, I never heard he had any friends. Even so, he would not tell me much, he did not trust me that far. But he showed me his box — it was full of rocks and specimens of minerals, all labelled in Latin — he was always picking up pieces here and pieces there. Did you know he was of some note as a mineralogist? A few of the pieces in the box were gold and he had them coated to disguise the metal beneath."

"If you've never been to the place where the mine is, how will you find it?"

"In the bottom of the box, his cabinet-maker had made a concealed compartment. The box was designed to be carried, you see — Froude meant to take it with him if he left Mount George. That's where he put the deeds to the land and instructions about where to find the vein." Wintour smiled, baring yellowing, wolfish teeth. "Nothing obvious, you understand — he always was a deep, subtle man. Even if someone found the papers they would not tell him much." The smile broadened, and I saw that in his way Jack was teasing me, which was perhaps a mark of affection. "Froude said I must ask a salamander for help."

"A salamander?" I stared at him. "Is this a jest?"

"If it is, it's none of mine. A salamander. That's what he said, and he told me the way to put the question." Wintour laughed at my confusion. "I shall explain all with a demonstration when we get back to New York."

I nodded towards the satchel. "You have the papers there?"

"Yes, they are what matter . . . But Edward, I . . . I shall make all right as far as I can, you know. My father and mother will grow old with every luxury about them. And Bella — why, she may have whatever she wants now." He swallowed. "And if Grantford leaves a widow or a mother, I shall settle a pension on them directly. I cannot call to mind if we own Abraham's mother — I believe Josiah is related to him somehow, but he's too old to be his father, is he not? — in all events, if there's a mother, I'll give her her freedom and set her up in a little shop or something. And as for you, who knows what we may be able to achieve? Wealth means influence and in the long run influence brings a man whatever he desires."

Wintour ran on in this vein, building castles in the air, for several minutes. The lure of gold had robbed him of his common sense. It seemed not to occur to him that if his gold mine was behind enemy lines there was no chance of his profiting by it until after the war; and even then, since the war's outcome was uncertain, it might not be possible.

I said nothing. The sun shone down on us from a hard, blue sky. A trickle of sweat ran down my neck. I closed my eyes and listened to the rustle of the stream and the incomprehensible chatter of the birds.

Gold. Suddenly I recalled Pickett's body in Canvas Town twelve months earlier. The lure of gold could also lead a man to murder, his own or somebody else's.

Jack Wintour's dreams floated past me and drifted away in the void. At last he ran out of things to say and promises to make.

I slept. I dreamed of salamanders. They were biting me and making me itch infernally.

CHAPTER
FIFTY-SEVEN

We left our refuge when it was almost dark. We were rested but very hungry. My spirits were low. We faced a hard and dangerous future. I believed our expedition had been betrayed, perhaps before we had even left New York. As time passed, the shadow of what had happened at Mount George seemed to increase rather than diminish.

It took us more than three days to accomplish a journey that we should have been able to achieve in one. The days and nights blurred into one another. It was with difficulty that we kept track of the passage of time. We were never free from the fear of pursuit behind us and an ambush ahead.

We walked mostly by twilight and in the dark. I do not know the route we followed for our only map was in Wintour's head. The terrain was wild, hilly and inhospitable. We passed the second day on a rocky outcrop in the middle of a fetid swamp. Once we were obliged to burrow deep into a haystack to conceal ourselves from a large body of cavalry. Later, as we were scrambling down a precipitous hill, there was a storm. Heavy rain added to the sum total of our miseries. On another occasion, just before dawn, we nearly stumbled into a line of sentries guarding an encampment of militia.

Our lack of provisions was a constant difficulty. It forced us to forage for food, which meant in plain language that we were obliged to steal. We dared not approach anyone and offer to pay for fear they might report us.

Foraging was dangerous and time-consuming. It required stealth and the utmost caution. But it was worth it. We took part of a ham from an unguarded farmhouse. We plucked cabbages from a negro family's patch beside their cabin and ate it uncooked. We stole the bread and cider that a cowherd had put aside for his dinner.

"Shall we leave a coin or two in payment?" I suggested the first time, when we stole the ham. I wanted to soothe my conscience.

"No, of course not," Wintour said. "They'd probably smell a rat and run to the nearest militia officer or army post. We can't trust anyone. Let them think it was some vagabond or other."

I did not like it but I ate the food and was grateful.

One evening we came to a stream, which it was necessary to ford. Halfway across, Wintour stopped and turned back to me.

"Thank God," he croaked. "Look — can you see those two trees against the skyline there? Like the letter 'h', ain't they? I know where we are now. This stream is the Bronx."

I had not realized how low my spirits had sunk until I heard this news. Vigour flooded through me — and through Wintour, too. We were almost cheerful as we pressed onwards.

But we were still wary. We knew from our journey with Piercefield and his men that there were enemy outposts nearby. We would not be safe until we were within range of our batteries at Fort Charles.

It seemed an age before we reached the Heights of Fordham. We descended with great caution. After about a mile we came to the head of another stream, which Wintour said was the Musholu Brook.

The light was seeping from the sky. We walked faster and faster, sacrificing concealment for speed. This was indeed the true neuter ground, belonging to neither side but under the observation of both. The grey waters of Harlem Creek gleamed below us.

King's Bridge itself was in sight now, with the fortifications of Manhattan. The glow of lanterns gave a festive air to the scene. We broke into a stumbling run as we threaded our way through the buildings, decrepit almost beyond belief after the years of war, that huddled about the bridge. There were people milling about with great urgency but little sense of purpose, as there always are in such places. After spending days in near solitude it seemed strange to be among human beings again.

Wintour and I glanced at each other. Both of us smiled, great grins splitting our grimy faces in two. He clapped me on my shoulder.

"We've done it, Edward. We're safe now, by God."

The sentries had seen us approaching. A corporal ordered us to halt and identify ourselves.

"An officer of the Sixtieth and an official of His Majesty's American Department," Wintour called out. "Where's the Sergeant of the Guard? Take us to him at once."

The sentries' faces showed their surprise, as well they might. We must have looked a pair of ragamuffins in our torn and filthy clothes. But Wintour's voice and his demeanour changed this in an instant. He had the habit of casual command and, among the army, was quite at home.

The sergeant was already running towards us. "What's this? Who are you?"

"I'm Captain Wintour, Sergeant. This is Mr Savill, Lord George Germain's special envoy in New York. We have been conducting private business on behalf of General Clinton — here, you see his signature on our passes. Now, we wish to see your commanding officer directly. And above all we wish to have some supper."

CHAPTER
FIFTY-EIGHT

Perhaps the best thing — indeed, the only good thing — to come out of our journey in the Debatable Ground was the sense of rapture that both of us felt at our safe return.

The senior officer, Major Kendall, made us wait before he saw us. But he could not have been more obliging once he realized who we were. He was interested in our story, too, and so was the man who came with him, Mr Carne, an American gentleman with whom both Wintour and I were slightly acquainted. It was an open secret that Carne was an intelligence-gatherer. I knew that he was vouched for both by General Tryon and the Deputy Adjutant General at Headquarters.

It was too late for us to go on to the city that evening. Besides, Wintour and I were so tired we could barely walk. Two rooms were bespoken for us at a nearby inn. We were invited to sup with Major Kendall and Mr Carne. Kendall found us clean shirts, stockings and small-clothes. His manservant even produced two pairs of shoes which, though much worn, fitted tolerably well. When I asked the fellow how he had come by them, he laughed and said that people were always coming and going at King's Bridge; and usually they shed some of their possessions as they came and went.

Wintour and I spruced ourselves up as best we could at the inn. Our chambers were small and meanly furnished but the luxury of solitude and a bed of my own seemed a foretaste of paradise to me. Wintour finished his sketchy toilet first and came along to my room.

"We have had quite an adventure, have we not?" he said as he watched me fumbling with my neckcloth.

"I'm rejoiced that it's over," I said. "There were times when —"

"I know. I'm sorry for it, Edward, believe me. If I could turn the clock back, I would. But now we shall reap the benefit, hey? We shall celebrate our happy return tonight — and other nights as well. And tomorrow we shall be back in New York."

Back with the family in Warren Street, I thought, back with Mrs Arabella. And back with the mystery of Roger Pickett's death, which had only deepened since I had discovered the true significance of the box of curiosities. In our desperate flight from Mount George all these considerations, even Mrs Arabella, had retreated from my mind; but now they flooded back.

But tonight I would ignore them, I told myself — tonight Wintour and I were in our own debatable ground, a brief neutral space between past and future, between the perils of our journey to Mount George and the difficulties of our return to New York. Tonight, at least, tonight we might enjoy ourselves.

372

Shortly afterwards, we strolled the short distance to the Major's quarters. It was an extraordinary release not to be on our guard, fearful for our lives, and not to be in a desperate hurry.

Wintour was humming a marching song and beating time with his hand against his leg. He seemed almost drunk already.

I touched his arm. "Jack, for God's sake have a care what you say. Don't let slip your reason for going into the Debatable Ground. Not to anyone."

"I shall be as secret as the grave," he said. "Anyway, I'm famished. I shall have no time for talking."

We reached Kendall's door. I smelled the intoxicating scents of roasted meat. A few minutes later we were at table. The food was indifferent but we fell upon it like starving wolves. As for the wine, both of us drank deep and drank quickly.

The Major and Mr Carne were particularly interested to hear about the state of the country we had passed through, and about enemy troop movements there. They had heard that Piercefield and his men had been defeated in a skirmish, but they knew little of the circumstances apart from a rumour that Piercefield himself had been among the dead.

"It was coming to him sooner or later," Mr Carne observed. "I could never understand the trust that Governor Franklin placed in him."

The bottle continued to circulate. Mr Carne suggested a game of cards. Wintour agreed with enthusiasm. By now it was nearly one o'clock in the morning. My head was reeling from the unaccustomed wine. Weariness engulfed me like my feather mattress in Warren Street.

I made my excuses and left them to it. The major summoned a soldier to light me to the inn. I am sorry to say that I needed the support of his arm as well.

When at last I found myself in my chamber, I opened the bed-curtains and sat down on the bed. It took me a moment to struggle out of my coat, which seemed reluctant to be parted from me. I pulled off my necktie, unbuttoned my waistcoat and kicked off the borrowed shoes. This last exertion overbalanced me. I fell back on the bed. I looked up at the canopy, which was made of dirty green cloth and swayed to and fro like the branches of trees in the forest.

I do not remember more. I fell into a deep sleep. I did not hear Wintour's return. I did not hear anything until I woke the next day.

My mouth was dry. My head felt as if someone had cut it in two with an axe. I lay there, allowing consciousness to seep into my head by fits and starts. I knew from the sunlight that the day was already well advanced.

I eased myself into a sitting position and swung my legs off the bed. The movement intensified my headache and brought on a fit of nausea. When I had recovered I stood up, supporting myself on the bedpost, and looked about me for the chamber pot.

Ten minutes later, I buttoned my breeches with trembling fingers and hobbled like an old man along the passage to the chamber where Wintour lay.

The door was locked or bolted. I called his name. There was no answer. I called again and then hammered on the panels with increasing vigour. I bent down and looked through the keyhole. The key was not in the lock. I could see nothing but part of the bed-curtains. I thought I heard a susurration within. It was like the purring of a cat or the humming of bees.

I banged the door again. The racket I made brought the landlord puffing up the stairs.

"I can't rouse Captain Wintour," I said.

Still panting, the man grinned. "He was late last night, sir, and he was merry."

"Have you a spare key?"

The landlord fetched his keys and unlocked the door. I pushed it open. The buzzing sound was at once louder. There was a terrible stench. Sunshine streamed through the window, which was open. Dust motes danced in the air. Despite the open window, the room was very warm. Wintour's clothes were strewn across the floor. Somewhere in the yard below a woman was singing a ballad I did not know in a remarkably pure voice.

"Jack?" I said. "Come, you sluggard — it must be nearly midday."

The curtains were partly drawn about the bed. I crossed the room and pulled back the nearest one.

Jack Wintour was lying on his back with his head resting on a low pillow. His throat had been cut from ear to ear. The sheet beneath him was soaked red. On and above his body were scores, perhaps hundreds, of large black flies gorging on his blood, their constant movements lending a simulacrum of vitality to the mutilated body.

"Oh sweet Jesus," moaned the landlord.

He turned away and retched. The singing stopped. But the buzzing grew louder and louder.

The more I looked, the more blood I saw, and the more flies. Jack's cheeks had been slit from the outer corners of each eye to the corners of the mouth. He was clad only in his borrowed shirt. This had been sliced open from the throat to the genitalia.

So had the skin beneath. I glimpsed the shocking white of bone, the blood and the glistening organs. And above all, the flies.

CHAPTER
FIFTY-NINE

I have waking memories and, worse than these, I have dreams. I still see the pools of blood in my nightmares and the wide, staring eyes. The guts that spilled out of the belly, the genitalia almost severed from the body. And then the flies, always the flies, the endless, buzzing, feeding, bloated flies.

The landlord, when he had done retching, set up a great wailing and howling. I retained presence of mind enough to push him out of the room. The passage was crammed with domestics and idlers and drinkers, drawn by sounds he had made. I summoned one of the maids, a sensible-looking woman for whom the first blush of youth was only a distant memory, and sent her to find Major Kendall.

"Tell him," I said, "that Captain Wintour is dead and he must come at once."

My mind was still clear and rational. Indeed, it seemed to me that the crisis had had the effect, only temporary alas, of intensifying my intellectual faculties and accelerating their operation. I knew exactly what I must do, and also that there was little time to do it.

Giving the landlord into the charge of his wife and daughter, I ordered them to take him downstairs and give him a dram or two of rum. Then I set one of the serving men, a big, burly fellow with the belly of an alderman and the carriage of an ex-soldier, to clear the passage of bystanders and to stand watch with me until Major Kendall's arrival. When the situation was somewhat calmer, I slipped back into Wintour's chamber and locked the door behind me.

The singing outside had stopped but the buzzing of the flies seemed louder than before. The sour taste of bile was in my mouth. I looked away from the bed.

The room was still obscenely cheerful with sunlight. I went to the window and glanced out. A stationary wagon stood immediately below in the yard. It had a raised seat at one end and was carrying a part load of roughly trimmed logs. If the window had been open last night, it would have been perfectly possible for a reasonably agile man to enter the chamber by using the wagon and perhaps one of the logs to raise him within reach of the sill.

I steeled myself to look at poor Jack Wintour. I thought it probable that most of his injuries had been inflicted after death: for otherwise there would have been a deal of noise that would have aroused the house, and possibly more blood as well. A robber might conceivably have killed him if Wintour had disturbed him in the course of a robbery — but why such a violent and unnecessarily prolonged attack? Such wanton violence seemed to serve no purpose; in that quality, if in no other, it reminded me of the destruction of Mr Froude's laboratory: I simply could not understand the nature of it.

I turned aside and examined the clothes that were strewn on the floor. Some were stained with blood. Wintour had kept his purse in a concealed pocket inside his coat. I looked for it there and found it gone. So too were his pistols.

I searched the rest of the room, which was too small to have many hiding places. I went down on hands and knees and peered under the bed. Finally, I screwed up my courage and returned to Jack Wintour's mutilated body, to the congealed blood and the shifting veil of flies.

Something caught my eye — a glint of light at the end of the pillow nearer the window. I bent closer. It was a steel buckle.

Gingerly I stretched out a hand and pulled it free from underneath the pillow. With it came the strap it held together. There was a little blood on the leather, but not much because Wintour's head was on the other end of the pillow.

I tugged harder. The satchel itself emerged in a rush. The movement was violent enough to affect the whole pillow, which moved an inch or so. This in turn dislodged Wintour's head, which rotated a few degrees towards me, so his eyes stared sightlessly at mine and the great wound across his throat gaped at me like a second mouth.

I snatched up the satchel and turned my back on him. I knew at once from the weight that it still contained the ore. I removed the three pieces and placed them in the pocket of my coat.

At the bottom of the satchel was a square of oilskin, folded over and sewn roughly with coarse thread to make a small packet. I rubbed it between finger and thumb and it bent under the pressure. I put that in my pocket too. I dropped the unbuckled satchel on the floor and kicked the coat over it.

I unlocked the door, stepped into the passage and turned the key in the lock.

I do not think my absence had even been noticed. The serving man had persuaded most of the bystanders to leave, but one of the women had gone into a fit of hysterics. She was lying on the ground, weeping and drumming her feet on the bare boards. Two of her fellow servants were trying to calm her and to make her leave.

"We shall all be murdered," she was shrieking. "Murdered in our beds."

The serving man bent over her and slapped her so hard on the cheek that her skull knocked on the floor. The slap and the sudden, shocking silence that followed operated on my sensibilities like the tug of a lever.

My eyes blurred. I turned away and let the tears run unchecked down my cheeks.

Major Kendall arrived with Mr Carne at his heels. Four soldiers accompanied them to the inn but remained below.

I went back to my own room and sat near the window. The maid brought me rum, tea and bread, without my asking for them. I could not face the rum or the bread, but I was grateful for the tea.

Kendall and Carne examined the body and the chamber in which it lay. At length they came to interview me. There was, I noticed, a formality to their questioning; and Mr Carne made notes in his pocket-book as the conversation went along.

At first I answered their questions mechanically. They took me through the circumstances of my discovery of the body. It was when Mr Carne began to ask in minute detail about the door to Wintour's bedchamber that I paid more attention.

"Have you found Wintour's key?" I said, interrupting him.

"No, sir."

Carne's eyes met mine for a moment. Their irises were almost colourless, bleached of personality. He was an intelligent man and I believe that each of us had a fair notion of what was in the other's mind. He was trying to establish whether the killer might have entered from within the house rather than by the open window.

"Pray search this room if you wish," I said. "And my person."

"No, of course not," Major Kendall said, shocked by this ungentlemanly suggestion. "Upon my honour, sir, there's no need for that sort of thing."

"The man who brought you here last night said you were so drunk he had to carry you up the stairs." Carne's voice was cool and faintly scornful. "Having watched you last night, sir, I was not surprised."

I coloured but said nothing.

"We all drank our bottle, sir," Kendall said. "I dare say I was a trifle foxed myself by the end of the evening."

Carne gave a barely perceptible shrug. "Whoever killed Captain Wintour needed a clear head and a steady hand. To be quite candid, I do not think that you had either of those last night, Mr Savill. Even now, perhaps —"

"You've made your point, sir," I snapped. "Nor did I have any conceivable reason to kill him. And, even if I had wished to, I have had far more convenient opportunities since we went into the Debatable Ground. I should hardly have killed him now or in that way."

"No, no." Kendall said. "My dear sir, I'm sure that nothing could be further from Carne's thoughts. Eh, Mr Carne? To my mind, whoever did this came through the window and went out the same way. Probably locked the door to delay pursuit and pocketed the key."

"But it's curious, all the same," Carne said. "Curious that the murderer left no bloodstains behind him. He must have been covered in blood."

CHAPTER
SIXTY

Later that day I was taken under escort to New York. I was in no sense a prisoner, of course. I had not been charged with anything. But Kendall — or rather Carne, perhaps — was taking no chances.

The latter accompanied me. We exchanged hardly a word on the journey. I felt the pieces of ore in my pockets weighing down my coat. They made an unsightly bulge and I feared that they might arouse my companion's curiosity.

We had nearly reached the city when an orderly from King's Bridge caught up with us. He brought a note from Major Kendall. Carne broke the seal, read it and passed it directly to me.

Kendall wrote that a servant at the tavern had gone to the well in the yard to draw water. Something had snagged on the bucket which, upon investigation, proved to be a long nightgown. Despite its immersion in the water, it was clear that it had been badly stained with blood down the front, from the neck to the hem and also on the arms.

The Major had given orders to investigate the bottom of the well, if that were possible, and to bring up any items deposited there. He had made enquiries about the nightgown and discovered that it belonged to the landlord's wife, a woman of ample proportions and unusual height. It had been washed the previous day and hung out to air overnight in an outbuilding.

"I rejoice for you," Carne said to me as he scribbled a reply in pencil for the orderly to take back to King's Bridge.

"I beg your pardon, sir?"

The American looked up and, for the first time that day, smiled. He did not respond but handed the note to the orderly and gave the signal that we should ride on.

Carne was a man who did not waste words if silence would do. I understood him well enough, as he had known I would; in many ways he and I were two of a kind. If the murderer had put on a nightgown before the frenzied attack and then thrown it into the well, he must have left by the window. It would not have been possible either to leave or to re-enter the inn without rousing the house, for the doors were of course locked and barred at night.

Now that Carne was convinced that I could not be the murderer, his manner became markedly more cordial. Nevertheless we had little conversation during the rest of our journey. My mind was elsewhere and so, no doubt, was his.

For the nightgown had other implications than my innocence. It suggested that the murder had been carefully planned and that the killer had worked out every stage of it with care, including the violence of the attack and his line of retreat.

384

There was an element of calculation about this, a sense of steady, almost rational malevolence — and also a degree of stealth or caution. That last quality reminded me of those strange and inexplicable events in the Debatable Ground: not just of the two murders at Mount George, but of the hints I had had on our way back that we were not alone.

Was it merely coincidence that Jack Wintour had been killed at the very first moment we had relaxed our guard?

We reached New York in the evening and went straight to Headquarters where Major Marryot, alerted by a letter from Kendall, was waiting for us in his private room. Several other gentlemen joined us, including General Tryon and the Deputy Adjutant General.

We discussed the murder as if we had barely known the victim in life. Carne pointed out that the purse had been stolen, which at least suggested that robbery might be the motive, though it did not account for the violence of the attack.

"There may be another reason for that," he went on. "We have seen so much violence in this war, so much blood . . ." His voice died away.

"Well, what of it, sir?" Tryon demanded.

"I believe that a few men, sir, a very few, find that carnage creates a strange appetite for bloodletting within their bosoms. I have seen several cases of soldiers or old soldiers afflicted with a form of madness that drives them to commit terrible deeds." He rubbed his forehead. "I do not pretend to understand it at all, but it is a phenomenon I have observed. If you ask the surgeons at the hospital I believe they will tell you the same."

Marryot snorted but, mindful of his manners in this company, tried to turn the sound into a cough.

Tryon rose to his feet. "It seems there's nothing more we can do at present, gentlemen. Pray keep me informed if there's fresh intelligence. I shall call on Judge Wintour to pay my condolences in a day or two."

The others drifted away in his wake, leaving Marryot and me alone.

"The Wintours must be told," I said. "The news will be all over the city in five minutes, if it isn't already."

He bent his head and rubbed at a spot of grease on his breeches. "Will you do it, sir?"

"Yes," I said, for I thought it might make it a little easier to have the news from me, who at least knew more of the circumstances than anyone else.

"You will break it to them gently, I know," he said. "Is there anything I can do? Anything at all?"

I thought of the diminished family in Warren Street. "There's nothing anyone can do."

"I shall call on them, of course," Marryot went on. "Tomorrow, if it would not be too early. I should not wish to intrude on their grief. Do you think it would be too early?"

I did not know how to answer, so I said something vague about the Wintours needing their friends at a time like this.

386

As I took my leave, he said what I think he had really wanted to say all along: "Pray give my deepest sympathy to Mrs Arabella. I . . . She . . ."

He ran out of words to say or the courage to say them. He bowed and turned away.

I believe Judge Wintour knew from the moment he saw my face.

I stood in front of the empty fireplace in the library and told him in as few words as possible what had happened to his son. While I spoke he sat quite still at his open secretary. He stared at the quill lying before him on a sheet of paper. The paper was blank apart from a cluster of ink-drops that had fallen from the discarded pen.

Afterwards he tried to ask questions but on that occasion his heart was not in it. He had no room for anything except the fact of his son's death.

I waited a moment or two and then suggested gently that Mrs Arabella should be told. He did not hear me. I said the words again, and then again, until at last he gave a nod.

When I said I would ring the bell and send Josiah to fetch her, he nodded once more; he heard me but I am not convinced he understood what I was saying.

Josiah came almost at once. He had guessed the news must be bad when he opened the street door to me alone. He must have already said something of his fears to Mrs Arabella. Her face was unusually pale. She gave me the briefest of curtseys and went at once to her father-in-law.

"Well, sir? You have news?"

The old man swallowed. He glanced towards me and waved his hand, asking mutely for me to do it for him.

"Will you not sit down, madam?" I asked, drawing out a chair.

She shook her head. "You have come alone, sir." Her voice was flat, purged of expression, and she did not look directly at me. "Is that your news?"

"I'm afraid Captain Wintour is dead," I said bluntly and quickly, for I could not find a kinder way to do it. "I am so sorry."

She took Mr Wintour's hand in both of hers and squeezed it. "What — what happened?"

So I told her, and the Judge as well. I told them that we had survived many perils together on our journey to Mount George and back. I told them of Jack Wintour's courage and resource, of his kindness to the unfortunate Tippets and his desire to honour his dead child. I told them how Abraham and Corporal Grantford had died. I told them that Captain Wintour had brought the two of us safely through the lines and then been foully murdered when he thought himself among friends again. I told them that the killer was still at large.

Mrs Arabella listened without interruption. But when I stopped, she demanded to know more of the circumstances of the murder. So I told her, for it was better that this story of butchery should come from me now and as a plain narrative of events I had witnessed myself; and not later from a stranger and perhaps in a garbled form. At last her calm deserted her. Her body began to tremble. I took her arm and insisted that she sit down. She allowed me to bring a chair for her but she would not relinquish her hold on Mr Wintour's hand.

"Why, sir?" the Judge asked when I had finished speaking. "Why should anyone take the life of a fellow creature with such needless brutality? I simply cannot comprehend it, Mr Savill — it's beyond belief."

"Captain Wintour's purse was taken, sir, so we must assume that robbery was the motive. But, as for the violence of the attack, I understand that it may have been the work of a madman."

We sat in a dreary silence. It was a warm evening but the room felt cold and clammy.

Mr Wintour stirred. "We need to keep this from my poor wife," he said. "I believe the news would kill her. If she asks, we must say that John has rejoined his regiment. Will you warn the servants, my dear?"

"Yes, sir," Mrs Arabella said. She turned to me and for the first time looked straight at me. "Tell me, sir, do they have any idea who the murderer might have been? Any at all?"

"I believe not. The officer at King's Bridge suggested he might be a deserter."

"But they know nothing?" she said. "Not even a hint?"

Her persistence surprised me. But it was natural enough, I thought, for no one finds comfort in the inexplicable.

"Nothing," I said.

"Nothing," she murmured, like an echo.

CHAPTER
SIXTY-ONE

The inquiry was entirely a military affair. At the time of his murder, Captain Wintour had held the King's commission and he had been travelling, in theory at least, for military purposes and by the authority of the Commander-in-Chief himself.

Major Marryot was involved and so I believe were his superiors. Marryot summoned me to Headquarters on the day after my return to New York. He interviewed me formally with his clerk taking down my answers. Once again he took me through what had happened at King's Bridge in great detail. He also asked me about our journey in the Debatable Ground.

This put me in a difficult position. As a friend of the family, Marryot already knew of Captain Wintour's private desire to visit Mount George, though he was not aware of the reason for it.

In the American Department we know about preserving official decencies. General Clinton had signed our passes on the grounds that Wintour and I were gathering intelligence. If he had troubled to ask questions, which he almost certainly did not, he would have learned that Governor Franklin was involved and that we intended to travel with Piercefield's irregulars, which would have lent colour to this explanation for our journey.

So I emphasized what Wintour and I had ascertained of enemy troop movements, the state of the country and the condition of the remaining inhabitants. As a sop to Marryot's conscience, I also mentioned that Jack had wished to assess the damage at Mount George. By ill luck, I told him, the enemy had caught wind of us. Grantford and Abraham had been killed, and Wintour and I had managed to escape. It was a straightforward story which had the merit of being the truth, if not the whole truth.

"Is it possible that you were pursued through the lines?" Marryot asked.

"Why would anyone have done that?"

"Because the killer wished to silence Captain Wintour at all costs?"

"Once again — why?"

The Major put his elbows on the table and leant towards me. "If they feared you had seen something — evidence, maybe, that they were intending an attack on our positions."

"But we didn't," I said.

"As far as you know. But what if you did without realizing it? Concealed batteries? Naval preparations? The outworks of a new encampment? Think, sir, think."

"I have thought," I said, my voice rising. "I've done little else since I found him there except think. And I can think of nothing."

"I may tell you that Mr Carne is convinced that this must be the reason."

"I wish I could prove him right."

"But suppose for the sake of argument he is right, at least in part," Marryot persisted. "Suppose there was something you saw in the Debatable Ground but you do not yet realize the significance of it. Do you see what that means?"

"Spare me the riddles, sir," I said. "I'm in no humour for them at present."

"Why — if they killed Wintour to silence him, will they not try to do the same to you?"

Captain Wintour was buried beside his Uncle Francis in Trinity churchyard. There was a considerable crowd in attendance. I was with the Judge. He clung to my arm and was silent throughout the funeral service and interment. He did not even weep.

As we turned away from the open grave, the crowd shifted its composition: for a moment a narrow avenue opened through its middle; and I glimpsed a thickset man smoking a clay pipe.

I saw him only for a few seconds. He was standing in the further fringes of the concourse, close to Van Cortlandt's Sugar House. He had the look of a man enjoying the spectacle of a funeral. I was sure I had seen him before. His presence seemed to hint at something worse than itself, as does an omen or a bad smell.

Marryot passed along the path ahead of the Judge and myself. He was deep in conversation with Mr Townley and Mr Carne. For a moment the three of them blocked my view. When they were gone, the crowd shifted. The pipe-smoker had disappeared.

The Judge and I walked slowly away. Some negro children were playing in the road that bordered the churchyard, oblivious to the solemnity of the occasion. The sight of them frolicking by a graveyard touched a spring in my mind that brought a memory to the surface.

I knew where I had seen the man. It was just before I had gone into the Debatable Ground with Jack Wintour. He had slipped in a pile of horse droppings outside the negro burial ground and some children had been taunting him in his misfortune. It was the man who had laid a posy on Henrietta Barville's grave.

Jack Wintour's murder seized the public's interest for a week or two. But this soon evaporated when the inquiry failed to bring forth new information. It was wartime, after all, and New York had a surfeit of alarming news and violent deaths to feed on.

The days turned into weeks, and the weeks into months. I paid scant attention to Marryot's warning that I might be in danger. I was too tired to fear for my own safety and also too unhappy. Instead I tried to drug myself with work. I slept too little and I drank too much. And I had bad dreams.

Soon after my return to New York from the Debatable Ground, I wrote to Mr Rampton in his official capacity and gave him an incomplete account of our expedition to Mount George and its brutal termination. I chose my words with care for I knew that he would also see the reports that the army sent to Lord George Germain; he made it his business to see everything that was laid before the American Secretary. I could not expect to hear Mr Rampton's response until late September or even early October.

I told nobody the full story of what had happened. I locked away the three pieces of ore and the oilskin packet in the brassbound writing box in which I kept my private papers. It seemed to me that there was nothing to be lost by postponing my decision in this matter and perhaps much to be gained.

It occurs to me now that I postponed many decisions in the weeks following my return to New York, and that this was itself one of the consequences of what had happened at Mount George and King's Bridge. I was sick at heart. Nothing seemed to matter.

In the meantime, I tried to pick up the threads of my old life, which had become unfamiliar and curiously alien. It was as if our expedition had made me quite a different person. My previous existence hung awkwardly about me like a suit of clothes tailored for a wizened old man in the years of his maturity, when he was taller and plumper and happier.

The house in Warren Street was a sorrowful place now, though there were no outward signs that its inhabitants were in mourning. Mr Wintour had decided to fly in the face of convention for the sake of his wife's peace of mind.

The old lady rarely came down from her chamber. Mrs Arabella and Miriam tended to her. The Judge visited her two or three times a day. He found little to console himself in her company.

"She does not always know me now," he confided as we sat over our wine one evening in September. "She stares in my direction but looks straight through me. And she talks to the children."

"The children?" I said, startled.

"Yes. Jack and poor Baby Hetty. She sees them quite plainly. Sometimes it's as if Jack is a boy again and his sister the age she was when she died. She sings to them. But that is better than when she is distressed. Oh yes, much better."

"What does the doctor say?"

"What do they always say?" Mr Wintour said. "They bleed her, they purge her, they prescribe this and that. But it makes no difference, except to make her weaker. You cannot cure time and sorrow."

I had no words of comfort to say to him for he was so obviously correct in his diagnosis. Mrs Wintour's wits became increasingly disordered. It made it no easier that she had days when her mind was clearer, if only for an hour or so at most. In her lucid moments, she remembered that we had told her Jack had gone to war.

"When will he come home?" she would ask Mrs Arabella and her husband.

"Soon," they would say.

Mrs Wintour would weep and worry for his safety for a few seconds. Then her mind would flit away. Sometimes, a moment later, she would ask the same question. And they would give her the same answer.

395

CHAPTER
SIXTY-TWO

In the latter half of September, I came home in the evening to find Mrs Arabella alone in the drawing room with the tea-tray beside her and a book in her hand. The candles were lit but, even in the gloom, I knew that something was different.

She laid aside the book and offered me tea. "The Judge will be down directly. He is with Mrs Wintour."

I took the cup from her. The room seemed unexpectedly airier and clearer than usual. I looked about me and saw what had changed.

"That painting's gone," I said.

Mrs Arabella had been watching me. "I wondered how long it would take you." There was a hint of amusement in her voice. "I could not endure to see it there any longer. Josiah and the porter took it away this afternoon."

The great painting of Mount George had dominated the room from its proud position over the fireplace. A solitary candle on the mantelpiece revealed its ghostly traces, a pale oblong outlined in the smoky stains on the wallpaper.

"Will you have it hung somewhere else?" I asked. "Or will you store it?"

"I told Josiah to cut it up and burn it on the kitchen fire, sir. And the frame. At least we shall have some use from it then."

"You did not care for the house, I think? I remember you told me that once."

She did not reply at first. Then, seemingly inconsequentially, she said: "It is better to go forward than to go backwards. Sometimes one must leave the past where it is — in the past. Do you not agree?"

"Yes." I thought of Augusta and the mistakes that she and I had made. Perhaps Mrs Arabella was thinking of Jack. "But that is not always easy to do."

We drank our tea in silence. Somehow we had slipped into the fragile intimacy we had shared in the past — though rarely, and never for long. I think candlelight made it easier for both of us, for shadows favour confidences. In that moment I made up my mind.

"Madam," I said. "Before you leave it behind altogether entirely, there is something I must tell you about Mount George."

Mrs Arabella looked up. "Ah. I wondered."

"About what?"

"Whether there was something more. Something else."

"I needed time to consider what was best to be done," I said, aware that already she had placed me on the defensive.

"You're a man who knows how to keep secrets."

I inclined my head — a token bow in thanks for a token compliment. "Besides, I thought you had other matters that were more pressing."

"Does it concern my husband's death?"

"No. Or rather, I do not see how it can do. But I cannot be certain of that. Indeed, I cannot be certain of anything."

"You are quite the philosopher this evening, sir."

To my relief, there was a knock on the door at that moment, and Miriam entered with fresh candles.

"If you please, ma'am," she said, curtseying, "Master says to tell you he's gone to bed."

"It's very early."

"Yes, ma'am, but he's weary." A look of intelligence passed between the two women. "Terrible weary."

Mrs Arabella dismissed the maid.

"I'm afraid Mr Wintour is not well," I said.

"Is it any wonder, sir? But you were saying?"

If the Judge had retired for the night, then we were unlikely to be disturbed. I excused myself and went up to my bedchamber to fetch the packet of papers and the three pieces of ore from my writing box.

I returned to the drawing room, carrying the canvas bag in which I had put them. Mrs Arabella watched in silence as I set a little table beside her chair. I undid the drawstring of the bag and, one by one, took out the three pieces of ore and the oilskin pouch. I placed them on the table.

"This was why Captain Wintour was so desirous of going to Mount George."

She extended her right hand and touched the nearest piece with her forefinger. She picked it up and felt the weight and the texture. "Is it metal?"

"Permit me to show you." I took out my penknife, opened the blade and took up another piece of ore. I scored a scratch in the side of it. I gave her the piece. "Hold it to the candle flame, ma'am. Examine it."

She did as I bid. "It has a glint to it underneath," she said. "Like gold."

"Captain Wintour believed it was gold. And so, I think, did your father. But I do not know for certain. I have not had it assayed."

Mrs Arabella put down the ore on the table. "Where did it come from?"

"It seems that there is a vein of gold on some land that your father owned."

Her eyes widened. "But there is no gold in this part of America, surely? Where is this land? On the Mount George estate?"

"No, ma'am. In North Carolina."

Her head snapped up. She stared at me. "It's in rebel hands?"

"Yes."

Mrs Arabella was silent for a few minutes. Her face was now averted from me. Her intelligence, it occurred to me, was hard and rational; one might almost say it had a masculine cast to it. She wanted time to think the matter through and she would not hurry for me or anyone.

"What is in the bag?" she said at last.

"I have not opened it. Captain Wintour told me that it contains the deeds confirming your father's title to the property and instructions about where the mine is on the estate. But your husband believed the instructions would not be straightforward. 'Nothing obvious' — those were his words."

"My father liked puzzles and enigmas that challenged the mind. He worked at them for recreation." She spread her fingers. Her hand hovered, palm down, over the pouch and the three pieces of metal. "You found this at Mount George?"

"Captain Wintour did."

"He knew where to look." It was a conclusion, not a question.

"Mr Froude informed your husband of the discovery just before he went to join his regiment. He also showed the Captain where he had concealed the papers and the ore samples. In case he himself was prevented from going to New York."

Her mouth twisted. "In his box of curiosities? Is that where he hid all this?"

I stared at her in surprise. "How did you know?"

"There's no mystery — my husband mentioned the box to you when the fever was upon him. Do you remember? He asked if you'd brought it to him."

"Of course — you were in the room."

"And I recall the box — my father had it made to his design a few years before the war to transport his specimens." Mrs Arabella sat in her chair. The whites of her eyes gleamed yellow in the candlelight. "But what really puzzles me, sir," she went on, "is how you knew of it beforehand."

"Madam, you must be mistaken, I —"

"No, sir, I am not." She was speaking very quietly now, and I had to bring my head closer to hers to catch what she was saying. "When you questioned me about the death of Mr Pickett — a little roughly, I thought, sir, by the by — you tossed in a question at the end: you asked if he'd said anything to me about a box of curiosities."

"Did I?" My reply sounded lame even to me, and I tried to carry it off with a high hand. "That was quite another matter, ma'am, and it concerned government business that I really cannot discuss with a private individual."

"Nonsense. I am not a child — you cannot bamboozle me with that sort of foolishness. I thought better of you, Mr Savill."

"It's not nonsense. I have only your best interests in mind."

She leaned forward, bringing her face close to mine. "I don't believe in such coincidences, sir, and nor do you. You're not doing this as a kindness — you have some other end in view."

I smelled the otto of roses she wore. She was so very beautiful in a passion. I watched helplessly as she gathered up the ore and the unopened pouch. She placed them in the canvas bag. Without another word, she left the room, holding the canvas bag to her breast as though it were a baby.

CHAPTER
SIXTY-THREE

I had no opportunity for private conversation with Mrs Arabella during the next few days, partly because I had pressing business to transact on behalf of the American Department — but perhaps more because when I was at Warren Street she took care not to provide me with an opportunity to talk to her alone. She was perfectly civil when we met at meals or passed each other in the hall. But it was as if there were a sheet of glass between us.

Her unflattering opinion of my motives distressed me. Did she think I was a Government spy? Or merely a greedy individual whose scruples had been overturned by his lust for gold? The simple truth was that I pitied the situation in which she found herself and I valued her good opinion more than was sometimes convenient for my peace of mind.

I considered writing to her, but I had long ago learned the folly of rushing to commit confidential matters to paper where anyone might read them.

Better to wait, I thought, better to hope.

Later that week I had occasion to call on Mr Townley at his house. It was the anniversary of Their Majesties' coronation, I remember, and as I walked over to Hanover Square, I was for a moment startled out of my wits by the sound of a royal salute from the Battery, followed by an answering volley from the ships of war in the harbour. If any rebel heard that startling display of military power, I thought, he would tremble in his shoes.

My visit was by appointment but the porter told me that his master was still engaged with General Clinton's aide-de-camp; Mr Townley had left a message regretting the inconvenience and begging me to wait a few minutes in the dining parlour on the other side of the hall.

I had barely sat down at the table when a door in the panelling opened with such force that it smacked against a sideboard that stood by the wall beside it. A small child shot backwards into the room, tripped over the edge of the carpet and fell heavily, cracking his head on the leg of the table. He let out a howl of mingled pain and rage.

He was followed immediately by an older, taller child, a girl of seven or eight, who was wielding a broom with unmistakably hostile intent. She saw me sitting at the table and stopped sharply in the doorway.

Her behaviour alerted the boy, who scrambled to his feet and stared at me with huge eyes. For a moment none of us spoke or moved.

Then I laughed.

The children continued to stare at me. I believe my laughter came as a greater shock to them than seeing me here in the first place. They could not have looked more surprised if the table had showed signs of mirth.

I heard rapid footsteps in the room beyond the open door. Two women appeared — a lady, who seized the girl by the shoulders and shook her vigorously, and a black servant.

I rose to my feet. The lady saw me and gave a shriek.

I bowed. "Forgive me, madam — I did not mean to surprise you."

The lady blushed like a girl, and the change of colour was cruelly obvious because her complexion was very pale, almost translucent; the skin was smudged with freckles and pitted with the scars of smallpox. Strands of ginger-coloured hair trailed from beneath the cap on her head.

The servant's reactions were quicker. She seized the girl. The boy clutched at her skirts and she patted his head.

"No, sir, it's of no consequence," the lady said wildly. "That's to say, I'm distressed beyond measure — mortified — oh, sir, I'm so sorry, those naughty children will never do what they're told."

"Pray do not give it another thought, ma'am. I have a young daughter of my own."

The lady waved her hand at the servant, a wordless command for her to take away the children. She took an uncertain step into her own dining parlour. She was small and plump and wore a dress that to my uneducated eye had seen better days.

"No doubt you have called to see my — to see Mr Townley?"

404

"Yes, ma'am. The servant showed me in here to wait for a moment or two. My name is Savill. Have I the pleasure of addressing Mrs Townley?"

"Yes, indeed — Mr Savill, sir? Of the American Department? You lodge in poor Judge Wintour's house, I collect?"

I bowed again and Mrs Townley curtseyed in return. She was not quite sure what to do with herself next. Her duty as a hostess, however unintentional, urged her to stay while her retiring nature encouraged her to go. I felt for her predicament and tried to make it easier by enquiring about her children. Jack Wintour had told me that Townley was ashamed of his wife, whom he had married for her money. It was true that the lady was not the most elegant of creatures; but she was civil enough and seemed quite as genteel as her husband.

We did pretty well on the subject of children, so much so that Mrs Townley grew sufficiently emboldened to ask how I liked New York and how it compared to London. When we had settled these matters she returned to the Wintours and told me that she had often seen old Mrs Wintour at Trinity Church before the war, and that the Judge's wife had been very gracious to her.

"The poor lady," Mrs Townley went on. "Mr Noak tells me that she never leaves her own apartments now. Is it true that she does not even know that her son is dead?" Her hand flew to her mouth. "I beg your pardon, sir — my tongue does run on — the subject must distress you."

"It's no consequence now, ma'am. But I'm afraid Mr Noak is quite correct." It occurred to me that fate, in the person of Mrs Townley, had presented me with an opportunity. "Did you know that Mr Noak used to read the Bible to her before she was confined to her chamber? And of course even now he helps the Judge a good deal with his papers. He is the kindest of men."

She looked startled at this but nodded and smiled.

"As I myself have cause to know," I went on. "He and I made the passage from England on the same ship and he was benevolence itself when I was ill."

"Seasickness? I feel for you, sir — how I suffer from it myself."

I bowed to acknowledge both her suffering and her sympathy. "And it was a happy chance that your husband mentioned that he was in want of a clerk."

"Was he?" she said, a frown appearing between her eyebrows. "I don't recall that."

"I remember his telling me soon after I arrived that his clerk had just died. Of fever, I think it was. So I proposed Mr Noak for the place."

"But Mr Ingham is quite well, I believe. He manages the warehouse by the distillery on Long Island so we don't see as much of him as we used to."

"Mr Ingham was Mr Townley's clerk? In this house?"

"Yes. And he was my father's before that. When Mr Noak came, my husband gave Mr Ingham his new position. I believe he is very competent." Mrs Townley gave me an uncertain smile. "But of course Mr Townley would not employ him if he were not."

406

"I'm sure Mr Townley is a fine judge of men," I said. "Which is just as well, since he has so many responsibilities to discharge. Indeed, you must hardly see him for days on end."

I smiled to indicate that this should be taken as a pleasantry. Mrs Townley had struck me as being so sensitive to possible hidden meanings that she might take fright at the most innocuous remarks.

"Indeed, he is very busy and —"

She was interrupted by the sound of a door opening and voices in the hall. For a moment she was quite still, her eyes wide and her lips parted. She took a step towards the door in the panelling.

"Forgive me, sir, I forgot — I really must withdraw — and I should not have — I forgot to offer you any refreshments. What will you think of me?"

"Only what is good, ma'am," I said softly, in case our voices might carry to the hall. "Thank you for a most agreeable conversation. I was in no need of refreshments. Perhaps you would prefer me not to mention that I distracted you from your duties? It was most unkind of me."

Mrs Townley nodded violently and mouthed the words, "Thank you." She slipped from the room so quietly that I did not even hear the click of the lock.

The voices in the hall grew louder. Then came the bang of the hall door as the porter closed it. The parlour door rattled and Mr Townley swept into the parlour in a flurry of smiles and bows.

"Forgive me, sir — you remember my little *entrepôt* at Norman's Slip? I needed to ensure that a shipment to our gallant men at Paulus Hook would go out this evening. The military mind seems quite incapable of understanding that the movements of the tide are simply not within my control."

He took me into his private room and offered me wine. I had called on him partly for the monthly returns of arrests he compiled, which I would forward, with my comments, to Mr Rampton, and partly to discuss the billeting of certain refugees who had influential friends in Westminster.

We dispatched our business within twenty minutes and chatted for a while over our wine. I did not mention my encounter with Mrs Townley and his children. But I did raise the subject of the winter programme at the Theatre Royal. I told him I intended to take a box when the season began in December.

"The Wintours will not be able to come because they're in mourning of course. But I hope you will join me, sir."

"With pleasure," Townley said.

"And Mrs Townley, as well, if it would amuse her?"

"I thank you on her behalf, sir, but no," he said quickly. "She rarely goes out of an evening and, besides, she does not find the theatre agreeable."

I left the house soon afterwards. As he rose to show me out, Townley's eyes fell upon a paper lying on his desk. He took it up and waved it at me.

"I had almost forgot. A refugee was asking for you."

"Nothing surprising in that," I said. "I'll soon have another claimant waiting on the stairs at Broad Street."

"The officer who registered her arrival made a note. It appears that she said she knew you and that you would vouch for her."

"She?"

Townley tapped his great nose and affected to look roguish. "I wondered at first if you'd engaged in an affair of the heart. At last. But not in this case, I fancy — she's no more than a girl, it seems, and a shabby little thing at that." He peered at the paper, for he was a vain man who would not succumb to spectacles. "Mirabel something? No — Mehitabel. Mehitabel Tippet."

CHAPTER
SIXTY-FOUR

They were holding Mehitabel Tippet at the Provost, a bleak building on the north-west side of Bowling Green that was used mainly as a prison. I went directly there from Mr Townley's house.

Part of the establishment had been commandeered as temporary accommodation for refugees who arrived in the city without means of support or friends to vouch for them. These unhappy people eked out a miserable existence. They were detained in two long rooms, men in one and women in the other, and allowed to exercise in the yard between them.

The rooms were partly below ground level, which at least kept them cool in summer. Overcrowding was a problem for the city received far more refugees than it could handle and those without resources of their own put an intolerable strain on the government.

They knew my face at the Provost for I was frequently obliged to go there by way of business. A clerk conducted me down the stone stairs to the room where an official served as a sort of turnkey controlling the comings and goings of the refugees. He was a red-faced Virginian who had grown plump on the pickings from his position.

410

He had no bribe from me. But he was all bows and compliments and attempts at discreet self-advertisement for he had an inflated notion of my influence at Headquarters and of the perquisites within my gift.

"A girl was brought in either yesterday or earlier today," I said. "Her name's Mehitabel Tippet, and she's from Westchester County."

"I know, sir. Nearly bit my hand off when we admitted her."

Dear God, I thought, she makes a habit of it: she bit poor Grantford too.

"Bring her to me now."

"Yes, sir, of course. Will you talk to her in here?"

"You misunderstand me. She is to be released into my care."

His eyes narrowed. I wondered what construction he put on my order. There was a rumour that he was not above extorting sexual favours from the women in his custody; and the worse a man is himself, the more likely he is to impute the worst motives to others.

But he knew better than to try to find out. Puffing with exertion, he hurried away, calling to the matron who oversaw the women's wing. Ten minutes later the two of them returned, with the girl between them like a filbert poised between a pair of enormous nutcrackers.

I should not have known her if we had passed in the street, though it was not two months since we had met. She had been thin, I remembered, with a mass of dark hair. But a child still. Her gown had been patched and faded but it had been clean.

She wore the same gown, now stained and torn as well as patched and faded. She was as thin as ever; her hair was even more tangled than it had been when we caught her poaching fish by the lake at Mount George. Her face was no longer clean, though someone had made a rough-and-ready attempt to wash it, leaving smudges of moisture on her dress.

But the real difference was that, in the eight weeks since I had seen her, she had aged as many years. There was a wariness about her expression. Her tiny breasts pushed against the thin material of her gown. She was still young but she had lost what had been childish about her.

Lost? Or had it snatched away?

"What about her possessions?" I asked.

"Here, your honour," the matron said, holding up a frayed straw basket.

"Give it to her."

The matron obeyed. She and the turnkey moved away from the girl, who did not look at me and whose face had remained expressionless throughout.

"You are to come with me," I said. "I'm standing surety for your good conduct."

Mehitabel said nothing. But she followed a few paces behind, trailing behind me like a whipped dog. I led her out on to the green and then stopped. She stared around her at the crowds and buildings. I wondered whether this was the first city she had ever seen in her short life.

"Mehitabel," I said.

She ran her tongue over chapped lips. She rubbed her hand down her hip in a gesture that belonged to an older woman in a different place. "What do you wish me to do, sir?"

As she spoke, her face lost what colour it had and she began to sway. I took her arm. I felt her recoil against my touch but she made no resistance to it. I supported her to a bench nearby. Her body was as light as a shuttlecock.

"When did you last eat?"

Her thin shoulders twitched. "Yesterday, sir, I think."

There was a coffee house on Broadway between Barclay and Robinson streets. It wasn't crowded at this time of day. I took her to one of the booths near the back where there was more privacy. I sat at the table and gestured for her to sit opposite me. When the waiter came, I ordered bread and soup for her, with some porter for her to drink and sherry for myself.

It struck me as odd that she did not seem to think it strange I should allow her to sit at table with me. Was it because her miseries had rendered her impervious to surprise? Or because she, as the daughter of a tenant farmer, had known better things before the war? Or was it simply the American way to ignore the niceties and distinctions of rank?

When the food came I ordered her to take it slowly. But I might as well have thrown the words to the wind. Within less than a moment her bowl and her platter were empty. She dabbed at the crumbs with her moistened finger and asked for more.

"No. Let that settle in your belly first. Then you shall have more."

For a moment we drank in silence. Her head was bowed, with the black hair falling like a curtain to hide the face. Grey lice moved busily among the threads.

"You had better tell me what happened."

She did not look up. "Mr Varden came back after you left, sir."

"Varden?" Jack had mentioned the name. "The Presbyterian deacon? The colonel of the local militia?"

"Yes, sir. Someone must have played the spy and told him. He ordered Mother to be whipped until she told him where you'd gone, and why you were come into the Debatable Ground, and what you were about at Mount George."

"But she didn't know."

Mehitabel ignored me. "And she had a fit, sir, from the pain maybe, and she died under the lash. She used to have queer turns, sir, but not like that. And Mr Varden said it was God's judgment on a sinner and a traitor."

"What happened to you?" I asked.

"Mr Varden took me into his family to work in the scullery, sir. He said it was an act of Christian charity to return good for evil, and heaven would bless him for it."

Her voice was fluent but monotonous as if she was reading a tedious account concerning, and composed by, someone in whom she had no particular interest.

Shelter and food, I thought. At least she had been safe among people who knew her. Then why had she

414

left? I said, "Have you news of your brother? Is he still with their army in South Carolina."

"He's dead of the pox and I hope he's in heaven."

"Is that why you left the Vardens?"

Her voice did not alter. "They made me sleep in the barn, sir. Mrs Varden told me that if I was hungry I should eat the scraps they fed the pigs with. And Mr Varden came by night and lay with me in the straw."

"What? Are you telling me —?"

At last she looked up and her expression stopped me in mid-sentence. "He said he was like Eliphaz the Temanite, Job's friend, sir. He said he'd come to commune with me and assuage my pains and, if I complained or whispered a word of it to anyone, he'd have me whipped for thieving till I bled and then turn me out of doors in my naturalibus."

In my naturalibus: suddenly Mehitabel had become a child again. I remembered my daughter, Lizzie, shrieking with joy when they stripped her for a bath by the kitchen fire and crying out that she was in her naturalibus at last like Adam and Eve in the Garden.

"What did you do?"

"I stole some food and ran away. I wanted to come to New York and ask Captain Wintour for help."

"You came here all by yourself?"

She shook her head. "I fell in with three men who said they were coming here. I went with them."

Her eyes dropped again. The words were ambiguous, though perhaps she had not intended them to be. I guessed what had happened. War makes animals of us — and most especially of gangs of men freed from the restraints of morality and discipline. Mehitabel had paid for her protection in the only coin she had.

After a moment she stirred and took a long drink of porter. "At King's Bridge, they told me Captain Wintour had been murdered," she went on. "So I tried to find you instead."

"You did right," I said. "You need have no concern for your future now. I shall talk to Judge Wintour and Mrs Arabella directly and see what can be arranged."

"But Miss Bella might not like it, sir."

"Why ever not? She would not blame you for the Captain's death, child. You had nothing to do with it."

"No, sir, it's not that. It's because I'd remind her of the night the squire was killed." She looked at me with large brown eyes, as guileless as an animal's. "I was there, you see."

CHAPTER
SIXTY-FIVE

"Please, sir," the child said. "I'm famished."

I beckoned the waiter and asked what he had. We settled on salt beef, onions and beans for Mehitabel and another glass of sherry for me. In truth I was glad of the interruption.

I knew enough of Mrs Arabella and the Judge to be sure that they would not abandon this unfortunate child who had so large a claim on their charity. If necessary, I would help defray any expense they might incur on Mehitabel's account.

But I was reluctant to march out of the coffee house and take the girl to Warren Street without preparing the ground beforehand. The household was in mourning for the dead and, perhaps, for the living. Mehitabel Tippet would serve as a reminder of a past that they were trying to forget.

There was another consideration. Providence had seen fit to supply me with an independent witness to what happened at Mount George nearly three years ago, to the series of events which had culminated in Mr Froude's murder and Mrs Arabella's flight to New York.

Those events had led, in the end, to Captain Wintour's expedition to Mount George and possibly to his murder. I believed they might also have had other consequences, large and small, that might go some way towards explaining much that had puzzled and disturbed me ever since my arrival in New York.

The key to the mystery might lie in the memory of this frail girl. I needed to question her, to draw out every scrap of information she had, before taking her to Warren Street. There she would be drawn away from my control.

I sipped my sherry and watched her eat. She hunched over the plate like a cat over her prey and shovelled the food into her mouth. When she had done, she swallowed her wine in two long draughts. Her cheeks fired up with colour. She sat back and licked her lips. She yawned.

"Were you often at Mount George?" I said, keeping my tone casual as if nothing more than idle curiosity was behind the question. "Before it burned down, I mean."

Mehitabel looked up. "Yes, sir. My father had a good deal of business with Mr Froude and sometimes for a treat I went over with him. And sometimes he'd leave me there for a day or two because the housekeeper had a kindness for me, and I'd help her in the still-room."

"Was your father's business about the farm?"

"I suppose so, sir."

"This was after the war began?"

She nodded. "But we hardly noticed it at first, sir. Wasn't like later. I remember seeing Mr Jack riding off

418

to war and Mr Froude said he'd be back before the summer was over because rebels couldn't last long."

"That must have been in the spring of seventy-six." I paused. "When Mrs Arabella was with child."

"Oh yes, sir." She wiped her mouth with her sleeve. She seemed quite at her ease now, slumping back against the wall. "Poor lady. And Squire was cock-a-hoop — he was sure she'd give him an heir. Only it wasn't a boy, as you know, sir, and it was born dead or dying. That was a terrible time — I was all alone in that house because Father had left me there, and that's when the rebel soldier came, the very morning after the birth. He —"

"What? It was the same day as they fired the mansion?"

"Oh no, sir — that was later. This was the first time Sergeant Pickett came, when Squire was busy with Juvenal in the —"

"Stop a moment, child. Let me take this slowly. Can you recall when this happened? The day of the month?"

She screwed up her eyes in concentration while her fingers fiddled with the spoon on her plate. She seemed to remain in this state for minutes. I opened my mouth, intending to question her further. But there was an interruption, a sudden flurry of activity and oaths from the doorway.

Both of us looked in the direction of the noise. A soldier had bustled into the coffee house from Broadway. He was clearly in a hurry and had knocked into a waiter, sending a tray of empty tankards flying.

I recognized the soldier, an orderly who was often in attendance on Major Marryot. He marched smartly towards us, sweeping the protesting waiter aside with his arm.

"Your honour." He came to attention. "Letter from Major Marryot, sir."

He handed me an unsealed and roughly folded square of paper with my name in pencil on the outside, written in Marryot's hurried and almost illegible hand.

"Went to Hanover Square first, your honour, like the Major said, then they sent me to the Provost, and as luck would have it, the sentry had seen you and —"

"Hold your tongue," I said.

The paper contained one of Marryot's laconic communications:

Dear Savill, The fleet is arrived from Ireland under convoy of the *Roebuck*. An express for you. R.M.

An express? But this could not possibly be Rampton's reply to my report concerning the fatal expedition to Mount George and Captain Wintour's death. My letter to him had left New York barely six weeks earlier and he might not even have received it yet. Yet why else send an express?

We walked down Broadway to Fort George with the orderly several paces ahead, clearing our way through the afternoon crowd. When we reached Headquarters, I consigned Mehitabel into the orderly's care, gave the man a few pence and told him to take her down to the buttery. Mehitabel was reluctant to leave me, for mine was the one familiar face in this incomprehensible and uncomprehending crowd.

I went directly to the Post Room. The head clerk saw me enter and abandoned the officer he was dealing with and came across to me at once with the express from the Department. The direction was in Rampton's hand. I signed for the letter. Unable to wait, I tore it open and turned aside to read it.

Rampton's handwriting was a blotchy scrawl, as if he had written in a hurry and in bad light, perhaps on his travelling desk as he swayed and jolted in his coach. My eyes went to the date: 7 August. That was the very day I had begun to write my carefully worded report on the Mount George journey.

I read the letter, but I did not take in the sense — partly because of the speed at which I skimmed it and partly because the news it contained was so unexpected, so unbelievable, that my mind simply could not grasp it at first reading.

My dear Savill, I have most distressing news and I shall not beat about the bush with it. Mrs Savill is no longer in London. I regret to inform you that she left for the Continent by the Rotterdam packet on the 5th inst. Worse still, she was not alone. She was travelling with a man who in London has been passing himself off as the Freiherr George von Streicher, a Bavarian gentleman attached to the Court of the Elector Charles Theodore. Before she embarked, she wrote most impertinently to me saying that she intends to convert to Catholicism, which will enable the Pope to annul your marriage to her and permit her to marry von Streicher. She seems unaware that neither the Pope nor her lover is likely to oblige her in this. Von Streicher is no more a Freiherr than I am and is quite possibly married already. I shall write at greater length by the next packet. Needless to say the scandal is all over London and is causing many difficulties. It is a great pity you did not see fit to take the foolish woman with you to New York. H.R.

Lizzie, I thought — does Lizzie know she has been abandoned by her mother? Another, much worse notion flew into my mind: surely her mother would not have taken her with her to Rotterdam or even Munich? I crumpled the letter into my fist and hammered it against the counter. A hush fell. Men looked up from their letters and stared at me. The clerk took a step towards me, his hand outstretched.

I ignored them all. I left the Post Room and collected Mehitabel from the buttery. She peered strangely at me as we walked away from Headquarters but said nothing.

"What is it, sir?" the girl asked me.

"Nothing."

"You're very pale, sir."

I looked blankly at her. Then: "It need not concern you, child."

422

CHAPTER
SIXTY-SIX

We retraced our steps up Broadway. I had no plan of action, no destination in view. I walked quickly with my head down. The girl trotted beside me. After a few hundred yards, she touched my arm.

"Please, sir," she said. "May we go more slowly?"

By this time I had almost forgotten that Mehitabel was with me. I glanced down at her. She was breathing hard and her left hand was pressed to her side. It occurred to me belatedly that she must be weary and footsore, and that the heavy meal she had eaten must add to the discomfort that the exercise caused her.

We were passing the ruins of Trinity on our left. I led her through the gate into the churchyard. At that hour it was not crowded, apart from a group of workmen making ready for the evening festivities to mark the coronation.

I had not been there since the funeral. I crossed the grass to the railing that enclosed the square where the Wintours lay. The earth inside was dry and powdery from the heat of the summer. The stonemason had not yet fulfilled his commission so there was no marker to show that Jack's body lay a few feet below us.

The girl knew nothing of this. I sat on a nearby bench and gestured that she might join me. For a while we listened to the whistling of the workmen and the blows of their hammers.

I am a cuckold, I thought. And soon Rampton will deprive me of my position as well. I am only a hindrance to him now.

"Shall I go on, sir?" Mehitabel said quietly.

"What?" I barked.

She shied away as though I had hit her. That brought me to my senses, or at least part-way towards them. The child had suffered enough already and would suffer more in the future. There was no need for me wantonly to increase her sorrows.

"Go on with what?" I asked in a gentler voice.

"You were asking about Mount George, sir. In the coffee house, you remember — just before the soldier came."

I wonder now whether Mehitabel spoke by design — whether, with a woman's natural sympathy sharpened by the troubles she had herself endured, she divined that I needed distraction.

"Do you remember?" she repeated.

Indeed, I remembered: Sergeant Pickett.

The rebel soldier who had come to Mount George. My mind seized on the diversion. Here was Roger Pickett again — a sergeant, just as Dr Slype had told me that Pickett had been in the spring of 1776, when the rebels had garrisoned New York itself and Dr Slype had encountered him in the street.

424

But if Pickett had been at Mount George at the same time that Mrs Arabella had given birth, that must have been in November of the same year when General Washington and his beaten army had abandoned the city and were retreating from the British.

In this instant, a possible pattern emerged, as if it had been waiting only for this single hint to draw it out, for Mehitabel to say the words that linked Roger Pickett with the destruction of Mount George. Before the war, Froude had bought the Pickett estate, knowing that there was a vein of gold on the land. Had Pickett heard, or guessed, something of that? Had he thought himself cheated? A lawyer would say he had no case worth arguing. But a moral philosopher might well argue that Pickett had a point.

Finding himself in the vicinity of Mount George among the rabble of a retreating army, it was natural enough that Pickett should pay Mr Froude a visit in the hope of extracting more from him — or merely to plunder the place for what he could find. But Froude, from what I knew of him, would not have been an easy man to browbeat.

Had he brought his murder on his own head?

Perhaps Froude had been foolish enough to boast of his discovery; for at that stage of the conflict it must have seemed that the war was all but over, and that the King's authority would soon be restored throughout his North American colonies; and he must have felt himself safe, in his own house, surrounded by his own servants and slaves. In any case, I could safely infer that he had made some mention of his box of curiosities —

something that had linked it with the gold in Pickett's mind, which would explain the latter's reference to it in the letter to his sister in England.

"You said the first time the rebel soldier came," I said. "So this man Pickett came more than once. Was he alone?"

"Yes, sir — that first time. I heard him and Squire shouting at each other. It was a terrible day — we'd just heard that the babe wasn't likely to live."

I looked at Mehitabel. She told this story without emotion in her voice, with no trace of remembered fear. Yet surely she had been terrified?

"You heard them shouting? Pickett was in the house with you?"

"No, sir — he was outside with squire. You see, he came when they were gelding Juvenal so he went to the yard. He followed the screams."

I frowned, thinking I had misheard. "Whose screams? Was Mrs Arabella still in labour?"

"No, sir — Juvenal's."

"But *gelding* him? What do you mean by that?" Surely the girl knew what the word meant? She was a farmer's daughter, after all. "You geld a horse or a pig or a —"

"Or a man, sir. It is all the same."

I took a deep breath. "Tell me. As far as you can."

"Mr Froude was in a terrible passion that day because he'd hoped for an heir. Father said squire was the proudest man in America, sir, and he could never bear to be crossed. And when he flew into a rage he'd

426

lash out at anyone. He'd have the slaves whipped for the slightest thing."

"But gelding —?"

"He said Juvenal had stolen money and must be punished to make an example. So he had the men take him down to the yard . . . there was a building nearby they sometimes used for the animals."

The old scullery, I thought, that must be it. I remembered the brick floor sloping down to the central drain, the ovens, the rings fixed low on the walls with the decaying ropes still attached to them. Near the drain there had been a dented iron plate, a hammer and a pair of pincers.

I remembered too how I had spat out a fly and how I had rubbed at a spot of spittle on the plate. I remembered the tint of rust-red on my fingertip. But had it been rust or the last trace of Juvenal's emasculation?

"What happened then? Did Pickett see all this?"

"I don't know, sir. I was at the window of the housekeeper's room. I saw the sergeant going towards the yard. And after a while squire and his men came out with him and sent him packing. That's when they were shouting at each other."

"When did Pickett come back?" I asked.

"A night or two later, sir, with a dozen men or more. Rebel soldiers. They stole what they could take and defiled some of the women and they set fire to the house. I hid behind a mattress in the slave quarters. That's where they had taken Juvenal — he was lying there, crying out and groaning like a madman. They'd

427

given him opium and rum for the pain but it wasn't enough."

A memory stirred: something did not quite agree with what I had heard previously. I tried to pin down the anomaly but it slipped away like a retreating fish in the dark waters of a pond.

Defiled?

The implications hit me at last. "Where was Mrs Arabella?"

"I don't know." The child's brittle composure was cracking. The muscles of her face worked. "Then Mr Froude came running, sir," she went on. "He came into the slave quarters to hide. And Juvenal reared up and stabbed him."

CHAPTER
SIXTY-SEVEN

A great trouble has one advantage: it casts out a lesser one.

I had been considerably exercised in my mind about how to provide for Mehitabel in view of the possibility that Mrs Arabella might refuse to take her in. But the difficulty was trivial in comparison with the news that I was a cuckold and that I had lost the support of my patron at the American Department. So I simply ignored it.

When we reached Warren Street, I told Josiah to take the girl down to the kitchen and give her into the care of the cook. I sent up a few lines to Mrs Arabella, explaining that I had brought Mehitabel Tippet to the house at least for temporary refuge; I reminded her that Mehitabel and her mother had helped Captain Wintour and myself, and that her poor mother had paid for this with her life. In a quarter of an hour, Miriam brought me her mistress's reply, a cold little note saying that this was quite in order.

Having settled the matter, I went out again and walked aimlessly to and fro — down to the harbour, round by the Battery and up towards Greenwich. By the time I returned home, it was growing dark. Mrs

Arabella and the Judge were upstairs. I told Josiah to bring me something to eat in the parlour.

Though I was footsore and weary I knew I would not sleep for hours. I also knew that doing anything is generally preferable to doing nothing, so I fixed on the plan of writing letters to Lizzie, her aunt and Mr Rampton. I had pen and ink brought to me in the parlour, where the light was better than in my chamber, and ordered up a bottle of claret in case my sorrows needed drowning.

The immediate difficulty that faced me now was distance. Lizzie was three thousand miles away. Any letter I wrote would not reach her and her aunt for five or six weeks at the very least. In a way my problem was identical to that which, in another sphere, bedevilled Lord George Germain in London and General Clinton in New York. Communication between England and America was necessarily so slow that in many respects it was almost worse than no communication at all.

The daylight faded. I tried to write to Lizzie, to assure her that I should soon be home and that we should be together again. Knowing Augusta as I did, I did not think it likely that she would have taken our daughter away with her, though the possibility lingered to haunt my nightmares.

I had barely reached the second sentence when I heard footsteps in the hall. The door opened and Mrs Arabella entered with a book under her arm. I rose and bowed. Josiah followed her, bringing candles.

I drew out a chair for her. Josiah lit the candles and withdrew. I waited for Mrs Arabella to open her book.

She looked up, raising her chin. "Are you at leisure for a moment, sir?"

"Of course." I laid down my pen, wondering if she intended to continue our conversation about the gold.

"I wished to thank you for bringing Mehitabel Tippet to us."

"Will it inconvenience you to have her here?"

Her eyebrows rose. "Not in the slightest. Why should it? Besides, we have a duty to care for her — she's the daughter of one of our tenants. We shall let her find her feet with us and by and by I shall look about for a respectable situation for her."

Neither of us spoke for a moment. My eyes drifted down to the letter in front of me — not the one to Lizzie but Mr Rampton's to me.

It is a great pity you did not see fit to take the foolish woman with you to New York.

"Forgive me, sir — and I do not wish to intrude — but you do not look at all well. Are you ill?"

"No, madam. I am quite well. It is merely that I have had distressing news from home."

"Your daughter?"

"No, thank God. As far as I know, she is in good health." I hesitated. Then, before I could put a brake on my tongue, I heard the terrible truth spilling out of my mouth. "It appears that my wife has eloped with a German gentleman. Though 'gentleman' is too kind a word for him."

431

I did not dare look at her face but I heard her sharp intake of breath. I did not mind her disgust. But I could not support it if she showed pity for me.

"And your daughter?" she said again.

"She has been living with her aunt. I hope and pray she is there still."

Mrs Arabella gestured towards my writing materials. "I'm afraid I am a distraction."

"That is an advantage at present, madam. I'm trying to write to Lizzie, but it may be days until the next mailbag goes."

"Then let us play a game to occupy ourselves."

I stared at her. "A game?"

She stared back at me — directly, as a man does, with no pretence of modesty. "Why not? You want distraction and so do I. Backgammon?"

I agreed to this and rang the bell for the servant. In theory, Mrs Arabella was in mourning so it was scarcely decent for her to play at backgammon, even in private. But hers was a strange sort of mourning. Besides, I reminded myself, this was America, where they did things differently.

Josiah brought us the board and set the chairs so we faced each other across the table with the candles burning on either side of the board. Mrs Arabella told him to bring another wine glass.

I remembered the time I had played backgammon with Jack Wintour on the occasion that he had threatened to sell Miriam to pay his debts. I opened the board and spread the counters. The shaker was there, and the pair of bone dice.

432

When I was done, I sat back and pushed two fingers into the pocket of my waistcoat. I felt the outlines of the two ivory dice: one from Pickett's body, the other from the belvedere at the bottom of the garden; discovered in different places and eleven months apart; yet alike as peas in a pod.

"Well, sir," Mrs Arabella said. "Do we play for love or money?"

The words were capable of more than one interpretation. There was nothing flirtatious about her demeanour. On the contrary, she sat back in her chair as she spoke and her tone was unemotional, almost uninterested.

"For love perhaps." I did not look at her as I spoke. I drew out the two ivory dice from my pocket and dropped them on the open board: a pair of sixes. "Will you indulge me, madam? These are my lucky dice."

I raised my eyes. Did a flicker of emotion cross her face when she saw them? It might so easily have been merely the shifting of light and shadow on her cheeks, caused by the swaying candle flames.

"Why not?" She picked up the wooden dice and set them to one side. "But I had not put you down as a gambler, sir."

"Not from choice."

I set the pieces in their places. Mrs Arabella sipped her wine. She rarely took wine, even with dinner. Like so many of the American ladies I met in New York, there was something of the puritan about her. I felt a contradictory surge of desire for her, as shameful as it was inconvenient.

We played the first game. I won, though the victory could have gone either way until the last throw.

"Your dice have brought you good luck," Mrs Arabella said.

"Then perhaps we should use the other pair for the next game."

"I think not. These may bring me luck this time."

My attention wandered from the game and returned to Mr Rampton's letter and its implications. Augusta had eloped with her German lover. By law, her adultery was grounds for divorce. But I knew that in practice a divorce decree required a private member's bill in Parliament, which was both expensive and time-consuming; divorce was not a luxury that was open to a person in the middling rank of society. I could not allow myself to hope for Augusta's death. Yet unless she died, I should never be free to marry again. My future seemed bleak indeed.

I looked up and found Mrs Arabella staring at me.

"You are wool-gathering, sir," she said with an affectation of severity. "I've nearly gammoned you and you haven't noticed. You see I was right about your lucky dice. They are as fickle as fate."

With an effort, I smiled at her. "Shall we make it the best of three games?"

We set the board for the third time. This time I concentrated on the game. It was another close-run affair but fortune was unkind to Mrs Arabella in the closing stage of the game and I won comfortably.

"It was not very gallant of you, sir," she said. "But I shall be forgiving and blame it on your dice. How glad I am that we were not playing for money."

She rose to her feet as she was speaking. We said goodnight and I opened the door for her. I sat down again at the table. I noticed that she had barely touched her wine.

I slipped the ivory dice into my pocket, placed the backgammon counters on the board and closed the box.

As I took up my glass, her words recurred to me: *How glad I am that we were not playing for money.* But now I saw the possibility — the hope? — of a double entendre.

We had agreed not to play for money. We had agreed to play for love.

CHAPTER
SIXTY-EIGHT

In the middle of war, New York slumbered in its own dreary peace.

We did not forget the dead. Jack Wintour's absence left a wound in the Warren Street house that affected all of us. But in a week or two the wound began to scab over. It itched and ached but it no longer bled unless we could not resist the temptation to scratch it.

Early in October, I received another letter from Mr Rampton, as chilly in tone as its predecessor. He had received a report confirming that Augusta was now in Munich. He also eased my mind, perhaps unintentionally, by enclosing letters from my sister and my daughter, who were still in Shepperton.

I felt a sadness for my poor wife. Augusta could never be received in polite society again. Respectable people would close their doors to her. She was in all probability condemned to a half-life on the Continent. I knew I could not quite abandon her for she was still the mother of my child. I must discover whether she was in actual want and, if necessary, send her money.

Mr Rampton wrote that the elopement continued to delight the gossips in London and cause distress and inconvenience to himself. More to the point, Lord

George had intimated that he did not at all like the notion that the American Department was connected with such a disagreeable scandal. Worse still, Mr Rampton hinted, news of my wife's behaviour had reached the ear of the King himself, who was not pleased. The royal marriage was notably happy and His Majesty did not see why the marriages of his subjects should be any different.

That being so, Mr Rampton continued, it had been found necessary to review my employment at the Department. His Lordship had reluctantly concluded that it would not be in the Department's best interests for me to remain in my clerkship. Though I was not of course directly to blame for Augusta's behaviour, I must accept some of the responsibility for it for a man should direct his wife in all things. Another clerk would be sent out to replace me in the spring; I should return as soon as possible after his arrival.

Rampton made no mention of finding me a post in a different department, though I knew such a transfer would be a simple matter for a man of his influence. He had never liked his niece and had helped me only reluctantly into a place. Now her behaviour gave him all the reason he needed to sever connections with both of us.

He did not actually say that in so many words. He was too wily a man to commit to anything unless there was a clear advantage to himself in doing so. That was one reason why he was an under secretary.

The weeks passed and autumn slipped away. Mehitabel settled in the household, though I rarely saw her. Mrs Arabella told me that the girl was competent with her needle and was making herself useful.

In November, I heard again from Mr Rampton. This time there was no mention of my unhappy wife for he had received my report of the Mount George expedition and of Captain Wintour's as-yet unsolved murder. This would have set the seal on my disgrace if the seal had not been set on it already.

It was at about this time that I began to notice that I was no longer received so warmly at Headquarters as I had been. Even the provincial and city officials grew cool towards me.

Nobody said anything directly. Gradually, however, I realized that I had ceased to be considered the coming man whose friendship it might be useful to cultivate. The news that I was to be recalled in the spring had become widely known. To make matters worse, my wife's elopement conferred a vicarious taint on me. The flow of invitations to concerts, supper-parties and dinners diminished to a trickle and then stopped altogether.

I still saw Noak, who continued occasionally to act as Judge Wintour's secretary and sometimes came to Warren Street. But he avoided unnecessary conversation. As for his master, Townley confined our intercourse to the bare minimum required by his responsibilities and mine.

On the whole my unpopularity did not distress me unduly: I knew that my time in New York was coming to an end and that, in all probability, I should never meet my acquaintance here again. I consoled myself with the thought that at least I should see Lizzie soon. As for the loss of my employment, I hoped there would be an opening for an honest man in the prime of life who could cast accounts and write a fair hand. While I found my feet again in England, my sister would not allow Lizzie or me to starve.

It was the change in Major Marryot's manner that surprised me most and, I own, made me a little unhappy. During the last twelve months, I had come to believe that he and I had put aside the coldness of our early relations in favour of something warmer that was, if not quite friendship, at least mutual esteem.

He and I were still obliged to work together but there was no longer any hint of our former intimacy. I encountered him once or twice in Mrs Arabella's drawing room and was tempted to smile at the quandary that his emotions placed him in: he was drawn to her like an iron filing to the positive pole of a magnet; and yet I took the part of the negative pole and repelled him.

On one occasion at Headquarters, Marryot and I happened to pass in the crowded passage outside the Post Room. He jostled against me, pushing me at the wall. He paused and, for a moment, our eyes met.

He stared at me, daring me to make something of his rudeness, even hoping that I would, so it would give him an opportunity to vent his hostility against me more effectively. Duels were officially frowned upon in New York but they were not unknown.

Neither of us spoke. I held his gaze for a moment but refused to allow him to provoke me. I turned on my heel and walked away.

CHAPTER
SIXTY-NINE

Towards the end of the month I had occasion to go across to Long Island, where a gang of irregulars from the mainland had murdered a Loyalist refugee from Connecticut in front of his family for the sake of a few guineas. I took depositions from witnesses and did what I could for the victim's widow and children.

Afterwards, I had an hour or two in hand. The day was fine, though very cold. En route back to the Brooklyn ferry I made a detour to the south that took me a mile or so out of my way. The distillery was here beside its own jetty, with a stumpy mole poking out to sea in the direction of Nutten Island.

I enquired of a fisherman where I might find Mr Townley's warehouse. He directed me to a large low building a couple of hundred yards back from the coast. Here I found Mr Ingham, the manager, in an office that overlooked the grey waters of the bay.

He was a stooped man a few years older than myself. His features were mobile and not without charm, though the vertical lines that scored his forehead hinted at habitual anxiety. The warmth of his welcome suggested that he seldom saw company in this place.

He knew of me by reputation, but seemed unaware of my recent fall from grace.

I explained that the Townleys had mentioned him and I had called in as I happened to be in the neighbourhood on business. He immediately asked me to dine. I said I was pressed for time but we drank a glass or two of very tolerable sherry and chatted for half an hour.

"I'm surprised we have not encountered each other before," I said as Mr Ingham poured the second glass.

"I'm rarely in the city these days," he replied, with a twitch of his head as though the subject of himself embarrassed him. "I'm obliged to live here because there is constant danger of thieves and, besides, deliveries may come and go at any time. We are so dependent on the weather, are we not, sir?" He darted a glance at me and ventured a pleasantry. "That and the caprice of our masters and the uncertainties of this war."

"Have you been here long?"

"Nearly fifteen months now. Not that I grumble, you understand — the position is a most responsible one. I was Mr Townley's confidential clerk before that, as you may know, but he wished to assist an American gentleman from England into the place. But that was only part of his reason — he told me that I was wasted as his clerk. He was kind enough to say that I should have more scope for my talents here."

I bowed my head in acknowledgment of Mr Townley's acumen. "The American gentleman must be Mr Noak," I said. "I've come across him a good deal."

442

"I'm sure he is a most competent man of business," Mr Ingham said with an air of uncertainty, as if he would have been delighted to hear the opposite.

"No doubt, sir. But he strikes me as a man who works best under orders, under close supervision. Whereas yourself . . ."

I left the flattery unsaid, secure in the knowledge that my host would fill in the blanks more effectively than I could ever do.

Mr Ingham's face was pinker than it had been, perhaps because of the sherry. "I — ah — I like to think that Mr Townley realized that I would be equal to the added responsibility. And indeed Mrs Townley too."

I raised my eyebrows in polite surprise.

"Oh yes," he went on. "I have known her for much longer than Mr Townley because her father was my old master. She has a surprisingly good head for business — like her father before her, of course, in his prime." He gestured out of the window, at the looming bulk of the warehouse. "All this was his, you know, and came to her on his death. That's why Mr Townley needed to install a manager. Mark you, I have not found it easy."

"The war?"

"That has caused us many problems, sir, but it has also brought many opportunities in its wake. No, I'm afraid the profits had suffered in the last year of the old gentleman's life because he'd become foolish and absurdly secretive. He saw rebels behind every bush. He was so terrified of spies that he would not do his accounts in ink; he insisted on using lemon juice to render the figures invisible. He slept with an armed servant lying across his doorway and with pistols under his pillow. Why, sir, the stories I could tell you."

I could not prevent my host from telling me some of his stories about Mrs Townley's father in his dotage. When at last I rose to leave, declining yet another invitation to stay to dinner, Mr Ingham saw me to my horse, talking all the way.

"Pray give my compliments to Mr Townley," he said as I prepared to ride off into the gathering gloom of the afternoon. "And to Mrs Townley."

"A charming lady," I said by way of a venture.

Mr Ingham nodded vigorously and his face flushed an even darker shade of pink. "Yes, sir, indeed she is."

The winter besieged New York more effectively than the Continental Army was ever able to do. The weather forced inactivity on both sides. Little of note, in the military sense, took place after our forces repelled a rebel attack on Savannah in October. Washington set up his quarters in Morristown in New Jersey, where he remained for many months.

The snow began to fall in November. It fell heavily and continuously throughout the winter. Great drifts clogged the gutters and banked up against the buildings. The traffic crawled through the streets and often stopped altogether. Soldiers and prisoners of war, organized into gangs, tried to keep the main roads clear, fighting a losing battle with the snow and ice. Even the whores were driven off the streets.

The rivers, creeks, harbours, ports and bays around Manhattan Island were choked with ice. Judge Wintour told me that he had never seen the like of it in all his years. As the ice thickened and spread, this led to another difficulty for the city: it hindered the passage of victuals from eastern Long Island and, worse still, from England.

General Clinton managed to sail for Charleston in late December with as much of the army as could be spared. After that, the cold steadily worsened and the ice extended its grip. By the middle of January, ice formed a broad if irregular bridge across the Hudson to the shores of New Jersey. Manhattan was no longer an island. Deserters from Long Island crossed over the ice from Lloyds Neck to Connecticut.

It was an anxious time for we lived in fear that the rebels would take advantage of our weakness and simply walk across the Hudson and into the city, whose garrison was now seriously reduced thanks to General Clinton's expedition to South Carolina.

Morale was low. It is difficult to keep up one's courage when one is cold and often hungry. To make matters worse, the authorities were completely unprepared for the severity of the winter. The stocks of timber had already been depleted in the previous winters of the war. What little remained was terribly expensive and it tended to be reserved for the army and for senior officials.

It was colder than ever in Warren Street. Major Marryot did his best to help for the sake of the *beaux yeux* of Mrs Arabella. To know that every cord of timber he managed to find for her would also provide warmth for me must have been wormwood to his jealous soul.

Even inside the house, we wore greatcoats or cloaks as well as hats and gloves. The chamberpots froze solid and the windows caked with opaque sheets of ice on the inner side of the glass. We spent long hours in our beds, burrowed beneath mounds of blankets, furs and quilts.

The Wintours did their best to keep three fires alight. We needed the one in the kitchen for the cooking; it also warmed the domestics, who found it more comfortable to sleep there, the two sexes jumbled together in defiance of decency. There was another fire in Mrs Wintour's room; she was now permanently confined to her bed, which had been moved into a small closet that communicated directly with her daughter-in-law's chamber. Mrs Arabella, the Judge and I spent our waking lives in the library, which was smaller than the other apartments and therefore easier to heat.

The cold weather threw the three of us into a curious intimacy. I confess I came to like it for I am not by nature a solitary animal. We huddled round the small fire, each with our feet on the fender, with a kettle always warming on the hob at the back of the grate. We often took our meals in this inelegant position. More than once, I suspect, the Judge did not bother to retire to his cold bedroom but spent the night in the library, dozing in his chair and wrapped in an old cloak that had once belonged to his son.

Sometimes Mr Noak would battle his way through the streets and join us, ostensibly to assist with the Judge's labours on his history of New York. In practice this meant that the Judge would talk about the unwritten portions of the book, meandering through the decades and centuries; he would discuss the people he had known as a young man and describe long-past conversations he had had with them. He would send Mr Noak to fetch particular items from his research materials; but, by the time he had the item to hand, he would often have forgotten why he wanted it in the first place.

"There is so much to do," he would say to us, wringing his hands at the immensity of the task. "So many documents to consult, so many men to write to, so many words to set down. I truly believe it will run to four volumes rather than three by the time I am done."

For all his labours, and those of Mr Noak, the Judge had not yet reached the year 1664, when the Duke of York's men had wrested control of the city from the Dutch West India Company.

Sometimes in the evening Mr Wintour would ask me to read from his manuscript. I read by the light of a candle made from spermaceti smuggled in from Rhode Island; it gave a better light than one made of wax, which I sorely needed to decipher the ever-increasing tangle of emendations, additions and footnotes.

On one occasion, the sound of his own words drove the Judge to slumber. When his breathing became stertorous and regular, I stopped reading. Mrs Arabella and I exchanged glances.

A few minutes later, Mr Wintour twitched violently and awoke in a rush. He stared about him as if uncertain where he was. Mrs Arabella took his hand and stroked it. Blinking, he looked first at her and then at me. He rubbed his eyes with the unselfconsciousness of a child.

"I am become a refugee in my own city," he said in a clear, distinct voice. "I never thought it would come to this, my dears. It pierces my heart."

CHAPTER
SEVENTY

There was little enough to celebrate at Christmas. In the first week of the new year, I received a letter from Mr Townley asking me to sup with him at Mrs Chawley's on the following Monday. "These are sad times," he wrote, "and we must find ways to enliven them."

In earlier days I would have been intrigued and even flattered. I knew the house only by reputation. It was both expensive and select. One did not go there except by invitation.

After Mr Townley's coolness to me during the last few months, his offer of hospitality was unexpected. I wondered whether it had anything to do with my visit to Mr Ingham, his former clerk, and my suspicions concerning Mr Noak. I accepted the invitation, nevertheless.

A day or two later, Mrs Arabella and I were sitting in the Judge's library. Josiah had taken away our supper trays. Only the two of us were there, for Mr Wintour was in his wife's chamber, encouraging her to eat a bowl of soup and take a sip of sherry.

The wood on the fire was unseasoned apple, stripped from someone's orchard. It crackled and spat as it burned. The kettle was on the hob, heating the water for tea. Apart from the flames from the fire, the only light came from a single candle at Mrs Arabella's elbow, which made it difficult for me to see her face.

We had not exchanged a word for at least ten minutes. The silence did not feel unnatural and neither of us rushed to break it. In the intervals of wondering how on earth I should contrive to make a living when I returned to England, I was thinking of Mr Noak. When I had returned to the house earlier this evening, I had found him in the library, sharpening pens at the secretary with a file of letters open in front of him. There was nothing out of the way in this. The Judge now allowed him an entirely free hand among his papers.

Mrs Arabella stirred in her chair. Her head turned towards me. "May I ask you something, sir?"

"Of course."

"I do not want to pry but what is your opinion of Mr Noak?"

I sat up sharply, dislodging the blanket which was draped over my knees. "How strange. I was turning over just the same question in my mind."

"And what were your conclusions?"

"I haven't reached them yet, madam."

She laughed. "Nor have I."

"Why do you ask?"

"He's about the house a great deal. Why should he spare us so much time? Tell me — have you known him long?"

"I met him by chance on the passage from England."

"You shared a cabin, I think?"

"Yes — Mr Noak was travelling privately, not on public business. I was very seasick at the start of the voyage and he was kind to me."

"So you had no previous acquaintance with him?"

"Not in the least."

I leaned forward, lit a spill at the fire and used it to light a second candle. Her face leapt out of the darkness.

I sat back in my chair and said, "As it happened, I knew of Mr Noak's previous employer by reputation. He is a Mr Yelland of the Temple — a lawyer who conducts a good deal of business for Loyalist gentlemen. Mr Noak was coming to New York because he had a position waiting for him here in a contractor's house. But when we arrived he found the man had died and the business had been wound up." I hesitated. "At least that's what he told me."

"And so he applied to you to use your influence on his behalf?"

"Yes — he came to me at breakfast on my very first morning here and told me of his difficulty. Later that day I saw Mr Townley — you remember we were engaged in that sad business with Mr Pickett at the time? — and he let fall that he was in want of a clerk because his own had just died of fever."

"And so you proposed Mr Noak," Mrs Arabella said. "That was obliging of you."

"Very. It seemed an easy way to repay a kindness. But I thought nothing more of it until a few weeks ago. I chanced to meet Mrs Townley —"

"Mrs Townley?" she interrupted. "In flesh and blood? I had thought she was a figment of Mr Townley's imagination."

"You are pleased to make fun of me, madam. Mrs Townley is a very agreeable lady, though retiring by nature and rather overwhelmed by her family cares. She happened to let fall that her husband's previous clerk, a Mr Ingham, is alive and well — he now manages a warehouse they own near Brooklyn."

"Perhaps this is a different clerk. Mr Townley may well employ more than one."

"Very true but, when I pressed the point, Mrs Townley said that Mr Noak had filled the vacancy that Mr Ingham had left. Before Christmas I encountered Mr Ingham himself, who told me quite categorically that Mr Noak had filled the position he had vacated as confidential clerk. More than that, he added that Mr Townley wanted to oblige an American gentleman from England: who proved to be Mr Noak."

"So it would seem that they were acquainted already," Mrs Arabella said.

"More than that, ma'am, I think. It suggests that Mr Townley and Mr Noak wanted me to believe — and the rest of the world, also — that their connection was through me. Indeed, that I had instigated it. In other words I was their puppet. I do not at all like that."

We were silent for a few minutes. The kettle emitted a gentle puff of steam, tinted orange by the flames.

"Then the question is why," Mrs Arabella said. "Do you propose to tell someone?"

452

"Who would listen?" I said. "Townley and Noak would deny it. It would be my word against theirs. And I do not think my word is worth very much in New York at present."

Mrs Arabella was far more in my thoughts than Mr Noak.

The worsening winter conditions forced the two of us closer and closer together. Augusta's elopement and Jack Wintour's death had removed two invisible barriers: these two events liberated my desires, though they did not license them.

I tried to persuade myself that I should have felt the same for any woman who lived in similar proximity to me, had she not been forbiddingly old or ugly. After all, it had now been a year and a half since I had lain with a woman, my wife. Some men find celibacy comes easily to them. I do not.

New York itself seemed to enflame the itch, to tease me, to play upon my weakness. During the war the city's population of whores grew ever larger, for soldiers attract them as dogs attract fleas; and as one died of pox or poverty, two or three more would arrive to take her place. They came in many guises, from the drabs who worked the alleys of Canvas Town to the elegant Cyprians who clung to the arms of generals.

I was tempted sorely but I did not succumb. My body took what petty revenge it could with nocturnal *emissiones seminis*. These formed an uneasy and unsatisfactory compromise between the rule of the will and the lusts of the flesh.

Mrs Arabella did not play the coquette. She was distant and frequently sullen in my company. She smiled rarely and was never completely frank. I thought that she treated me with suspicion, that I was an unwelcome guest in her house.

But she interested me. She fascinated me. She intrigued me.

First I allowed myself to think that I liked the woman, despite her obvious faults. Then I found excuses for those faults. Next I admitted to myself that I wanted her as a man wants a woman; for the thought of her slipped into my mind, particularly at night when I was defenceless; and by day I found ways to seek out her company.

Finally, on Monday, 10 January, the day appointed for my supper with Mr Townley, I admitted the truth to myself: I was in love with Mrs Arabella Wintour.

CHAPTER
SEVENTY-ONE

Mrs Chawley was known for the elegant suppers she provided for gentlemen and for the concerts she held in her big drawing room on the second Tuesday of every month. She was also known for her whores.

Her house was not far from Trinity churchyard in one direction and from the outskirts of Canvas Town in the other. The establishment was, as it were, poised between the two, precariously balanced on the cusp.

I went there by sedan chair from my office in Broad Street. The bearers slipped and swore all the way, for the streets were still crowded at that hour as well as treacherous with ice and frozen snow.

Mrs Chawley's porter, a huge black man, had been told to expect me. He ushered me into the hall. A pair of footmen converged to strip away my outer layers. Nothing was allowed to disturb the fiction that this was a lavishly appointed private house where I was a welcome guest.

As the servants were removing my greatcoat, Townley came bounding down the stairs like an overgrown schoolboy.

"My dear sir," he cried. "What a pleasure this is! It's been an age since we have had time for anything but business."

I played my part and greeted him with every appearance of happiness. When the footmen had finished with me, he drew my arm through his and took me upstairs to the drawing room, where he introduced me to our hostess.

Mrs Chawley was a very handsome woman, particularly by candlelight, who owned to thirty but was probably nearer forty. She was the widow of a major in the Queen's Rangers, whose death had left her without support for herself and her children.

A large fire burned in the grate, which was an unusual sight in any house in New York that winter. Also in the room were three younger ladies, newly arrived in the city, who were variously introduced as Mrs Chawley's cousins and the friends of her cousins. They were American but perfectly well-bred in the colonial way. There was also an officer in the 17th Regiment of Dragoons, whom I knew by sight; he bowed distantly to me but at once retired to converse with one of the ladies, drawing her away to the shadows at the far end of the room.

A footman served champagne. Townley and I chatted for a few minutes with Mrs Chawley and her other two young friends. There was nothing untoward in the conversation, though one of the ladies, a graceful brunette, was a little free with her gestures with me, sometimes touching my arm and laughing very loudly at any pleasantries I ventured; and I could not help noticing that her gown was unusually low-cut.

The genteel illusion that this was a private house came to an end when a footman entered with the news that, if Mr Townley pleased, supper was on the table in a nearby room.

We left the ladies where they were with many polite regrets and promises to return. The footman showed us into a neat, warm dining parlour on the same floor. Townley told the servants we would serve ourselves.

"You will not object if we rough it like a pair of old campaigners, sir," he said with smile. "We shall be more comfortable without the people of the house always coming and going."

We ate and drank very well — indeed, the food was so good and so varied that one would not have known that winter and General Washington had the city in their grip. I said as much to my host.

"Mrs Chawley is a fascinating woman," Townley replied, caressing his great nose. "She has many friends at Headquarters who are anxious to oblige her in any way they can. One can do nothing in this town without friends, can one?"

I nodded and smiled, sensing that Mr Townley was steering our conversation into deeper waters than before.

"It must be the same in London, of course," he went on. "Which reminds me: I heard a rumour that Mr Rampton has foolishly grown cool towards you. I trust it's no more than tittle-tattle? You have only to say the word and I shall contradict it."

"It's always hard to know what they are thinking in London."

I helped Mr Townley to wine to give myself a moment's grace. The news of Augusta's elopement had been in the parcel of London papers that reached New York in October. Newcomers from England must have garnished the scandal with further details, real and imaginary.

"But I will not conceal from you, sir," I went on, "that matters in London are not quite as I should wish them."

"Ah well." He refilled my glass and then his own before going on in the same casual tone: "Of course London is not the world."

"For me it is, sir, in a sense: it's where the American Department is."

"But a man of your parts could settle anywhere, Mr Savill, and do anything. When this tiresome war has run its course you might even consider settling in America. There are fortunes to be made in New York with a little application — and with the assistance of a few friends."

I bowed. "As you said earlier, one can do nothing without friends."

He smiled at me and sipped his wine. He had drunk at least twice as much as I had but there was no trace of intoxication in his manner or his speech.

"The young lady you were talking to just now — what was her name? Miss Clarissa? — She seemed greatly taken with you."

"No doubt she is easily pleased," I said.

"I doubt that. But she's a lovely girl, is she not?"

458

"Charming in all respects."

"I am sure she would be enchanted to continue your conversation. Would you like me to have a word with Mrs Chawley and see if something can be arranged? It would be no trouble. There are some quiet and very comfortable rooms upstairs where a lady and a gentleman may converse undisturbed for as long as they wish."

"Thank you but no," I said, though I was tempted. For who would care a jot if I said yes?

"Perhaps you may change your mind later," Townley said. "But to go back to our discussion of friendship. You have made many friends in New York, you know, and you have it in your power to make many more if you wish it."

"Is this to do with Mr Noak?" I said.

Something changed in Townley's face: the eyes momentarily narrowed, I think, and movement made the candlelight flare in the black reflections of his pupils.

"Noak?" He laughed. "Good God, no, of course not — though he has always stood your friend, ever since you came over together. He sings your praises. And he's not alone — he tells me the Wintours confide in you quite as if you were one of the family."

I did not speak. Mr Townley had not said whether Ingham had told him of my visit to the warehouse in Long Island. But these flattering overtures only made sense if he had learned that I had been enquiring about his connection with Mr Noak.

"We could do so much together," Townley said; and his drawling voice had a hypnotic quality, like the purring of a great cat. "You and I. The war will not last for ever. We should look beyond it. In a sense, it does not matter if the thirteen colonies govern themselves or not. The inhabitants of North America have far too much in common with the mother country to sever their ties with it."

"No doubt, sir." The wine tasted sour now. "But — would you excuse me? — I have had a long day, and I fear I cannot be good company."

He tried to persuade me to remain. When that failed he suggested that I might find Miss Clarissa's company a soothing distraction, and that if I felt sleepy he was sure that Mrs Chawley would be delighted for me to stay the night.

But I would not be dissuaded. Townley accepted my decision with the best of grace. I said my farewells to the ladies and then he accompanied me downstairs. The footmen wrapped me with tender solicitude against the cold. Townley told the porter to find me a hackney chair.

"You will not want to walk on a night like this," he said, turning back to me. "And of course you cannot go alone." He smiled and raised his eyebrows. "Unless you do not go at all. It's not too late to change your mind."

I declined but with an answering smile, for Townley was very charming and there was a part of me that felt I had been churlish — or even foolish — to treat his hospitality so ungraciously.

A knock announced the arrival of the sedan chair. The porter swung open the street door. The chairmen set down their burden. There was a third man holding aloft a lantern; the chairmen often worked in teams of three for they knew there was safety in numbers. The lantern-bearer was a tall fellow with what looked like a weighted stick in his belt. With his free hand he opened the door at the front of the chair for me.

"Warren Street," Townley told them from the house doorway. "Judge Wintour's house. Mind you don't slip, my men. Good God, it's colder than ever."

I climbed into the chair and sat on the narrow bench. "Thank you and goodnight," I said.

"A safe journey, my friend. And God bless you."

I knocked at the ceiling of the chair with the head of my stick as a signal to depart. The man with the lantern closed the door. The other men lifted the poles and I lurched a foot into the air. I lowered the glass at the side and waved to Townley, who raised his hand in farewell. I pulled up the glass and sat back on the unyielding seat.

One of the men slipped as we rounded the corner towards Trinity. The chair canted sharply to the right. The glass clattered down, for I had failed to secure it properly with the strap at the top. I swore, fearing that in another moment they would overset the chair and throw me into the freezing filth of the street.

The lantern-bearer, who was still walking alongside, glanced at me. Like the other two men, he was muffled to the eyes against the cold. But the sudden movement had loosened the scarf around the lower part of his face. He and I were only a few inches apart, staring at each other through the open window. His face was illuminated by his own lantern.

I saw a large black man with angry scars running from the corners of his eyes to the corners of his mouth.

CHAPTER
SEVENTY-TWO

Scarface.

I had no inclination for bravery. I acted with the instinctive desperation of a terrified rabbit.

I kicked the door open. I threw myself out of the chair. The door collided with the broad back of the leading bearer. I was outside now but trapped by the chair behind, the poles on either side and the fellow in front of me.

He had already begun to turn his head. I had my stick in both hands. I rammed its weighted head up against his jaw. He cried out and dropped the poles. The bearer at the back lost control. The chair tipped sideways, colliding with the man with the lantern.

Scarface.

I pushed the man in front of me aside and burst free. For a few precious seconds, the three men were entangled with the chair and its poles.

It was almost entirely dark. I ran forward, skidding on ice. I nearly fell but righted myself and plunged onward. The men behind me were shouting.

After a few yards there was an intersection with a wider street. At the far end of it I saw flickering lights.

I swung towards them. The freezing air tore at my lungs. The running footsteps were gaining on me.

I could barely distinguish the outlines of the buildings on either side. Hardly any lights were showing. Were they part of the ruins of Canvas Town? If so, I was running away from safety.

There was the sound of a heavy fall behind me. A man shouted, a wordless, angry howl.

I staggered on. My chest was a mass of pain. A woman in a doorway laughed at me.

The lights ahead were nearer. A shadowy man on a shadowy horse moved slowly across the mouth of the street. I heard the distant strains of a drinking song.

The footsteps behind me had stopped.

I ran on, driven by fear and by the strange energy it provides. The lights came from a lantern suspended over a tavern door and from the window of a pie-shop over the road.

I thrust open the tavern's outer door and stumbled against a burly porter, who sat smoking a clay pipe and guarding the inner door that led to the barroom. His face flared with anger. He stood up, his hand tightening around his staff.

He would have thrown me out if my clothes hadn't proclaimed that I had a certain station in life. But it was a near thing — I was hatless, panting like a winded horse; and my expression must have looked truly desperate. He tried to question me but I waved him into silence until I had recovered.

"I was set upon by footpads," I said at last. "Where's this place?"

464

"Corner of Queen Street, sir."

Thank God. In a moment I could be in Broadway. I felt for my purse, which was in a inner pocket.

"Tot of rum, sir? Settles the nerves."

"I want to go to Headquarters. I need a man who will escort me there." I took out the purse and weighed in my gloved hand. "In case the rogues are minded to try their luck again."

The porter's manner became markedly more respectful. "If you allow me a moment, your honour, I can take you there myself."

We came to an arrangement soon enough. Ten minutes later we walked side by side up to Broadway and turned right towards Fort George and the Battery. The street was still busy, even in this weather and at this time.

I retained my bodyguard until I had reached the sentries and shown my pass to the sergeant of the guard. I gave him half a guinea for his trouble.

Once I was within the gates, a blessed sense of security washed over me. I found the duty officer and learned that Major Marryot was still here. This did not surprise me for he often worked late and indeed sometimes would have a camp-bed set up for himself in his private room.

I found him at his papers, huddled over his stove with a blanket over his legs and a muffler round his throat. The air in the room was fragrant with the smell of rum punch. Glass in hand, he rose to his feet and bowed awkwardly, swaying as his wounded leg refused to obey him.

"I've been attacked," I said without preamble, coming forward to warm myself by the stove.

"Eh? By whom?"

"The black man we called Scarface. You remember?"

He motioned me to a chair and we sat down. He did not offer me a bumper of punch, though the bowl was steaming on the hearth at the foot of the stove.

"I thought he was long gone," he said. "Where was this?"

"Outside Mrs Chawley's. I took a chair from there tonight. He was carrying a lantern to light the bearers. The three of them were working together."

Marryot frowned. "Mrs Chawley? The . . . the lady who has that establishment near Trinity church?"

"Yes. Townley had asked me to sup with him there."

"I see," he said, in a tone suggesting that he saw something he did not much care for. "Well, in that case I suppose it's not to be wondered at."

"I don't take your meaning."

He toyed with his glass. "Rogues are drawn to an establishment of that nature. They queue at the door and wait for the gulls to fall into their hands. What happened?"

"We'd just left and I glimpsed his face. I realized what they were about and I ran off."

"Thank you for informing me," he said stiffly. "I'll put the word out again for him."

"You don't think it was more than coincidence?"

"That he attacked you, sir? You suggest that the people of the house were in collusion with Scarface?" Marryot's face twisted into a sneer. "It hardly seems likely, does it? Mrs Chawley's engaged in quite a different line of business."

"But —"

I broke off. Another moment and it would have been too late: I should have blurted out more than I wanted Marryot to know. For I knew there had been nothing coincidental in this attack. I had just turned down Townley's ill-defined offer of an alliance. He had been aware that I was suspicious of his connection with Mr Noak. He had learned this evening that I was not easily to be cozened or bribed into silence. He had summoned the chair for me; no doubt the porter was in his pay.

But I could not say this to Major Marryot because, in order for it to make sense, I should also have to tell him the whole — including those things I had concealed from him earlier. He knew nothing of the connection between Roger Pickett and Mrs Arabella's father, nothing of Mr Froude's murder and Captain Wintour's real motive for going to Mount George, and nothing about Noak's prying and his secret connection with Townley.

Even if I could convince him of the truth, that would mean admitting that I had concealed the information for months, which would lay me open to the severest censure from the authorities both here and in London. Besides, the gold was not my secret, I reminded myself, but Mrs Arabella's. In any case, I already had done my duty by telling Marryot the important point, the one he needed to know: that Scarface was still at large in New York.

"No, sir," Marryot said, "I cannot believe that Mrs Chawley is in league with a gang of footpads. She has no need of that. But I'm obliged to you for warning me that Scarface is about." He took up one of his papers and pretended to glance over its contents. "And now, sir, if there's nothing else . . .?"

I stared blankly at him. The implications were wider and more disturbing than I had at first thought. Every way I looked, there was danger. It was as if I had woken from a bad dream only to find myself trapped inside another, far worse nightmare.

CHAPTER
SEVENTY-THREE

On payment of a small fortune, three soldiers escorted me back to Warren Street. At the Wintours' house, everyone was in bed apart from the porter dozing in the hall.

As I went upstairs, however, the closet door opened and Miriam came on to the landing. In her quilted dressing gown, she looked like a clumsy rag doll. She curtseyed awkwardly and whispered that her mistress begged the favour of a word.

I concealed my surprise — it was nearly two o'clock in the morning. The maid showed me into the small room where old Mrs Wintour lay. The bed-curtains were drawn around the bed. Mrs Arabella was sitting by the fire, swathed in a cloak. She looked up as I entered.

"I know it's late, sir, but could you spare me a moment?"

She indicated the chair on the other side of the fireplace. I put down my candle and sat. I heard the click of the door lock; Miriam had left the room. I was alone with Mrs Arabella, apart from the steady snores and gurgles from the bed where our invisible chaperone was lying.

I held out my hands to the fire. "How is Mrs Wintour?"

"There's no change. Not yet. Will you have tea? There is some in the pot."

I accepted for I was very cold.

"I was worried," she said almost petulantly as she busied herself with the teapot.

I was too tired to be polite. "Why?"

"About you. Miriam told me where you had gone."

"Why should that worry you, ma'am?"

She handed me my cup. "Mrs Chawley's has a certain notoriety. And since our conversation the other day, I do not quite know where we are with Mr Townley. Or Mr Noak." She drew her cloak more tightly about her. "Mr Noak was here again today and was most attentive."

"To Mr Wintour?"

"And to me. Do you remember our conversation three months ago? When you gave me the — the items that had been my husband's?"

"Yes," I said. "As if it were yesterday."

"I believe I was harsh to you then," she said in a rush. "Unkind, even."

"Not at all."

"Come, let us not fence. I distrusted your motives, sir, and I think I was right to do so. I distrust Mr Noak's and Mr Townley's too." She hesitated, looking at the fire. "Indeed, I trust no one completely now except perhaps my father-in-law. But he is too feeble, too distracted, for me to rely on him." She turned her

470

gaze on me. "But I must confide in somebody. So may I make the best of a bad job and trust you?"

I laughed softly. At first she looked shocked but then she smiled. But anger was stirring within me. She seemed not to realize that trust should be mutual if it was to be worth anything at all.

"Madam," I said, "I shall take that as a compliment. Perhaps it will make it easier if I tell you that I was attacked tonight after I left Mrs Chawley's."

"Good God!" Her hand flew to her mouth. "Are you hurt?"

"Not at all. I ran away, most ingloriously."

"Who attacked you?"

"Three ruffians — chairmen, in fact. The point is, I believe Mr Townley must have had a hand in the matter or at least foreknowledge of it. If we're right about a concealed understanding between them, that means Mr Noak probably knew as well."

"Does this have a connection with the gold?" she asked.

"I can't see what else this could be about."

"Roger Pickett was looking for a box of curiosities. Does that indicate that he knew of the gold as well?"

"I believe so." I could not see any reason not to tell her more. "He used to own the land in North Carolina where Mr Froude found the deposits. I think Mr Pickett considered that your father had cheated him. But you know all this, don't you?"

She sat up in her chair. "What do you mean?"

The snores of Mrs Wintour stopped. The old woman made a rattling, gargling sound, as if clearing phlegm. For a few seconds there was silence. Her breathing became heavy and regular. The snores and gurgles began again.

I said in a voice not much above a whisper: "Mr Pickett must have reminded you about his claim on the gold when he called at this house."

"He did nothing of the sort," she said in a low voice. "Besides, we were not alone for a moment. I do not like your —"

"Then why did you not tell Judge Wintour that you knew Pickett was, or had been, a rebel soldier? That he had quarrelled violently with your father and then burned down Mount George?"

"Because it's nonsense from start to finish. Has that foolish Tippet girl been talking to you? Don't you realize that Mehitabel's wits are addled? And no wonder, after what she's endured."

"I also have it upon the unimpeachable authority of a clergyman in this city that Roger Pickett was a sergeant in the Continental Army in 1776. Moreover, a letter that Pickett wrote to his sister refers to a box of curiosities as a source of great wealth. So this does not rest on Mehitabel's word alone. I regret, madam, that we cannot help each other at all unless you tell me the truth."

She did not reply. I put down my cup. I waited a moment and then rose to my feet and bowed. Still she did not speak. I took up my candle and left the room without another word.

I did not sleep that night. In my bedchamber, I kicked off my shoes and threw off my coat, waistcoat and

472

breeches. The cold made me whimper. I clapped on my nightcap, climbed into bed and burrowed under a mound of covers. Josiah had brought up a heated brick to take the chill off the bedclothes but the warmth had long since seeped away from it.

The darkness frightened me tonight. Like a child, I kept the candle burning and left the curtains open a crack so the light fell in a bar across the pillow. If I turned my head I saw part of the shadowy room beyond the bed.

My mind was in turmoil. For a moment I had allowed myself to speak frankly to Mrs Arabella about my suspicions before storming out. But it had gained me nothing beyond a temporary glow of righteous indignation succeeded by a terrible, gnawing sense of regret.

I had not known that it was possible to love a woman one did not trust. I wished I did not know it now. Was it conceivable that I had wronged Mrs Arabella? After all, this business of the gold and Pickett's murder was as formless and impenetrable as a cloud. I could no more grasp it in my hand than I could a puff of steam from a kettle.

The night wore on. I had no way of measuring the hours except by the diminishing candle, for my watch was in a pocket of my waistcoat on the floor. Though I could not sleep, I drifted into that unhappy borderland on the edge of wakefulness where thoughts lose their hard edges and acquire a simulacrum of autonomous life quite separate from the consciousness that produces them.

Until I heard the scratching.

Suddenly I was fully awake again and my thoughts, for good or ill, were once more my own. The scratching was a regular sound which came in groups of three, separated by a short pause from the next group. At first I attributed the noise to a rat behind the panelling; there were far more rats in this crowded city than there were people.

But there was something too regular about the movements, too calculated.

I had only just come to that conclusion when the scratching became a tapping that followed the same rhythm as the scratching. As I listened, it grew louder.

Scratching and knocking . . .

Someone was at the door.

I pulled back the curtain, draped a blanket over my shoulders and left the shelter of the bed. Taking up the candle, I walked silently on stockinged feet across the floor. Draughts of freezing air played about my ankles. I stood by the door. The tapping had become faster, more frantic.

"Who is it?" I whispered.

The tapping stopped. A floorboard creaked on the other side of the door.

"For God's sake," I said in my normal voice. "Who is this?"

"Hush — it's I."

I pulled back the bolt and opened the door, holding the candle high so that a wedge of light spilled on to the landing beyond. Mrs Arabella was waiting there. She wore a black hooded cloak that reduced her to a

474

shadow, apart from the pale oval of her face. She was carrying a candle that trembled in her hand, making the shadows dance about the landing like mad things.

I stared at her in disbelief.

"For God's sake let me in," she said. "Mrs Wintour is dead."

We talked in whispers.

"Her breathing stopped. Then she gave a gasp, a long, long rattle. After that nothing."

"Are you sure she is dead?"

"Of course I am. I went to the bed and saw her face. You do not mistake death when you see it." She pulled the cloak more tightly about her. "Dear God, this cold. I believe it will kill us all."

I said, "Let me put this blanket around your shoulders. Sit on the bed."

She obeyed me like a child. And, like a child, she tucked her legs under her when she sat down. "I did not wish to wake Mr Wintour," she whispered. "He's exhausted. He will hear soon enough."

"What about Miriam?"

"She's in the same condition. She sat up with Mrs Wintour these last three nights. You — you do not object?"

"Of course not. You're shivering. Get under the covers."

Again, she obeyed me. I was still standing by the bed, shaking with cold.

"For God's sake, sir," she said. "Don't be foolish. It's not the weather for scruples."

She shifted across the bed and lifted the edge of the covers. Her meaning was plain enough and I was too cold to care about decorum. I climbed into the bed.

We lay side by side with six inches or so of mattress between us. I listened to her ragged breathing and stared up at the shadowy canopy above our heads. Mrs Arabella's candle, which I had placed on the mantelshelf, was burning steadily. But my own candle was guttering, its flame flickering through the gap in the curtains. The scent of otto of roses filled my nostrils.

Mrs Arabella was crying softly. Again, it was as a child cries, without fuss. "I do not like to be alone with the dead," she said in a while. "I fear they are watching me. But they say one should sit with the dead, don't they? A soul is vulnerable just after death. The Devil may snatch it away as it leaves its earthly body."

"Mrs Wintour's soul is in God's care now," I said. "You must not distress yourself about that."

Later, she stirred again. "I hardly remember my own mother."

Time passed. I knew she was awake. As for me, I had never been more alert in my life.

The overstuffed feather mattress sank beneath our weight and curled around our two bodies. Imperceptibly it brought us closer together. I did not realize this until my right hand brushed her left hand under the covers. I did not move it away. She did not move hers.

I said, a little breathlessly, "When I first came here, I wrote to my daughter Lizzie and told her that in

America I lay in a featherbed that was as big as an elephant."

Arabella gave a snort of laughter.

Gradually the featherbed finished what it had begun. Our forearms touched, and then our shoulders. My breathing became fast and shallow. I heard her swallow.

I turned my head to look at her and saw that she had turned hers to look at me.

My candle guttered and slowly died.

She moved a little in the bed but she did not break the contact between us. I took her fingers in mine. She squeezed my hand gently.

"Well?" I whispered.

"Well," she said. "Very well."

CHAPTER
SEVENTY-FOUR

The dreary business that follows death took its course.

The effects of the weather and the war mercifully limited the trappings of mourning. Two days after Mrs Wintour's death, her corpse went to its rest in Trinity churchyard. The sexton told me that the ground was frozen so hard that it broke the diggers' spades. But at least she had a grave. The dead lay unburied all over the city, waiting for a thaw. There were few mourners at the funeral. Mrs Wintour had lived a retired life for several years. Most of her friends had died or fled the city.

The Judge was now a mere husk of his former self. With his wife's death following so soon upon his son's, all the heart and vigour had been hammered out of him. The servants, particularly old Josiah and Miriam, seemed almost equally affected by grief as their master. Mrs Wintour might have diminished to insignificance in life but, absent in death, she coloured the existence of the entire household.

These melancholy surroundings made me feel guilty for my own secret happiness. They also lent a strange relish to it. So too, I think, did those unanswered questions about Mrs Arabella's connection to Roger Pickett.

478

All I cared for was this: that Mrs Arabella came to my bed by night. I was like a starving child turned loose in a pastry-cook's shop. Indeed, I believe she was in much the same condition.

We knew this could not last. We lived in constant fear of discovery, which perhaps added to our pleasure. It would not have been possible for us to conceal the liaison if the times had not been so topsy-turvy. But the household was smaller than before; the conditions of war had disrupted its routines beyond repair; and the cold kept people huddled wherever they could find warmth. We were not disturbed.

I believe that only one person suspected us: Miriam. Arabella said this did not matter for the girl was devoted to her and also had a great kindness for me since I had prevented Captain Wintour from selling her to pay his backgammon debts.

She may have been right about the maid's devotion to her but I was not so sure about the girl's feelings towards me. I was aware that Miriam sometimes watched me when she thought she was unobserved.

I told myself, what did it matter if the girl was loyal to her mistress? I forgot that a person may have more than one loyalty.

One evening, Arabella and I found ourselves alone before the fire in the Judge's library. For once the room was almost warm, for an old friend of the family had sent Mr Wintour several hundredweight of coal, a considerable luxury during the war. Her proximity to me was both a pleasure and a torment — people were constantly coming and going; I dared not risk touching her.

Five days had passed since Mrs Wintour's death. Arabella and I sat a discreet distance apart with our feet on the fender. The Judge had retired for the night; he now slept in the closet where his wife had died, as if lying on the very spot where she had drawn her last living breath would bring him closer to her.

On the floor beside her chair, Arabella had a large sewing bag made of tapestry with wooden handles. She reached into it and brought out the oilskin pouch which Captain Wintour had found at Mount George. The stitching across the top had been cut. She glanced at me and saw me watching.

"I must come to a decision," she said.

"Must you? Not now, surely."

"Yes — now." She let the pouch fall to her lap. "We have so little time, you and I. You will be going back to England before we know it. And as for me — well, God knows what will happen."

"Come to England," I said. "Throw that pouch on the fire and come with me."

"I can't leave my father-in-law. It would kill him."

"Bring him too."

She smiled and shook her head. "He wouldn't come. Anyway, how should we live?"

"I don't know. We'd find a way."

"I won't live under the same roof as you, sir." She feigned horror at the very thought. "A married man."

Neither of us spoke of love. Neither of us mentioned Roger Pickett.

She took several folded papers from the pouch. "Perhaps these will give us the answer," she went on. "After all, if I'm a lady of fortune, then anything is possible."

"Does it not depend which side wins? And on whether this vein of gold can be found? If it actually exists at all."

She flared up at me. "I have no other ground for hope, sir. So this will have to do."

I leaned over and took her hand, violating our pact that we would not touch except in my bedchamber. "Then I shall hope, too. May I examine the papers?"

She gave them to me willingly. "You were right about there being a puzzle. You will see."

First there were the title deeds to the estate that Mr Pickett had sold to her father, Henry Froude. It comprised of a house, slave quarters, an overseer's house, various outbuildings and messuages, and seven hundred acres of land. I looked over the deeds, which seemed quite in order, and returned them to Arabella.

There remained only a page torn from a printed book. It was headed "The Conclusion" and contained about twenty lines of verse that began:

Now, reader, I have told my dream to thee;
See if thou canst interpret it to me,
Or to thyself, or neighbour; but take heed
Of misinterpreting . . .

All of a sudden I had a picture of my father, dead these twenty years, sitting in the parlour and reading aloud to us children. In memory it had been one of those endless summer evenings of childhood, and the sound of the words in his deep, quiet voice had made me drowsy until at last I had slept.

As I walked through the Wilderness of this World, I lighted on a certain place . . .

"Are the lines familiar to you?" Mrs Arabella asked.

"Yes," I said, surprised that she had not recognized them herself.

And as I slept, I dreamed a Dream.

"They come from *The Pilgrim's Progress*," I went on. "It must be the end of the first volume. Was Mr Froude a religious man?"

"He followed the forms and observances of the Established Church," she said drily. "When he found it convenient or desirable to do so."

"So Bunyan was not a particular favourite of his?"

"I never saw the book in his hands or anything like it. It might have been my mother's, I suppose."

I turned over the page. The other side of the sheet was blank apart from a pencilled list of dates, names and figures. *To R. Pickett, Esqre: 120 guineas.*

"The payments must relate to his purchase of the Pickett estate," Arabella said. "It's as if he did not have his account book by him and he made these notes as a temporary record."

The explanation made sense. But it did not quite satisfy me.

"Then why include it with the deeds?" I asked.

"It must mean something. My father thought himself cleverer than the rest of humanity and he did nothing by chance. He enjoyed mystifying those around him. It confirmed his opinion of his own superior understanding."

I turned the page over again. My eyes ran further down the lines of verse. The word "gold" snagged my attention.

"Listen," I said.

"What of my dross thou findest there, be bold
To throw away, but yet preserve the gold.
What if my gold be wrapped up in ore?
None throws away the apple for the core."

"He's toying with us," Arabella said. "How I disliked my father. Indeed, I still do."

A memory surfaced in my mind. On our way back from Mount George, when Jack Wintour had told me of the box of curiosities, he had also mentioned something that Froude had said to him when he had shown his son-in-law the box.

That's what he said, and he told me how.

"Mr Froude suggested that your husband should ask a salamander for help. Does that mean anything to you?"

"A salamander?" She burst out laughing. "That's droll if nothing else. We have enough of those wretched lizards in the Catskills. I detest them."

"Did he refer to something at Mount George? A painting of a salamander, perhaps? An exhibit in his laboratory?"

She thought for a moment. "I cannot bring anything to mind, sir."

I held the paper up to the candle in case there were pinpricks or indentations in the paper that might reveal a hidden message. There was nothing, only the lines of the paper and, at the top, the watermark, an inverted fleur-de-lys.

"Have a care," Arabella said. "It'll burn."

I jerked the paper away. She was right: at the top the paper was just beginning to darken with the heat.

"You would not let my fortune go up in smoke, I hope."

I did not reply. I held the paper up to the candle flame again, this time at a safer distance. My eyes had not misled me. At the head of the page was a decorative bar of printer's flowers whose type consisted of a pattern of arabesque foliage. A little above this bar a tangle of fine lines, smudged and brown, had appeared to the right of the watermark. It was about an inch in length. I could have taken my oath that it had not been there earlier.

At that moment I recalled the garrulous Mr Ingham, Townley's clerk to Long Island, exiled so that Noak might have his post in New York; I remembered how he had prattled of Mrs Townley's father in his dotage; and how the old man had tried to conceal his accounts from prying eyes.

I held the paper nearer the flame again.

"Sir," Arabella cried. "It will burn, I tell you."

"No, ma'am." I watched the brown tangle expand towards the right-hand margin; I saw another appearing below it, dimly visible through the bar of printer's flowers. "I believe I have solved your father's riddle. And it is not so very difficult after all."

"Then tell me," she said.

"They say salamanders are creatures of fire, do they not? The ancients certainly believed it — is it not in Pliny, and in Aristotle before him? Mr Froude was telling us that we should apply heat to the paper."

I turned the sheet over to its blank side. It was not blank any more. The brown tangle had grown to six lines. The words were run together and written in a narrow, confined scrawl. I could decipher only a few words here and there — *to, entry, dead*.

"I can't read it," I said.

"Give it me," Arabella said. "My father's hand was as crabbed as his heart."

I handed the paper to her. Frowning, she cast her eyes over it and then read aloud:

> "*From brewhouse,*
> *NNE ¾ mile to second*
> *stream. Upstream abt. 300 paces.*
> *Two dead trees make cross.*
> *Creek. Entry cave*
> *concealed among rocks.*"

That night, as we lay in a warm muddle of limbs in the depths of the feather mattress, I broached a subject that had niggled at me like an insect bite for several days. At first it had been an almost impalpable irritation but it had grown steadily worse, as if the miniature wound had become infected by the events of the last few months.

"Arabella?" I called her that when we were alone; the Wintours called her Bella.

She stirred in my arms.

"I am a little puzzled in my mind about Miriam."

She muttered something I could not catch.

"I think she may be spying on me," I said.

"You imagine it."

"Someone searched my possessions the other day."

"What?" Arabella's voice was more distinct now. "How do you know?"

"My papers were disturbed. Nothing that mattered, of course — I lock away anything of importance. But I think it may have been her."

"Servants always pry," Arabella said, as if stating a self-evident truth that a child would have grasped. "It's nothing to be wondered at. It's why God invented locks and keys."

"Tell me, has she ever had a child?"

Arabella sat up with a jerk, dislodging the bedclothes and letting a current of cold air invade our warmth. "Why do you ask?"

"I saw her one evening on Broadway last winter. She was with a black child — a girl. But when I chanced to mention it later, she denied she had been there at all, let alone with a child. It was very young — two or three years old, no more."

She lay down again and pulled the covers over us. "Slaves breed all the time. But it can't have been her child — it was probably a friend's. No doubt Miriam

486

was out of the house without leave, so of course she would deny it. Sometimes, my love, you are such a simpleton."

It was the first time she had called me "my love."

I said, "I chanced to pass the negro burial ground in the summer. There was a child's grave there. The infant's name was Henrietta Maria Barville. I understand that Barville is the surname that Miriam uses. The next of kin in the sexton's register was one Miriam Barville. It must be the same person, surely?"

"Perhaps she was kin," Arabella said with a shiver that rippled through her like the wind on water. She turned towards me. "Slaves are all related to each other, you know. Brothers lie with sisters, and mothers with their sons. You must not expect refinement of behaviour from them. The truth is, they have no morals, no restraint."

"How unlike us, my dear," I said; and I brushed my hand gently against her breasts.

CHAPTER
SEVENTY-FIVE

We lived in a fool's paradise. But it was a paradise nonetheless.

The following Tuesday, 18 January, was the night of the great fête at Hicks Tavern. The army had subscribed above four hundred guineas towards it, which set up a considerable murmur in the town; for many said that the money would have been better spent of procuring fuel and food for the poor, who were suffering so terribly. Every day there were reports of people freezing to death in their sleep.

But the army was above such considerations. Besides, this was a patriotic affair that demanded the approval and support of every loyal citizen: for the entertainment was designed to celebrate the queen's official birthday.

By virtue of my position I was obliged to attend as the representative of the American Department. The Wintours could not go, even if they had wanted to, because they were in mourning for the deaths of Mrs Wintour and the Captain.

The fête was an extravagant, splendid affair. Baroness von Riedesel, the wife of a Hessian general newly arrived in New York from captivity, represented

Her Majesty, which annoyed many of the ladies there who felt they had a better claim to temporary royalty. The Baroness, vastly pregnant, was welcomed at the tavern with drums and trumpets. She opened the ball with the commandant, General Pattison, and afterwards at supper sat like a plump partridge on a great chair under a canopy. Outside the tavern, the city's beggars gathered until the soldiers drove them away.

I watched the dancing. I bowed low to the Baroness. I drank the loyal toast and those that followed. Most of my New York acquaintance was there — I even noticed Mr Carne, the American intelligence-gatherer, deep in conversation with General Pattison in a window embrasure. I myself had little conversation with anyone. Though there had still been no public announcement about my recall to London, disgrace clings invisibly to a man like an infection; it repels those around him.

I contrived to leave shortly before midnight. I had arranged to share a hackney coach with a gentleman who lived near King's College. I ordered the coachman to drop me not at the front door of the house but at the garden gate in the wall near the belvedere. The Judge was sleeping badly at present and my entering by the front door would have disturbed him, for the closet where he lay was immediately over the hall.

At my request, the postillion jumped down with his lantern and waited while I unlocked the gate. I saw a light burning behind the shutters of the belvedere; one of the slaves would be waiting there to conduct me to the house.

Once inside the garden, I closed, locked and bolted the gate. I heard the coach drive away. A lantern burned faintly in the fanlight above the garden door to the house. In the slave quarters, a man was singing softly in a very deep voice, one of those strange, sad melodies that the black people croon as they go about their lives.

I mounted the short flight of steps to the belvedere, meaning to upbraid the slave for not coming out to assist me; he must have heard the sounds of my arrival.

I pushed open the door. A lantern stood on the table. Miriam was sitting beside it, resting her head and arms on the table. She started up when I entered, her cloak and a blanket fluttering to the floor.

"What are you doing here?"

"Beg pardon, your honour. Madam sent me."

"Why?"

At that moment, a current of cold air touched my cheek. I heard movement. Pain sliced through me like sheet lightning in a night sky.

The terrible brightness lasted only an instant. I tumbled into a black pit where nothing was.

In the beginning was the pain. I became aware of it before I was aware of anything else. It was worse, far worse, in my head. But it stretched down the entire length of my body.

The next item of information to force its way to the attention was the fact that my bladder was bursting. This was followed by the realization that, although I was lying on an unpleasantly hard surface, I was at least tolerably warm. The air stank of urine and sweat, of stale spirits and ill-tanned hides.

I forced my arm to move slowly up to my head. I could not feel a nightcap. Or a wig or a hat. I felt the bristle on my scalp and a very painful, swollen spot above and slightly behind my right ear. I was still dressed in the evening clothes I had worn at Hicks Tavern. My feet were cold. I flexed my toes. I discovered that I was not wearing shoes.

I'm a man with no shoes — like poor Roger Pickett all those months ago on my first day in New York City.

The memories returned. I remembered coming back to Warren Street after the fête. I remembered Miriam sitting in the belvedere, waiting to light me up to the house. But nothing more, not then.

At last, and with a considerable effort, I opened my eyes. Not twelve inches away from me was a small malevolent face.

I gave a cry and sat up in a rush. The sudden movement intensified the pain a hundredfold. The place where I lay was filled with a dirty-yellow radiance, a murky glow that was a near neighbour to fog. I saw beside me a line of small animals, the size of squirrels or even large rats, hanging like vermin on a board outside a gamekeeper's cottage.

Dead, I thought, and left to rot as a warning to others.

I stretched out my hand and felt a wall of cold, damp bricks. The mortar between them crumbled at my touch. I brushed the side of the nearest figure, which swayed and turned.

Alive?

I pulled back my hand sharply, fearing a bite or a scratch. The light shifted to the head of the moving figure. I glimpsed a wizened face with a nose like a blade. The nose reminded me of Mr Townley's. A thought stirred in the depths of my mind, pushing its way through the pain.

A face with a great nose.

I was fully awake now. I remembered the puppet theatre at the Brooklyn races, with the one-legged barker and the squat fellow who carried the booth and managed the puppets. I realized suddenly that I had seen the latter again — more than once, indeed, and when he was unencumbered by his booth. He was the moon-faced man who had laid the flowers on the child's grave in the negro burial ground. I had glimpsed him again in the depths of the crowd at Jack Wintour's funeral, when he had been smoking a clay pipe.

A voice said, "Mr Punch at your service, sir."

I turned my head sharply. What light there was came from two candles behind the man who had spoken. His face was in shadow. He was tall and broad-shouldered. He towered over me.

"This is his town residence. Where he comes to rest after his labours. Along with Mrs Punch and their acquaintance."

The man's voice was American, not unlike Judge Wintour's in intonation but deeper in pitch. He and I were alone in a chamber perhaps ten feet long by six feet wide. It appeared to be lined entirely with

492

brick, even the barrel vault of the ceiling. I could not see a window or a door.

At the other end from the dangling marionettes and myself was an old stove of the Dutch pattern, the source of the warmth. To the right of it, I made out the shape of a low wide door.

"If that's Mr Punch," I said, "have I the pleasure of addressing the devil?" I was so thirsty that it felt as if I were speaking through a mouthful of fine sand. "They usually appear together, I believe."

He laughed. "You may call me whatever you like, sir."

"Who are you? What are you doing? Where are we?"

"We are in Canvas Town, sir," he said. "This was once the strong-room of a merchant who traded in furs. The house above us is reduced to a heap of rubble. If you scream, no one will hear."

I summoned up my strength and tried to scramble to my feet. I discovered that a rope attached to the wall had been tied to my ankles. I sprawled on the floor and the pain in my head made me cry out.

Once again, my captor laughed.

I struggled into a sitting position and then, with infinite care, stood up. The man did not move. When the pain had subsided, I asked if I might have a drink of water.

He considered the request for a few seconds. "No."

My wits were still addled. "Those men with the puppet theatre on Long Island . . ."

"How observant of you, sir. Yes, you have met Mr Punch and his friends before. My little deputies, in a manner of speaking."

"You speak in riddles."

"Few of us talk plainly, Mr Savill. Have you not noticed that? Allow me to gloss it for you: the men with the theatre were my eyes and ears in New York while I had business elsewhere. Hence my deputies, though sadly unintelligent ones."

"But who the devil are you? And why —"

"Perhaps you would care to observe me more closely."

He turned, picked up one of the candles and came closer. For the first time I saw his face. To my surprise I discovered that he was a black man. But that surprise was instantly elbowed aside by a far greater one. The negro's face was scarred from the outer corner of each eye to each corner of the mouth. The flesh had not healed properly and the scar tissue was raised and pink.

"I see you recognize me now, sir, and you will understand why I have been obliged to act through intermediaries for the last few months — in New York City, at least."

"Listen to me," I said, "I have no animosity towards you and you can have none towards me. Restore my shoes, let me go and we shall say no more about it. You already have my purse, I'm sure, and you may keep it. I have nothing else of value on my person."

He laughed. "I don't want your purse. I want you."

I peered through the gloom at him. "Do you hope for a ransom? I'm of no particular importance and I'm almost entirely without resources or friends. So I'm afraid you hope in vain."

"I hope for very little nowadays," he said. "If anything."

"Then oblige me in this, at least," I snapped. "Tell me what you're about. Was it not you the other night at Mrs Chawley's with the sedan chair? Does that mean you are Mr Townley's creature? And is Miriam Barville your ally, your lover?"

He hit me then — a punch with all his weight behind it, which landed full on my mouth. The force of it drove me back against the line of hanging puppets on the wall. The rope around my ankles trapped me like a rabbit in a snare. I fell heavily to the ground, bringing Mrs Punch with me. The pain made my vision blur. My mouth filled with blood. I touched the front teeth with the tip of my tongue. One of the incisors rocked in its socket.

"Hetty-Petty," I said, the blood in my mouth distorting and thickening the sound of the words. The pain made me reckless. Despair made me angry. Fear made me talkative.

"What did you say?"

"Hetty-Petty. I saw one of your damned theatricals at the negro burial ground in the summer. A white man bringing a nosegay for a dead black child. Her name was Henrietta Maria Barville. Was she yours? If she was, I'm sorry for it. It's a bad business, the death of a child."

I tensed myself, expecting another blow or a kick or worse. But nothing came.

"Was it her I heard crying in Warren Street?" I said. "Of course — she was the child who died of the smallpox in the slave quarters, was she not? That was where Miriam hid her."

"You know nothing," he said, moving nearer the stove.

"I thought Miriam was loyal to her mistress," I went on, probing further. "No doubt she is, in her way. But what's a slave's loyalty worth? Not very much, it seems. Because the pair of you laid a trap for me this evening. You and Miriam."

Scarface crouched by the stove. He had his back to me. He opened the door. I thought he was warming himself. He did not speak.

I shifted as far as the rope would let me, my hands feeling for a weapon, any weapon. "Loyalty is a strange, immaterial thing, is it not? Perhaps Miriam finds that a greater loyalty outranks a lesser one. I should be obliged if you could explain this to me. Do slaves have loyalty as free people do? Or is it something that can be bought and sold just as they themselves can?"

He turned back to me. He had wrapped a cloth around his right hand and used it to grip a pocket knife with a dark wooden handle. The tip of the blade glowed a dull red colour in the gloom of the chamber.

I scrambled to my feet. As I did so, he seized my neck in his left hand and pushed me back against the wall. I flailed my arms towards him. But his arms were longer and stronger than mine.

Still gripping my neck, he pushed me down to the floor. The rope pinned my legs. He knelt heavily on my upper arms.

"So," he said in his deep, melodious voice. "Loyalty. Let us see how loyal you are."

He shifted his grip, wedging my head in the angle between floor and wall. I felt the heat of the knife before it touched me. He drew the tip down my right cheek from eye to mouth.

"I could make you deny Christ himself if I had a mind to it, sir. Just like St Peter."

The pain was exquisite. I screamed, my body bucking beneath his weight, trying to throw him off. He adjusted the position of his left hand, forcing me to rotate my head.

"Can a slave feel loyalty?" he murmured.

He stood up, leaving me whimpering on the ground. I covered my face with my hands.

"Indeed they can," he went on. "A slave has sentiments just as a free man has. He feels love, he feels hate, he feels the desire for revenge. Do you think we learn these elevated sentiments from our white masters, sir? It is indeed a nice philosophical question."

My cheek stung and was wet with blood.

"Why did you kill Mr Pickett?"

That at least is what I meant to say. But the words emerged as a sort of muffled gasp. I swallowed some of the blood in my mouth and tried again.

"Why did you kill Mr Pickett?"

By this time the black man had retreated as far as the stove. I felt my muscles tense in anticipation of pain:

did he intend to heat the blade again as a preliminary to another attack on me?

But he shut the door of the stove and closed his knife.

"Why do you think I killed him?" he said.

"Revenge?" I hazarded. "Or to stop him talking?"

"Talking? About what?"

I strained to see his face but I could not make out his expression. "Why, about the box of curiosities."

He shrugged his massive shoulders. "Maybe it was revenge after all. After all, that's why I was obliged to slash your cheek, Mr Savill. It is barely more than a scratch. In an hour or two, when the wound has begun to scab, I shall make a deeper cut because it will be more painful then. Then I shall oblige you to turn the other cheek, as Our Lord advises, and I shall do the same to that side of your face." He paused and slipped the knife into his pocket. "All of which you should consider merely as a preliminary. I shall do worse to you, by and by. Much worse."

At that moment I knew precisely what he was about and what he meant to do to me. He intended to make me as himself.

To emasculate me. As he himself had been emasculated.

"I have been no better than a blockhead." My voice sounded unnatural in my ears and, to my surprise, strangely calm. "I thought you were dead. That's what everyone said. But you're as alive as I am, Juvenal. Aren't you?"

498

"Indeed I am, sir," he said with that unsettling urbanity of address. "And I fear that I may soon outlive you."

He blew out one of the candles. He took up the other and left me in the dark with the taste of blood in my mouth.

CHAPTER
SEVENTY-SIX

I drifted towards insensibility but did not quite succeed in getting there. My world was made of pain and darkness. I tried to count, both to measure the time and as a distraction, but somehow lost my way among the numbers.

What roused me was the sound of the door opening.

First an oblong of light spilled into the room. Juvenal followed, carrying a jug and a wooden platter, which he set on the floor just out of my reach. The tang of spruce beer joined the other smells in the chamber. I scrambled slowly to my feet.

Juvenal picked up the lighted candle he had left at the threshold, brought it over and used it to light the second candle. He shut the door. He held out his hands to the stove and looked at me for the first time since his return.

"I believe you mentioned loyalty, sir," he said.

I bowed politely. My overburdened bladder made a savage pain in my guts.

"I consider it the guiding principle of my life," he went on. "But the point I should have made to you earlier is that loyalty must be freely given. It is not an attribute or moral adornment that can be forced on a man. You cannot, as it were, make him wear it as you can a silver collar."

I thought of the double portrait I had seen in Jack Wintour's bedchamber: the boy in green, the boy in blue; the white master and the black slave.

"Captain Wintour told me you did everything together when you were boys," I said. "You shared his lessons and his games. He said that you were a far better scholar than he was."

"That was not so difficult."

"He also told me you were dead." I swallowed with difficulty for my mouth was now very dry. "And the Judge said that Miriam shot you after you had stabbed Mr Froude."

He gave a quick nod, as if my remarks were so much a matter of course they were hardly worth his notice. "The Tippet girl told you about Froude, no doubt. Mehitabel. She was there, you know."

"Why did he hate you so?"

"Squire Froude was a brute. He didn't need a reason to be cruel. But in this case he had a very good reason. I had stolen something from him."

"That's no reason why you should have killed him."

Juvenal hawked and spat at my feet, an action that was all the more shocking for the quietly genteel tone of his conversation. "After what he did to me, sir," he remarked in the level voice he had used before, "Froude deserved far worse than death."

"Indeed," I said. "But why should Miriam say she had shot you? Unless —"

Loyalty must be freely given. I saw the truth in all its blindly obvious simplicity.

"Of course," I said, answering my own question. "Because you and she were lovers. And so she told her mistress she had killed you. To protect you. In the confusion of the fire and their flight from Mount George, there was no one to gainsay her. And eventually you followed them to New York, where everyone but Miriam believed you were dead. But were you not afraid that someone would recognize you in the street?"

"I am much altered from what I was, sir," Juvenal said. He touched his right cheek. "People see the scars, not the man, as you will discover yourself." He paused. "And I have undergone other changes."

He meant his castration, I thought: I did not know how that would alter the appearance of an adult; or perhaps the alterations had as much to do with the mind as the body.

Juvenal opened the stove and threw some fragments of floorboard inside. I interpreted this to mean that he meant to heat the knife again. I shrank back against the line of puppets. The prospect of more pain spurred me to keep talking.

"But then there came the Pickett business," I said in a rush. "Just as I arrived in New York. Miriam must have told you that Roger Pickett was here in New York, that he'd called at Warren Street. He'd been at Mount George on the night you killed Froude, so he knew you weren't dead — or at least that Miriam hadn't shot you. Is that why you killed him? Or was it —?"

I broke off. I had been about to say *Or was it because he knew about the gold?* But it came to me in a flash that Juvenal had not mentioned the gold.

"Or was it revenge?" I went on so quickly that my hesitation must have been barely perceptible. "But what had Pickett ever done to you?"

The only answer I had was that Juvenal hawked again and spat, this time at the stove. The spittle hissed as it evaporated. It was so very quiet in this place. No sound reached us from the outside world. The rubble of the merchant's house above sealed us off from the rest of the city, the rest of the world.

"You attacked me in the street, did you not? That time the two soldiers came to my rescue? Was that because Miriam told you that I had seen her with your little girl on Broadway? Or were you there too, and you feared I had seen you together with them? If I had, a word from me to Judge Wintour and —"

Juvenal spat a second time. The spittle hissed. He opened the stove again. Pale flames were licking the piece of board.

"And then Captain Wintour came home," I said. "Your master."

"I have no master," Juvenal said softly, as he closed the stove door.

"You attacked him on his own doorstep. That was after he threatened to sell Miriam to pay his debts, was it not? Did you hate him, too, for what he was and what he had been to you?"

For loyalty, I thought, is like milk: it may curdle and become something quite different in both taste and consistency.

"The consequence of all this," I continued, "was to bring you to the notice of the authorities. You avoided Major Marryot and his patrol in Canvas Town. But your face could not easily be concealed, not in New York, even in Canvas Town."

Loyalty is a sort of love, I thought: and the reverse of love is hate.

"Where were you? In the Debatable Ground?"

Juvenal actually laughed. "I see I have no secrets from you, sir."

"Miriam must have told you that Captain Wintour and I were coming there," I said. "You were waiting at Mount George."

He did not reply.

"Was it you who killed poor Grantford and that boy, Abraham?"

"If you kill a man," Juvenal said at last, speaking slowly as if testing each word beforehand to see whether it would bear the weight of his meaning, "you should do so for one of three reasons. For your own preservation, for loyalty, for revenge."

Not for gain, I thought, not for gold?

"It was a pity about your man and Wintour's negro," he was saying. "But they were in the way."

"So was I, I apprehend."

He shrugged.

"You followed us through the lines," I said. "You killed Captain Wintour at King's Bridge. You mutilated him most cruelly."

"I did as I was done by, sir."

A silence fell between us. I was about to ask whether Juvenal was Townley's ally, for that was still the great unanswered question. But he distracted me by opening the door of the stove again. The new fuel was ablaze now, the flames snapping and crackling like wild things. He patted his coat. I guessed he was looking for his knife.

I blundered into speech. "Sir, I have a terrible thirst. Would you have the goodness to let me drink something?"

It was the first time I addressed him as "sir" in the manner of an equal, though he had addressed me as "sir" at several points; not in a servile way but as one gentleman to another.

With the toe of his boot, Juvenal pushed the jug within my reach. I stooped and picked it up. It was a quart-size earthenware vessel, a third full of beer.

"Forgive me, but may I trespass on your good nature and ask for a pot to piss in before I drink? If I do not do it soon, I fear I may explode."

He laughed and took up a bucket for ashes that stood near the stove. "Here — use this."

It was, in its way, a kind action. I shall always remember that. He could have told me to piss against the wall or even in my breeches. For an instant, perhaps, he forgot that I was his prisoner. Such is the power of civility on a man of his breeding. For Juvenal was a sort of gentleman, albeit in a partial and vicarious way; he had acquired more than a little Latin when he shared the education of Jack Wintour.

He took a step forward with the bucket in his hand.

"Thank you, sir," I said, swinging the jug against his skull with all the force I could muster.

It was the only chance I had. The blow was a lucky one. It caught Juvenal on the side of the head. The jug shattered, the base falling from it, the beer cascading over him. He gasped and staggered to one side, tripping over the wooden platter and dropping the candle.

I fell forward with all my weight on him. My right hand touched the candlestick. I seized it and dashed it against his head. He fought back feebly. The candlestick was made of metal and had a weighted base. I hit him again and again with it. At last he was still.

I felt in the pockets of his coat until I found the knife he had used on my cheek. I opened it and cut his throat. The blade was sharp but it was harder work than I imagined, to cut a man's throat. The door of the stove was still open. The flames cast a shifting, twitching orange light over our little hell.

Juvenal cried out so I stabbed him in the neck and in the chest, in the region of the heart. His limbs thrashed. I returned to the neck and sawed to and fro until I had cut through the artery.

The blood splashed out of him. It made my hands so slippery the knife slid from my grasp. The blood spattered my fine evening coat and puddled on the floor with the beer.

I took up the knife once more, rolled away and cut the rope around my ankles. I was trembling. It was as if I was a child again and an angry parent had picked me up and was shaking me so hard that my teeth rattled.

I rested my head against the wall to steady myself. I unbuttoned my breeches and at last let out a stream of urine. It rustled in a broadening stream down the brick wall and pooled on the ground around the fallen, graceless figure of Mrs Punch. It spread a liquid shadow that mingled with the blood and the beer and came at last to rest against the barrier of Juvenal's body.

By degrees I grew calmer.

If you kill a man, I thought, you should do it for one of three reasons. For your own preservation, for loyalty, for revenge. I suppose I killed Juvenal for all three.

But I wished I had not.

CHAPTER
SEVENTY-SEVEN

Murder.

Let us not beat about the bush. That is what it was. For a few seconds, I had a choice. I chose to cut Juvenal's throat.

I tell myself no jury in its right mind would convict me of murdering him. That in another moment he might well have overcome me — he was far stronger than I — and that my life probably depended on his death.

Also, that he intended to castrate me, which might have proved fatal in itself quite apart from the fact that it would have caused me suffering beyond belief and destroyed my manhood.

Also, that he had shown himself to be capable of nursing his homicidal hatred for years until the right opportunity presented to him to take his vengeance.

Also, that he had killed at least five men to my certain knowledge — Froude, Pickett, Corporal Grantford, Abraham and Jack Wintour; he had shown them no pity and he therefore deserved none from me.

Also — well, all these arguments and more are valid. Nevertheless my heart tells me that what I did was murder. I had a choice. I chose to kill Juvenal and I did so with deliberation.

In the same moment, therefore, I chose also to make myself into a murderer for the rest of my natural life.

Of course these thoughts did not pass through my mind in the immediate aftermath of the deed. Moral philosophy had no interest for me whatsoever, for my terrors circled like wolves, ready to attack if I showed the slightest weakness.

I did not know who or what awaited me on the other side of the door beside the stove.

Somehow I contrived to remain calm, though I was in considerable pain from the cut in my cheek. The trick was to think only of the immediate future: to deal with the next five minutes and let the rest take care of itself.

My actions were considered, even methodical. Sweating from exertion and from the heat of the stove, I relit the candle that had been extinguished in the course of the struggle, though I could not bring myself to replace it in the candlestick I had used with such violence. But I wiped the blade of Juvenal's knife, closed it and put it in my pocket.

I still had my purse and my watch. The two dice were in my waistcoat. Like a superstitious fool I touched them in the hope they would bring me luck. The Departmental commission signed by Lord George

Germain and my passes were safe in the concealed inner pocket of my coat.

The watch had stopped with its hands at ten past three. I had no idea of the time or even whether it was night or day. The cellar was as private as a tomb.

My shoes, hat and cloak were bundled up by the stove. I found beside them a small axe of the sort used for chopping kindling. On the floor by the wooden platter were fragments of the hard, gritty biscuit that forms part of sailors' rations.

But I did not eat. My thirst was worse than ever.

I examined the door. It was stoutly made of dark, solid wood that had grown darker and harder with time; it was bound with iron; and a ring controlled the latch. On this side of the door there was no sign of a bolt or of a lock requiring a key.

Slowly I twisted the ring. I felt the weight of the latch and felt it move. I tugged gently. The door edged towards me. It scraped on the floor, but not loudly. It made no other sound.

It was dark outside. Cold air rushed into the cellar, chilling my bare hands and my naked scalp. I listened, counting the beats of my pulse until I had reached a hundred and twenty.

Someone was shouting in the distance. There was no sign of daylight. I heard a dull report, probably a musket shot but far away. Nearer, there were voices — men arguing loudly but without real heat. I could not distinguish their words. Elsewhere I heard laughter and a solitary scream, cut off suddenly as a knife lops off the end of a piece of string.

510

I opened the door a few inches further so the gap between the door and the jamb was wide enough for me to slip through. A narrow flight of steep brick steps climbed upwards between jagged walls of brick. The treads were coated with frost. The cold and the exertion made my wounded cheek throb to the beat of my pulse. Above me was a night sky. It was so clear one could have counted the stars. The air smelled of smoke and salt water.

Steadying myself on the wall, I crept up the steps, pausing at every one. I made some noise — it was impossible not to — but there was no sign that anyone had heard me.

The higher I climbed, the more sounds I heard. What worried me most of all was the possibility that Juvenal's confederates might be close by. I knew that he had worked with at least two people apart from Miriam — the one-legged man and his colleague with the puppet theatre. On the other hand, he would have been confident of his ability to restrain me single-handed and he might not have wished to have witnesses for what I might have said or what he intended to do to me.

The steps led into a heap of debris, coated with more frost and frozen snow. I kept in the lee of a broken chimney stack.

On a night like this, any movement would be clearly visible against the skyline.

Axe in hand, I looked out on a scene that might have come from the last days of the world. The ruins of Canvas Town stretched before me. Fires glowed in the darkness. Other lights were visible from the inhabited buildings beyond. I heard snatches of songs, shouts, wild cries and a woman weeping in great gasping sobs.

At this moment, five or six men began to move among the campfires. They were clearly very drunk. They shouted, traded insults and sang. They blundered through the vagrants and heaps of rubbish. The racket they made gave me the opportunity I needed. I climbed over the rubble of the house and descended to a lower level, an area of pitted, frozen mud.

In the darkness I trod on something soft that might have been a man; but he did not respond and there was no way of knowing whether he was alive or dead. Thirty yards on, someone must have seen me, for they shouted "Ben, you old devil, come over here!" I waved, and passed on. I swerved away from them and stumbled into a group of three or four people who appeared to be engaged in some form of copulation around a glowing brazier.

All at once — and this was typical of New York City where such extraordinary opposites lived side by side — I passed from the barbarous wilderness of Canvas Town into a paved street of prim, shuttered houses. A few minutes later I was on Broadway.

The shops had closed for the night but many taverns and coffee houses were still doing a brisk business. I concealed the axe beneath my cloak and walked rapidly back to Warren Street. Juvenal's knife was in my hand, the blade already open.

On any other occasion I should have felt the danger of my being out alone at night. Now I did not give the matter a thought. If anyone had tried to stop me, I think I would have killed them too.

CHAPTER
SEVENTY-EIGHT

My head ached. But exercise stimulated still further my already agitated brain. The thoughts crowded into my mind at great speed, jostling feverishly against each other. By and by, however, they settled into groups and formed patterns, like dancers assembling to take up their places and tread a measure.

At last I thought I glimpsed the truth. Or rather, I glimpsed the two sets of truth that intersected, as it were, in the person of Mrs Arabella Wintour. I had stumbled into two mysteries, not one, though conjoined at the hip like those twins that emerge fused together from their mother's womb.

The business began with Froude's purchase of the Pickett estate in the knowledge that he was also buying a vein of gold. After the rebel army withdrew from New York late in 1776, Roger Pickett had visited Mount George in search of recompense or even vengeance. He had chanced upon Froude punishing Juvenal for his theft. Froude had bragged of his box of curiosities — and possibly even shown it — to Pickett. Pickett had returned with his men and destroyed Mount George. But he hadn't found the box.

Nearly two years later, Pickett came back to New York, this time in the guise of a Loyalist refugee. When he called at Warren Street, Miriam had seen him. Servants know everything about the business of their betters. She would have known that he threatened the happiness of her mistress; and Miriam was nothing if not loyal. She had told Juvenal, her lover and the father of her daughter.

This was more than speculation: there was proof. When Marryot and I had revisited Pickett's lodgings, the mulatto maid had told us that a negro in a red coat with a scarred face had left a letter for him on the day of his death. A summons to a rendezvous, perhaps, somewhere convenient to Canvas Town where we had found his body.

But — and this was the point on which the whole matter turned — Juvenal knew nothing of the gold or of the box of curiosities. Nor had Mrs Arabella until I had told her.

Unlike Noak and Townley.

The more I considered it, the more likely it seemed that the gold was the motive that had animated the pair of them from the start. There was no doubt whatsoever that there was an alliance between them and that it had begun before Noak and I had set sail from England. Nor could I doubt that they had plotted to use me as an innocent means of bringing them together in New York, in a way that would place their connection beyond suspicion. But they had selected me for another reason: I was to lodge at Warren Street. I gave them their *entrée* to the Wintours.

What else could draw Noak and Townley to Warren Street apart from the gold? Why else would Noak spend so much time there? Why else would he pry among the Judge's papers and in Mrs Arabella's sitting room?

Congress was desperate for gold. You cannot fund a revolution with paper money. That fact alone made almost any risk worth running, any chance worth taking, if it might bring the rebels a source of gold under their own control.

I turned into Warren Street and ran into the teeth of a crosswind that nearly knocked me over. It knocked some doubts into my mind as well. I could account for most of Juvenal's actions but not quite all. Was it really possible that he had been in league with Townley? It beggared belief. But how else could I account for the timing of his attack on me as I left Mrs Chawley's?

Juvenal was dead. I could not ask him anything now. But as soon as I reached the Wintours' house I would rouse Arabella and together we would confront Miriam and at last wring the truth from her.

I mounted the steps and rapped violently on the door.

What of the dice? Were they another flaw in the pattern?

The door opened an inch or two, still on the chain. The porter's face peered out at me. The light from within must have shown him my face. I saw his expression changing and the shock in his eyes.

"For God's sake, man, let me in," I said. "I'm freezing to death."

★ ★ ★

In the hall there was a mirror in a tarnished gilt frame with a candle in a bracket on either side. I caught sight of my reflection as the porter was taking off my cloak. I would not have recognized myself in the street.

I had become a spectacle fit for a booth in a fair. In the absence of hat or wig, my bony skull gleamed like a death-head. My eyes were sunk deep in their sockets. Most striking of all was the angry stripe on my right cheek. I was like a Red Indian — or, worse, a wild man, one of those savage creatures reared by the light of nature alone that emerge from the depths of forests and both fascinate and appal the savants.

When the porter took my cloak, he saw the axe in my left hand and the knife in the right. His eyes widened and his mouth dropped open.

I handed the weapons to him. "Put them on the table there for now."

There were footsteps on the landing above. I looked up and saw Josiah hobbling down the stairs. He was out of livery but still in his day-clothes. He wore a fur hat that had once belonged to his master and a muffler round his neck. He was carrying a weighted stick.

"Thanks be to God, master," the old man cried when he saw me. But then he caught sight of my face and stopped, clinging to the rail.

"I met with an accident," I said.

He came down the rest of the stairs. "Sir, we've searched everywhere — where have you been?"

"It doesn't matter." I glanced at the clock. It was almost two o'clock. "Tell me — what day is it?"

517

The porter made a sound that might have turned into a laugh had he not strangled it at birth.

Josiah peered at me. "Wednesday night, sir. That's to say, early on Thursday morning."

So I had been unconscious for nearly four-and-twenty hours. "Have the Judge and Mrs Arabella retired?"

He shook his head, clearly bewildered and at his wits' end. "I thought you might have come from there, sir."

"From where?"

"Why, sir, from Mrs Arabella. From Mr Townley's."

I stared at him. "What the devil do you mean?"

"Mrs Arabella went there this evening, sir. Mrs Townley collected her and Miriam in their coach. Sir, you are injured. What has happened? Were you robbed? And my poor, dear master —"

"Josiah," I said. "Why did the Townleys call for Mrs Arabella? Why did she go?"

"Because my master is dead, sir."

The candlelight made large, liquid gleams in his eyes. I saw the tear tracks on his cheeks.

"How?" I said. "When?"

Josiah gestured upstairs. "Master was sleeping in the closet. In the bed where . . ."

I nodded, frowning, as his voice trailed away — I knew this already, of course, for that was the reason I had come to the garden gate and not the front door on Tuesday evening.

"When I went to call his honour in the morning, he was dead. He was cold. Sir, he should not have died

518

alone. Someone should have been there. I should have been there."

I touched his arm. "Stop that, my friend. Tell me, how did he die?"

Josiah shrugged thin shoulders that curved inwards in a weary droop that spoke of decades of bowing and stooping. "What do I know of these things, sir, except that we must all go when God pleases?"

I gestured up the stairs. "His body has not been moved? I shall go up."

"They have not come to lay him out — he is scarcely decent, sir. This weather —"

"I know. It doesn't signify."

Josiah lighted me upstairs. I slowed my pace to accommodate his. I had not realized how lame the old man had become of late and how his vigour had diminished. He showed me into the closet where his master lay.

The room was very cold and smelled of death; for in the moment of dying the body releases more than its soul. The curtains were drawn close about the small bed. At a sign from me, Josiah drew back the nearest of them and held up the candle so I might see.

The Judge lay on his back, his head raised by a single pillow. He wore a heavy gown and a thick flannel nightcap. His eyes were closed. His mouth was slightly open. His skin had a pale, waxy patina like ageing alabaster.

Sometimes death makes a man look foolish. It had been kinder to Mr Wintour. It smoothed away the wrinkles, stilled the tics and twitches of age and restored to his face something of what he had once been in the prime of life. His features were handsome, stern and regular, but not unkind or mean in any way. He looked like a judge.

I stooped and kissed his forehead.

CHAPTER
SEVENTY-NINE

I was desperate to find Mrs Arabella. I wanted to rush through the streets to Hanover Square and hammer on Mr Townley's door until the people of the house let me in. But I am a clerk by training and experience, and clerks have this to be said for them: they think before they talk, and they talk before they act.

I made Josiah tell me what had happened. Yesterday morning, the boy who did the fires was the first to enter the closet but he had not realized his master was dead because the bed-curtains were still closed. It was Josiah who had made the melancholy discovery when he went to wake Mr Wintour at about nine in the morning.

Mrs Arabella was informed at once, which was when it emerged that I had not returned home the previous evening after the fête. Miriam said she had waited up for me until three o'clock. As I had not come, the maid explained, she had assumed that I had drunk more deeply than usual and that I had stayed the night at the tavern or with friends.

The news of the Judge's death had brought both Mr Townley and Major Marryot to the house during the day. Both men reported having seen me among the crowd at Hicks Tavern but neither of them could shed light on what had happened to me afterwards.

"Mr Townley came just as Major Marryot was leaving," Josiah told me. "Mrs Arabella took him up to the closet — I heard him say he must pay his respects to his honour. He came back to the house at about three o'clock with Mrs Townley. They were with my mistress in the library for some time, and then she sent for me and told me to tell Miriam that they were going to stay with the Townleys and that she should pack what they would need for a few nights."

"Did you chance to hear anything of what Mr Townley said?" I asked. "On either occasion?"

Josiah looked shocked. "No, sir."

"And how did your mistress seem?"

"In great distress, sir." There was a hint of reproof in the old man's voice.

"Did she leave a message for me?"

"No, sir."

I could not understand it. I knew that Mrs Arabella distrusted the motives of Mr Townley and Mr Noak. It was inexplicable that she should agree to go to the Townleys' at all; and to go without leaving a message for me was beyond belief.

I told Josiah to have the library fire made up and to bring me a tray of supper there, together with a bottle of wine and a pot of coffee. First, however, I wanted a bowl of warm water in my bedchamber. I think he was glad to be doing something he understood.

When the boy who looked after the fires brought up the water, I washed my face and hands and changed my clothes. I covered my head with my second-best wig and felt approximately myself again. Before I went downstairs, I studied myself in the mirror and was relieved to discover how unremarkable I appeared, if tired and careworn. Only the cut in my cheek placed a limit on my respectability. It had scabbed over but I was aware of it every time I moved a muscle in my face.

As I was crossing the hall towards the library door, there was a rustling in the shadows behind me. I spun round, my fists clenched. But it was only Mehitabel Tippet, the refugee child from Mount George.

"Please, sir," she said in a whisper so the porter in his chair near the door would not hear. "Please, sir, begging your pardon, but may I speak a word in your private ear?"

In its way, nothing better illustrated the chaos of the household than Mehitabel Tippet's presence in the hall in the early hours of the morning. The girl should not have been out of her bed. She should not have been in the hall without having been expressly commanded to go there. She should not have been so bold as to speak to me without having been spoken to first. Any of those offences would in normal circumstances have earned her a whipping.

As it was I told her that she might follow me into the library and speak to me while I ate. Josiah frowned when he saw her entering the room but he did not say anything. After he had served me my supper, I sent him away.

Despite the fire, it was cold in there. I sat in my usual chair. I made Mehitabel stand by the fender, for she was shivering. She was a little plumper than she had been four months earlier when I had taken her away from the Provost and brought her to Warren Street. But she was still a small, sad thing, liable to start at shadows.

I ate swiftly and in silence, shovelling the food into my mouth because I did not want to waste a moment more than was necessary. At the first taste, I realized that I was starving. It was poor fare — the usual gritty bread made from adulterated flour and a few slices of tough, salted pork garnished with a mound of currant jelly — but it tasted ambrosial to me.

After a moment or two, I laid down my fork and knife and took up the glass of wine. "Well, child? What is it?"

"If you please, sir, it was when I was putting the mended sheets away in the cedarwood chest in the mistress's bedchamber. That's when I heard them."

"Heard whom? And when was this?"

Even the dim light could not conceal the fact that the girl had blushed. "The mistress, sir. And the tall gentleman with a big nose."

"Mr Townley?"

"Yes, sir. This was the first time — when he came this morning to pay his respects. Not later when he came in the coach with his lady and took madam away. I heard them on the stairs almost directly. I couldn't leave the room because I'm not meant to be seen in the family side of the house."

524

I sat up and pushed aside the plate. I was beginning to follow her drift. "Your mistress's chamber communicates directly with the closet, does it not? There's an inner door between them?"

"Yes, sir — it was open an inch or so for air, but you couldn't tell that from the other side on account of the curtain in front. I dared not move when they were in the closet for fear they'd hear me. But I could not help hearing them."

I began to eat again. "What were they saying?"

"The gentleman said all that was right and proper about poor Judge Wintour. And then he said he had a proposal for Mrs Arabella. Said he knew all about Mr Pickett."

I choked on a piece of gristle. "Mr Pickett? Are you sure, child? Quite sure?"

She nodded. "It's not a name I'd forget, sir. Not after that night at Mount George."

"What did he say next?"

"I couldn't make head nor tail of it, not for five or ten minutes. They were still in there, still talking, back and forth, but in whispers." Mehitabel's face crumpled like a dirty rag. "And the poor judge lying there dead before them. Then Mr Townley said your name, sir, and my mistress said, loud and clear, 'Where is he, you devil?' "

In my agitation I pushed aside the tray, rose from the chair and began to walk about the room. "What else?"

"I couldn't hear, sir. Not until the end, when my mistress repeated something he'd said. 'Norman's Slip,' she said. And he said, 'When the tide is on the turn, that's the best time.' "

"Norman's — are you quite sure that's what he said?"

"Yes, sir. I heard him as clear as a bell. But the strangest thing was that Miriam laughed when he said it. I've never heard Miriam laugh since I came to New York."

"She was with them in the room? You didn't say."

"Of course she was, sir. It wouldn't have been seemly otherwise."

"No," I said. "Of course it wouldn't." I took up a candle and rummaged among the muddle of papers on the table, looking for a tide-table. "But why should Miriam laugh?"

"I don't know, sir. But she was cheerful later too, while she was packing the clothes for her mistress. It's not like her."

"What's she like?" I asked suddenly. It was not a subject I had troubled to think much about because Miriam was a servant and a slave at that.

"Sour as a crab-apple now, sir. She's very close with the mistress but keeps her distance with everyone else. But she used to be different when her brother was alive. I remember them when I was a girl at Mount George — the two of them were always laughing and singing. They were twins, you know. That must have made it worse when she had to kill him."

"What?"

Mehitabel stared at me. "That's what changed her, sir, having her brother's blood on her head."

"Her brother?"

I sat down heavily. I was in a desperate hurry to be gone but I knew I could not go without knowing more. "Are you telling me that Juvenal and Miriam are brother and sister?"

"Yes, sir." Surprised, the girl stared at me. "Everyone knows that. Miriam said he was going to kill the mistress next, which was why she had to shoot him. Her own brother — how could she? But you have to choose sometimes, don't you, sir? You have to choose who you love more, who you owe your duty to. And she chose to kill Juvenal."

Juvenal. My dark shadow.

The intellectual faculty has a curious capacity for making sudden discoveries. Or, rather, in a blinding revelatory flash, for placing a new interpretation on the data it already has at its disposal. Is this what the poets call inspiration?

In an instant I was on my feet. In the time it took me to reach the hall, shouting for Josiah, the truth and its implications had burned themselves on my mind.

Juvenal had met Arabella when she married his master, Jack Wintour, in a union that had brought neither party happiness. True, Juvenal was a negro but he had the address of a gentleman and I knew he had been well enough to look at as a young man.

What if Juvenal and Arabella had lain together? What if the result had been a girl-child with dark skin? Henrietta Barville.

Now the idea had hatched itself, the rest followed in an instant. In those days at Mount George, early in her marriage, Arabella must have hoped that the child growing in her belly would be Wintour's. But the girl had been black and Arabella's adultery was written for all to see in the colour of her child's skin.

So much now became clear that had been obscured. When Froude discovered his long-awaited heir was a black bastard, no wonder he had inflicted such a savage punishment on Juvenal, one that made it impossible for him to father another child. When Froude wrote to Judge Wintour, no wonder he said their grandchild had been stillborn.

Nor was it strange that Juvenal had killed Froude when he had the opportunity.

Miriam falsely claimed to have killed Juvenal to protect her mistress on the night when Froude died and Mount George was destroyed. Arabella had supported her. The truth was that the mistress and the maid had conspired to allow Juvenal to escape. The women had brought Henrietta Barville with them to New York — a negro infant of no account; a slave's child. There was no one left to provide another version of events.

No one except Roger Pickett.

Even in his mutilated state, Juvenal had remained a jealous lover. Miriam became his eyes and ears in the Wintours' household. When Pickett became a threat to Arabella and her child, Miriam would have told him, which had led to Pickett's murder in Canvas Town. When Jack Wintour returned, she would have reported on his behaviour to her brother. It had been soon after

Wintour had hit his wife in the garden that he had been attacked, almost fatally, on his own front doorstep.

Similarly, both his nocturnal assaults on me had been because, even in his ruin, Juvenal did not brook rivals, particularly one who had been enquiring about the death of the young informer, the mulatto Taggart. I realized now that Juvenal had been responsible for two other deaths — that of Virgil, the runaway who had been hanged for Pickett's murder; and that of Taggart, who had borne false witness against Virgil and thereby brought him to the gallows.

Juvenal's child had died and been buried with his surname for all the world to see. Surely that must have hardened his heart still further?

For then had come his attack on our expedition to Mount George, culminating in his murder of Jack Wintour, his former master and his lover's husband.

Yes, Juvenal had been a jealous lover. Hence his desire to castrate me when he learned from Miriam that Arabella and I had become lovers.

Oh yes. I understood everything now as I stood in the hall and pulled on my greatcoat while barking orders at Josiah and the porter. Everything, though I did not know it, except the most important thing.

CHAPTER
EIGHTY

A savage wind was blowing off the river. The moon was up but its light was fitful, for clouds were moving steadily across the sky. It was very cold, colder than I had ever known.

When I had left Warren Street, the grandfather clock in the hall was striking half-past three. The tide had turned almost half an hour earlier. There was no one I could take with me from the house for the only male servants who remained to us were old Josiah, the porter, who was even older, and the boy who did the fires. I scribbled a note for Marryot and left it with Josiah for him to send round as early as he could in the morning.

Under my cloak I had a pistol in my pocket, one of the pair I had carried when we were in the Debatable Ground. I had also brought Juvenal's axe, which I had thrust into the belt securing my coat. My hat was tied to my head with a scarf that had the additional benefit of concealing and protecting the cut on my cheek.

I met no one until I encountered the patrol manning the barrier near Vauxhall Gardens on the Greenwich road.

"There's a woman," I said with a wink as I showed the sergeant my pass. I swayed slightly. "Lovely girl. She hates waiting, Sergeant."

He chuckled and handed back my papers. "Don't we all, sir?" He gestured to his men to move the barrier aside for me.

I gave him a shilling. "Get yourself something warm to drink," I advised him. "It's a cold night."

"Not if there's company in your bed, sir," he said.

I walked on. I had chosen a plausible excuse to be out at this hour for several houses in this direction had become little better than bordellos; others provided lodgings for gentlemen who preferred the convenience of keeping their mistresses at a safe distance from the temptations of the city.

My eyes adjusted to the lack of light and I made good time on the road, which the authorities had recently cleared of snow for the benefit of the army. Norman's Slip was out towards Greenwich, a short way beyond the foundry. I had been there once last summer with Townley. The slip itself was protected by a small mole and there was a yard containing a warehouse on the shore beside it. The yard was surrounded by a high brick wall set with spikes and broken glass. Though it was close to the city, Norman's was a secluded place. A short lane serving nowhere else connected it to the road.

Mr Townley held the slip and the yard on a five-year lease from a Loyalist merchant who had fled to England at the outbreak of hostilities. There was a good deal of trade, legal and illegal, between New York and

Jersey throughout the war. Our outposts in New Jersey, at Paulus Hook and elsewhere, were in constant need of supplies. Major Marryot had told me once in his cups that they found Norman's Slip useful at Headquarters for it served as a private place for people to cross the river without the tedious necessity of official sanction.

To this day, I do not know whether I made the right decision in going directly to Norman's. The terms of my commission from the American Department gave me the powers of an observer, nothing else. I was not authorized to order soldiers hither and thither. But perhaps I should have gone to Headquarters, roused Marryot if he was there and then tried to persuade him to intervene with a sufficient force to make a difference. That would have been the prudent course of action, appropriate to a clerk in a government department; that would have been what Mr Rampton would have done. But, even if my efforts had gone as smoothly as possible, it would have taken me until dawn to reach Norman's Slip with a party of soldiers.

By then it would have been too late. Even the geography of the affair was against me: Norman's was not far away from Warren Street, whereas Headquarters was much further and in the opposite direction.

I could be certain only of this: there was a bridge of ice across the Hudson to the Jersey shore, and Norman's Slip was a secluded spot from which to make the crossing. I could not be sure that this was the night chosen for the attempt but, whatever Townley's plan might be, delay could only make it riskier for him.

The going became harder when I turned into the lane. It was covered in frozen snow, which had fixed itself into hard, unforgiving ruts. On either side were thick hedges that reduced the light still further but at least gave some protection from the biting wind.

At last I came to the double gates into the yard. They were shut fast. But in front of them was a pile of fresh horse-dung that had not lain there long enough for it to freeze. It was a good omen. I waited a moment and listened. I heard nothing.

I knocked on the wicket set into the gate. A dog began to bark inside. Its chain rattled as it leapt about in a frenzy. There was the sound of a door opening.

"Who is it?" a man demanded. He snarled at the dog, which fell silent.

"Message for Mr Townley," I said, wondering if Townley would have been alerted by the dog. "Open up, man, and quick — I'm chilled to the bone."

"Who are you? What message?"

"It's Mr Savill," I said. "Hurry — Government business, and I'm pressed for time."

The man drew back two bolts and opened the wicket. Two men, one armed with a musket, the second with a heavy stick, studied me by the light of a lantern. One of them was probably the watchman. The other I recognized from my visits to Mr Townley's house, where he served as the porter. Hope surged through me: his presence must mean that Townley was here; and if Townley was here so, almost certainly, was Arabella.

"It's Oliver, isn't it?" I said. "I've seen you often enough at Hanover Square so I should know your face by now."

"Beg pardon, sir," he said, opening the wicket for me to step through. His breath smelled of rum. "Didn't realize it was you."

"No matter. Where's your master?"

"Down by the slip, sir."

"With the others?"

"Yes, sir."

I don't believe he had any suspicion of me. I was fortunate — Townley's habit of secrecy was so ingrained that he kept his own counsel whenever he could. The porter knew me merely as an honoured visitor to the house. I guessed that this was not the first time that he had been called upon to assist on one of these nighttime expeditions and that such comings and goings had become almost routine to him.

"Are they all here?"

"Just his honour and Mr Noak, sir, and the lady and her maid. I came over with them from the house."

"Excellent. I know my way from here. Stay in the warm while you can."

With obvious relief, the two men retired into a cabin with a stove that had been built against the wall by the gate. In the grey half-light, I struck out towards the river with a confidence I did not feel. The bulk of the warehouse lay between me and the slip itself.

I rounded the corner of the building, which took me out of sight of anyone who might be watching from the cabin by the gates. Footsteps were approaching from the direction of the slip. Pulling off my gloves, I ducked into a recessed doorway leading to the darkened warehouse. I took out the pistol but did not cock it for fear of the sound the mechanism would make.

A tall man came into view. It was too dark to see his features but I guessed it was Townley coming to see what the dog's barking was about.

I stepped out of the doorway and rammed the muzzle into his cheek. "Be silent."

He gave a start but recovered himself instantly. "Good God, sir. But — but it's Mr Savill, isn't it? You took me quite —"

I let him hear me cocking the pistol and he fell silent. I jabbed the muzzle harder into his face. "Hold your tongue. Where are they?"

"Who, sir?"

I drew him into the embrasure and placed the pistol under his chin, forcing his head back against the door. "Mrs Arabella. Noak."

"Why, at home with Mrs Townley, of course, and I hope fast asleep. Poor Mrs Arabella was quite —"

I pushed harder and he gave a cry.

"Pray be careful with that, sir," he said in a strangled whisper. "The slightest touch might lead to an accident."

I pushed harder still. "Pistols behave unpredictably sometimes, especially in this weather."

Townley's breathing became rapid and laboured. He tried to speak but could not.

"Where are they?" I said again. "On the ice already?"

"Yes. Not long, though. If you hurry . . . But, sir, allow me to say one thing at least. When Noak was at his London attorney's, he intercepted a letter from Pickett to his sister that revealed the existence of a great gold deposit. May we not come to an understanding? You and I will be as rich as —"

"Hold your tongue." I eased the axe from my belt. "Is it just the three of them out there, the two women and Noak?"

"Yes, sir. I swear it on my mother's grave."

I believed him. The more people in a party, the greater the risk of being either betrayed or observed.

"Are they being met?"

"A patrol's coming from the other shore." Townley hesitated and then added in a rush, his voice soft and hoarse: "I never meant that any harm should come to you. It was merely necessary to keep you out of the way for a day or two. For your own safety as much as anything. I don't know how you —"

"Juvenal slashed my cheek," I said.

"Juvenal? Who?"

"Your gaoler — a runaway slave with a grudge." I realized suddenly that Townley knew no more of Juvenal and his significance than Juvenal had known of Townley, Noak and the gold. "He was going to emasculate me and leave me for dead. That is not safety, sir."

"I'm more distressed than I can say. It was Miriam's idea that the man should keep you out of harm's way until she and her mistress were safely away. She said he was entirely trustworthy and devoted to the interests of

Mrs Arabella. On my honour, sir, I had no dealings with him myself —"

I brought up the axe and swung its blunt side against Townley's exposed head. The blow caught his skull between the iron of the axe and the hard wood of the door. The haft twitched in my hand. Something cracked. He crumpled to the ground.

CHAPTER
EIGHTY-ONE

The slip was encrusted with icy snow. I stared down its frosted slope to the cold, grey world of the river, which stretched away towards that other America I knew so little about.

The night was full of noises. The tide was ebbing rapidly, causing the great sheets of ice to move restlessly against each other. The river creaked and groaned and grated like a living thing in pain. The wind hissed and howled, sweeping upstream towards the empty heart of the country. A bank of high clouds now occluded two-thirds of the sky and hid the moon completely.

I did not like the ice. When I was a child, I had seen a boy fall through the ice on the river near our village. None of us could swim. They did not find the body, what was left of it, until the spring.

So I had not ventured on the ice that year or during the previous winter. But many people did, walking and skating. They took sledges on the frozen river and even horses.

This winter, the worst of the war, the cold had been so intense that the army was able to move a twenty-four-pound cannon, which weighed three tons on its carriage, across the ice from the city to Paulus

Hook. On another occasion, two hundred sleighs laden with provisions, each drawn by two horses, crossed from New York to Staten Island, with an escort of two hundred light horse to guard them.

But one could never be sure of the ice, even in that long, hard winter. The movements of the tide and the fluctuations of the water temperature subjected it to unpredictable stresses and varied its thickness from place to place. There were stories of refugees who had drowned as they fled from the rebels to the safety of New York. Cracks and holes sometimes allowed water to wash over the surface of the ice, where it would form new layers and freeze in its turn.

In the distance, on the further shore, a light flashed on and off some way to the north of Paulus Hook. After a pause of perhaps twenty seconds, it happened again. And then once again.

It must be a signal to the party on the ice, I thought, a marker to show them their direction. The discovery broke the spell that had held me. I scrambled down the slipway, holding on to the iron railing fixed to the side of the quay to prevent myself from falling.

I stepped gingerly on to the sheet of ice at the bottom and walked out beyond the lee of the mole. A faint yellow glow made a puddle of light on the ice. Hanging on a hook at the end of the mole was a lantern. When I drew nearer, I discovered that the glass was shielded so the flame could only be seen from the ice and the opposite shore.

It was another navigation marker, I realized, the twin to the flashing light across the river.

The full force of the wind struck me as I moved away from the shelter of the mole. It came in gusts that made me stagger like a drunken man. I stumbled over the frozen corpse of a duck and pitched forward on my hands and knees.

The light flashed three more times on the Jersey side.

I scrambled to my feet. I must reach Arabella before the rebel patrol. That was all that mattered.

I did not think of what would happen next if I succeeded in reaching her or what would happen if I did not. I did not think of any of the unanswered and perhaps unanswerable questions. I plodded onward, my mind emptied of thought.

The ice was as solid as a marble floor. The wind was my enemy, cruel and insatiable in its malice. It pushed me off-course, it buffeted me, it set my eyes watering, and it found its way into the smallest crevice in my clothing.

But the snow was my ally: it offered better purchase for my boots than the ice and also, as my eyes adjusted to the conditions, it showed me where the others had gone before me.

Three sets of footsteps marched abreast in a wavering line towards New Jersey. Noak's were in the centre, slightly ahead of the others. He had Miriam and Arabella close on either side, probably hanging on to his arms. Their travelling cloaks were longer than his and they trailed along the ground behind them, the marks they made partly obliterating the prints of their feet. The women would slow him down.

Following their footsteps lessened the fear that I might stumble on to one of the thinner patches of ice in the river or fall into one of the cracks between the sheets of ice. I began to run — slowly and awkwardly at first, like a child in leading strings discovering a new means of locomotion, but then with increasing confidence.

Again the flashes of light came from the Jersey shore.

The wind pushed the clouds away from the moon with the speed and transforming effect of a curtain rising to reveal a brightly lit scene on the stage.

Suddenly the North River was a sheet of silver and white under the night sky. Beyond it lay a long, grey blur, the coastline of New Jersey. Not a hundred yards away, outlined like the principal actors in the drama seen through the wrong end of a telescope, three linked figures were walking over the ice.

I shouted wordlessly. The wind whipped the sound from my lips. But they heard something for they stopped and looked back.

I ran on.

I drew closer. The little group had separated, the two women standing side by side. Though the women were shrouded in their hooded cloaks I knew the one on the right was Arabella because she was taller than Miriam.

Beside them was Noak. They must have recognized me now for he drew a pistol and levelled it at me. He did not shout that I should stop or he would fire. He didn't say anything at all. He merely cocked the pistol.

I knew then that Noak meant to shoot me. He would kill me as efficiently as he had treated my sea-sickness when we shared a cabin on our passage to New York. There would be nothing personal about it when he pulled the trigger and, in a sense, nothing malicious, either. But he was always a practical man who looked for a practical solution to any difficulty he encountered. His purpose was patriotic; and as far as he was concerned his end justified any means he was obliged to employ to secure it.

But I ran on for I had nowhere else to go and nowhere to hide.

The moonlit figures dissolved into a flurry of movement. Arabella threw herself towards Noak. He sprawled sideways on the ice with her on top of him. The pistol went off but the shot was wide.

In a moment I had reached them.

Arabella scrambled to her feet. I held out a hand to her but she backed away. Noak was in the act of getting up. Miriam was standing to one side. She spat at me like a cat.

I took out my own pistol and cocked it with clumsy fingers. The barrel trembled and I was obliged to steady my wrist with my left hand. I was not at ease with firearms.

"Madam," I said. "Pray stand aside from the other two." My words emerged jerkily, interspersed with gasps for air. "Miriam, move towards Mr Noak."

The women obeyed me. Noak rose unhurriedly to his feet and brushed the snow from his cloak. All three of them had been encumbered with bundles and bags, some of which now lay abandoned on the ice.

"Mr Noak and Miriam, you may continue to Jersey," I said. "For all I care the two of you may go to the devil as long as you do not come back. But Mrs Arabella stays with me."

Noak coughed. "Forgive me, sir, but does not that depend on the lady herself?"

Arabella's face was in the shadow of her hood. She did not move.

"Well, ma'am?" said Noak.

"You cannot go with them," I said.

"I must," she said. "If you knew all, sir, you would not wish me to stay."

I saw at once how Noak had forced her cooperation. "Is that how this spy made you come with him?" I said. "Blackmail?"

She did not reply.

Keeping the pistol trained on Noak and Miriam, I moved closer to Arabella. I murmured two words in a voice that I hoped only she would be able to hear.

"Henrietta Barville."

Arabella moaned softly.

"I believe I know who she was," I went on. "She was your daughter. But the poor girl does not matter now, I promise you."

Arabella lifted her head and said very clearly, "She matters to me, sir. She will always matter."

"But what happened is over. It is all forgotten now. Besides, they can prove nothing."

"Would you say the same if it were your Lizzie lying in her grave? That she's all forgotten?"

"Where's Juvenal?" Miriam cried suddenly. "What have you done with him?"

"He was about to castrate me," I said. "So I was obliged to kill him."

The woman launched herself at me across the ice. I turned the pistol on her and pulled the trigger.

The hammer fell but the gun misfired.

Miriam was upon me immediately, biting and scratching like a Fury. Her hand caught at the wound on my cheek and tore it open. I screamed and swung the pistol barrel at her with all my strength, sending her flying backwards on the ice.

There was a cracking sound. I heard it. I felt it beneath my feet.

"Come away," Noak shouted. "The ice is weaker downstream. They were fishing there this morning."

The new danger briefly united us. The four of us drew together and retreated about thirty yards up the river.

I still had the axe under my cloak. As we moved, I took Arabella's arm and tried to coax her from the others. But she pulled herself away.

"We must go back to New York," I whispered. "I beg you, madam."

"Ah," Noak said. "The Lord be praised."

I turned. He was looking towards the Jersey shore. Dark figures moved against the silver and white of the river. There were five or six men. Two of them pulled a sledge over the ice behind them. They must have been downwind of us for they made no sound.

"Come with me, ma'am," Noak said in his precise, nasal voice. "You know what will happen if you stay. And it's not a pretty death, is it? To hang by your neck until you die."

CHAPTER
EIGHTY-TWO

I took out the axe. The edge of the blade glinted in the moonlight.

The men with the sledge had drawn closer. But they were still some way off.

"Why should she hang?" I said to Noak.

"For aiding and abetting His Majesty's enemies," he said. "The evidence will admit of no other interpretation. It's a capital offence."

"It was under duress. Besides, they would not hang a lady."

"Perhaps. But they would certainly hang an accessory to murder. Even if she is a lady."

I came a step nearer to him. "You cannot mean that."

"I mean everything," Mr Noak said. "It's quite simple. Mrs Arabella had a curious power over the negro, Juvenal. It would be indelicate of me to enquire too closely into its nature, but I have proof of it — I intercepted a letter he wrote to her which he had confided to his sister. When Mr Pickett threatened her, she bribed or coaxed the negro into acting as her agent in his murder. He did not do it for his sister, Miriam. He did it for her."

"You are quite wrong, sir," Mrs Arabella said.

"Give me the papers relating to the Pickett gold deposit, madam," Noak said to her, "and you may do as you please and I shall be as silent as any grave."

"No," she said.

"Madam," Miriam said. "Have a care, I beg you."

Noak glanced at me. "And let us not forget, sir," he went on, "Mrs Arabella allowed an innocent man to hang for Pickett's murder. We watched him die, Mr Savill. Do you remember? The runaway who stole Mr Pickett's ring and shoes. The evidence against the runaway came from an informer, no more than a boy. Juvenal primed him with what to say. And then Juvenal killed the informer to stop his mouth. I believe you went to inspect the lad's body when they pulled it out of the water near the Paulus Hook ferry. I knew you must have your suspicions."

At that moment there were two gunshots, so close to each other that the second sounded like the echo of the first. All four of us looked towards New York.

"We've been seen," Noak said. "It's this confounded moon."

There were more men on the ice now. A British patrol was making its way towards us, advancing in loose formation. The four of us were approximately the same distance from the rebels on one side and our own people on the other.

"Come, Mrs Arabella," Noak said, "further delay would be foolish. Let us declare a truce. We have time to continue our journey if we go now." He looked at me. "You will not try to prevent us, sir. Not if you care for this lady's happiness."

The runaway, I thought, had been called Virgil. Why did they give slaves those ludicrous names? Was it simply a form of mockery?

"Come, my love," I said. "Come back with me and we shall find a way to begin again."

"It's too late," Arabella said. "I wish with all my heart it was not."

She moved away from me. In the distance, someone shouted.

"It's not too late," I said. "Have faith in me."

"You don't understand."

"I understand enough to —"

"Mr Pickett came to Warren Street twice," she interrupted. "The second time was by my invitation — Juvenal took my note to Mr Pickett's lodgings. I told him I would meet him privately at the belvedere and he should come to the garden gate, not the house, and we would discuss our business there. It was in the evening, quite late."

"Madam —" Miriam broke off and turned her back on us.

"I was playing at backgammon with Miriam when he came," Arabella went on. "He was an odious man, sir, puffed up with his power over me. He had seen me with Hetty at my breast at Mount George. He wanted the land and he wanted the gold. He even wanted me. And when he touched me and tried to kiss me, I took up my scissors from my sewing basket and I stabbed him in the neck."

Blood on the backgammon board.

"He fell to the ground, bringing the table with him. And then I stabbed him in the back to make sure he was dead. Juvenal took the body away in the night and left it in Canvas Town."

I remembered my first visit to the belvedere, when I had sat there with Judge Wintour and Mrs Arabella. It had been the evening of the day they hanged Virgil for Pickett's murder.

The air in the belvedere that night had smelled faintly of lemon juice and vinegar. The murder must have left stains and odours behind it, which Arabella and Miriam had done their best to remove.

But they had forgotten the dice.

I had carried the solution to this mystery on my person for months: one die had been caught up among Pickett's clothing, the other in a crack in the floor; and now both dice were reunited in my waistcoat pocket.

Arabella cried out my name, *Edward*, and the wind snatched it away.

That was all she said. She turned and ran — but not towards the coast of New Jersey and not back to New York. She ran down the invisible stream, her heavy winter pattens tapping on the ice like hammers.

"Stop, madam, for God's sake, stop," Noak shouted. "It's unsafe."

Miriam watched her mistress. She did not move.

I ran after Arabella. Despite her pattens and the encumbrance of her clothes, she was already twenty yards ahead of me. I tripped over a jagged outcrop in the ice and fell. I pulled myself up. She had increased her lead. I heard Noak running behind me.

I heard and felt the ice cracking beneath my feet.

Arabella redoubled her efforts. I followed her. There was a burst of distant gunfire. Something hit my left leg just above the knee.

I fell forward. The ice gave way under the impact of my body. Freezing water enveloped my face and my chest. I let go of the axe and it glided into the darkness beneath. I slid inexorably after it.

Noak seized my legs. He tugged me backwards. It must have been him, though I did not see him. The wound in my leg made me shout in agony. But no sound emerged from my mouth, only freezing salt water.

Retching, I lay on my belly under the hard, metallic light of the moon. I remember the keening of the wind and the water that chilled my skin like liquid death. I remember the shots and then more shots.

I remember Arabella Wintour falling, floundering, her arms waving. She said nothing. She did not even scream. I remember thinking, I shall never know now if she cared for me.

I heard the sound of scratching and knocking. Ice speaks in its own language as it fractures and pulls apart. I thought of Arabella on the night that Judge Wintour died: how she came scratching and knocking at my chamber door; and how we lay together, warm and dry, in the featherbed that was as big as an elephant and smelled of otto of roses. Now she was scratching and knocking beneath the ice, begging me to join her.

How I hate memory.

I listened to the scratching and knocking of the ice. I wanted to take Arabella into my embrace and to lie with her, now and always.

Now and always.

Scratching and knocking.

When our soldiers came, I was quite alone.

CHAPTER
EIGHTY-THREE

"I had hopes that we might remove the leg. But we must not despair. No doubt we shall have another opportunity."

I did not recognize the man's voice. His words did not surprise or even interest me. I heard a door open and close. Then there were footsteps receding in the distance. My mind floated like a leaf on the surface of a great darkness and an invisible current bore me away.

Later, perhaps much later, I opened my eyes. Pale light dazzled me. A drum was beating in the far distance.

I saw an old man stooping over me. He had the window behind him and I could not see his face.

"Ah. You are awake at last." He had an Irish accent with a soothing cadence to it. It was the voice that had spoken in the middle of the darkness. "I thought it might be today."

"You were saying something about a leg, sir." My voice was rusty with disuse. "My leg?"

"Indeed."

"You want to cut it off?"

552

"Yes, there was swelling, you see, and it looked ugly. Had the infection gathered strength, we should have had no alternative but to amputate above the knee."

"But — but you said you might have another opportunity."

"My dear sir, I did not mean your leg necessarily. I hope that we will not be obliged to take it off. Besides, I am not at all particular about these things. Any leg will do, so long as it conforms to the general pattern of a leg, if you take my meaning. You must not concern yourself about it in the slightest."

His voice flowed softly. Some peculiarity of his mouth meant that every now and then a faint and not unmelodious whistle mingled with what he was saying. I grew more interested in the whistles than the words. What key were they in? Did the ghost of a fragmentary tune inform their apparently arbitrary nature? In a while I was asleep again, leaving these questions unresolved.

Later, it was dark. A candle burned on the table by the bed. Someone was washing my face in warm water, the cloth scraping over the bristle on my chin. My left foot was acutely painful. My nurse was a man who hissed like an ostler grooming a horse. He wore a long bloodstained apron over his clothes.

"Where am I?"

He paused in his wiping and hissing. "So you're talking now, eh? I'll tell the doctor." He folded up his cloth and picked up the basin of water. "This is King's

College, sir. Though you won't find much book-learning here apart from Dr Clossy's lectures."

Dr Samuel Clossy was the Irishman with the whistle in his voice. He was, I learned later, a distinguished physician who had served as the college's Professor of Anatomy in happier days. He had returned to the city when the rebels were forced to abandon it. The army had converted the college buildings to a combination of military hospital and barracks. He put his knowledge to good use and served as a surgeon's mate on the wards. He also found time to lecture to his younger colleagues on anatomy.

"They are sadly deficient in their knowledge, sir," he told me in one of our first conversations when my mind was lucid once more. "I was in hopes of dissecting both your knee and your foot on their behalves. The foot, as I'm sure you know, is remarkably complex in its anatomical organization. Quite fascinating."

Dr Clossy was an amiable old man who longed to return to his native Ireland. It was he who told me that it was now February. When they had brought me in, I had been suffering from cold and exhaustion, as well as from the wound in my leg. I had nearly lost a finger and two of my toes from frostbite.

He claimed to know nothing of the circumstances that had led to my admission. Indeed, for all his gossiping, he told me very little. But on the first day that I was allowed to leave my bed and sit by the fire for a few minutes, he mentioned with a casual air that I

554

need not fear unwelcome visitors during my convalescence because there was a guard on my door.

By now I remembered almost everything until the moment on the ice when the soldiers had come.

The very next day Major Marryot called on me. I heard him talking to the sentry outside and I recognized his voice. He limped into the room with a scowl on his face. I was propped against the pillows of my bed and staring at the rectangle of grey sky beyond the window.

"Good day, sir," he said with an awkward bow. "I'm glad to see you more yourself."

I acknowledged his greeting but could not be troubled to speak to him. I was still very weak and my mind, though perfectly clear, wearied quickly with any exertion.

He walked about the room for a moment and then stopped abruptly with his back to the window, blocking the light. "This is a bad business, Mr Savill. General Clinton is most concerned. The Commandant has ordered an inquiry. You will have to appear before it in due course."

"I wish to go home," I said.

Marryot chewed his lip for a moment. Then he limped over to the bed and sat down heavily in the chair beside it. "I can tell you confidentially," he said in a low voice, "that it would save a good deal of time if you were to speak frankly to me now, in private — before you go to the board, I mean. We need not make this worse than it is."

"Make what worse?"

"This Noak affair."

I was too tired for this so I fell back on ignorance. "Noak? What about him?"

"Surely you remember?"

"I remember very little at present."

He stared at me. He looked older than before and there was a sprinkling of grey among the stubble on his chin. "What do you remember then?"

"The fête at Hicks Tavern. I believe I was attacked on my return to Warren Street. But I did not see my assailant."

"In the street or in the house?"

I remembered Miriam waiting for me in the belvedere. "I don't remember. But I went in by the garden gate. I suppose they must have been waiting there."

"But the servants said you came back to the house the next night. And that you were distraught and had received that wound on your face."

I put my hand up and touched my cheek. A long, hard scab ran from the eye to the corner of the mouth. It itched infernally because of my own stubble, which was now almost a beard.

"Yes," I said. "I was held in a cellar in Canvas Town. But they left me alone and I contrived to escape."

"Who was it?"

"I never saw them. Not properly. It was dark."

"But surely you heard them?" he prompted. "They must have said something."

"Nothing of any account. I took them for rogues. They stank, I know that."

556

"Where was this cellar?"

"How should I know, sir? I told you, it was dark, and when I escaped I ran — I didn't ask for directions from passers-by."

Marryot scowled at me, his sickroom manners forgotten. "Very well. But tell me why you went out again almost as soon as you reached Warren Street."

"Because I found Judge Wintour was dead —" I broke off, for tears had welled into my eyes. I realized I was weaker than I had thought. After a moment I went on: "I learned from the servants that Mrs Arabella and her maid had gone to stay with the Townleys."

"Why should she have done that?"

"You must ask Mr Townley."

"I can't," Marryot said. "He's dead."

CHAPTER
EIGHTY-FOUR

As a clerk in government service I have learned that silence is almost always a better tactic than speech. I expressed shock and sorrow when I heard of Townley's death but said nothing more. Marryot told me that he had been murdered at Norman's Slip and that the circumstances were still under investigation.

Within a day or two I was able to walk with the aid of a stick across my room. I never discovered where the bullet that hit my left leg came from, their side or ours. Perhaps that was only to be expected. War is a foolish business at best.

If I had not been brought down by the bullet, could I have saved Arabella? And if I had, what then?

Dr Clossy had extracted the ball and the wound was at last healing. He told me that, in his opinion, it had not done much lasting damage. He recommended a regimen of gentle exercise as my health improved. I might not regain the full vigour of the limb but I would not be a cripple.

A soldier brought me a change of linen and a suit of clothes, which he had fetched from Warren Street. When I was dressed, I was permitted to leave my room under escort. I discovered that I was in a hospital ward on the second floor of the main block of the college. The ward had been allocated to patients who required, for one reason or another, the luxury of a room to themselves. Many of them were in great pain and I had often heard them crying out like the souls of the damned, particularly in the nighttime.

When Marryot returned, I told him that a servant at Warren Street had heard Mr Townley talking about Norman's Slip to Mrs Arabella. I believed that she wished to cross the lines and join the rebels. She had let slip something to that effect as I was leaving to go to Hicks Tavern. But she was talking so wildly in her grief that I had not taken her seriously.

Standing in the hard winter light by the window, Marryot's face was very pale. "I cannot believe it," he said. "It's impossible. Not Mrs Arabella." He had the stricken expression of a man forced to accept what he desires to deny.

"But you must have had my note," I went on. "I gave it to Josiah to send to you in the morning. I told you I was gone to Norman's Slip where I feared there was some villainy afoot."

"You did not mention Mrs Arabella," he said, clutching at a straw.

"Of course I did not. I hoped to persuade her to return, and that we could hush up the entire affair. You know as well as I do that the deaths of her husband and parents-in-law must have temporarily unhinged her reason. Even now, sir, I hope we can find a way not to sully the poor lady's memory. We who were her friends owe her that, if nothing else."

Marryot changed colour and turned very red. He limped about the room in silence for a moment. Then he turned back to me.

"Then what did happen at Norman's Slip?"

"When I got there I told the watchman and Townley's porter I had a message for their master. They let me into the yard and I found my own way to the slipway. Luckily the moon came out at that moment and I saw the three of them on the ice — Mrs Arabella and her maid, with Noak between them. They were making for a light on the Jersey shore."

"And Townley? Where was he?"

I remembered the recessed doorway of the warehouse where I had left his body. "I have no idea. And I was in too much of a hurry to find out. I followed the others on to the ice. Noak shot at me." I hesitated. "Mrs Arabella spoiled his aim and saved my life. I believe she regretted her decision to flee and I could have brought her back safely to New York. But she panicked and fled downstream where the ice was less solid. I — I pursued her but to no avail."

My sorrow bubbled beneath the surface. I turned my head away. But I did not weep.

Marryot cleared his throat. "I know the rest, Mr Savill. The patrol saw it all."

The following day, they let me outside to walk in the grounds of the college, now much disfigured by the impedimenta of war. This became a daily outing. Clossy or a medical orderly would walk with me, and the soldier guarding my door would trail after us. They kept me away from other patients. I was not quite a prisoner and not quite free.

In my former life, I should have chafed at the restrictions that hedged me about. I should have despised my weakness of body and mind. But now I felt numb.

During our walks I often glimpsed the North River, still sheeted with ice. It was probable that Arabella was still there, a prey to fish, in thrall to the dissolution of death, waiting to be drawn out to sea by the tide.

What remained of her body was no longer of any significance. She had become yet another victim of this foolish war. She was as one with the rebel prisoner whose rotting corpse Noak and I had seen from the deck of the *Earl of Sandwich* on our first morning in New York.

Aye, I told myself as I plodded along, there is a circularity in these things.

Four days after Marryot's second visit, an orderly came to my room and told me that I had a visitor. He conducted me to a small sitting room usually reserved, he informed me, for the use of the superintendent of the hospital.

The room was empty. I warmed myself by the fire as I waited. I assumed that my visitor was Marryot but, when at last the door opened, it was Mr Carne who entered. He was alone. He bowed briskly and motioned me to a chair. I had glimpsed him with the Commandant that night at Hicks Tavern but I had not talked or even bowed to him since the day I found Jack Wintour's body.

"Well, sir," he said in his brusque American way. "So you've fallen into a scrape again. The question is: did you in fact fall into it or did you jump? To put it another way: are you a fool or a knave?"

"Neither, I hope, sir."

He stared at me with his pale eyes. The skin on his face was seamed like a patch of sun-baked mud. "I've talked to Major Marryot and to the officer commanding the patrol that brought you in. I've searched the Wintour house in Warren Street and questioned the servants. I regret to say I was obliged to look over your private papers."

He paused but I did not speak. I knew he would have found little to interest him there.

"Were you attached to Mrs Arabella Wintour?" he said suddenly.

I did not reply.

"It would not surprise me at all," he went on. "Nor would it surprise some of the Wintours' remaining servants."

"I have lived with the Wintours for these last eighteen months. Of course I was attached to the family. And they, I believe, to me."

"I had in mind an attachment of particular warmth." He gave me a wintry smile. "It's a pity that the maid wasn't there. Miriam Barville. She would know. But she fled to the rebels along with Samuel Noak and God knows where she is now."

I shifted in the chair. My injured leg was growing stiff.

Carne sighed. "Which leaves you, Mr Savill, as my principal source of information. You know that Noak was a spy?"

"Yes," I said. "But I did not know until the end."

"You met him on the passage from England?"

"Yes. Quite by chance. He told me he had a clerkship waiting for him here. The morning after we landed he came to me and said the position was no longer available. He begged me to mention his name if I chanced upon a gentleman in want of a clerk. As it happened, Mr Townley said his own clerk had just died."

"Which was a lie, it seems," Carne said. "I've talked to his former clerk. So did you, I understand. If you are telling the truth, that would suggest that Noak and Townley used you to effect their meeting. But, if Noak was a rebel spy, then so was Townley. Would that surprise you?"

I shrugged. "Not particularly. I follow your reasoning."

"Then pray follow it a little further. We found papers at Townley's house that support this theory. Suppose it's true. Why should Noak spend so much time at Warren Street?" Carne looked up at the ceiling as if hoping he might find the answer there. "To spy on you? That's possible, but you do not strike me as a man who is careless about what he writes or says. Why else? Was the man consumed with passion for the charms of Mrs Arabella? Again, it's possible — but not likely. Or was

563

there some other reason? Was it connected in any way with the lady's inexplicable decision to flee across the ice with Mr Noak?"

"Perhaps they were eloping together," I said.

Carne looked sharply at me. "You speak in jest, I think. But indeed it's as likely as anything else."

"She was distraught, sir, I do know that. Everyone she loved had died. She was not acting rationally."

"Townley was murdered at Norman's Slip. Who killed him?"

"I don't know."

"He was hit on the head with a heavy implement," Carne said. "He was a tall man, too. So it's unlikely to have been one of the women. Say it was Noak. Why? Because he feared Townley would betray him? To shut Townley's mouth? If so, was it connected with whatever took Noak to Warren Street?"

"I don't know."

"Why did he keep visiting the Wintours' house? That's the question at the heart of this. Was there something there he wanted? Did he take it with him to Jersey?"

I did not speak. I wrapped myself in silence and tried not to think of anything at all. After a while, Carne stood up and clapped his hat on his head.

"To be frank, sir, this affair is more than a puzzle," he said. "It's an embarrassment. The alternative is that it was you who killed Mr Townley because he tried to prevent you from chasing after Mrs Arabella. And that would be even more of an embarrassment to us all, both here and in London. Good day to you."

564

CHAPTER
EIGHTY-FIVE

I did not see Mr Carne again. The following afternoon, I received a letter from Major Marryot, who wrote that the Wintours' house was now shut up and that he had given orders for my possessions to be removed to the Broad Street office. Three days later I was discharged.

Dr Clossy wished me well and gave me a pass which would ensure the guards would let me leave the grounds of the college. An orderly conducted me to the gates and, out of the goodness of his heart, offered to summon a chair for me. I had no idea where I would go or what I would do.

A coach was standing a few yards up the road. As I was waiting for the chair, a door opened and a man climbed down. His shoulders hunched against the wind, he took a couple of steps towards the gates. He saw me standing there with my valise beside me. He took off his hat and bowed.

I saw his face clearly then. It was Mr Ingham, the manager of Townley's warehouse in Brooklyn.

"Forgive me, sir, I did not mean to startle you," he said with a quick smile, for I must have betrayed my surprise. "My mistress ordered me to meet you with a coach."

My brains were still addled. "Your mistress?" I repeated.

"Mrs Townley, sir. Major Marryot told her that you would probably want to go to your Broad Street office at first. But if there's somewhere you would prefer?"

"No," I said. "That would do very well."

"She also reserved an apartment for you at Fraunces's Tavern. Major Marryot thought it probable you had not settled on where you would lodge when you left here and that it might serve you for a night or two. But the arrangement is easily countermanded if it's not to the purpose."

I was too weary to be suspicious. Besides, the orderly was standing by and had heard the entire conversation so what was there to fear? I allowed myself to be assisted into the coach. I had no more power to direct my actions than does an automaton that strikes the hour on the old clock at the bidding of invisible machinery.

I stayed several weeks at Fraunces's Tavern while I waited for my replacement to arrive from England. A curt note from the Commandant's aide-de-camp informed me that I should remove my belongings from the Broad Street office. He also told me that, since the affair of Mrs Arabella Wintour's death was in manner of speaking *sub judice*, I was not to speak of it to anyone on pain of imprisonment.

It gave me the strangest sensation to see my clothes, my books and my papers again. Many of them had come from Warren Street. Carne and Marryot had pawed over them in search of explanations and answers. Through these familiar things I glimpsed myself in another time and place. I saw a stranger.

I found one item there which was not familiar — a small, hard object like a brown rock; it had been tossed among the jumble of letters and memoranda as if it might once have been used as a paperweight for them. I opened my penknife and scratched its surface. I saw the sparkle of gold beneath.

Who but Arabella could have put it among my papers? She had left me a keepsake before she went.

I lowered my head and for the first time I wept. I wept for Arabella. I wept for Juvenal, even, and for Townley. I wept for me.

I was questioned again by both Carne and Marryot. Later, I was brought before a Board of Inquiry, which consisted of four senior officers with nothing better to do, and asked the same questions, to which I gave the same answers. They could not shake my story. They could prove nothing.

The following day Mr Carne paid a visit to me at Fraunces's.

"It has been decided that you may leave New York when your replacement arrives from the American Department," he said. "On one condition, sir: that you do not speak of this business to anyone, here or in England. You accept?"

"Yes, sir."

"We do not want scandal. We have heard nothing from the rebels or Mr Noak, which suggests they do not see any advantage in telling the world, either. So General Clinton thinks it best to let sleeping dogs lie."

I bowed and thanked him. As he left, he paused at the door. He looked at me steadily for a moment without speaking, as if searching for the truth in my face. He turned and closed the door behind him.

I set my affairs in order. On a cold morning, I walked to Warren Street and knocked at the familiar door. The house looked smaller and shabbier than I remembered.

I did not recognize the porter who let me in. I asked for Josiah and he came to me in the hall. To my great embarrassment he seized my hand and kissed it.

He told me that the house and the remains of the Wintours' estate now belonged to a remote cousin in Canada. In the meantime, the house had been requisitioned by the army and a dozen officers were billeted there. Josiah and the other servants, including Mehitabel Tippet, had been retained for the time being.

I gave him a present of money to distribute among them and wrote down my sister's address in Shepperton. I would have offered to buy him if I could.

I went to the negro burying ground where the child of Arabella and Juvenal lay. The flowers were long gone. Snow and ice had destroyed the little wooden cross, leaving its fragments by the side of the grave. I arranged for a stonemason to cut and install a small, plain marker. I ordered him to carve on it Henrietta Barville's name and the dates of her birth and death.

Hetty-Petty. In my mind, the lost children of the two Mrs Wintours mingled and became as one.

I had written to thank Mrs Townley for her kindness when I had reached Fraunces's Tavern. I heard nothing in reply for some weeks. Eventually, however, after the board of inquiry, I received a note inviting me to call at Hanover Square any morning of that week.

There was a new porter at the house — the man I had seen at Norman's Slip that night was no longer there. I was shown into the parlour on the left, which had formerly served as Townley's outer office. Mr Ingham was perched on the clerk's stool where Mr Noak had once sat. He greeted me cordially.

"Have you left Long Island?"

"Yes, sir," he said with a smile. "Mrs Townley asked me to return to my old post. She has assumed the direction of her late husband's affairs, you see, and she believed my knowledge of them might be of use to her."

He showed me into the inner office that had been Mr Townley's domain. Now the room belonged to his widow. She was sitting at her husband's desk with an account book open before her. She rose and curtseyed when I entered. She wore mourning, of course, but she looked far more cheerful and at ease than when I had last seen her.

I expressed my sympathy for her loss.

"Yes," she said briskly. "Mr Carne says he cannot say exactly how my husband died but he inclines to the theory that it was the work of Mr Noak." She looked directly at me and sometimes looks say more than words. "Still, we shall never know for sure, shall we? Perhaps it's better that way." She gave me the ghost of a smile. "At all events we who are left must get on with our lives."

When the compliments and condolences were done, she asked me what my plans were. I told her I should soon return to London and that I would be leaving the American Department.

"I thought as much, and so did Mr Ingham." Her colour rose. "Forgive me for asking, sir, but do you have another position in mind?"

"Not as yet."

"Then may I put a proposition to you? As it happens, I have some property in London, including a warehouse we use ourselves. It was my father's. We have an agent to manage it but Mr Cumnor is elderly and Mr Townley was not able to oversee his work as closely as my father had. The rents have declined quite markedly. There's an acre of market garden, too, just north of the City. They say the town is expanding at a great rate so I wonder if the land might be ripe for development in some way."

"What would you wish me to do, ma'am?"

"To assess the situation, look over the accounts and, if Mr Cumnor agrees, perhaps take over some of the work if we find we suit each other. I cannot say what may happen in the future, but Mr Cumnor will eventually retire and I shall need another man of business there."

Mrs Townley and I agreed terms, which were adequate rather than generous, and also subject to various safeguards. The lady had a generous spirit but she drove a hard bargain. Mr Ingham would draw up a contract and write the letters of authorization. We fixed a day for me to return for the documents.

I hardly recognized the self-assured little creature at the other side of the desk. It was as if her husband's death had freed her from invisible chains. Moreover, Mr Townley's death seemed not to have damaged her circumstances in any material way. A widow, of course, is unique among women in that she has the power to control her own affairs without reference to husband or father.

"I'm sensible of your kindness, ma'am," I said as I was about to leave. "But why me?"

"My husband once told me you were a capable man. And an honest one, too." She hesitated and for an instant I glimpsed the shy, awkward creature I had encountered at our first meeting. "And because you were kind to me once, sir, which is always a powerful recommendation."

My replacement arrived on 13 March, a man named Thorpe. I had never met him before and I did not meet him now because he communicated solely in writing with me.

There were letters from England on the same ship. Mr Rampton, of course, had not yet heard of what had happened on the ice of the North River in the early hours of 20 January. He merely instructed me to hand over everything relating to my office in New York to Mr Thorpe and to return home as soon as possible. Once in London, I was to report to the American Department to account for the monies I had disbursed and for a final interview. There was no mention of Augusta. Nor, to my relief, was there anything about her in the London newspapers.

Both Lizzie and my sister had written. Their letters made happier reading.

Since I was still travelling on official business, I was able to take passage on a frigate, HMS *Lydmouth*, bound for Canada and then England. It would be a long voyage, but I would rather be at sea than linger in New York.

I went aboard the night before we sailed because we were to leave with the tide before dawn. That evening after supper I wrapped myself in my cloak and walked on deck, looking at the lights of the city across the water and the lanterns bobbing up and down on the other ships that crowded the harbour.

Many of the ship's company had been granted shore leave. A boat passed to and fro between the ship and the city, bringing them back. One of them was a very young midshipman, no more than twelve or thirteen years of age. I watched him climbing the ladder up the side with much assistance from his friends.

When he was safely on deck, however, he looked about him, saw me and then staggered towards me, pursuing a zigzag course as if tacking against the wind. He stopped beside me and leant heavily against the rail. He sketched a salute.

"Mr Savill, sir?" he said. His voice had not quite broken and went from low to high in three words.

I agreed that I was. The ship twitched unexpectedly beneath our feet, as ships are wont to do, and the boy lost his grip on the rail. I steadied him.

"A gentleman asked me to give you this, sir."

The boy felt inside his coat and drew out a small package. As I was thanking him, he turned aside and vomited copiously over the rail.

I did not open the little parcel until I had returned to my cabin. The packet was irregular in shape, wrapped in brown paper and tied with string. It yielded slightly to the touch.

I cut the string and unwrapped it. Inside I found about half a pound of tea. There was also a scrap of paper with a few lines written on it.

Pray remember the value of a piece of pork with the fat on it, swallowed again and again until it comes up no more.

Later, Souchong tea with a little rum in it, taken by the spoonful.

It was the remedy for sea-sickness that had restored me on the voyage out. There was neither salutation nor signature on the letter. The handwriting was unfamiliar. But I knew who had sent me this parting gift from America. I knew that Mr Noak had said goodbye.

Afterword

The British deserved to lose the American War of Independence for many reasons, not least because they fought it with remarkable ineptitude and they were woefully slow to understand the real issues.

From their point of view, however, the defeat could have been much worse. First, this was an unnecessary war that many of them hadn't wanted to fight. Second, in the context of Britain as a whole, her burgeoning economy and her rapidly expanding empire, the fate of the Thirteen Colonies was a significant blow to pride rather than to the national interest.

The real losers of the Revolutionary War were those Americans who had supported the British. In one sense, this was a civil war, with all the bitterness and internal contradictions associated with the term. When it was over, yesterday's rebels became tomorrow's patriots. Yesterday's loyal Americans were driven from the country they had helped to create, only to find that they had become something of an embarrassment to the British government whose claims they had tried to support.

Loyalist opinion had many shades, from hardline Tories who hankered for a form of government which no longer worked to those who welcomed change and wanted a negotiated peace that would leave intact the formal ties between Britain and America. After the war, some went north to Canada to build a new life in difficult conditions. Others went to Britain, where many of them received neither the welcome they deserved nor the compensation they had been promised. Still others found ways to reach an accommodation with the new order.

One of the aims of this novel was to give a glimpse of these unfortunate Loyalists, many of whom thought of themselves with some justification as patriotic Americans. Their loyalty cost them all they had.

Loyalty is generally accounted a virtue but the war and its bitter aftermath revealed it for what it truly is: not an absolute but a relative quality, contingent on external factors, changeable as the weather.

For most of the war, His Majesty's superficially loyal city of New York was the British Headquarters in North America. Before the war the city covered an area of about a square mile at the southern tip of Manhattan and may have housed about twenty thousand people. During the first phase of the war, many of the original inhabitants fled. But Loyalist refugees poured in from other parts of America. It has been estimated that at one point the city contained over thirty thousand civilians, many of them black.

New York was also an occupied city — first, at the beginning of the war, by the army of Congress and later by British and Loyalist troops. Though the soldiers (and sailors) were, in the main, billeted outside the city, thousands of them swelled the numbers of those who ebbed and flowed through the streets.

To make matters worse, the two great fires of 1776 and 1778 destroyed nearly six hundred houses. There was no significant rebuilding during the war. The temporary slums of Canvas Town spread over the blackened ruins.

The city and the British-held hinterland around it were surrounded by hostile territory that was held, more or less, for Congress. The entry of the French navy into the war seriously hampered Britain's ability to supply New York from the sea. Starvation was a very real danger, particularly in the long and exceptionally hard winters of the war.

Conditions were hard; life was precarious. Still, until the British were resoundingly defeated at Yorktown in October 1781, Loyalists in New York had considerable grounds for optimism. Britain was then the world's leading power, with the ability to devote enormous financial and military resources to the war. It must have seemed inconceivable that the rebels could win.

Even after Yorktown, Britain in theory had the option to fight on, though the Americans and their French allies had evolved into a formidable opponent. What was lacking was the will. The Government had at last come to realize just how expensive and how difficult it would be to win this war. British public and political opinion had never wholeheartedly supported it. Perhaps Britain's leaders also sensed that, even if they achieved victory, it would only be a fragile and partial one.

History had moved on. The war had redefined what it meant to be a loyal American.

Congress was desperately in need of gold, not least to pay and equip its own soldiers. In 1799, only sixteen years after the end of the war, a substantial deposit was found on a farm in North Carolina. There's an irony in the fact that it was discovered by John Reed, a former Hessian mercenary who had fought for the British but settled in America after the war.

Acknowledgements

Novels are joint efforts. It's a pleasure to thank the team at HarperCollins again — in particular, Julia Wisdom for her superhuman patience and very valuable suggestions; Anne O'Brien for her meticulous copy-editing; and Emad Akhtar for coping so courteously with the production process. The book wouldn't have emerged at all without the encouragement of my agent, Vivien Green of Sheil Land, and, as ever and most of all, my wife, Caroline.